About the Authors

Maisey Yates is a *New York Times* bestselling author of over one hundred romance novels. Whether she's writing strong, hardworking cowboys, dissolute princes or multigenerational family stories, she loves getting lost in fictional worlds. An avid knitter with a [illegible] yarn addiction [illegible] lives with her h[illegible] Check out her w[illegible] or find her on Facebook.

Fiona Brand lives in the sunny Bay of Islands, New Zealand. Now that both of her sons are grown, she continues to love writing books and gardening. After a life-changing time in which she met Christ, she has undertaken study for a bachelor of theology and has become a member of The Order of St. Luke, Christ's healing ministry.

Clare Connelly was raised in small-town Australia among a family of avid readers. She spent much of her childhood up a tree, Mills & Boon book in hand. Clare is married to her own real-life hero, and they live in a bungalow near the sea with their two children. She is frequently found staring into space—a surefire sign that she's in the world of her characters. She has a penchant for French food and ice-cold champagne, and Mills & Boon novels continue to be her favourite ever books. Writing for Modern is a long-held dream. Clare can be contacted via clareconnelly.com or at her Facebook page.

Royal Scandals

December 2021
His Royal Heir

January 2022
The Playboy Prince

February 2022
Seducing His Queen

March 2022
Forbidden Passions

April 2022
Royally Wed

May 2022
Royal Intrigue

Royal Scandals: Forbidden Passion

MAISEY YATES

FIONA BRAND

CLARE CONNELLY

MILLS & BOON

First Published in Great Britain 2022
By Mills & Boon, an imprint of HarperCollins*Publishers*, Ltd
1 London Bridge Street, London, SE1 9GF

www.harpercollins.co.uk

HarperCollins*Publishers*
1st Floor, Watermarque Building,
Ringsend Road, Dublin 4, Ireland

ISBN: 978-0-263-30445-9

HIS FORBIDDEN PREGNANT PRINCESS

MAISEY YATES

To Nicole Helm.

Ask and you shall receive. Dare and I shall deliver.

Can I make a children's cartoon a romance novel?

Yes. Yes, I can.

CHAPTER ONE

SHE WAS BENEATH him in every way. From her common blood to her objectively plain appearance—that years of designer clothing, professional treatments from the finest aestheticians and beauticians and the work of the best makeup artists money could buy had failed to transform into true beauty—from the way she carried herself, to the way she spoke.

The stepsister he had always seen as a particularly drab blot on the otherwise extravagant tapestry of the royal family of San Gennaro.

The stepsister he could hardly bear to share the same airspace with, let alone the same palace.

The stepsister he was now tasked with finding a suitable husband for.

The stepsister he wanted more than his next breath.

She was beneath him in every way. Except for the way he desired most.

And she never would be.

There were a thousand reasons. From the darkness in him, to the common blood in her. But the only reason that truly mattered was that she was his stepsister, and he was a king.

"You requested my presence, Luca?" Sophia asked,

looking up at him with a dampened light in her blue eyes that suggested she was suppressing some emotion or other. In all probability a deep dislike for having to deal with him.

But the feeling was mutual. And if he could endure such an indignity then Sophia—in all her borrowed glory—certainly could.

"I did. As you know, it was my father's final wish that you be well cared for, along with your mother. He wrote it into law that you are part of this family and are to be treated as a daughter of his blood would be."

Sophia looked down, her lashes dark on her pale cheek. She had visible freckles that never failed to vex him. Because he wanted to count them. Because sometimes, he wanted to kiss each one.

She should cover them with makeup as most women of her status did. She should have some care for the fact she was a princess.

But she did not.

Today she wore a simple shift that made her bare legs seem far too long and slender. It was an ungainly thing. She also wore nothing at all to cover them. She had on flat shoes, and not a single piece of jewelry. Her dark hair hung limp around her shoulders.

He could only hope she had not gone out in public that way.

"Yes," she said, finally. Then those dark eyes connected with his and he felt it like a lightning bolt straight down to his stomach. He should not. For every reason cataloged in his mind only a moment before. She was not beautiful. Not when compared to the elegant women who had graced his bed before her. Not when compared to nearly any other princess the world over.

But she captivated him. Had done from the moment he had met her. At first it was nothing more than feeling at turns invaded and intrigued by this alien creature that had come into his life. She had been twelve to his seventeen when their parents had married.

Sophia had possessed a public school education, not a single hint of deportment training and no real understanding of the hierarchy of the palace.

She had a tendency to speak out of turn, to trip over her feet and to treat him in an overly familiar manner.

Her mother was a warm, vivacious woman who had done much to restore his father's life, life that had drained away after the loss of his first wife. She was also a quick study, and did credit to the position of Queen of San Gennaro.

Sophia, on the other hand, seemed to resist her new role, and her new life. She continued to do so now. In little ways. Her bare legs, and her bare face, as an example.

His irritation with her had taken a sharp turn, twisting into something much more disturbing around the time she turned sixteen. That sense of being captivated, in the way one might be by a spider that has invaded one's room, shifted and became much more focused.

And there had been a moment, when he had found her breathless from running out in the garden like a schoolgirl when she had been the advanced age of seventeen, that everything had locked into place. That it had occurred to him that if he could only capture that insolent mouth of hers with his own she would finally yield. And he would no longer feel so desperately beguiled by her.

It had only gotten worse as the years had progressed.

And the idea of kissing her had perverted yet further into doing much, much more.

But it was not to be. Not ever.

As he had just told her, his father had decreed that she was family. As much as if they were blood.

And so he was putting an end to this once and for all.

"He asked me to take care of you in a very specific fashion," Luca continued. "And I feel that now that it has been six months since his passing, it is time for me to see those requests honored."

A crease appeared between her brows. "What request?"

"Specifically? The matter of your marriage, *sorellina*." Little sister. He called her that to remind himself.

"My marriage? Shouldn't we see to the matter of me getting asked to the movies first, Luca?"

"There is no need for such things, obviously. A woman in your position is hardly going to go to the movies. Rather, I have been poring over a list of suitable men who might be able to be brought in for consideration."

"You're choosing my husband?" she asked, her tone incredulous.

"I intend to present you with a manageably sized selection. I am not so arrogant that I would make the final choice for you."

Sophia let out a sharp, inelegant laugh. "Oh, no. You're only so arrogant that you would inform me I'm getting married, and that you have already started taking steps toward planning the wedding. Tell me, Luca, have you picked out my dress, as well?"

Of course he would be involved in approving that selection; if she thought otherwise she was delusional. "Not as yet," he said crisply.

"What happens if I refuse you?"

"You won't," he said, certainty going as deep as his bones.

He was the king now, and she could not refuse him. She would not. He would not allow it.

"Why wouldn't I?"

"You are welcome, of course, to make a mockery of the generosity that my father has shown to your mother and yourself. You are welcome, of course, to cause a rift between the two of us."

She crossed her arms, cocking one hip out to the side. "I could hardly cause a rift between the two of us, Luca. No matter what you might say, you have never behaved as a loving older brother to me."

"Perhaps it is because you have never been a sister to me," he said, his voice hard.

She would not understand what that meant. She would not understand why he had said it.

And indeed, the confusion on her face spoke to that.

"I don't have to do what you tell me to." She shook her head, that dark, glossy hair swirling around her shoulders. "Your father would hardly have forced me into a marriage I didn't want. He loved me. He wanted what was best for me."

"This was what he thought was best," Luca said. "I have documentation saying such. If you need to see it, I will have it sent to your quarters. Quarters that you inhabit, by the way, because my father cared so much for you. Because my father took an exceptional and unheard-of step in this country and treated a child he did not father as his own. He is giving you what he would have given to a daughter. A daughter of his blood. Selecting your husband, ensuring it is a man of impeccable pedigree, is what he would have done for his child. You are welcome to reject it if you wish. But I would think very deeply about what that means."

Sophia didn't have to think deeply about what it meant. She could feel it. Her heart was pounding so hard she thought she might pass out; small tremors running beneath the surface of her skin. Heat and ice pricking at her cheeks.

Oh, she wasn't thinking of what this meant in the way that Luca had so imperiously demanded she do.

Luca.

Her beautiful, severe stepbrother who was much more king of a nation than he was family to her. Remote. Distant. His perfectly sculpted face only more desperately gorgeous to her now than it had been when she had met him at seventeen. He had been beautiful as a teenager. There was no question. But then, that angular bone structure had been overlaid by much softer skin, his coal-black eyes always formidable, but nothing quite so sharp as crushed obsidian as they were now. That soft skin, the skin of a boy, that was gone. Replaced by a more weathered texture. By rough, black whiskers that seemed ever present no matter how often he shaved his square jaw.

She had never in all of her life met a thing like him. A twelve-year-old girl, plucked up from obscurity, from a life of poverty and set down in this luxurious castle, had been utterly and completely at sea to begin with. And then there was *him*.

Everything in her had wanted to challenge him, to provoke a response from all of that granite strength, even then. Even before she had known why, or known what it meant that she craved his attention in whatever form it might come.

Gradually, it had all become clear.

And clearer still the first time she had gone to a ball and Luca had gone with another woman on his arm. That acrid, acidic curling sensation in her stomach could have only been one thing. Even at fourteen she had known that. Had known that the sweep of fever that had gone over her skin, that weak sensation that made it feel as though she was going to die, was jealousy. Jealousy because she wanted Luca to take her arm, wanted him to hold her close and dance with her.

Wanted to be the one he took back to his rooms and did all sorts of secret things with, things that she had not known about in great detail, but had yearned for all the same. Him. Everything to do with him.

As Luca had said not a moment before, he had never thought of her as a sister. He was never affectionate, never close or caring in a way that went beyond duty.

But she had never thought of him as a brother. She had thought of him in an entirely different fashion.

She *wanted* him.

And he was intent on marrying her off. As though it were nothing.

Not a single thing on earth could have spoken to the ambivalence that he felt toward her any stronger than this did.

He doesn't want you.

Of course he didn't. She wasn't a great beauty; she was well aware of that. She was also absolutely and completely wrong for him in every way.

She didn't excel at this royal existence the way that he did. He wore it just beneath his skin, as tailored and fitted to him as one of his bespoke suits. Born with it, as if his blood truly were a different color than that of the common people. As if he were a different creature entirely from the rest of the mere mortals.

She had done her best to put that royal mantle on, but much like every dress that had ever been made for her since coming to live at the palace, it wasn't quite right. Oh, they could measure it all to fit, but it was clear that she wasn't made for such things. That her exceedingly nonwaiflike figure was not for designer gowns and slinky handmade creations that would have hung fabulously off women who were more collar and hip bone than curves and love handles.

Oh, yes, she was well aware of how little she fit. And how impossible her feelings for Luca were.

And yet, they remained.

And knowing that nothing could ever happen with him, knowing it with deep certainty, had done nothing to excise it from her soul.

Did nothing to blunt the pain of this, of his words being ground into her chest like shards of glass.

Not only was he making it clear he didn't want her, he was also using the memory of his father—the only man she had ever known as a father—to entice her to agree.

He was right. King Magnus had given her everything. Had given her mother a new lease on life, a real life. Something beyond existence, beyond struggle, which they had been mired in for all of Sophia's life prior to her marriage to him.

He had met her when she was nothing more than a waitress at a royal event in the US, and had fallen deeply for her in the moment they met.

It was something out of a fairy tale, except there were two children to contend with. A child who had been terrified of being uprooted from her home in America and going to a foreign country to live in a fancy palace. And another child who had always clearly resented the invasion.

She had to give Luca credit for the fact that he seemed to have some measure of affection for her mother. He did not resent her presence in the way he resented Sophia's.

She had often thought that life for Luca would have been perfect if he would have gotten her mother and his father, and she had been left out of the equation entirely.

Well, he was trying to offload her now, so she supposed that was proven to be true enough.

"That isn't fair," she said, when she could finally regain her powers of speech.

Luca's impossibly dark eyes flickered up and met hers, and her stomach—traitorous fool—hollowed out in response. "It isn't fair? Sophia, I have always known that you were ungrateful for the position that you have found yourself in your life, but you have just confirmed it in a rather stunning way. You find it unfair that my father wished to see you cared for? You find it unfair that I wish to do the same?"

"You forget," she said, trying to regain her powers of thought. "I was not born into this life, Luca, I did not know people growing up who expected such things for their lives. I didn't expect such a thing for mine. I spent the first twelve years of my life in poverty. But with the idea that if I worked hard enough I might be able to make whatever I wanted of myself. And then we were sort of swept up in this tidal wave of luxury.

And strangely, I have found that though I have every resource at my disposal now, I cannot be what I want in the same way that I imagined I could when I was nothing but a poor child living in the United States."

"That's because you were a delusional child," Luca said, his tone not cruel in any way, but somehow all the more stinging for the calm with which he spoke. "You never had the power to be whatever you wanted back then, Sophia, because no one has that power. There are a certain number of things set out before you that you might accomplish. You certainly might have improved your station. I'm not denying that. But the sky was never the limit, sorely not. Neither is it now. However, your limit is much more comfortable, you will find, than it would have been then."

Her heart clenched tight, because she couldn't deny that what he was saying was true. Bastard. With the maturity of adulthood she could acknowledge that. That she had been naive at the time, and that she was, in fact, being ungrateful to a degree.

Hadn't her position in the palace provided her with the finest education she could have asked for? Hadn't she been given excellent opportunities? Chances to run charitable organizations that she believed in strongly, and that benefited all manner of children from different backgrounds.

No, as a princess, she would never truly have a profession, but with that came the release of pressure of earning money to pay bills.

Of figuring out where the road between what she dreamed of doing, and what would help her survive, met.

But the idea of marrying someone selected by her

stepbrother, who no more knew her than liked her, was not a simple thing.

And underneath that, the idea of marrying any man, touching any man, being intimate with any man, who wasn't Luca was an abomination unto her soul.

For it was only him. Luca and those eyes as hard as flint, that mouth that was often curled into a sneer in her direction, those large hands that were much rougher than any king's ever should have been. It was only him who made her want. Who made her ache with the deep well of unsatisfied desire. Only him.

Only ever him.

"I will be holding a ball," Luca said, his tone decisive. "And at that ball will be several men that I have personally curated for you."

"You make them sound like a collection of cheeses."

"Think of them however you like. If you prefer to think them as cheese, that's your own business."

Something burst inside her, some small portion of restraint that she had been only just barely holding on to since she had come into the throne room. "How do you know I like men, Luca? You've never asked."

Luca drew back slightly, a flicker in his dark eyes the only showing that she had surprised him at all.

"If it is not so," he said, his tone remote, "then I suggest you speak now."

"No," she responded, feeling deflated, as her momentary bit of rebellion fell flat on its face. "I'm not opposed to men."

"Well," he said, "one less bit of damage control I have to do."

"That would require damage control?"

"How many gay princesses do you know?" he asked.

"The upper echelons of society are ever conservative regardless of what they say. And here in this country it would be quite the scandal, I assure you. It is all fine to pay lip service to such things as equality, but appearances, tradition, are as important as ever."

"And I am already a break with tradition," she pointed out.

"Yes," he said, that tone heavy. "My father's actions in granting you the same rights as I have were unheard of. You are not his by blood, and in royal lines blood is everything. It is the only thing."

"I will go to the ball," she said, because there really was no point arguing with Luca once he had made pronouncements. But whatever happened after that… It would be her decision.

But she was too raw, too shocked, from this entire conversation to continue having a fight with him.

He wanted to marry her off to another man. He wanted her to be someone else's problem.

He felt nothing about doing it.

He did not want her.

He's your stepbrother, and even if he did he couldn't have you. As he just said, tradition is everything.

She squared her shoulders. "When is this blessed event?"

"In a couple weeks' time," he responded.

She blinked. "Oh. I'm not certain my mother will be back from France before then."

"She will be. I have already spoken with her."

That galled her. Like a lance through her chest. Her mother, of course, had no idea how Sophia felt about Luca. She told her mother everything. Everything except for that. Everything except for the completely forbidden lust she felt for her stepbrother. But even so, she couldn't believe that her mother had allowed Luca to have this conversation with her without at least giving her a call to warn her first.

"I told her not to tell you," Luca said as if he was reading her mind.

She sniffed. "Well. That is quite informative."

"Do not be indignant, *sorellina*," Luca said. "It is not becoming of a princess."

"Well, I've certainly never been overly becoming as princesses go," she said stiffly. "Why start now?"

"You had better start. You had better start so that all of this will work accordingly."

He looked her up and down. "We need to get you a new stylist."

"I use the same stylist as my mother," she said defensively.

"It doesn't work for you," he said, his tone cold.

And with a wave of his hand he dismissed her, and she was left somehow obeying him, her feet propelling her out of his royal chamber and into the hall.

She clutched her chest, gasping for breath, pain rolling through her.

The man she loved was going to marry her off to someone else. The man she loved was selecting from a pool of grooms for her to meet in two weeks' time.

The man she loved was her stepbrother. The man she loved was a king.

All of those things made it impossible for her to have him.

But she didn't have any idea how in the world she was supposed to stop wanting him.

CHAPTER TWO

"WHAT IS *THIS*?" The disdain in Sophia's tone when Luca presented her with a thick stack of files the following week was—in his estimation—a bit on the dramatic side.

"It is the list of possible husbands to invite to the upcoming ball. I feel strongly that an excess of five is just being spoiled for choice. Plus, you will not have time to dance with that many people. So I suggest you look it over, and find a way to pare them down."

"This is..." She looked up at him, her dark eyes furious. "These are dossiers of...*men*. Photos and personal profiles..."

"How else would you know if you're compatible?"

"Maybe meeting them and going out for dinner?" Sophia asked.

She crossed her arms, the motion pushing her rather abundant décolletage up over the neckline of the rather simple V-neck top she was wearing.

They really needed to get ahold of that new stylist and quickly. She was, as ever, a temptation to Luca, and to his sense of duty. But soon it would be over. Soon he would have his problematic stepsister married off, and then she would be safely out of his reach.

He could have found a woman to slake his lust on, and over the years he had done just that. After all, whatever was broken in him… Sophia should not have to suffer for it.

But during those time periods he had not been forced to cohabitate with Sophia. Always, when he had spent too much time with her, he had to detox, essentially. Find a slim blonde to remind himself that there were other sorts of women he found hot. Other women he might find desirable.

And then, when it was really bad, he gave up entirely on playing the opposite game and found himself a curvaceous brunette to pour his fantasies into. The end of that road was a morass of self-loathing and recrimination, but on many levels he was happy to end up there. He was comforted by it.

But this… Sharing space with her. As he had done since his father had died. No other woman would do. He couldn't find it in him to feel even a hint of desire for anyone else. And that was unacceptable. As all things to do with Sophia invariably were.

"You are not going on dinner dates," Luca said. "You are a princess. You are part of the royal family. And you are not setting up a Tinder profile in order to find yourself a husband."

"Why not?" she asked, her tone defiant. "Perhaps I want nothing more than to meet a very exciting IT guy who might swipe me right off my feet." He said nothing and she continued to stare at him. "Swipe. Swipe right. It's a dating app thing."

"That isn't funny in the least. As I said, you are part of this family." Perhaps if he repeated it enough, if he drilled it into both of them that they were family, his body would eventually begin to take it on board. "And as such, your standards of marriage must be the same as mine."

"Why aren't you looking for a wife yourself?" she asked.

"I will," Luca said. "In due time. But my father asked that I make your safety, your match, a priority."

He would marry, as duty required. But it would not be because of passion. And certainly not because of love. Duty was what drove him. The preservation of reputation, of the crown. If that crumbled, his whole life was nothing.

He would choose a suitable woman.

Sophia was far from suitable.

"What about the production of an heir?" Sophia lifted a brow. "Isn't that important?"

"Yes. But I am a man, and as such, I do not have the same issues with a biological clock your gender does."

"Right," she huffed. "Because men can continue to produce children up until the end of their days."

"Perhaps not without the aid of a blue pill, but certainly it is possible."

For a moment she only blinked up at him, a faint pink tinge coloring her cheeks. Then Sophia's lip curled. "I find this conversation distasteful."

"You brought up the production of heirs, not me."

She scowled, clearly having to take his point, and not liking it at all. "Well, let me look through the dossiers, then," she said, lifting her nose and peering at him down the slender ridge, perfecting that sort of lofty look that was nothing if not a put-on coming from Sophia.

Though, possibly not when directed at him.

"Erik Nilsson. Swedish nobility?"

"Yes," Luca responded. "He's very wealthy."

"How?"

"Family money, mostly. Though some of it is in sheep."

"His money is in sheep?" Sophia asked, her expression completely bland. "Well, that is interesting. And one would never want for sweaters."

"Indeed not," he said, a vicious turn of jealousy savaging his gut. Which was sadistic at best. To be jealous of a man whose fortune was tied up in sheep and who had the dubious honor of being a minor noble in some small village that wasn't part of the current century.

A man he had not expected his stepsister to show the slightest interest in. And yet, here she was.

"So he will have access to…wool. And such," Sophia said. "And…he's quite handsome. If you like tall and blond."

"Do you?" he asked.

"Very much," she said with a strange injection of conviction. "He's on the table." She set the folder aside. "Let us get on with the next candidate, shall we?"

"Here you are," he said, lifting up the next folder and holding it out toward her. "Ilya Kuznetsov."

She arched a brow. "Russian?"

He raised one in response. "Very."

Sophia wrinkled her nose. "Is his fortune in vodka and caviar?"

"I hate to disappoint you but it's in tech. So, quite close to that IT guy you were professing to have a burning desire for."

"I didn't say I had a burning desire for anyone," she pointed out, her delicate fingers tracing the edge of the file.

He couldn't help but imagine those same fingers stroking him.

If he believed in curses, he would believe he was under one.

"I don't know anything about computers," she continued, setting the folder off to the opposite side of the first one. "I prefer sheep."

She was infuriating. And baffling. "Not something you hear every day. Now, to the next one."

She set aside the next two. An Italian business mogul and a Greek tycoon. Neither one meeting up to some strange specification that she blathered on about in vague terms. Then she rejected an Argentine polo player, who was also nobility of some kind, on the basis of the fact that a quick Google search revealed him to be an inveterate womanizer.

"You're not much better," she said mournfully, looking up from her phone.

"Then it is a good thing that I am not in the files for consideration."

Something quite like shock flashed through her eyes, and her mouth dropped open. Color flooded her cheeks, irritation, anger.

"As if that would ever happen. As if I would *consider* you." She sniffed very loudly.

"As my sister, you could not," he bit out.

"Stepsister," she said, looking up at him from beneath her dark lashes.

His gut twisted, his body hardening for a moment before he gathered his control. The moment seemed to last an eternity. Stolen, removed from time. Nothing but those eyes boring holes through him, as though she could see right into him. As though she could see his every debauched thought.

Every dark, terrible thing in him.

But no, there was no way she could.

Or she would run and hide like a frightened mouse.

"In terms of legality, in terms of my father's will, you're my sister," he said. "Now, the next one."

She went through the folders until she had selected five, though she maintained that the Swedish candidate was top of her list.

It did not escape his notice that she had selected all men with lighter features. Diametrically opposed to his own rather dark appearance.

He should rejoice in that.

He found he did not.

"Then these are the invitations that will be sent out," he said. "And I will be reserving dances with each of the gentlemen."

"Dances?" She blinked. "Are we in a Regency romance novel? Am I going to have a card to keep track?"

"Don't be ridiculous. You can keep track of it in an app."

She barked out a laugh. "This is ridiculous. You're ridiculous."

"Perhaps," he said, "but if you can think of a better way to bring together the most eligible men in the world, I'm all ears."

"And what happens if I don't like any of them?"

"You're very excited about the sweaters."

"What if I don't like any of them?" she reiterated.

"I imagine something will work out."

"I'm serious," she said, her blue eyes blazing with

emotion. "I'm not marrying a man I don't like because you have some strange time frame you need to fulfill."

"Then we will keep looking."

"No," she said. "I promise that I will be fair, and I will give this a chance. But if it doesn't work, give me six months to make my own choice. If I can't find somebody that is suitable to me, and suitable to you, then I will let you choose."

"That was not part of the original bargain."

Six months more of her might just kill him.

"I don't care," Sophia said. "This isn't the Dark Ages, and you can't make me do what I don't want to. And you know it."

"Then you have a bargain. But you will have to put in serious effort. I am not wasting my time and resources."

"Well I'm not marrying a man just to suit you, Luca. I want to care for the man I marry. I want to like him, if I can't love him. I want to be able to talk to him. I want him to make me laugh."

Luca braced himself. Braced himself for her to start talking about passion. About wanting a man who would set her body on fire.

She didn't.

She had stopped at a man who made her laugh, and had not said she wanted a man who would make her come. He shouldn't think such thoughts. Shouldn't want to find out why that didn't seem to occur to her.

Why attraction didn't come into her lists of demands to be met.

It made him want to teach her. Didn't she understand? That physical desire *mattered*?

And if she didn't understand…

Some Swedish sheep farmer would be the one to teach her.

Luca gritted his teeth. "But do you need to want him, *sorellina*?"

He should not have asked the question. He shouldn't entertain these thoughts, and he certainly shouldn't give voice to them.

Cursed.

If he weren't a logical man, he would swear it.

"Want him?" she asked, tilting her head to the side.

"Yes," he bit out. "Want him. His hands on your body. His mouth on yours. Does it matter to you whether or not you want him inside you?"

He hadn't realized it, but he'd moved closer to her with each sentence. And now he was so near her he could smell her. That delicate, citrus scent that always rose above the more cloying floral or vanilla perfumes the women around the palace typically favored. A scent he was always assured he could pick out, regardless of who else was around. Always Sophia, rising above the rest.

"I… I…" Her cheeks blushed crimson, and then she stood, her nose colliding with his cheek before she wobbled backward. "I've only ever wanted one man like that." The words seemed to be stuck in her throat. "I never will again. I'm sure. And I refuse to discuss it. Least of all with you."

And then she turned and ran from the room.

CHAPTER THREE

SINCE MAKING A fool out of herself in front of Luca days earlier, Sophia had done her best to avoid him. It wasn't that difficult. Luca was always busy with affairs of state, and it was actually for the best. The problem was that every time she heard heavy, authoritative footsteps on the marble floors of the palace, her heart caught, and held its position as if it was waiting, waiting to bow down to its king.

She did not want Luca to be the king of her heart. Being King of San Gennaro was quite enough power for one man. But her heart didn't listen. It beat for Luca, it stopped for Luca, tripped over itself for Luca.

It was starting to feel like she was running an obstacle course every time she made any movement in the palace. One wherein Luca was the obstacle that she was trying desperately to avoid.

But she wanted to see him, too. That was the real conundrum. The fact that she wanted to both avoid him and be with him all the time. Foolish, because he wasn't even nice to her. He never had been. But still, he captivated her in ways that went beyond sanity.

And today there would be no more avoiding him as he had engaged the services of a new stylist to help her prepare for the ball. The ball wherein she was supposed to choose a husband.

Luca and those dossiers had enraged her. She had picked every man who was completely opposite to him, to spite herself, mostly.

She highly doubted that she would marry any of these men. But one thing she knew for certain was that she would not marry a man who was simply a pale carbon copy of her stepbrother. She would not choose a man who was tall, dark and handsome, who had that kind of authority about him that Luca possessed. Because it would simply be an effort at giving her body a consolation prize. And that was far too tragic, even for her.

She shouldn't be tragic, she mused as she wandered down the labyrinthine hall toward the salon where she was meeting the new stylist. She had been a commoner, and she had been raised up to become the princess of a country. She had been adopted by a king. A man who had loved her, and had loved her mother. Who had shown them both the kind of life that neither of them had ever dreamed possible.

But Luca. Always Luca.

It was as though her heart was intent on not being happy. As though it wanted to be tragic. In the same way that it had determined that Luca would be its owner.

In a palace, a life of luxury, and with that came a fervent, painful love for the one man she could never have.

And, he didn't like her.

Star-crossed lovers they were not. Because Luca could hardly stand to share the same space as she did. He thought she was silly, that much was apparent from their exchange yesterday. They were from completely different worlds. The man couldn't understand why she found it off-putting to be looking through file folders filled with profiles of men she had never met, trying to work out which one of them she could see herself marrying.

Although she supposed it wasn't entirely different from online dating.

No. She refused to pretend that any of this was reasonable. It wasn't.

She wondered if she would ever find someone who just wanted *her.* These men, who had agreed to come to the palace, would never have done so if she wasn't a princess.

It was the only reason her biological father had ever spoken to her. After he'd seen her mother in the media, marrying King Magnus.

King Magnus had loved her. But…he had only strived to love her because of her mother.

And Luca…

Well, nothing seemed to make Luca like her at all. Not status, or herself.

He was consistent, at least.

She took a deep breath, bracing herself for the sight of him. That was another problem with Luca. Too much exposure to him and her poor heart couldn't recover between moments. Not enough, and it always flung itself against her breastbone as though it were trying to escape. Trying to go to him. To be with him.

Her heart was foolish. And the rest of her body was worse.

She gathered herself up, drew in the deepest breath possible, hoping that the burning in her lungs would offset the rest of her physical response. That it might drown out the erratic tripping of her pulse.

Then, she pushed the door open.

And all the breath left her body in a rush.

There was no preparing for him. No matter how familiar she was with his face, with that imposing, muscular physique of his, it was like a shock to her system every time. Those dark eyes, eyes that she sometimes thought might see straight through her, but they couldn't. Because if they did, then he would know. He would know that she was not indifferent to him. He would know that her feelings toward him were in no way familial.

He would be disgusted by her.

It took her a while to notice that there was a woman standing next to him. The new stylist, presumably. It took her a while, because as far as she was concerned when Luca was in the room it was difficult to tell if anyone else was there at all.

"You must be Princess Sophia," the woman said. "I'm Elizabeth."

"Nice to meet you." Belatedly, she decided that she should try and curtsy or something, so she grabbed the edge of her sundress and bent forward slightly. She looked up and saw that Luca was watching her with a disapproving expression on his handsome face.

If she bowed down and called him King of the Universe he would disapprove. He was impossible.

"She needs something suitable for an upcoming event," Luca said. "She must look the best she ever has."

"I am confident that I can accomplish such. It is simply a matter of knowing what sort of energy Sophia should be projecting. All these colors that she's wearing now are far too drab. And from what I have seen in pictures and publications over the years, her overall color palette doesn't suit her. I have plans."

Suddenly, Sophia felt very much like she was being stared down by a hungry spider. And she was a fly caught in the web.

"Just leave it to me," she said, shooing at Luca.

"I must approve the selection," he said. Obviously not taking kindly at all to being shown the door in his own palace.

"You will approve," Elizabeth said, her tone stubborn. "You will see soon."

The rest of the afternoon was spent styling and plucking and scrubbing.

Sophia felt as though she had been exfoliated over every part of her body. This woman did not try to have her hair completely straightened, but rather, styled it into soft waves, which seemed to frame her face better, and also—so she said—would not revert halfway over the course of the evening. Which was the problem that Sophia usually had with her hairstyles. Her hair wasn't curly, but it was not board-straight, either, and it could not hold such a severe style for hours on end. It became unruly when she got all sweaty. And she supposed it was not a good thing to sweat when you were a princess, but she did.

Then there was the matter of the gown she chose. None of the navy blue, black or mossy-green colors that her mother's stylist favored. No, this gown was a brilliant fuchsia, strapless with a sweetheart neckline that did nothing at all to cover her breasts. It draped down from there, skimming her waist, her full hips. Rather than making her look large like some of the high-necked gowns that had been chosen for her before, or blocky like the ones that hit her in strange places at the waist, she actually looked…curvy and feminine.

Typically, she didn't show this much skin, but she had to admit it was much more flattering when you could see that she had cleavage, rather than a misshapen mono breast.

Her lipstick matched the dress, and her eye makeup was simple, just black winged liner. Her cheeks were a very bright pink, much brighter than she would have normally done, but all of it created a very sophisticated effect. And for the first time she thought maybe she looked like she belonged. Like maybe she was a princess. Not a girl being shoved into a mold she resolutely could not fit into, but one who'd had a mold created just for her.

"He will approve of this," Elizabeth said.

"You know he is my stepbrother," Sophia pointed out. "He doesn't need to approve of it in that way."

The very idea made her face hot. And that she wanted him to…that she wanted him to want her was the worst humiliation of all.

"I know," the woman said, giving her a look that was far too incisive. "But you wouldn't mind if he did."

Sophia sputtered. "I… He can't."

"That has nothing to do with what you feel. Or what you want."

Sophia felt like she had been opened up and examined. Like her skin had been peeled away, revealing her deepest and most desperate secrets. She hated it. But she didn't have time to marinate in it because suddenly, the door was opening, and Luca had returned. Obviously, Elizabeth had texted him to say that Sophia was ready.

But she wasn't ready. She wasn't ready to face him, not with the woman next to her knowing full well how Sophia felt about Luca. Because now she felt like it was written across her skin, across her forehead, so that it could clearly be read by the man himself.

Her earlier confidence melted away, and her skin began to heat as Luca stopped, his dark eyes assessing her slowly.

Her body tingled, her breasts feeling heavy, her nipples going tight as though his fingertips were grazing her skin. As if he was doing more than simply looking.

"It will do," he said, his tone as hard as his features.

Her throat felt prickly, and she swallowed hard, feeling foolish, her heart fluttering like a caged bird trying to escape. How could she feel so much when he looked at her, while he felt nothing for her at all? While he clearly saw her as an annoyance.

He didn't look impressed; he didn't look awed or surprised with what she had felt was a total transformation.

"I am glad that I reach at least the bottom of your very lofty standards, Your Majesty," she said stiffly. "I can only hope that a certain Swedish noble has a slightly more enthusiastic response."

"I said that it will do," he reiterated. "And it will. What more do you want from me, *sorellina*?"

"I spent the entire day receiving a makeover. I would have thought it would garner a response. But it seems as if I am destined to remain little more than wallpaper. It is okay. Some women are never going to be beautiful."

She grasped the flowing skirt of her dress with her fists and pushed past Luca, running out of the room, down the hall, running until her lungs burned. The sound of the heels she was wearing on the floor drowned out the sound of anything else, so it wasn't until she stopped that she heard heavy footsteps behind her. And she was unprepared for the large, strong hand that wrapped around her arm and spun her in the opposite direction. It was then she found herself gazing up into Luca's impossibly dark and imposing eyes.

"What is it you want from me?" he asked, his voice low and hard. Shot through with an intensity she had never heard in his voice before. "What do you want me to give you? What reaction would have been sufficient? In the absence of the one man you have ever wanted, what is it you expected *me* to give you? Do you want me to tell you that you're beautiful? Do you want me to tell you the curves would drive any man to distraction? That every man in that ballroom is going to imagine himself holding you in his arms? Feeling those luscious breasts pressed against his chest? Kissing those lips. Driving himself inside you? Is that what you want to hear? I can give you those words, Sophia, but they are pointless. I could tell you that any man who doesn't want you was a fool, but what is the point in saying those words? What could they possibly mean between the two of us?" He released his hold on her, and she stumbled backward. "Nothing. They mean nothing coming from me. It will always be nothing. It must be."

"Luca…"

"Do not speak to me." He straightened then, his expression going blank, his posture rigid. "It will do, Sophia. You will wear that dress the night of the ball. And you will find yourself a husband. I will see to that."

It wasn't until Luca turned and walked away, wasn't until he was out of her sight, that she dropped to her knees, her entire body shaking, her brain unwilling to try and figure out what had just passed between them. What those words had meant.

He said it could be nothing. It was nothing. She curled her fingers into fists, her nails digging into her skin.

It was nothing. It always would be.

She repeated those words to herself over and over again, and forced herself not to cry.

CHAPTER FOUR

He had acted a fool the day that Sophia had received her makeover. He had... He had allowed his facade to crack. He had allowed her to reach beneath that rock wall that he had erected between himself and anyone who might get too close.

He never acted a fool. And he resented the fact that Sophia possessed the power to make him do so.

His entire life was about the crown. The country.

His mother had driven the importance of those things home before she died. In an exacting and painful manner. One that had made it clear it was not Luca who mattered, but San Gennaro. The royal name over the royal himself.

He had shaped himself around that concept.

But Sophia had looked...

Thankfully, it was time. The guests had all arrived for the ball, with Sophia scheduled to arrive fashionably late so as to draw as much attention as possible.

His attention had been fixed on her far too much in the past few days. Sadly, everything his body had suspected about her beauty had been confirmed with this recent makeover. This stylist had managed to uncover and harness the feminine power that had always been there. And she had put it on brilliant display. Those curves, not covered anymore, but flaunted, served up as if they were a rare delicacy that he wanted very much to consume.

And of course, other men were going to look at her this way. Other men were going to dance with her.

Another man was going to marry her. Take her to his bed.

It was the plan. It was his salvation. Resenting it now… Well, he was worse than a dog in the manger, so to speak. Much worse.

He made a fox and a hen house look tame. Of course, if he were the fox he would devour her. He would have no one and nothing to answer to.

He was not a fox. He was a king.

And he could not touch her. He *would* not. He would honor that final request his father had made. To keep her safe. To see her married to a suitable man.

He was not that man, and he never could be.

Even if their relationship wasn't as it was, he would not be for her. He might have been, once. But that possibility had been destroyed along with so many other things. He had very nearly been destroyed, too. But as he had set about to rebuild himself, he had made choices. Choices that would redeem the sins in the past. Not his sins to redeem. But that mattered little.

He was the one who had to live with the consequences. He was the one who had to rule a country with strength and unfailing wisdom.

And so, he had purposed he would.

But that did not make him the man for her.

Thank God the ball was happening now. Thank God this interminable nightmare was almost over.

She would choose one of the men in attendance tonight. He would be certain of that.

He stood at the back of the room, surveying the crowd of people. All of the women dressed in glorious ball gowns, none of whom would be able to hold a candle to Sophia, he knew. None of whom would be able to provide him with the distraction that he needed.

"This is quite lovely." He turned to see his stepmother standing beside him. She had been traveling abroad with friends for months, clearly needing time away to process the loss of her husband. Though she was back now, living in a small house on palace grounds.

It suited her, she said, to live close, but no longer in the palace.

She had lost a significant amount of weight since the death of his father, and she had not had much to lose on that petite frame of hers to begin with. She was elegant as ever, but there was a sadness about her.

She had truly loved his father. It was something that Luca had never doubted. Never had he imagined she was a commoner simply looking to better her station by marrying royalty. No, there had been real, sincere love in their marriage.

Something that Luca himself would never be able to obtain.

"Thank you," he said.

"And all of this is for Sophia?"

"Yes," he said. "It is as my father wished. He wanted to see her in a good marriage. And I have arranged to see that it is so."

"Yes," she said, nodding slowly. "But what does Sophia think?"

"She has agreed. In that, she has agreed to try to

find someone tonight. And if she does not, she has six months following to choose the man that she wishes. But I have confidence that one of the men tonight will attract her."

"I see," she said.

"You do not approve?"

"I married your father because I loved him. And one of the wonderful things that came with that marriage was money. With money came the kind of freedom that I never could have hoped Sophia to have if we had remained impoverished. I hate to see it curtailed."

"This is not curtailing her freedom. It is simply keeping with what is expected of those in our station. I have explained this to Sophia already."

"Yes, Luca. I have no doubt you have. You are very like your father in that you are confident that your way is always correct."

"My way is the best for a woman in her position. You must trust that I am the authority on this."

"You forget," his stepmother said, "I have been queen for a sizable amount of time. I did not just leave the village. So to speak."

"Perhaps not. But I was born into this. And you must understand that it is difficult to marry so far above your station. That is not an insult. But I know that it took a great deal for yourself and Sophia to adjust to the change. I know that Sophia still finds it difficult. Can you imagine if she married someone for whom this was foreign?"

"You make a very good point."

"This ball, this marriage, is not for my own amusement." It was for his salvation. However, he would leave that part unspoken.

Suddenly, the double doors to the ballroom opened, and all eyes turned to the entryway. There she was, a brilliant flash of fuchsia, her dark hair tumbling around her shoulders. She was even more beautiful than he had remembered. Golden curves on brilliant display, her skin gleaming in the light.

"Oh, my," her mother said.

"She got a new stylist," he said stiffly.

"Apparently."

Sophia descended the staircase slowly, and the moment one foot hit the bottom of the stair, her first suitor had already approached her. The Swede.

Sophia would probably be disappointed he didn't have a sheep on a leash to entertain her. Or a sweater.

"You do not approve of him?" his stepmother asked.

"Of course I approve of him. I approve of every man that I asked to come and be considered as a potential husband for Sophia."

"Then you might want to look less like you wish to dismember him."

"I am protective of her," he said, straightening and curling his hands into fists.

"If you say so."

He gritted his teeth. He did not like the idea that his stepmother of all people would find him transparent. He prided himself on his control, but Sophia tested it at every turn.

And so he told himself that the feeling roaring through him now was relief when the man took hold of Sophia and swept her around the dance floor.

The other man's hand rested perilously low on her waist, on the curve of her hip, and if he was to move his hand down and around her back he would be cupping that lovely ass of hers. And that, Luca found unacceptable.

He will not stop there if he marries her. He will touch her everywhere. Taste her everywhere. She will belong to him.

He gritted his teeth. That was the point. The point was that she needed to belong to another man, so that he could no longer harbor any fantasies of her.

As the song ended, another man approached Sophia, and she began to dance with him. Another of her selections.

Luca approached a woman wearing royal blue, and asked her to dance. Kept himself busy, tried to focus on the feel of her soft, feminine curves beneath his hands. Because what did it matter if it was this woman, or another. What did it matter. Sex was sex. A woman's body was a woman's body. He should be able to find enjoyment in it. He should not long for the woman in pink across the room. The woman who was tacitly forbidden to him. But he did.

The woman he held in his arms now might well have been a cardboard cutout for all that she affected him.

But still, he continued to dance with her, knowing that he should not. Knowing that dancing with any single woman this long would create gossip. He didn't even know her name. He wouldn't ask for it. And tomorrow he would not remember her face until he saw it printed in the paper. She didn't matter.

Suddenly, Sophia extricated herself from her dance partner's hold, excusing herself with a broad gesture as she scurried across the ballroom.

"Excuse me," he said, releasing hold of his dance partner, following after his stepsister.

Sophia wove through the crowd and made her way outside. He followed. But by the time he got out to the balcony, she was gone. He looked over the edge and saw a dark shape moving across the grass below. He could only barely make her out, the glow from the ballroom lights casting just enough gold onto the ground to highlight her moving shape. He swung his leg over the edge of the balcony and lowered himself down to the grass below, following the path that Sophia had no doubt taken.

He said nothing, his movements silent as he went after her. To what end, he didn't know. But then, he had no idea what she thought she was doing, either. It was foolish for her to leave the ball. And it was foolish for him to go after her. All of this was foolish. Everything with her. Always.

And yet, he couldn't escape her. That was the essential problem. She was unsuitable because of their connection. She was inescapable because of their connection. And for that reason, he had never been able to master it.

He could not have her; neither could he banish her from his life.

And here he was, chasing after her in a suit.

He was the king of a nation, stumbling in the dark after a woman.

Finally, she stopped, her pale shoulders shaking, highlighted by the light of the moon. He reached out, placing his hand on her bare skin. She jumped, turning to face him, her eyes glistening in the light. "Luca."

And suddenly, he knew exactly why he had gone after her. He knew exactly what the endgame was. Exactly why he was here.

"Sophia."

And then he wrapped her in his arms and finally did the one thing he had expressly forbidden himself from doing. He claimed her lips with his own.

CHAPTER FIVE

LUCA WAS KISSING HER. It was impossible. Utterly and completely impossible that this was happening. She was delusional. Dreaming. She had to be.

Luca *hated* her.

Luca saw himself as being so far above her that he would hardly deign to speak to her if they weren't related by marriage.

He didn't want to kiss her. He didn't.

Except, with the little bit of brainpower that she had, she recalled that moment in the halls of the castle days ago. When she had gotten her makeover. He had grabbed hold of her arm and had told her he could not tell her how beautiful she was because it was pointless. Because nothing could come of it.

Did that mean he wished it could?

It had all felt like something too bright and too close then. Something she couldn't parse and didn't want to. Not when the end result would only be her own humiliation. Even if he didn't know what she was thinking, entertaining the notion that Luca might want her had always seemed horrific, even if no one ever found out.

It was so surreal a thought that she was still asking

it even as those firm, powerful lips thrust hers apart, his tongue invading her mouth.

She had never been kissed like this before. Had never received anything beyond polite kisses that had seemed to be a testing of her interest.

Luca, true to form, was not testing her interest. He was *assuming* it. And she imagined that if he found her disinterested, he would work with all that he had to change her mind.

Except, his assumption was correct. And she did not possess the strength to deny that. Not now.

Not when her most cherished fantasy was coming to life, right here in the darkened garden of the palace.

Luca cupped her face, large, hot hands holding her steady as he angled his face and took her deeper.

He kissed exactly like what he was. An autocratic conqueror. A man who had never been denied a single thing in his life.

A man who would not be denied now.

"I cannot watch this," he rasped. "I cannot watch other men dance with you. Put their hands on you."

"You said… You said you had to find me a husband." Her voice was wobbly, tremulous, and she hated that. She wished—very much—that she could be more confident. That she could sound sophisticated. As if this was simply another garden tryst of many in a long line of them. Rather than the first time she had truly, honestly been kissed by a man.

Rather than a girl on the receiving end of something she had desired all of her life.

She didn't want him to know that. She didn't want him to know how she felt.

But then she imagined that she betrayed herself with

each breath, with each moment that passed when she didn't slap his face and call him ten kinds of scoundrel for daring to touch her in that way.

Of course she betrayed herself. Because, though he had been the one to instigate, she had kissed him back.

She had been powerless to do anything else. She had been far too caught up in it, consumed by it. By him.

The story of her life.

Things went well, and then Luca. And it all went to hell. It all belonged to him.

"I am going to find you a husband," he said. "I swore it to my father." He dragged his thumb along the edge of her lip. "But I cannot pretend I don't want you. Not any longer."

"You… You want me?"

"It is like a disease," he ground out. "To want my *sister* as I do."

"I'm not your sister," she said, her lips numb. "We don't have the same parents. We don't share blood at all."

"But don't you see? To my father you were. And you would be to the nation. An affair between the two of us would have disastrous consequences."

She closed her eyes, swallowing hard. "How?"

"Think of the headlines. About how our parents were married, and I debauched you likely from the moment you were beneath my roof. As a child. Or, you seduced me to try and hold on to your place. The nation has accepted you as a princess, without a blood relation, but reminding them so starkly that you do not carry royal blood is only a mistake. Can you imagine? An affair between two people who must thereafter remain family? It would be a disaster," he reiterated.

"Then why did you kiss me?"

"Because I no longer possess the power to *not* kiss you. He had his hands on you," he growled, grabbing hold of her hips and drawing her up against his body. "You may have only ever wanted one man before me. But I will make you forget him."

She gasped. She could feel the aggressive jut of his arousal against her stomach, could feel the intensity in the way he held her. His blunt fingertips dug into her skin, and she was certain that he would leave bruises behind. But she didn't care. She would be happy to bear bruises from Luca's touch. Whatever that said about her.

And then, he stopped talking. Then, that infuriating, arrogant mouth was back on hers, kissing, sucking and tasting. He angled his head, dragging his teeth along her tender lower lip before nipping her, growling as he consumed her yet again.

Sophia didn't know this game. She didn't know what to do next. Didn't know how to use her lips and tongue just so as Luca seemed to do.

So she battled against inexperience with enthusiasm, clinging to the front of his jacket with one hand, the other wrapped around his tie as she raised herself up on her toes and kissed him with all the needs she had inside her. She found herself being propelled backward, deeper into the garden. There was a stone bench there, and Luca gripped her hips, sliding his large, warm hands down her thighs, holding on to her hard as he lifted her so that her legs were wrapped around his waist. Then he brought both of them down onto the stone bench, with her sitting on his lap.

Her thighs were spread wide, the quivering, needy

heart of her pressed hard against that telltale ridge that shouted loudly to her that this wasn't a hallucination. That Luca did want her. That no matter it didn't make any sense, that no matter it went against everything she had always believed about him, about herself, about who they were, it was happening.

He moved his hands back to cup her rear, drawing her even more firmly against his arousal. Heat streaked through her veins, lightning shooting through her body. She had never felt anything like this. Like the all-consuming intensity of Luca. That sure and certain mouth tasting her, the friction slick and undeniably intoxicating. Like those big, hot hands all over her curves. His length between her thighs. He was everywhere. All around her. Flooding her senses. It wasn't just his touch. It was his flavor. His scent.

Familiar and so unfamiliar all at the same time. She knew Luca. From a distance. He had been in her life for so many years. Part of so many formative feelings that she'd had. He had most definitely been her very first fantasy. But those fantasies had been muted. They had not come close to the reality of the man himself. Of what it meant to be held by him, kissed by him, consumed by him.

This was no gauzy fantasy. This was something else entirely. It was harsh, and it was far too sharp. She was afraid it was going to slice her in two. The feelings of pleasure that she felt were nothing like the fluttery sensations that had built low in her stomach when he used to look at her across a crowded room. Were nothing compared to the swooping feeling she would get in her stomach when she would allow herself to imagine something half as racy as him kissing her on the mouth.

No. This was pain. Sharp between her legs. A hollow sensation at her core that terrified her, because she didn't feel as though he had created it just now so much as uncovered it. That she was hollow until she could be filled by him. That if he didn't, she would always remain this way.

Luca.

This was a raw, savage uncovering of desire. Desire that she had always known was there, but that had been muted, blunted, by her innocence. By the sure certainty that nothing could ever happen between them.

But now he wanted her. And she didn't know if she was strong enough to bear it.

Because it wasn't just what might happen next. No. It was what would happen when it ended. Then it would end. He had said as much.

He might have confessed his desire for her, but there were no other feelings involved. He had spoken of nothing tender. No. It was nothing but anger in Luca's eyes. Anger and lust.

That was what had been on his face when he had chased her down in the corridor days ago. Anger. Rage. And lust. The unidentified emotion in his eyes. The one she had not been brave enough to identify.

He moved his hand up the back of her head, cupping her skull, then he plunged his fingers deep into her locks, curling his hand into a fist and tugging hard, forcing her head backward, pressing his lips to the curve of her throat. And she felt like wounded prey at the mercy of a predator. Her most vulnerable parts exposed to him.

And yet she allowed it. Didn't fight against it. Wanted it.

Needed it.

That was the worst part. This was something more than want. This was part of her essential makeup.

She had been exposed to Luca at such an early age that he had been formative to her. That he was part of her journey to womanhood. So maybe this was apt. Terrifying though it might be, maybe this was something that needed to happen.

This wasn't the Middle Ages. None of those men out in the ballroom had been promised a virgin princess.

She owed them nothing, for now. For now, it was only Luca.

For now.

And that would have to be enough.

"Dear God," he rasped, dragging his tongue along the edge of her collarbone, down lower to where the plump curve of her breasts met the neckline of her dress. "I've lost my mind."

"I..." She was going to say something witty. Something about the fact that she had lost hers right along with him. But she couldn't speak. Instead, she heaved in a sharp breath, bringing that wicked mouth into deeper contact with her breast. He growled, jerking the top of her dress down, exposing her to him.

She had never been naked in front of a man before. She found she wasn't embarrassed. Certainly, the darkness out in the garden helped, but she knew that with the aid of the moonlight he could still see plenty. But it was Luca. The only man that she had ever been prepared to have seen her naked body. The only man she had ever fantasized about. This was terrifying. It went far beyond anything she had imagined. But it was with him.

And that made all the difference. It made every difference.

He said some words in Italian that she didn't understand. She was fluent enough, having lived in San Gennaro for so much of her life, but she didn't know these words. Hot and filthy-sounding, even without the translation. He scraped his cheek along that tender skin, his whiskers abrading her skin. And then he drew one aching, tightened nipple deep into his mouth, sucking hard.

She arched her back, crying out as pleasure pierced her core like an arrow.

He brought one hand up to cup her breast, rough and hot. She wanted to ask him why his hands were so rough. Wanted to ask him what he did to keep his body so finely honed. Why a man who should have the body of any man with a desk job looked as he did.

But she couldn't ask. All of her words, all of her questions, were bottled up in her throat, and the only thing that could escape was one hoarse cry as he moved from one breast to the next with his mouth, sucking the other nipple in deep, teasing her and tormenting her as he did.

For a moment she had the thought that this was too much too soon. She wasn't ready for this. How could she be? She had never even kissed a man before, and now she was in the arms of King Luca, her top pulled down, her breasts exposed. Riding the hard ridge of his arousal. How could that not be too much? How could she possibly withstand such a thing?

But suddenly, perhaps in time with the flex of his hips upward—that iron part of him making contact with the place where she was softest, most pliant and most sensitive—perhaps it was that that crystallized everything for her. It wasn't enough. And she had waited a lifetime for it. It didn't matter what experience or lack of it she'd had before. Not in the least. What mattered was that it was him.

That she had longed for, craved, desired this very thing for what felt like an eternity.

Luca. Her stepbrother. The man who seemed for all the world to find her utterly and completely beneath his notice, was kissing her. And she could not deny him anything that he wanted.

She could not deny herself what she wanted.

Luca's large, warm hands slid down the shape of her body as if he was taking her measurements with those strong fingers. Then they moved down farther, to her thighs, finding the hem of her dress, already pushed up partway, and shoving it up farther, exposing her even more.

He made a low, feral sound. Hungry. Untamed. Perhaps he was like this with all women; that was a possibility. One that she didn't want to think about. At least not too much. She would like to be special. But she had no idea how she could be. Anything between them was impossible, and she knew it. She had always known it. That didn't mean her feelings disappeared.

"I have wanted you," he said, his voice rough, as rough as the scrape of his whiskers against the side of her neck as he dragged a kiss down her throat. "It is a madness. It is like a sickness. And nothing…nothing has ever come close to banishing it from me. You are like a poison in my blood."

The words sounded tortured. Tormented. And for a moment she wondered if he felt even the slightest bit of what she had felt over the past years. And if he did… Then whatever this could be, and she had no illusions that it could be anything remotely close to permanent, she knew it was the right thing.

Madness. Sickness. Poison.

Those words described what she felt for Luca far too closely. They resonated inside her. They were her truth. And if they were his…how could she deny it?

She was no longer content to simply sit on his lap and be kissed. No. She wanted him. She wanted this. And she was going to have him.

She returned volley with a growl of her own, biting his lower lip as she moved her hands to that black tie that held his crisp, white shirt shut. With trembling fingers she undid the knot and pulled it open, then made quick work of the top button of that shirt. Followed by the next. And the next. She pushed the fabric apart, exposing muscles, chest hair and hot, delicious skin to her touch.

She had heard people talk about desire. But they had never said that it was so close to feeling ill. So close to feeling like you might die if you couldn't have what you wanted.

So close to pain.

There was a hollow ache between her legs, running through her entire body, and she felt that if it was not filled by him she wouldn't be able to go on. It was as simple as that.

She traced her fingertips over his chest, across his nipple, gratified by the rough sound of pleasure that exited his mouth as she did so. He wrapped his arms around her tightly, lowering his head again, tasting and teasing her breasts as he did. She had never imagined that insanity could be blissful. But hers certainly was. Magical in a way that she had not imagined it could be.

She had not thought that there could be beauty in torment. But there was. In this moment.

In this world they had created in the rose garden, separate from the concerns happening in the ballroom. The concerns of their lives, real lives, and not this stolen moment.

There were men in there that she was expected to consider seriously as husbands. A whole raft of duties and responsibilities waiting for both of them that had nothing to do with satisfying their pleasure under a starry sky with only the moon as witness.

But she was glad they had found this. This quiet space. The space where only they belonged. Where their parents' marriage didn't matter. Where their titles didn't matter. Where—whatever that could possibly mean to a man like Luca—they simply were Luca and Sophia, with nothing else to concern them.

He kept on saying things. Rough. Broken. Words in Italian and English. Some of which she couldn't understand, not so much because of the language barrier but because of the intensity in his words, the depth of them. The kinds of things he said, talking about doing things she had never imagined, much less spoken about.

But they washed over her in a wave, and she found she wanted them all. That she wanted this.

Him.

Broken, and out of control in a way that she had never imagined it was possible for Luca to be. At all other moments he was the picture of control. Of absolute and total certainty. And in this moment he did not seem as though he had the power to be that man.

It made her feel powerful. Desired.

His hands moved between her thighs, sliding between the waistband of her panties and teasing her where she was wet and ready for him. For a moment she felt a fleeting sense of embarrassment, a scalding heat in her cheeks. Because certainly now he would know how much she wanted him. How much she felt for him. What woman would be like this if she didn't? And there, he found the incontrovertible evidence. But if it bothered him, he didn't show it. Instead, he seemed inflamed by it. Seemed to want her all the more.

"Perhaps later," he rasped, kissing her neck, her cheek, making his way back to her lips. "Perhaps later I will take my time. Will be able to savor you as you should be. But now… I find there is not enough time, and I must have you."

She wanted him to have her. Whatever that might mean. She needed it.

He shifted, undid the closure on his pants and wrapped his arms tightly around her, angling her hips so that she was seated above him, the head of his arousal pressing against the entrance to her body.

And then he thrust up into her, deep and savage, giving no quarter to her innocence at all. It hurt. But Luca didn't seem to notice. Instead, he began to move inside her in hard, decisive thrusts. She couldn't catch her breath. But then, she didn't want to. Even as she felt like she was being invaded, conquered, she didn't want him to stop. Even as it hurt, she didn't want him to stop. Gradually, the pain gave way to pleasure, an overwhelming, gripping sense of it that built inside her until she thought she wouldn't be able to take it much longer.

When it broke over her it was like a wave containing a revelation, pleasure like she had never known bursting through her. If she had looked up to find fireworks in the sky she wouldn't have been surprised. But the only thing above her was stars. The fireworks were in her.

They were the fireworks.

She and Luca together.

She held on to him tightly as she rode out her release, pulsing waves that seemed to go on and on crashing inside her endlessly. Then he gripped her hips hard, driving himself up into her with brute force as he found his own release, a growl vibrating through his chest as he did.

And then somehow, it was over. Nothing but the sound of their breathing, the feel of his heart pounding heavily against her hand, where it rested against his sweat-slicked chest.

The night sky no longer seemed endless. Instead, it pressed down on them, the reality of what had just occurred lowering the blackness but leaving the stars out of reach.

She felt dark. Cold.

She was cold. Because she was naked in a garden.

Luca moved her away from him, beginning to straighten his clothing. "We must go back," he said, his tone remote and stiff.

"How?" she asked. Because she had a feeling he did not just mean to the ball, but to the way things had been before he had touched her. Before that rock wall had broken between them and revealed what they had both desired for so long.

"It doesn't matter how. Only that it must be."

She looked at him, searching his face in the darkness. "I don't know if I can."

"But you must," he said, uncompromising.

The light from the moon cast hollows of his face

into light and shadow, making it look as though he was carved out of the very granite his voice seemed to be made of.

"You will go back into that ballroom and you will dance with the rest of the men you said you would dance with. Then you will choose a husband," he continued.

"Luca," she said, her voice breaking. "I can't do that. Not after I was just…"

"It is only sex, *sorellina*," he said, the endearment landing with a particular sharpness just now. "You will find a way to cope."

Panic attacked her, its sharp, grasping claws digging into her. "I was a virgin, you idiot."

That stopped him. He drew back as though he had been slapped.

"You said…you said you wanted a man."

She looked away, her shame complete now, her face so hot she was sure she was about to burst into flame. "Who do you think I wanted, you fool?"

The silence that fell between them was heavy. As if the velvet sky had fallen over the top of them.

"Not the choice I would have made my first time. But the choice was yours. You had every chance to say no. You did not." Suddenly his tone turned fierce. "Am I to assume you didn't want to? Are you trying to imply that you didn't know what you were doing?"

"No," she said. "I knew what I was doing."

"Then I fail to see what your virginity has to do with any of it. This is hardly Medieval times. No one will expect a virgin princess on their wedding night anyway."

"I suppose not."

"I must go back. I am the host, after all. Take all the time you need to gather yourself."

He said that as though she should be impressed with his softness. With his kindness. She was about to tell him how ludicrous that was, but then he turned and walked away, leaving her there, half-naked on a stone bench, having just lost her virginity to her stepbrother. To her king.

Her lungs were going to cave in on themselves. Collapse completely, along with her heart. It was shattered anyway, so it didn't matter where the pieces landed.

This was her fantasy. That bright little spot of hope that had existed somewhere inside her, a glimmer of what could be that kept her warm on the darkest of nights.

Now it was gone. Snuffed out. As dark as the night around her.

When she went to bed at night, she would no longer wonder. Because she knew. It had been better than she had imagined. Had transformed her. In more ways than the physical. He had been inside her. Joined to her. This man that had held her emotions captive for half of her life.

This man she'd spent nights weaving beautiful, gilded stories about in her head before she fell asleep. If only. If maybe. If someday.

But it had happened. And now there was no more rest in *if only*.

Nothing remained but shattered dreams.

He acted as though they would be able to go back to normal. But Sophia knew she would never be the same again.

CHAPTER SIX

SOPHIA HAD AVOIDED him for the past few weeks. Ever since she had gone back into the ballroom and proceeded to dance with every man he had commanded her to.

She had been pale-faced and angry-looking, but gradually, it had all settled into something serene, though no less upset.

But he did not approach her. Not again. And she moved around the palace as if she were a ghost.

He had failed her. Had failed them both. But there was nothing to be done. There was no use engaging in a postmortem. His control had failed him at the worst possible moment.

He had done the one thing he had purposed he would never do. And it had been all much more a spectacular failure than he had initially imagined it would be.

A *virgin.*

He had not thought she would be that.

She had gone to university. Had moved out in the world for quite some time, and she was beautiful. In his mind, irresistible. Hell, in practice she was irresistible. Had he been able to resist her, then he surely would have.

No man could possibly resist her. If his own ironclad control had failed…

So perhaps that was his pride. Because clearly she had somehow remained untouched all this time.

And he had failed at maintaining that particular status quo.

But that other man had been touching her. Holding her in his arms.

Perversely, he was satisfied by the fact that he had been the first man to touch her. It was wrong. And he should feel a deep sense of regret over it. Part of him did. But another part of him gloried in it.

As with all things Sophia, there was no consensus between desire and morality.

The only contact he'd had with Sophia had been for her to tell him that she wanted to speak with him today. And so he sat in his office, his hands curled into fists, resting on the top of his desk while he waited for her to appear.

The fact that she never failed to put him on edge irked him even now.

There'd never been a more pointless and futile attraction in the history of the world. Or, perhaps there had been, but it had not bedeviled him, and so, it didn't concern him now. No, it was Sophia who had that power over him.

And she was not for him.

There was no way he could reconfigure their fates to make it so. No way that he could switch around their circumstances. Even if she weren't his stepsister…

He was not the man for her.

The door to his office cracked slightly, and she slipped inside, not knocking. Not waiting for an announcement. Because of course she wouldn't. Of course she would break with protocol, even now. Not allowing the blessed formality inherent in royal life to put some distance between them when it was much needed.

"You wished to come and speak to me?"

"Yes," she said. "But I should think that was self-evident. Considering that I made an arrangement to come and speak to you, and now I am here doing it."

"There is no need to be sarcastic, Sophia."

"I'm surprised you recognized it, Luca."

For a moment their eyes caught and held, the sensation of that connection sending a zap of electricity down through his body.

She looked away as though she had felt that same sensation. As though it had burned.

"I recognize it easily enough. What did you wish to speak to me about?"

"I wanted to tell you that I've made my selection. I've decided who I will marry."

That was the last thing he had expected, and her words hit him with the force of a punch squared to the chest. So intense, so hard, he thought it might have stopped his heart from beating altogether.

"You have?"

"Yes. I hope that you value an alliance with Sweden."

He had not been aware that he possessed the ability to feel finer emotions. Until he felt a last remaining piece of himself—one he had not realized existed—turn to stone. "I'm surprised to hear you say that."

"That I selected him specifically? Or that I have selected anyone at all?"

"That you have complied at all. Rather than making this incredibly difficult."

She clasped her hands in front of her, her dark hair falling down into her face. The outfit she was wearing was much more suited to her than her usual fare. Tight, as that ball gown on the night he had first kissed her had been. A tangerine-colored top that shaped exquisitely to her curves, and a skirt with a white and blue pattern.

But the pattern was secondary to the fact that it hugged her body like a second skin. As he wished he could hug her even now. What he wouldn't give to span that glorious waist again, to slide his palms down to those generous hips.

Having her once had done nothing to eradicate the sickness inside him.

But this marriage… Perhaps it would accomplish what he had hoped it would.

And in the end, he would still have been the one to have her first.

Yes. But he will have her second, if he hasn't had her already, and you will have to watch the two of them together.

He had always known that would be his fate. There was no fighting against it.

"I had some very important questions answered the night of the ball," she said, making bold eye contact with him. "I have no reason to fight against this marriage. Not now."

There was an unspoken entreaty in those words, and it was one he could not answer.

He would have to marry, yes, that was certain. But it would never be a woman like her. It would be a woman who understood. One who didn't look at him with hope in her eyes.

One who wouldn't mind that the part of him that could care for another person, the part of him that loved, had been excised with a scalpel long ago.

That he was a man who ruled with his head because he knew a heart was no compass at all. Least of all his.

It felt nothing. Nothing at all.

"Excellent," he said. "I'm glad there's no longer a barrier."

Color flew to her cheeks, and he did nothing to correct her assumption that he had made an intentional double entendre. He had not. But if it made her angry, all the better.

"Let me know how soon you wish for the wedding to be, and I will arrange it."

"In a month," she said quickly. "We are to be married in a month."

"Then I will prepare an announcement."

Sophia's head hurt. Her heart hurt. Everything hurt. The depression that she had fallen under since the ball was pronounced. It made everything she did feel heavy. Weighted down.

The engagement to Erik hadn't helped matters. The courtship in general hadn't helped at all. And she felt like a terrible person. He was solicitous, kind. Their interactions had not been physical at all. The idea of letting him touch her so closely to when she and Luca had…

Though part of her wondered if she should. Like ripping off a Band-Aid.

The mystery was gone from sex anyway.

A tear slid down her cheek and she blinked, shocked, because she hadn't realized she had been so close to crying. She wiped it away and swallowed hard, attempting to gather herself.

She was currently getting a wedding gown fitted. That meant she had to look a little bit less morose. Though, right now, she was sitting in the room alone, wearing nothing but a crinoline.

Both the seamstress and her mother would be in the room soon, and she really needed to find a way to look as if she was engaged in the process.

But then, she felt as if she had not been engaged in the process of her life for the past few weeks, so why should this be any different?

It had been foolish, perhaps, to jump into marrying Erik, simply because she wanted to do something to strike back at Luca. Simply because she wanted there to be something in her life that wasn't that deep, yawning ache to be with him.

They couldn't be together. It was that simple. He didn't want to be with her. Oh, he had certainly revealed that he lusted after her in that moment in the garden, but it wasn't the same as what she felt for him.

And furthermore, he was allowing her to marry another man.

Another tear splashed onto her hand.

Was that why she was doing this? Was that why she was going through with the engagement? Because she wanted him to stop it?

That was so wholly childish and ridiculous.

And yet she had a feeling she might be just that ridiculous and childish.

The door to the dressing room opened, and the designer and her mother breezed inside at the same time.

Her mother was holding the dress, contained in a plastic zip-up bag, and the designer was carrying a kit.

"Let's help you get this on," the woman said briskly.

Sophia's mother unzipped the bag and helped Sophia pull the dress over her head as the designer instructed. There was much pinning and fussing and exclamation, and Sophia tried very hard to match those sounds.

"Are you okay?" her mother asked as the designer was down on her hands and knees pinning the hem of the gown.

"I'm…overwhelmed." She figured she would go for some form of honesty. It was better than pretending everything was fine when it clearly wasn't, and her mom wasn't going to accept that as an answer.

"It is understandable. This wedding has come together very quickly."

"It's what Luca wants."

"I see."

"It's what Father wanted."

"And what do you want, Sophia? Because as much as I loved your stepfather, and as much as I know he had your best interests at heart… I didn't marry him because I wanted to be queen. I didn't marry him for money, or status. I married him because I loved him. And I want nothing less for you. I understand that he did this because it is what he would have done for his biological daughter if he'd had one. You are not from this world. And you don't have to comply to the dictates of it if you don't wish to."

What was the alternative? Living life with Luca glowering down at her. Wanting him. Watching him get married and have children…

Well, it was that or cutting herself off from her family altogether.

For a moment she stood adrift in that fantasy. Blowing in a breeze where she was tied to nothing and no one. It made her feel empty, hollow. Terrified.

But at least it didn't hurt.

"I want this," she said, resolute. "It's the right thing. And he's a very nice man."

Her mother sighed heavily. "I'm sure that he is."

"You know that Luca wouldn't allow this if he wasn't suitable. If he wasn't good."

"Certainly not," she said. "I know Luca would never allow any harm to come to you. Not physical harm, anyway."

Sophia gritted her teeth, wondering, not for the first time, if her mother suspected that there was something between Luca and herself. If she did, she was not saying anything. Resolutely so.

And Sophia certainly wasn't going to say anything.

She looked down and kicked the heavy skirt of her dress out of the way, and then she straightened, looking at herself in the mirror. Suddenly, she felt dizzy, wobbling slightly as she took in the sight of herself wearing a wedding gown. A wedding gown.

She felt ill.

"Excuse me," she said, clamoring down from the stepstool and dashing into the adjoining bathroom, slamming the door behind her as she collapsed onto her knees and cast up her accounts into the toilet.

She braced herself, shaking and sweating, breathing hard. She had never been sick like that. So abruptly.

She felt terrible. Throwing up hadn't helped.

She pushed herself up, afraid that she had damaged the gown, but it looked intact.

There was a heavy, sharp knock on the door. "Sophia?" It was her mother. Worried, obviously.

"I'm fine," she said. "Just a little bit…nauseated."

"Can I come in?"

"Okay."

The door opened and her mother slipped inside, her expression full of concern. "Are you ill?"

"I wasn't," Sophia said.

"You just suddenly started to feel sick?"

"Yes."

"Sophia…" Her mother looked at her speculatively, "forgive me if this is intrusive… Is it possible that you… Are you pregnant?"

The tentative grasp that Sophia had on the ground beneath her gave way. And she found herself crumbling to the floor again.

"Sophia?"

"I…"

"Are you pregnant?" her mother asked.

"It's possible," she said.

"I suppose the good thing is that the wedding is soon," she said, bending down and grabbing hold of Sophia's chin, her matching dark gaze searching Sophia's. "Are you happy?"

"I'm scared," Sophia said.

She couldn't organize her thoughts. She was late. It was true. She hadn't given it much thought because she had been stressed out with planning the wedding. But she was quite late. And she and Luca had not used a condom that night.

One time.

She'd had sex one time.

With the last man on earth she should have ever been with, and she had gotten pregnant. What were the odds of that happening?

Of course, now she was engaged to another man, a man whose baby it couldn't possibly be, because she had never even kissed him.

But there was going to be a wedding. Invitations had been sent out. Announcements had been made. She was being fitted for a dress.

"Of course you are," her mother said. "It's a terrifying thing facing a change like this. But wonderful." She put her hand on Sophia's face. "You're the best thing that ever happened to me, Sophia."

Sophia tried to smile. "I hope I'll be even half as good a mother as you have been to me."

"You will be."

"I wish I had such confidence."

"You will have help from your husband," her mother said. "I didn't have any help. It will be so nice for you to start with more in life than we had."

Sophia's mouth felt dry as chalk. How could she tell her mother that it wasn't her fiancé's baby?

That it was Luca's.

She couldn't. So she didn't. Instead, she let her mother talk excitedly about the wedding, about being a grandmother. Instead, she went outside and finished the fitting.

When it was over, she walked down the empty halls of the palace, back in her simple shift dress she had been wearing earlier. Then she pushed the door to her bedroom open. She looked around. At this beautiful spectacular bedroom that it was still difficult to believe belonged to her.

She stumbled over to her bed, a glorious, canopied creation with frothy netting and an excess of pillows.

Then she lay across that bed and she wept. She wept like her heart was breaking.

Because it was.

And she had no idea what to do about it.

CHAPTER SEVEN

ULTIMATELY, SOPHIA FELT it was wisest to procure a test through the official palace physician. The princess was hardly going to go to a drugstore to acquire a pregnancy test. It would be foolish. Things like that could never stay secret, not for long. Not in a media-hungry society, always looking for scandal.

One of the many things she'd had to learn, because it wasn't ingrained. That anyone would be interested in the life and times of a girl like her. But they were now. Because of who her mother had married.

Because of who she was, all thanks to a piece of paper. Nothing more.

Oftentimes, she appreciated what had come from that marriage.

This was one of the times she appreciated it less.

Fortunately, she trusted the woman that she had seen for years, recommended to her by palace staff. And she knew that her confidentiality was in fact one of the most important parts of her role as the physician to all members of the royal family, and palace staff.

Unfortunately, no matter how good the doctor was, she could not change the test results with skill.

Sophia paced back and forth while she waited. She

knew pregnancy tests didn't take *that* long. Still, the doctor was certainly taking her time in the makeshift lab, AKA, Sophia's en-suite bathroom.

When the door finally did open, the doctor looked blank. Sophia couldn't read a plus or negative sign on the woman's face. "The test is positive," she said. "Congratulations."

Sophia didn't want to be congratulated. Why should she be? She'd made a massive mistake and put everything Luca believed in in jeopardy. She was risking public embarrassment, wasted money on a wedding…she…she deserved something. But it wasn't congratulations.

"Thank you," Sophia said, instead of any of the things she was thinking. "The wedding is soon at least, so all will be sorted."

Except, she had no idea how to sort it out. This wedding was happening. All of the moving parts were at critical mass.

Tomorrow. The wedding was tomorrow. People were coming from all over to attend.

She was going to have to go to him. She was going to have to see Erik and let him know exactly what transpired. Likely, he would want to break it off. But it was entirely possible that…

She had no idea what she was supposed to do. Was she going to hide Luca's child from him? And what would he think? There was no way he would believe that she had immediately gone to bed with another man. He would know the child was his.

Would he?

It was entirely possible she could convince him she had played the role of harlot. That she had gone straight from Luca, on a garden bench, to Erik's bed.

But Erik was blond, while Luca was dark, darker than she was. The child would not look like Erik.

"I just need some time alone," Sophia said finally. "That's all I need."

The doctor nodded, collecting things and leaving Sophia in her bedroom. Leading her to solve a problem that might well be utterly and completely unsolvable.

She walked over to the closet and opened it up, letting her hands drift over the silk fabric of the wedding gown that was hanging there.

She was carrying Luca's baby. And she was supposed to walk toward another man tomorrow and say vows to him. Promise to love him, stay with him forever. She was supposed to have her wedding night with him.

A violent wave of nausea rolled over her.

She had been lying to herself this entire time. Thinking that she could do this. Thinking that she could be with another man. That she could make all of her feelings for Luca go away if she only tried hard enough. That if she replaced him in her bed she could replace him in her heart, but she didn't know how that could possibly be.

She swallowed hard, her throat dry. There was no going back. Not now.

There couldn't be. There was so much riding on this. Luca was right. Deals had already been made with Erik regarding his holdings, based on this marriage. Luca's reputation…in the eyes of the people, of the world, it mattered.

San Gennaro's reputation depended on Luca's. And…this could potentially compromise that.

And she had to think of that.

It had nothing to do with her being afraid. With her

feeling raw and wounded. Nothing at all. It was the greater good. Not…not the fact that thinking of Luca hurt.

Yes, Erik she was going to have to talk to. Because she owed her future husband honesty if nothing else.

Luca…

She had a feeling it would not be a kindness to give him honesty.

Her head throbbed, her entire body feeling wrung out. She knew that her logic was fallible at best. She knew that she was wrong in so many ways, but she couldn't untangle it all to figure it out.

She picked up the phone, and she dialed the number she needed to call most.

"Hello?"

"Erik," she said, not sure if she was relieved or terrified that he'd answered. "There's something I need to tell you."

"You are not running out on the wedding, are you?"

"*You* might. When you hear what I have to say." She swallowed. "I'm pregnant."

There was nothing but silence for a moment.

"Well," he said, his tone grim. "We both know it isn't mine."

"Yes. We do. But…no one else has to know that. It would be for the best if the baby's father didn't know. And I can't have anyone… I can't have anyone knowing." She tightened her hold on her phone, her heart hammering so hard she could scarcely hear herself speak. "But only if that… If it doesn't offend you in some way."

"I cannot say I'm pleased about it. Though I appreciate the fact that you did not try to pass it off as mine."

"I wouldn't have done that," she said quickly. "Before we get married, you have to know the truth."

"Whose is it?" he asked.

She hesitated. "I cannot give you *that* truth. That's the one thing I can't tell. Trust me on this one thing. I know I made a mistake, but I told you this much. I'm not trying to trick you."

"I see," he said, his tone brave. "You didn't know you were pregnant before now?"

"I swear I didn't."

There was a long pause, silence settling over her, over the room, the furniture groaning beneath its weight.

"It is too late to turn back," he said at last. "I require this union with your country. The alliance and the agreements that were promised to me… I want to see them honored. And if we were to cancel the wedding at such a late date the resulting scandal would be a serious issue."

"Yes," she replied, her lips numb. "That is my feeling on it, as well."

"Then we will go ahead with the wedding."

She must have agreed, but she couldn't remember what she said the moment after she'd spoken the words.

Sophia hung up the phone, not feeling any sense of relief at all. She curled up into a ball on the bed as hopelessness washed through her. Tomorrow it would be finished. It would finally be over.

Except, it never would be. Because whatever the world believed, whatever anyone knew…

The child in her womb was Luca's. A part of him. A part of her. The evidence of their passion, of her love. A bright and shining thing that she would never be able to ignore.

But Luca had been clear. There can be no scandal. She would not subject their child to that. She would not subject him to it.

And so she would have to subject herself to this.

For the second night in a row, Sophia cried herself to sleep.

The morning of the wedding dawned bright and clear, and Sophia awoke feeling damaged. Empty.

Except she wasn't empty. She was carrying Luca's child.

That fact kept rolling through her mind on a reel all while her hair was fixed, her makeup done, her gown given its final fittings.

Her mother looked at her with shining eyes, pride in them. Misplaced.

So badly misplaced.

"Are you all right?" she asked.

"Nervous," she said honestly.

It echoed the exchange they'd had during the fitting. But it was all the more real now. Her tongue tasted like metal, her whole body like a leaden weight.

"Did you take a test?" her mother asked.

"Yes," Sophia said.

"And?"

"It's positive," Sophia returned. "I'm having a baby."

Her mother held her for a long time before letting her go finally. "Have you told Erik?"

"Yes."

If her mother thought something was amiss—and Sophia thought she might—the other woman said nothing. Instead, they continued readying themselves for the ceremony. Then, a half hour before everything was set to begin, Sophia was ushered into a private room where no one could see her. Where the big reveal of the bride would be preserved.

It was dark in there. Quiet. The first moment of reflection she'd had all day. Her veil added an extra layer of insulation against reality. And gave her too much time to think.

She resented it. She didn't want to reflect on anything. She wanted all of this to be over.

She wanted it done, so that there was no going back. She wanted her wedding night done.

Wanted that moment to pass so that Luca would no longer be the only one who'd had claim on her body. So that perhaps she could start building some sort of bond with Erik.

As if you believe that will work.

She had to. What other choice did she have? Tell her *stepbrother* she was having his baby? A stepbrother who didn't seem to want her as more than a physical diversion? Even if it wasn't for the potential scandal…

Luca had been more than willing to send her straight to the arms of another man out of his sense of duty, after taking her virginity in an open space where anyone could have caught them.

Yes, on some deep level she felt this was a betrayal of Luca, but she felt as if he had betrayed her first.

He had made no move to stop this wedding. None at all. He was truly going to let her marry another man.

Then she realized that all this time she had been hoping he would stop it. That he would step in. He said he could not stand to have another man touch her, as he had done the night of the ball.

In the end she had hoped, beyond reason, beyond anything, that he would make this stop.

But he had not.

The realization was like a hot iron through her chest. What a fool she was. She'd been clinging to hope, even now. Hope was why she was here. Because she kept imagining…

She squeezed her eyes shut, a tear streaming down her cheek.

She would be damned if she would go crawling to him. Confess to him she was pregnant with his child when he had already made it clear he did not want her.

And perhaps it was wrong. Perhaps she had no right to those feelings.

Perhaps, as the father, regardless of the fallout, he should be made aware of the baby.

But she couldn't.

Because what if he stopped it all then? What if that was the only reason?

How could she live with herself after that? How could she live with him?

Suddenly, the door to her little sanctuary burst open. His hands clenched into fists, his expression unreadable.

Luca.

CHAPTER EIGHT

RAGE ROLLED THROUGH Luca like a thunderstorm. There she was. His duplicitous stepsister. Her expression obscured by a veil, her figure a stunning tease in that virginal-looking gown.

They both knew she wasn't a virgin.

He had been the one to ruin that, to ruin her. He was well aware.

And then there was the other bit of evidence that she was not as innocent as she currently appeared to be.

"Are you here to give me away?" she asked, her tone maddeningly calm.

"Is that what you want? You want me to march you out of here and pass you off from my arm to his? Fair enough, as you seem to have gone from my bed and straight into his."

He waited for her to correct him on that. But she did not.

"It's a bit late to be acting possessive, *fratello*."

The word *brother* stabbed into him. Sharp. Enraging. The reason she was here prepared to marry another man in the first place.

"Is it now?" It did not feel too late. It felt altogether like just the right time.

She took a step back, stammering. Wondering if she had overplayed her hand. "I'm in a wedding gown. The guests have all arrived. I assume there is a priest."

"You know as well as I do that there is."

"Then unless you intend to give me to my groom, symbolically, of course, I suggest you step aside."

He crossed his arms, standing between Sophia and the door. "Absolutely not."

"I need to go, Luca," she said, her tone pleading with him.

"Answer me one question first," he said, taking a step toward her. His heart was pushing the limits of what a man could endure, he was certain, his stomach twisted.

"What question?" she asked.

"Have you slept with him?" He asked the question through gritted teeth, his entire body tense.

She turned to the side, the veil a cascade of white and bland separation, concealing her expression from him. "I don't see how that's any concern of yours."

"It is my concern if I say it is," Luca returned. "Answer the question, Sophia. And if you lie to me, I will find out."

Suddenly, her posture changed. She came alive. As though she'd been shocked with a live wire.

"Oh, no," she said, delicate hands balled into fists. "I haven't slept with him. But I intend to do so tonight. I would show you the lingerie I selected, but that would be a bit embarrassing. After all, you are only my very concerned stepbrother."

A red haze lowered itself over Luca's vision.

Anger was like a living thing inside him, roaring, tearing him to pieces. He had no idea what answer he would have preferred. One that proved she had been touched by another man, but might not be attempting to deceive them both…or this.

She was doing exactly what he had suspected. And by admitting that, she had also confirmed what he had suspected, his heart raging, when those lab results had come across his desk only an hour ago.

He had imagined…

He had imagined that she would come to him if the news was relevant to him.

She had not. But there was a chance. He had known that. Even if she had slept with Erik the day after she had been with him, there would be a chance.

And here, she had made it very clear, that there was only one possibility.

Still, she hadn't come to him. As if on some level she knew. Knew she should not bind herself to him. As if she could see the cracks in his soul.

If he were a good man, if any of his outward demonstrations of royal piety were deeper than skin, he would let her be.

Would let her go off and marry Erik.

But he had reached an end. An end to the show he had lived for the past two decades.

An end to anything remotely resembling *good.*

"We will have to send our regards to Erik," he said, taking a step forward.

"Why is that?"

"Because I…" He reached forward, grabbing the end of her veil, lifting it and drawing it over her head, revealing that impossibly lovely face that had called to him for years now. That was his constant torment. His constant desire. "I am about to kiss his bride for him."

Luca drew her into his arms; she was his now. There was no denying it. There was no other alternative.

When they parted, she was staring at him, wide eyed.

"And he," Luca continued, his voice rough, "is about to find himself without a wife."

Then he lifted her up and threw her over his shoulder, ignoring the indignant squeak that exited her lips.

"What are you doing?" She pounded a fist against his back.

They were turning into a bad farce of a classic film. And he didn't care. Not one bit.

"Well," he said, continuing to hold her fast. "It seems that we have skipped a few steps. Here you are, in a wedding dress, but our relationship has already been consummated. And it appears that you are pregnant with my child."

"Luca!"

"Did you think I wouldn't find out?" He carried her out of the chapel and across the lawn. It was private back here; paparazzi and guests both barred from coming into this section of the grounds, where the bride might be disturbed. And here, Luca had a private plane waiting.

Just in case.

Just in case of this exact moment.

It felt like madness. Like something that had overcome him in the moment. Strong enough he'd had to pick her up and haul her off.

But obviously some of his madness was premeditated.

Though he had not envisioned this exact scenario, it was clear to him now there had never been another possible outcome.

"Forgive me," he said, not meaning at all. "But I feel as though at this moment in time a wedding ceremony is a bit redundant. We are headed off on our honeymoon."

"We can't," she protested, beating against him again with one closed, impotent fist.

A rather limp, ineffective protest, all in all. When the poor creature could scarcely move.

"I am the king, *sorellina.* And I can do whatever I want."

Yes. He was king. And he could do whatever the hell he wanted. He had been far too caught up in being honorable. In being dutiful to his country. In doing as his father had asked. In doing as his country expected.

In protecting Sophia. Making sure she had the life that would best suit her, not the one that would best please him.

What the hell was the point of being king if you didn't take everything that you desired?

And he desired his stepsister. She was also carrying his heir.

That meant that she would be his.

Regardless of what anyone thought.

It was all clear and bright now. As if the sun had come out from behind the clouds.

"What if I refuse?" she asked.

He carried her up the steps, onto the plane, holding her still while his staff secured the cabin. None of them daring to question him. "You're not in a position to refuse," he said as he placed her in one of the leather seats and solicitously fastened her seat belt. "You are only in a position to obey."

She didn't speak to him for the entirety of the flight. He supposed on some level that was understandable.

She simply sat there and looked at him, radiating rage and tulle, resembling an indignant cake topper. Disheveled, from his carrying her out across the lawn and onto the plane, her hot eyes bright and angry, that lovely lace wedding gown making her look the perfect picture of a bride.

She would need a new wedding gown for when they married. As beautiful as she looked now he would be damned if she walked down the aisle toward him in a dress she had meant for someone else.

That was not something he could endure. He found that he was quickly getting to the end of his endurance where she was concerned.

Scandal was something to be avoided at all costs. It was something his mother had drilled into his head even after she had known…

She had protected the reputation of the family.

And now he was about to destroy that. Then it called into question a great many things.

But here was the point where he had to break from his desire to prevent scandal.

Because if there was one thing, one bitter shard of anger that existed in his chest that cut deeper than all the others, it was the fact that his mother had prized reputation over protecting her son.

Over pursuing retribution for him.

She had cared more for her marriage. More for her paramour.

He would not care more for a clean slate than for this child that Sophia carried. He had needed to marry. Had needed to produce an heir, and it seemed that he was halfway there already. Why should he preserve the nation, their sensibilities, and ignore the fact that this was a moment to seize on something that would be an important asset. Truly, he could not have planned this better.

Because there was only one way that he would be able to justify claiming Sophia as his own. Only one way he would be able to justify having her in his bed for life.

The child.

That, no one would be able to argue with. And yes, it would come at the cost of an ugly scandal. The things that would be written about them…

They would not be kind.

Those headlines would exist, and it was something that their child would have to contend with. Something they would have to contend with.

But in the end, the memory would fade, and they would be husband and wife longer than they had ever been stepbrother and stepsister.

In the end, it would work.

Because it had to.

He was not in the mood to allow the world to defy him. He was not in the mood to think in terms of limits.

He had, for far too long.

He was a king, after all.

And for too long he had allowed that to limit him.

No more.

"Do you want to know where we're going?" he asked, leaning back in his seat and eyeing the bar that sat across the cabin.

"I don't wish to know anything," she said, pale of face and tight-lipped with rage.

"Did you love him so much that this is an affront to you?"

"I tried," she said, whipping around to face him, her dark curls following the motion.

"I tried to do the right thing. I tried to do what you asked of me. I was willing to—"

He could not hear her lies. He held up a hand and stopped her speaking. "You were willing to try to pass my child off as another man's. For that, I cannot forgive you."

"You were willing to let me marry another man," she said. "Only when you found out that I was carrying your child did you try and stop it. You took my virginity in a garden. You gave no thought to protecting me. You took advantage of my innocence. You were going to let another man have me. For that, I cannot forgive *you*." She looked away from him again, pressing one hand to her stomach. "He knew it was not his child, Luca. Whatever you think of me, I would not try and convince another man that this baby was his."

"Does he know it's mine?"

She looked toward him, her dark eyes flashing. "I told him it was the one thing we could never speak of."

"I know you only found out yesterday," he said.

"How did *you* find out?" she asked.

"The palace physician reports directly to me, Sophia. In these matters, there is no privacy."

Her face drained of the rest of its color, her entire frame shaking with rage. And perversely, even in the moment, he found his eyes drawn, outlined to perfection by the sweetheart neckline of the gown, to the delicate swell of her breasts.

A sickness. Sophia would always be his sickness.

"How dare you?"

"I dare *everything*," he said, his voice like granite

even to his own ears. "I am the King of San Gennaro. You are pregnant with my heir. You would have me leave that to chance?"

"I was trying to prevent a scandal. And I don't want your obligation, Luca."

"You have it," he bit out. "Endlessly, *sorellina*, and there is no way around that."

"Would you have let me marry him?"

His throat tightened, adrenaline working its way through his veins. He closed his hands into fists and squeezed them. "Of course," he said. "Because when it comes to matters of the flesh, you can hardly allow them to dictate the course of a country."

"Except, apparently, when that flesh takes shape as a child."

"Naturally," he bit out. "I will hardly allow another man to raise my child. I will hardly sacrifice my son's birthright on the altar of my reputation. On this you are correct, Sophia. I was careless with you. And that carelessness should not come back on our child."

"It might not be a son. It might be a daughter. In which case, you might wish you had allowed me to marry someone else."

"Never," he said, his voice rough.

"You don't seem overly happy."

"Happiness is not essential here. What is essential is duty. What is essential is that I do what is right by my child."

"Yes, I suppose it is what your father tried to do for me. Bundle me up and sell me off to the most worthy of men."

"Yes, and sadly you seem to be stuck with me."

She said nothing to that. He imagined she didn't think he meant it. He did.

He had his darkness. He had his trauma, and he would never have chosen to lock Sophia into a union with him. But the fact remained, it was unavoidable now.

And if that meant he got to sate his desire in her lovely body, then so be it.

"You will be my wife now, Sophia," he said.

"When?" She said it like a challenge. As if she didn't believe him.

"Oh, as soon as we can arrange it. We're going to San Paolo."

Her expression went strangely…soft. Very odd in the context of the moment, when before she'd been looking nearly feral. "Your father's island?"

"It is *my* island now." A soft, firm reminder that his father was gone.

That, though he would have strongly disapproved of this, he was not here to see it. No one was. Not now.

How easy it would be to lay her back on that chair, to push up that wedding dress and lose himself inside her. Talking was a pointless exercise when it was not what he wanted.

Heat lashed through him. He wanted her. Even in this moment, when all should be reduced to the gravity of the situation, he wanted her.

"This will not be easy," she said, her voice shaking.

"Denying me my child would have been simple, Sophia?"

"That isn't what I mean. Don't be dense, Luca. The world will be watching us. Will be watching and judging and we will be bringing a baby into that. It seemed kinder in some ways to try and avoid all of that."

Rage was like a storm inside him. By God, he couldn't cope with not having power. With having his choices taken from him. "You don't have a biological father of your own. The man couldn't be bothered to raise you. How dare you visit the same fate upon your child?"

"Biology doesn't matter," she snapped. "All that matters is that a man is good. Your father was the best father I could have ever asked for. My own father… He didn't want me. He didn't care for me. He didn't matter. Not when I had your father to call my own. He *earned* that place. He wasn't born with some magical right given to him by blood you can't even see. That's how I thought I could do it. Because I know full well that it's not genetics that make a parent."

"And what about me? You think so little of me that you think I am like the man who sired you? That I am like a man who could walk away from his child and never think of her again?"

"I figured what you didn't know couldn't hurt you. Or your goals. Or the country."

"How cavalierly you played with our fates," he bit out.

"How cavalierly you played with my privacy," she shot back.

"You don't deserve privacy," he returned. "You proved that with your betrayal."

Silence descended on the plane. Luca stood up and made his way across the space, heading over to the bar and pouring himself a measure of scotch.

"None for you," he said, his tone unkind. He was well aware of it. He didn't care. She did not deserve his kindness at the moment.

"You hate me," she said softly. "You always have. Or, if you don't hate me, it's a kind of malevolent indifference the likes of which I have never experienced. I would have said it was impossible. To dislike and not care at the same time. But you seem to manage it."

He shook his head, laughter escaping in spite of himself. Then he took a drink of scotch. "Is that what you think?"

"It is what I *know*, Luca."

"You are a fool," he said, knocking back his drink, relishing the burn all the way down to his gut. At least that burn was expected. Acceptable.

Then he stopped over to where she was seated, leaned forward, bracing his hands on the arms of the seat, bracketing her in. His eyes met hers, electricity arcing between them. His skin tingled with her being this near, his entire body on high alert. His heart was pounding heavily, his blood flowing south, preparing his body to enter hers.

He wondered if every time he was near her it would be thus. And concluded just as quickly that as it had been this way for nearly a decade it was likely not to change anytime soon.

"You think I hate you? You think I am indifferent to you? If I behaved that way, Sophia, it was only because I was attempting to protect your innocence. Attempting to protect you from my lust."

"Luca…"

He stood up, running his hands through his hair. "I have always known there was something wrong with me," he said. "That I could not trust my own desires. I proved it to be so the other night. But I quite admirably steered clear of that destruction for a very long time."

"You want me?" she asked, her voice small.

"Did I *want you*? I wanted no one else. Do you have any idea how many delightfully curvy brunettes I have taken to my bed and attempted not to make them you in my mind as I made love to them?"

Her face was white now, her lips a matching shade. "Am I supposed to be flattered by that? That you used other women and thought of me?"

"No one should be flattered by it," he said darkly. "But I feel strongly that no one should be flattered by my attentions, either."

"Why?"

The question was simple, and he supposed it was the logical one, and yet, it surprised him. He had not expected her to come back at him with the simplest and most reasonable question.

"It is not important."

"I think that it might be," she said.

"Truly it is not. All you need to know is that you will marry me. It is nonnegotiable. You will be my queen, and our child will be the heir. If you feel regret over it, you should've thought of that before you climbed on my lap in the garden."

"If you feel regret then perhaps you should've thought of that before you took me without a condom," she shot back.

Heat, white and sharp, streaked through him like a lightning bolt, and he had to grit his teeth, plant his feet firmly on the floor and tighten his hands into fists to keep from moving toward her. To keep from claiming her. To keep from doing just what she described now again.

"I have no regrets," he said. "I'm not so certain you'll feel the same in the fullness of time."

Sophia felt drained, utterly bedraggled by the time the plane landed, and she trudged off and onto the blaring heat of the tarmac. Her gown was beginning to feel impossibly heavy, but Luca had not offered her anything to change into.

Had she not just spent an extremely cool three hours on the plane with Luca, alternating between stony silence and recrimination, she would have thought she was in some kind of a dream.

An extremely twisted one.

It was far too hot on San Paolo for layers and layers of lace and chiffon. For the crinoline she had on beneath the gown.

The sky was jewel bright, reflected in the clear waters that stretched out around them, like an impassible moat, cutting them off from the world. The beach was bleached white by the sun, shrubby green grass and broken shells the only intrusion of color along the shoreline. And beyond that was the magnificent palatial estate that Luca's father had built just for their family. She had spent part of her childhood here on this island, and she had always thought it to be like heaven on earth.

Right now she did not feel so enamored with it.

But then, right now she did not feel so enamored with anything.

On the one hand…she had never been so relieved in her life. To have been carried out of that wedding before it had a chance to take place. Because truthfully, she did not want to marry Erik.

But it was difficult to think about marrying Luca. When she knew that he was only doing it for the child. When she knew that he would have let her walk down the aisle toward another man, that he would have done nothing to stop Erik from claiming her. Touching her. Kissing her. Joining his body to hers.

It was almost unimaginably painful. That full realization. That on her own she had not been enough.

It was that feeling of fantasy, of being in another time and space, that carried her through. That allowed her to breathe while they were driven from the landing base to the villa.

It was all white stucco and red clay roofing, brilliant and clean construction amidst the spiky green plants that surrounded the house.

The home itself was three floors, making the most of the fact it was built into the side of the mountain, that it overlooked the sea. She knew there was a large outdoor bathtub that faced out over the water, made of glass, as if to flaunt the exclusivity of the location.

She could not understand this as a child. It made no sense to her why someone would take their clothes off outdoors. Or why one person would get into a bath that size when there was a pool to swim in.

As an adult, she more than understood.

Because she could well imagine the hours she and Luca could spend in there, naked and slick, with nothing but the sea as witness to their time spent there.

She ached for it, shamefully. Even knowing that he did not want her. Not like this. Not forever.

They stepped inside the cool, extensive foyer, and Sophia looked around, nostalgia crashing into the present moment like a tidal wave. It was so strange. She could remember walking into this place as a girl. With her stepfather and her mother holding hands as a couple, with Luca the stormy and electric presence that made her feel strange and out of sorts. One that she wanted to run away from as much as she wanted to linger here.

That, at least, was the same.

She wanted to run from them as much as she wanted to run to heaven. Wanted his hands on her body, and wanted to shout and scream at him about how he was never permitted to touch her again.

He had devastated her.

And the worst part was, even as he had fulfilled the fantasy of rescuing her from the wedding she had not wanted, he had shattered her completely by doing so. Because of the reasons surrounding it.

She supposed it would be a wonderful thing if she could simply be happy to have Luca. If she could simply be grateful that he had come for her, regardless of the circumstances.

But she couldn't be.

Was it so much to ask that something be about her, and not someone else?

The fact of the matter was she hadn't been enough for her biological father. He hadn't wanted her. Not in the least. She loved her stepfather dearly, but she had been more of an impediment to his marrying her mother than she had been an attraction. He had certainly come to love her, and she didn't doubt that. But still…

She was loved circumstantially.

With Luca, she wasn't even loved.

How much more romantic that had seemed when he was out of reach.

"It seems my phone has… I believe they say blown

up?" Luca said, the words hard and crisp as he looked down at his mobile phone.

That felt strange. Wrong. Because she had been lost somewhere in the veil of fantasy and memory. And neither of those contained cell phones.

"Why?"

"Really?" he returned.

He had one dark brow raised, his handsome face imbued with a quizzical expression. And then suddenly it hit her. She had been so lost in her present pain that she had forgotten. Had forgotten that of course Luca's phone would be lit up with phone calls and text messages. With emails from members of the press, trying to find out what had happened.

By now, everyone knew that the wedding hadn't happened.

Suddenly, her arms felt empty, and she looked around. Realizing then that she had no purse, that she had not taken her phone. She had nothing. Nothing but this wedding dress for a wedding that hadn't happened.

"Luca," she said. "My mother is going to be frantic."

"Yes," he said, scrolling through his phone. "She is. She is deeply concerned that you've been kidnapped."

"I *have* been," she all but shouted.

"By me," he said simply.

"As if that doesn't make it kidnap?"

"I am the king of the nation," he said. "No one is going to arrest me over it."

"That is an extremely low standard to hold yourself to."

"I find at the moment I don't care overmuch."

"Are you going to tell her?" Sophia asked.

"Well, eventually we're going to tell everyone."

"Let me call my mother," she said.

Luca arched a brow. "I do not want your mother on the next flight here."

"You've kidnapped her daughter, what do you expect?"

"I don't want company."

"Why?"

Suddenly, she found herself being swept up off the ground once again. "You have made a bad habit of this."

"I don't find it a bad habit."

He began marching up the stairs, her wedding gown trailing dramatically behind her as they went.

"What are you doing?"

"Claiming your wedding night."

"There was no wedding. And anyway, it wasn't supposed to be *your* wedding night."

"It is about to be." He growled, and he leaned down, claiming her lips with his own.

The moment his mouth made contact with hers it was like the tide had washed over her. And she and her objections were left clinging to the rocks. With each brush that swept over her, she lost her hold on one of them. Her anger washed away. Her doubt. Her resilience. Her resolve.

Whatever Luca felt for her—and she didn't think it was anything tender at all—he wanted her. There was no denying that. He had said as much on the plane, hadn't he?

She had been so lost in her head over the fact that the baby was what had stopped him from letting the wedding go forward, that she hadn't fully taken that part on board. But it was real. It was true.

This was honest. If nothing else between them was. It was real, if the rest could not be.

This was why they were here. The electric, undeniable chemistry that existed between them, in defiance of absolutely everything that was good and right in the world.

She did not taste love on his tongue as it swept over hers. But she tasted need. And that, perhaps, could be enough.

His hold tight on her, he carried her all the way to the top of the stairs and down the landing toward the master bedroom, a room that they had certainly not stayed in before. Well, perhaps Luca had, but she had not. He all but kicked open the double doors, sweeping them inside and depositing her down at the foot of the bed.

"Where is… Where is everyone?" she asked, feeling like she was in a daze. She had only just realized that there seemed to be no servants present.

"I had everyone vacate. Supplies were left, including clothing for you, so you won't need for much. But we need privacy."

"Why?" Tears stung her eyes, an aching pain tightening her throat. She could not understand why he needed this.

This was all too much. She hadn't appreciated fully the protection that had been built into wanting a man she could never have. For her heart. For her body.

Now he was here. Looming large and powerful, so very beautiful.

It all felt too much. Like she would be consumed. Destroyed. Nothing at all of Sophia remaining.

"Because that bastard was going to put his hands on

you tonight," he said, his voice rough. "He was going to touch you. He was going to kiss you. Perhaps you were even fantasizing about it. But I will not have that. I will be the only man to touch you. No other. I will be the only man you want. The only desire in your body will be for me. I will be what you crave. Your body is mine."

"You didn't want me," she said, choked.

"No," he said. "I wanted… I prayed…to not want you. There is nothing that will take it from me. And so there is nothing but this. To take you in any way that I can. To have you. Fate is sealed where we are concerned. There is no reason now not to glory in it."

He reached behind her and grabbed hold of either side of the wedding gown, and he wrenched the corset top open. She gasped as it loosened, felt free as the fine stitching that had been so carefully conformed to her body came loose, and her breasts were left bare to him.

"So beautiful," he said, his dark head swooping down, his tongue like fire over one distended nipple.

How she ached for him. For this. Even as she hurt. Even as her desire threatened to destroy her, she wanted nothing more than to give in to it.

She breathed his name, lacing her fingers through his hair as he sucked her indeed. As he moved his attentions to her other breast, tracing a circle around one tight bud with the tip of his tongue.

"You're right," she said, her voice trembling. "This is madness."

"I knew it would destroy us, Sophia. I knew it could bring down an entire kingdom. But now here we are. There is nothing on earth I have wanted to be rid of more than this desire for you," he said, his voice low, tortured. "And good God I want to burn."

It was like fire. His touch branding her as he removed the layers of clothing from her body. As he left her completely naked except for her high heels, as he pushed her down onto the bed and spread her thighs wide, exposing the most intimate part of her body to his gaze.

He got down on his knees then, grabbing hold of her hips and forcing her toward his mouth.

"Luca," she said, shocked, appalled that he would do such a thing.

"This has been my greatest desire," he said. "Even more than sinking into your tight, wet body, I have wanted to taste you. I have wanted you coating my tongue, my lips. Sophia..."

He dipped his head then, that wicked, electric tongue swirling over the bundle of nerves at the apex of her thighs, tracing a line down to the entrance of her body and drawing the evidence of her desire from her. He added his fingers then, penetrating her, coaxing pleasure from deep inside her. It was too much. It was not enough. It was like a sharp pain that ran deep inside her. That could only be satisfied by him. Only him.

He pressed two fingers into her while he continued to lave her with the flat of his tongue, and she shattered completely. There were no thoughts in her head. Not about a wedding that might have been, not about the man who was supposed to strip this down off her tonight, not about scandal, not about anything. Nothing but this. The extreme heat bursting through her like light in the darkness.

He moved away from her then, his gaze predatory as he unbuttoned the crisp white shirt he wore, as he pushed his jacket from his shoulders and the shirt followed suit.

She could only stare at him. At the beautiful, perfect delineation of his muscles, the dark hair sprinkled there. Could only watch as his clever, masculine fingers made quick work of his belt, of his pants, as he left every last inch of his clothing on the floor, revealing powerful, muscular thighs and the thick, hard part of him that made him a man.

She'd had him inside her once. She would again. Even now, it seemed impossible.

If she had been able to see him the night she had been a virgin she would've been much more apprehensive.

At least now she knew that such fullness in size brought pleasure.

He growled, moving toward her with the liquid grace of a panther. Then he grabbed hold of her hips again, lifting her completely off the bed and throwing her back, coming to settle himself between her legs and thrusting into her with one quick, decisive movement.

Their coupling washed away everything. Like a cleansing fire, destroying the hay and the stubble, all of the temporary things, and leaving behind what was real.

This.

This connection between them that existed for no reason she could see other than to torture them. That remained.

Because whatever it was, it was real.

Each thrust of his powerful body within hers brought her to new heights, and she met each and every movement. With one of her own.

Until he shattered. Until, on a harsh growl, he spent himself deeply within her, and she was powerless to do anything but follow him over that precipice. When it was over, she held him. Because holding on to him was the only way to hold things together.

And she feared very much that the moment she let go, everything was going to fall apart.

Including her.

CHAPTER NINE

HE LEFT HER there in the expansive bed all by herself. Her dress was torn, past the point of fixing, and though he had mentioned there would be a new wardrobe supply for her here, she had no idea where said wardrobe was. Not that she had gone poking around.

She felt too…something. Sad. Bereft, almost, but also boneless and satisfied in a way she never had been before. Or, if she could compare it to anything, it was the way she had felt after their first time. Not happy, no. There was no room between them for something so simple as happy.

It was more like she was lying in the rubble of a building that had needed demolition.

That didn't make it easy. It didn't make it less of a pile of rubble. But there was something inevitable about all of it that made something in this a relief.

Even as it was a sharp pain, like being stabbed in the center of her chest.

She needed to call her mother. She knew full well that Luca did not want her to divulge their location. But he had left her. And there was a phone on the desk. Unless he had done something truly diabolical and cut the line, there was nothing stopping her from getting in touch with the one person who truly needed to know that she was okay.

She wrapped herself several times in the feather-soft white sheet, making sure it was secure at her breasts, before going to the phone and with trembling hands picking up the receiver and listening for the dial tone.

It had one. So, provided she could dial off the island, she should be able to get in touch with her mother.

"Let's see," she mumbled as she typed in the country code for San Gennaro followed by her mother's number.

The phone rang just once before her mother answered. "Hello?"

"Mom," Sophia said.

"Where are you?" her mother asked, panic lacing each word. "Are you safe?"

"Yes," she said.

It was true that she was physically safe. Emotionally was another matter.

"What happened? You were at the chapel and ready, and Luca went in to fetch you and… Is Luca with you?" her mother asked.

"Luca…" The rest of the sentence died.

"What is it?"

"Luca is the reason that I've gone missing," Sophia finished.

The silence on the other end was brittle, like a thin pane of glass that she was certain would splinter into a million pieces and shatter if she breathed too deeply.

"Is he?" her mother asked finally.

"There's something I have to tell you…"

"Oh, Sophia," her mother said, the words mournful. "I had hoped… I had hoped that you had put your feelings for him behind you."

"It's his baby, Mother," she said, the words coming out raw and painful.

More silence. But this one was full. Of emotion. Of words left unspoken. Sophia couldn't breathe.

"I see," the queen finally responded.

"We didn't mean for… I tried… He tried." She closed her eyes, swallowing hard. "We did try."

"Just tell me he never took advantage of you when you were younger." There was an underlying venom in her words that left Sophia in no doubt her mother would castrate Luca if the answer was yes.

Sophia shook her head, then realized her mother couldn't see. "No. Never. It was just… This time was the first time. The time that we…the pregnancy, I mean. That was the first time"

"I knew," her mother whispered. "But I hoped that it would pass. For both of you."

"You knew that he… That he had feelings for me?"

"I knew that he *desired* you. Far sooner than he should have. And I told his father to keep him away from you. There was no future for the two of you, Sophia. You have to understand that."

"I do," she said. "Why do you think I was prepared to marry another man?"

"Yes, well, that has created quite a scandal."

"Just wait until they find out what actually happened. I imagine my running off before the wedding is not half as salacious as the fact that I have run off with my stepbrother because I'm having his baby."

Her mother groaned, a long, drawn-out sound. "Sophia… The scandal this will cause."

Sophia cringed, feeling desperately sad to hear such

distress in her mother's voice. "I'm so sorry. So very sorry I disappointed you."

Her mother's voice softened. "I'm not disappointed. But it's a hard road, Sophia. Being married to a king. And that's simply when you're a commoner. I cannot imagine how difficult things will be for you and Luca. All things considered. I had hoped that you could avoid it."

"We did. Until we couldn't."

She was embarrassed to be talking with her mother in this frank fashion. Until only recently she had been a virgin, after all, and now she was confessing that she had been overwhelmed by a state of desire. Her mother knew full well what that meant.

"If it was love…" Her mother trailed off.

Sophia's shoulders stiffened, her back going straight, a pain hitting her in the stomach. "If it was love, I never would have pretended I might be able to marry Erik. Luca does not love me."

But she did wonder if perhaps marrying Erik had been about running away. Not from scandal, not even from this conversation with her mother.

From all that Luca made her feel. All he made her want.

"He is a good man," her mother said as if trying to offer her some consolation.

"I know he is. Too good for such a scandal."

"But too good to turn away from his responsibility. Still… I have to wonder if it would've been better if he would have allowed you to marry Erik."

Those words went through her like a lance. "Why?"

"If he can't love you…"

Her mother's choice of words there was interesting.

If he couldn't love her. Did that mean that her mother thought she was difficult to love, too? Or did she believe that Luca had a difficult time loving?

In many ways Sophia wondered if they were both true.

She didn't want to love him. That much was certain. Whatever she felt was far too bright and painful all on its own.

"I'm not sure I love him," she said truthfully. "I only know that whatever this is between us is undeniable. And he has chosen to make a scandal. I will only go so far to protect him. I'm not going to force him to disavow his child."

"Of course not. But, Sophia, it's going to be such a difficult life. Where are you? I feel like I should come and get you."

"I—"

The door opened and she turned sharply. Luca was standing there, regarding her with dark eyes. His expression was like a storm, his mouth set into a firm line.

"I have to go."

She hung up the phone, much to her mother's protests. And then Luca walked over to the phone and unplugged the power cord from the base. "I do not wish to be disturbed," he said. "How much did you tell your mother?"

"I told her that I'm having your baby."

He chuckled, bitter and hard. "I imagine her faith in me is greatly reduced by this news."

Sophia wrapped her arms around herself. "She said that she always knew. That you wanted me. That I wanted you."

"Fascinating," he said, not sounding at all fascinated. "But you had no idea, did you?"

"I didn't," she said truthfully. "I thought you despised me."

"You refused to be any less attractive to me, no matter how the years went on. You refused to shrink. You refused to be invisible. I certainly despised you, Sophia, but my desire for you is not exclusive from that."

"That's beautiful, Luca. Perhaps you should take up poetry."

"How's this for poetry? You're mine now." He took a step toward her, grabbing hold of the sheet that she had resolutely wrapped around her curves, and he pulled her to him, wrenching the soft, exquisite cotton from her body. "There is to be no doubt of that."

She stood there, naked and trembling, feeling hideously exposed in ways that went well beyond her skin.

"Then that makes you mine," she shot back, feeling run out and fragile after the day she had had. "Doesn't it?"

His dark eyes sharpened. "I'm not sure I get your meaning."

"If I belong to you, then I require nothing less. If we are to be married, Luca, I will be the only woman in your bed. You have all of me or you have none of me."

"I was never going to be unfaithful to whatever wife I took. I would hardly be unfaithful to you."

Electricity crackled between them, and neither spoke what was so patently obvious. So obvious that it lit the air between them with electricity.

That at least for now, there was no chance either of them would take another to their beds. They would have to exhaust the intense desire between the two of them first, and at the moment Sophia could not imagine it. Granted, she was new to sex, but she had a feeling that what existed between herself and Luca was uncommon in every way.

"What are you going to do?" she asked, her voice small, taking a step away from him.

"Tonight? Tonight I intend to take you back to my bed, spread you out before me and feast on you until you're crying out my name. Until my name is synonymous with *lover*, not *brother*."

His words set a rash of heat over her body. "I mean, about us. About telling the world about us. About our upcoming marriage. About…what we are going to do next."

"I'm going to make a press release to go out tomorrow morning. And you and I will stay here incommunicado until some of the furor dies down. Then I will marry you. Not in that dress," he said, looking at the scrap of white on the floor.

"I think that dress is beyond saving now," she mused.

He looked at her, his dark eyes suddenly bleak. "Who knew I would have something in common with a gown."

But before she had a chance to question such an odd statement, she was back in his arms, and he was kissing her again. And she had a feeling that there would be no more talking tonight.

The next morning Luca was full of purpose when he awoke. Sophia was naked, soft and warm, pressed up against his body, one breast resting at his biceps. She was sleeping peacefully, her dark hair a halo of curls on the pillow around her head. He had done it. He had destroyed everything.

It was strangely satisfying. A perfect and sustained string of curses directed to his mother even if it was going to have to make its way into the beyond.

A scandal she would not be able to squash.

He supposed it was unkind to think poorly of one's dead mother. But he could not find a kind thought for his own.

Strange, how he spent very little time thinking about her. He had already made decisions about himself, about his life, based on the events that had occurred in his childhood. He didn't have to think about them every day.

Truthfully, he didn't even have to think about them yearly. He spent a great deal of time not pondering the ways in which he was damaged, and even when he didn't think of it, typically in reference to why he had to keep his hands off Sophia—a horse that had well and truly left the barn now—it was only in terms of his scarred soul, not in terms of actual events.

This forced him to think of it. The fact that his responsible, pristine image was about to be destroyed, made him think of it.

No one can ever know about this. If your father knew about Giovanni our marriage would be over. And can you imagine what people would think of you? They would never forget, Luca. It is all you would ever be.

He gritted his teeth and got out of bed, staring out the window at the ocean below.

He had a press release to prepare.

He set about to doing just that, contacting his palace staff and letting his majordomo know exactly what had transpired. Exactly what would be happening from here on out. If the other man was shocked, he did not let on. But then, he supposed it was in the other man's job description to remain impassive about such things.

Luca also left instruction to keep his and Sophia's location secret.

With that taken care of, Luca decided that he needed to figure out what he was going to do with his fiancée. That was how he would think of her from now on. Until, that was, he was able to think of her as his wife. She was no longer first and foremost his stepsister.

In his mind, she never had been.

And that meant that he had to get to know her.

He had avoided that. For years he had avoided that. Of course he had. He had not wanted to foster any kind of attraction between them.

It had turned out that was futile anyway, because the attraction between them had been hell-bent on growing no matter what either of them did.

Now the fact remained, he was going to marry her, and he didn't know her at all.

That was not actually a point of contention for him, but he would have to be able to make conversation about her. They would have to be able to come to an accord on how they talked about their relationship.

And he had a feeling that Sophia would want to feel as if she knew him.

He had done what he had intended to do by bringing her here to the island. He had isolated her. And he had managed to get her into proximity with him. To keep her from marrying Erik. But he would not be able to keep her here forever. That meant that something other than kidnap was going to have to bind them. Eventually. Something other than sex would help, as well.

Although at the moment the sex was enough for him.

His staff had generously stocked the kitchen with a basket of croissants. Opening the fridge, he found a tray of fruit, figs and dates. Cheeses. Then, there was a pot of local honey in a small jar on the counter. He cobbled those things together, along with herbal tea, and brought them up to the bedroom. When he opened the door, Sophia shifted, making a sleepy sound.

She opened her eyes, and he could see the exact moment her vision came into focus.

She frowned. “Is that for me?”

“Yes,” he said, sitting down on the edge of the bed.

He was gratified to see that her gaze drifted away from the food and onto his chest, which was still currently fair. Her cheeks flushed, and she looked away.

It pleased him to see that she was not immune to him.

That someone so soft and lovely could be so affected by him.

He shoved that thought to the side.

“That’s…kind of you.” She shifted, pushing herself into a sitting position, holding her sheets against her breasts modestly. “What is this?” She opened up the pot sitting on the tray and frowned deeply. “This isn’t coffee.”

“You’re pregnant,” he pointed out. “I believe I recall hearing that pregnant women should not drink caffeine.”

“Not *too much* caffeine.” She sounded truly distressed. “That doesn’t mean I have to drink…herbs.”

“I was only doing the best I could. I’m not an expert.”

“That might be a first,” she said.

“What?”

She treated him to a smile that was almost impish.

Something he wasn't used to having directed at him. "You admitting that you don't know everything."

"Sophia..." he said, his tone full of warning.

"You can't tell me it isn't true."

"I was raised to be arrogant. It's part and parcel to being in charge."

"Really?" she asked.

"Nobody wants an uncertain king."

"Perhaps. But no one wants an insufferable husband, either."

Neither of them spoke for a moment. Sophia reached into the basket and procured herself a croissant.

"You like coffee," he said.

She lifted a shoulder. It was gloriously bare and he knew now from experience that her skin was as soft as it looked. He wished to lick her. If only because he had spent so many years not licking her. "Yes."

"I didn't know that."

"Almost everyone likes coffee. Or needs it, if it comes down to it."

"But we have never discussed what you like. Or what you don't like."

She looked thoughtful for a moment, and that should've been an indicator that this was not going according to plan, as he really should have guessed that Sophia was never going to be anything like compliant.

"Well," she said, "I like coffee, as established. My hobbies include getting fitted for wedding gowns that will eventually be torn off my body, and being kidnapped and spirited away to a private island."

Luca cast her a hard look. "Much more exotic than stamp collecting, you have to admit."

"Indeed. Although, my wretched dress is not going to increase in value. A stamp collection might."

"I beg to differ. By the time news of our union hits global media I imagine that torn gown will be worth quite a bit."

Sophia frowned, grabbing a strawberry from the fruit tray and biting into it angrily. "Global media," she muttered around the succulent fruit.

"There is no way around it. We are a headline, I think you will find."

"I tried *not* to find."

"Sophia," he said, suddenly weary of games. "There was no other alternative. No other outcome, and you know that. It was always going to be this."

He meant because of the baby. And yet, he couldn't escape feeling that there was something else in those words. Some other, deeper truths being hinted at.

"We tried," she said, sounding desolate.

"Not that night. Not the night of the ball."

She looked up at him, her expression quizzical. "Really?"

"You know it's true," he said. "Had I tried, I would never have touched you. But I didn't. It was simply that what I wanted became so much more powerful than what I should do. And I could not… Could not allow him to touch you."

"We would have allowed him to touch me last night," she said quietly, picking at a fig.

"He didn't," Luca said. "That's all that matters."

"Luca," she said, looking up at him, her expression incisive. "Why is reputation so important to you? I mean, beyond the typical reasons. Beyond the reasons that most rulers have. You have never been… I knew your father.

I loved him. As my own father. He was the only father I ever knew. He was serious, and he treated his position with much gravity. But it's not like you. You do everything with such gravity. And I… Truthfully, whether you believe me or not, part of the reason I didn't tell you is that I didn't want to put this on you. I know how much your country means to you…"

"Not more than my child," he said, fire rising up in his chest, bile in his throat. "Nothing matters more than my child, Sophia, you must know that. The moment those test results came across my desk I had to know. I will not sacrifice my child on an altar with my country's name stamped onto it. With my reputation on it. My name is only a name. The baby you carry is my blood." He took a deep breath. "What good is a legacy if you don't defend the ones who are supposed to carry it out when you die?"

"I'm sorry," she said, and she sounded it. "You're right. For all that we…" She squeezed her eyes shut. "For all that I have carried a certain fascination for you for a great number of years, I don't know you." She opened her eyes, tears glistening in them. "If I could guess at this so wrong, then it is apparent there are things I don't know."

"You're not wrong," he said, the word scraping his throat. "On any score with this, I would have protected the name. But not at the expense of a child."

It was the breaking point. Because if the name didn't matter, then what he had endured, then the lack of action his mother had taken to defend him, would be null and void, and that was unfathomable to him in many ways. This was where the corner turned. Where it became far too close to what had been done to him. And that, he could not allow.

"What are we going to do today?" The question was open, honest, and it made him feel strange.

"I had not given it much thought."

That was a lie. What he wanted, what he wanted more than anything, was to strip her completely naked, rip that sheet right off her as he had done last night, and keep her that way for the entire day.

"Your wardrobe should arrive soon," he said instead of that. "And then of course, there is the beach, and the pool."

"Badminton," she pointed out. "We used to play badminton."

"You cannot be serious."

"We're rather cut off here, Luca," she said. "I was thinking of all the things we used to do to entertain ourselves."

He treated her to a scorching look, and he watched as her face turned scarlet all the way up to the roots of her hair.

"We can't do that the entire time," she protested, her hand flinging out wide like an indignant windmill.

He leaned forward, gripping her chin with his thumb and forefinger. "Why not?"

Her eyes widened. "Because… Because… We can't." Her protest was beginning to sound weak.

"I'm going to need a better reason than that, Sophia. As we have spent years not doing it, and I feel that we have much time to make up for."

"Well," she said, sniffing piously. "It's not done."

"I assure you, *cara*, that it is done quite frequently."

"You would *die*." She sounded entirely certain of this assessment.

He couldn't help himself. He laughed. "That's a bit overdramatic, don't you think?"

"No," she protested. "There is nothing dramatic about it. You've been there both times we've, well, you know. I can't breathe for nearly an hour afterward. If we did it all day..."

"It would be different," he said. "But no less impacting."

"Is it always like this, then? Does it just naturally shatter you less and less each time? Is this how it's been with all your lovers?"

He could lie to her. But then, a lie would neither bring him joy nor accomplish anything. Truth was the best option.

"It has never been like this with any of my previous lovers," he said. "I already told you that you have been my obsession for far too long. And there has been nothing that I could do to put a dent in that hunger. And before you... I didn't know such hunger at all."

"Oh," she said, sounding subdued.

"I wished often that it was simple enough to just want another woman," he said. "But it is not."

He shook his head. "There is no way around it. We must go through."

"Perhaps after badminton."

"If you get out a badminton racket, I will break it over my knee." Possibly, he could break it over another part of his body, given how hard he was at the moment.

It didn't take much. He was held in thrall, just for a moment, as the sunlight broke through a crack in the curtains, streamed onto Sophia's lovely upturned face, catching the light behind her wild curls. Sophia was naked in his bed. After so many years of lust.

She was his. There was triumph in that, to be certain.

He was Nero. Fiddling while Rome burned, he supposed. But Rome was going to burn no matter what at this point. He supposed he might as well play away.

“There is one thing I’m curious about.”

“Whether or not I take cream in my coffee?”

“No. Why were you a virgin, Sophia?”

She drew back, pressing her hand to the center of her chest, the expression almost comically missish. “Does it matter?”

“The very fact that you would ask that question says to me that it must.”

“I never found anyone that I felt… Luca, if no other man could make me feel what I felt just looking at you, if he kissed me, if he touched me, what was the point of going to bed with him? I would be thinking of you.”

He was humbled by that. Shame. A familiar, black fog rolling over his shoulders and down his spine. Yes, shame was his constant companion. And sex was…

It never occurred to him to deprive himself of sex. His introduction to it—such as it was—had not been his choice. And he had set out to make a choice after that, and every time thereafter.

It had become a way of putting distance and bodies between that first encounter.

To prove to himself that in truth, the two experiences were not even the same. But what had been done to him against his will that night was something dark. Something ugly.

Control. A deep contempt for another person’s autonomy.

“I was with other people and thought of you,” he pointed out. “Unless I made it a point not to. And then,

I made sure it was someone who was quite different to you."

"I suppose that's the difference between men and women, then," she said.

"Or simply the difference between you and me," he responded. "Sophia… There are many reasons that I never allowed myself to touch you for all that time."

"Your reputation."

"My reputation, the reputation of San Gennaro, is only a piece of the puzzle."

"Then tell me what the puzzle is, Luca. I feel like I should understand since we are supposed to be married. I feel like I need to understand you."

"We have a history," he said slowly. "One that has been difficult. I cannot… I cannot adequately express to you the way it was when I first noticed you as a woman. The way that it hit me. You were always…reckless and wild in a way that I could not fathom, Sophia, and yet the fact that it bothered me as it did never made any sense. Until you turned seventeen. And suddenly…everything that you were, this vivacious, irrepressible girl, crashed into what you had become. I knew I couldn't have you. I knew that it was impossible. And so, as much as there was never closeness between us, I pushed you away. I don't regret that. It was my attempt at doing what was right. I failed, in the end. And so, those years, that history, is useless to us. Let us forget who we were in the past and why. We have to make a way forward, and I don't think there are answers lurking behind."

She narrowed her eyes, looking at him with total skepticism. He could see that she did not agree with him, not remotely.

But there was no point talking about the shadows

in the past. He didn't want her to know him. He didn't want anyone to know him. They could have a life, like this. One where they made love and she teased him. Frankly, it was a better life than he had ever imagined for himself.

He had not ever fathomed that his duty could be quite so pleasurable.

He had resolved himself to a life without the woman that he wanted most. Now he had her. There was no point dragging skeletons out of the closet.

"You have an objection, *cara*?"

"You want to act as though we haven't known each other for most of our lives? You don't want to go back and try to understand who I was?"

"Isn't it most important that we understand who each other is now?"

"Can we do that? Can it be accomplished if we don't actually know what each other was built with?"

"There are no surprises in my story. I was born into royalty." He shrugged his shoulders. "Here I remain."

"You lost your mother when you were sixteen. I suppose that was very painful for you."

"Yes," he responded, the word sharp like a blade.

It was painful. But perhaps not in the way she meant. Not in any way he could put into words.

Losing someone you were meant to love, someone you had grown to hate, was its own particular kind of pain. There had been guilt. Such guilt. As if it were the hatred in his heart that had poisoned her to death. As if he had somehow caused her car to go off the road that day.

He knew better than that now.

But that, too, was a discussion they would not have.

"Today I thought we might have a walk on the beach," he said. "What do you think of that?"

She nodded slowly. "That sounds nice."

Though she still didn't sound convinced.

She would see. It would be better his way.

And if Sophia wanted to share herself with him, he was more than happy to allow it. In fact, he found he was quite hungry for it.

But he would not poison her with the stories of his past.

The poison in his own veins was quite enough. He refused to spread it.

On the score of protecting the family reputation, of protecting her from a life with him, he had failed.

He did not have to fail when it came to everything else.

Sophia was hot and sweaty after spending an afternoon combing through the white sand beaches, finding seashells and taking breaks from the sun to soak her feet in the water.

True to his word, her clothing had eventually arrived, and she had found a lovely white dress that seemed suited to the surroundings. They had walked together, and he hadn't touched her.

It occurred to her that Luca had *never* touched her without sexual intent. Nothing intentional anyway.

There had been no casual handholding. He'd never moved to touch her with affection, only to strip her of her clothes.

Which was why when they had been on their return trip to the estate she had looped her fingers through his and taken control of that situation.

She had almost immediately wished that she hadn't. It had been so impacting. So very strange. To hold Luca's hand. Like they were a couple. Not just secret, torrid lovers, but something much gentler and sweeter, too.

Strange, because there was no real gentleness in their interaction.

Although, it had been quite a nice thing he'd done this morning with the fruit. The herbal tea notwithstanding.

When they returned to the villa, dinner had been laid out for them on the deck that overlooked the sea. A lovely spread of fresh seafood and crisp, bright vegetables.

All a little bit healthy for her taste. Though that concern was answered at the end of the meal when Luca went into the kitchen and returned a moment later with the truly sinful-looking dessert made of layers of cream, meringue and raspberry.

Sophia took a bite of the decadent dessert and closed her eyes, listening to the sound of the ocean below, the sun still creating warmth, even as it sank down into the sea. A breeze blew gently through her hair, lifting the heavy curls off the back of her neck, cooling her.

For a moment she had the horrible feeling that if she opened her eyes she would find that Luca wasn't really there. That she had somehow hallucinated all of this in order to survive the wedding.

That in reality she was on her honeymoon with Erik. Because of course it had to be a fantasy that Luca had come to claim her. That he had whisked her out of that waiting room in the back of the chapel and spirited her off to a private island.

But no. When she opened her eyes there he was. Regarding her closely, his dark, unfathomable eyes assessing her. The remaining light of the sun shone brilliantly on his razor-sharp cheekbones, highlighting the rough, dark whiskers that had grown over his square jaw. She did not think he had shaved since they had arrived.

She suddenly had the urge to watch him shave. To watch him brush his teeth.

To claim all those little intimate moments for herself. Those routine things that were so easy to take for granted. She wanted to be close to him.

That was the sad thing. She had made love to him a few times now, and still, she didn't feel…like they were close.

Physically, they had been as close as two people could be. But there was still a gulf between them. She wanted to know what had created him. This good, hard man who clung to his principles like a mountain climber holding on to the face of a rock.

He fascinated her, this man. Who only ever let his passion unleash itself in the bedroom. Who was otherwise all things reserved and restrained.

That he had been hiding his desire for her for so many years was a revelation.

But he didn't *want* her to know him. He had made that clear.

She understood now why her mother had sounded so upset on the phone. It wasn't simply the issues that they would have with the press. But the pain she would experience, having feelings for her husband that far outweighed the feelings he had for her. Of wanting more of him than he would ever share. Luca desired her. He wanted her body. He'd had it. But sex and intimacy were not the same things.

That fact had become clear when they held hands on the beach and it had rocked her world in a wholly different fashion than being naked with him had.

One thing was clear: sex was certainly the way to reach him.

Because it was the only time when his guard was down. Of course, hers was equally reduced when they were making love. He did things to her… Made her feel things… Things she had not imagined were possible. And she wanted more. She had never thought of herself as greedy, not really.

How could a woman who had been born into poverty and become a princess overnight ever ask for more out of life? And yet…she wanted more. Being with him, finally having what she had held herself back from for all that time, had only made her more greedy.

There was something about today, about the beautiful afternoon spent walking on the beach that ended with holding hands, and this magical dinner, that made her feel a sense of urgency. Or maybe it wasn't the dinner, or the handholding. Maybe it was simply the fact that they were to be married. And if they were going to get married then it meant this was forever. And if this was going to be her forever…

It had been a certain kind of torture, wanting Luca and not having him. But having him in some ways, but never in others, was worse.

Or if not worse, it was simply that it was closer. She couldn't pretend that there was nothing between them, not when she was sharing his bed.

He was beautiful. And physically, he made her feel so very much. It wasn't enough.

And maybe she was so perfectly aware of how not

enough it was in part because she knew full well that it could be more.

She had seen that passion. She had felt it. Had been over him, beneath him, as he had cried out her name and lost himself completely in their lovemaking.

She wanted *that* man out of bed, too.

But in order to reach him, she imagined she had to appeal to him first in bed.

Not a hardship as far as she was concerned.

But it would perhaps require her to be a bit more bold than she had been previously.

After all, she had been a virgin until only recently. But the fact remained that what she had told Luca earlier was true. She had been a virgin because of him. Because of the way he had made her feel.

That meant he could have any of her. All of her. Because he was the one her body had been waiting for, so truly, there was no reason for her to be timid. Not where he was concerned.

"Just have some business to attend to," Luca said, rising from his chair. "I will meet you in our room."

The meaning behind his words was clear. But if Luca thought he was going to be in control of every interaction between them…well, she was about to prove to him otherwise.

CHAPTER TEN

LUCA WAS QUESTIONING the wisdom of checking the way their story was being played out in the headlines before he and Sophia left the island. What was the point? He could have simply left it all a mystery. Could have spent this time focused on her.

But no, the ugly weight of reality had pulled on him, and he had answered. So he had done some cursory searches to see if they had been splashed all over the tabloids yet.

He had underestimated the intensity of the reaction.

The headlines were lurid. Bold. Scandal in the palace. A borderline incestuous love affair between stepsiblings that had been going on for… God knew how long.

A good and handsome groom had been left at the altar, the King of San Gennaro finally snapping and claiming his illicit lover before she could marry someone else.

There were one, maybe two, stories that shed a more romantic light on the situation. Forbidden lovers who had been in crisis. Who had not been able to choose to be together until it had been decided for them by fate. By a pregnancy.

The truth was somewhere in the middle. He and Sophia certainly weren't in love.

He looked out the window, at the clear night sky, the stars punching through the blackness. It reminded him of being with Sophia. Little spots of brightness that managed to bring something into those dark spaces.

There was so much more darkness than light. And it was amazing that the blackness did not consume it.

For a brief moment he felt something like hope. Like perhaps it would be the same with her. That *his* blackness would not cover her light, but that her light would do something to brighten that darkness.

But no.

It could not be. Not really. He was not fool enough to believe it. Hope, in his experience, was a twisted thing.

Was for better men than him.

Suddenly, he was acutely aware of the pitch-dark. Of the way that it stretched out inside him. Yawning endlessly.

He needed to get back to her. Needed to have her hold him in her arms.

A wretched thing. Because he should be the one carrying her.

It was amazing, but somewhere, amidst all the granite inside his chest, there was softness for her. A softness he had never allowed himself to truly focus on before. He had been too obsessed with pushing her away. With keeping his feelings for her limited.

It was over now.

He had her. So he supposed…

The headlines once again crowded his head. It wasn't fair. That Sophia should be subjected to such a thing. Already, there had been many unkind things written about her mother and about her when she was young. And yes, gradually, the tide had turned in their favor. And even then, most had seen it as a fairy tale. He doubted very much that people would ever see this as any kind of fairy tale.

In that world stepsiblings were always wicked. And they certainly didn't get a happy ending.

Least of all with the princess in the story.

No. Theirs was not a fairy tale.

Theirs was something dark and frightening, obsession and lust creating a cautionary tale.

One he certainly wasn't going to heed. It was far too late for that.

He turned and walked out of the office, heading down the long hallway toward the room he was sharing with Sophia.

She might be asleep. She might not have waited up for him.

He pushed the door open without knocking, and did not see her in bed. In fact, he did not see her anywhere.

He frowned. And then he looked up and saw her standing in the doorway of the balcony that contained the large bathtub he had built several fantasies around.

She was wearing nothing more than a white gown, diaphanous and insubstantial. He was certain that—even in the dim light—he could make out the shadow at the apex of her thighs. Of her nipples.

"What are you doing?" he asked.

Her dark brown hair was a riot of curls, those generous curves calling to him.

Every time they'd been together it had been frantic as if they were both afraid one or both of them might come to their senses and put a stop to everything. This was different. There was a look in her eye that spoke of seduction. Seduction certainly hadn't been involved in any of their previous couplings.

He swore, beginning to undo the buttons on his shirt, until Sophia held up a delicate hand. "Not so fast."

"You will not tease me," he growled, taking a step toward her.

"I don't want to tease you."

"Then why are you stopping me from ravishing you? Because you know all I can think of is ripping that dress off you."

"You keep doing that to me," she scolded.

"Perhaps I think white isn't your color. Or perhaps I think the clothing doesn't suit you. But then, the conclusion could be drawn that I simply don't think clothes in general suit you. I've often wondered why I never cared for the image that the palace stylist had cultivated for you. And obviously the new one has done better. But I think the real reason is quite simple. I like you better naked. And part of me always knew that I would."

She looked down for a beat, those long, dark lashes fanning over her cheekbones. The only sign that she was perhaps not as confident as she appeared.

But then she looked up at him, those brilliant, defiant eyes meeting his. Sophia. Always there to challenge him.

"I'm happy to get naked for you, Luca," she said, the way her lips formed the sounds of his name sending an illicit shiver down to his manhood, making him feel as though she had licked him there.

"But what?"

"I require a forfeit."

"A forfeit?" He paused for a moment, the only sound

coming from the distant waves crashing on the rocks below, and the thundering of his heart in his ears. "Well, now, that is very interesting. Do you wish me to get down on my knees and worship at the cleft of your thighs? Because I'm more than happy to spend an evening there."

"No. That would be too easy. For both of us. I will take off this gown in exchange for one thing."

"What is that?"

"You have to tell me one thing you have never told another soul. It might be enough for you to pretend that we only just met, Luca, but it is not enough for me."

His stomach curdled. Going sour at the thought. Because there was only one thing that sprung readily to his mind. There was no other living soul who knew what had happened to him, even though at one time someone certainly had known.

Well, perhaps there was another living soul who knew. Whether or not Giovanni was dead or alive wasn't something Luca was privy to. He didn't want to find out. He hoped the man was dead. If he wasn't, Luca would be far too tempted to see to his demise himself.

Though, considering the scandal that had just erupted, perhaps murder would be surmountable. Or at least not so glaring in the face of all this.

Still. He was not going to tell Sophia.

He gritted his teeth, casting his mind back to something… Anything that he might be able to tell her. So desperate was he to have her naked.

"I was rejected by the first girl I ever cared for," he said. "Though I use the words *cared for* euphemistically here, considering I didn't know her at all."

That wasn't something he often thought about. What

had happened the night of the ball. Before he had been violated. When everything had been simple and he had been innocent in many ways.

"What?"

"There was a girl who came to a ball that my father threw. There were dignitaries from all around the world." Which was what had allowed his mother to sneak her lover into the palace.

A man that Luca had met on a few occasions and had gotten a terrible, sick feeling in his stomach whenever he spoke. He had sensed that he knew the relationship between Giovanni and his mother. But then later he wondered if really that disquiet that he felt had to do with the fact that Giovanni was a predator. A predator who had set his sights on Luca.

"There was a girl called Annalise. She was beautiful. Her father was a dignitary in Morocco and they were visiting the palace for our grand party. I was entranced by her. She refused to dance with me. But then we spoke for a while. I led her out to the garden, and I tried to kiss her. She dodged me, and I ended up kissing a rosebush instead."

Sophia laughed, clearly not expecting the story. "You were a prince."

"And she was unimpressed with me."

"How old were you?"

"Sixteen. I believe she was eighteen."

"Oh, no," Sophia said, laughing. "You were punching above your weight."

"I had imagined that being the prince in the palace in which her family was staying might lend me an edge."

Sophia giggled, ducking her head, the expression making her look young. Making him feel young. As if perhaps he were that boy he had been that night. Innocent. Full of possibilities. To love, to be loved.

Living a life that would not ultimately culminate in the moment when his mother proved her lack of care for him.

But perhaps living the life that his head appeared to be at that point in time. Golden. Glittering. One of a privileged, infinitely fortunate prince who had the world at his feet.

Though, in this moment, he would give the world in place of Sophia.

"I like her," Sophia said. "A woman who was not impressed with you just because of your title."

"The same can be said for you, I think," he said, taking a step toward her. She took a step back.

"If anything," Sophia said, "I have always found your status to be a hindrance. Imagine what it would have been like if we would have met under different circumstances."

"You would still be younger than me," he said. "So it would still take time for me to see you differently."

"All right. What if you met me at seventeen, instead of at twelve?"

"Perhaps I would have asked you for your phone number."

She laughed. "That's so startlingly benign. You and I have never been afforded anything quite so dull."

"No, indeed."

"I must warn you," she said. "I don't intend for tonight to be dull, either."

"I believe we have started as we mean to go on."

"I suppose so."

"Your dress," he said. "I have given you my forfeit. You owe me mine."

She said nothing. Instead, she raised her hand, brushing the thin strap of her dress down so that it hung loosely over her shoulder. And then she did the same to the other side. The diaphanous fabric barely clung to her body, held up by those generous breasts of hers. He wanted to wrench it down, expose her body to his hungry gaze.

But this was her game. And he was held captive by it. Desperate to see what her rules might be.

He had grown into a man that most would never dream of defying. That was by design. But Sophia… She dared. And he wanted to see what else she might dare.

"I believe it was for the entire dress," he pressed. He stood, curling his hands into fists, his heart thundering so hard he thought it might burst through a hole in his chest.

She made him…

She made him wild. And he had not been wild for a very long time.

"I suppose it was," she returned. "Though I see that you are standing there fully clothed. And it doesn't escape my notice that the first time we were together you were also mostly clothed, while I…"

"Your dress was still on. Technically."

"I was exposed."

"All the better to enjoy you, *cara*."

She shivered, and he was gratified by that response. "Well, I want to enjoy you. I want you naked."

She lifted her chin, her expression one of utter defiance. Defiance he wished to answer. Though he had a feeling that his little beauty's boldness might end if he actually complied with her request.

For all that she was playing at being in charge here, for all that she was a responsive and generous lover, she was still inexperienced.

He wondered how long it would take for that to not be the case. How many times. How many kisses. The number of moments he would have to spend in her bed in order to strip that inexperience from her. That innocence. Until she would look at him boldly when he removed his clothes, until she would no longer blush when he whispered erotic things in her ear.

He looked forward to the progression, but he was not in a hurry. For now, he would enjoy this.

More than anything, he looked forward to the fact that there would be a progression, rather than a one-off and a garden alcove, like he had imagined it would be.

He gripped the hem of the black T-shirt he was wearing and dragged it over his head, casting it to the floor, making similar and quick work of the rest of his clothes. Until he stood before her with nothing on.

She did shrink back, only slightly. He had been correct in his theory that she might still find the sight of him without clothes to be a bit confronting.

He spread his arms wide. “And here I am for you, *cara mia*. Where is my reward?”

She turned around quickly, and if it wasn’t for the heavy rise and fall of her shoulders, he might have thought it an extension of the game, rather than a moment where nerves had taken over.

But then she lifted her arms, taking a slow, indrawn breath, the fabric of the gown slipping, falling to her waist. Exposing the elegant line of her back, the twin dimples just below the plump curve of her ass. Still covered by that flowing dress.

He gritted his teeth, holding himself back. He wanted nothing more than to move to her. Than to take control. He ached with it.

But he waited. Still, he waited.

She placed her hands at her hips, pushing the fabric down her slender legs, revealing the rest of that tempting skin.

And then, his control was lost.

He walked up behind her quietly, careful not to give her any indication of what he planned to do next.

Slowly, very slowly, he reached out and swept her dark hair to the side, exposing her neck. And he kissed her. His lips pressed firmly against the center of the back of her neck, careful not to touch her anywhere else.

She gasped, a sharp sound of need winding its way through the breath.

He drew back, pressing the back of his knuckles to that spot between her shoulder blades, following the indent of her spine down low. She squirmed, wiggling her hips, and he gripped her left side with his hand, holding her still as he followed his journey down all the way until his fingers pressed between her thighs, finding that place where she was soft and wet just for him.

He moved his hand back upward to cup one rounded cheek, squeezing her hard as he slid the hand that gripped her hip around her stomach, pulling her up against him so that she could feel the evidence of his arousal pressing against her lower back.

"I'm growing impatient of games," he whispered into her ear, capturing her lobe between his teeth and biting her gently.

She arched against him, her lovely ass pressing into him.

She wiggled.

"If you keep doing that, Sophia," he said, "you're going to push me to my limit."

"Perhaps I want to find it."

"I'm not sure you do."

"I don't want your control," she said softly. "I don't want you to be solicitous and careful. I know that you are a man of honor, Luca. But I feel that there is no place for honor between us just now." She arched even farther into him. "Indeed, there's not much room for anything between us. It's just our skin, our bodies, pressed against each other."

He pushed his hand down toward the apex of her thighs, those downy curls beneath his fingers the filthiest pleasure he'd ever experienced in his life.

He pushed down farther, brushing his fingers over that sensitive bundle of nerves, through her folds, finding the entrance to her body and pressing his fingers inside her. She let her head fall back against his shoulder, relaxing on an indrawn breath.

"Is this what you wanted?" he asked. "You want me uncontained? You want me out of control? As if it has not been so from the moment I first laid my hands on you in that garden?"

"You are far more controlled than I would like," she gasped.

"Control is a good thing," he said. "I think you will find."

He swept his free hand up to cup her breast, teasing her nipple with his thumb. "You will benefit from my control," he rasped, drawing his cheek down the side of her neck, over her shoulder, well aware that his whiskers were scraping delicate skin. She moaned. A clear sign that she quite liked his control in the right venue.

"But I don't have any," she whispered.

"Is that what you think? Sophia, you have had control of me for far too long. My thoughts turn on the sway of your hips, my focus shifting with each breath you take in my presence. How can you not know this?"

"You said I was your sickness," she breathed.

"And indeed it is true." He kissed her shoulder. "There is no cure. I am a terminal case. But I have accepted this."

"I'm not sure how I'm supposed to—" she gasped, her breath hitching as he pressed his fingers deeper inside her "—feel about that."

"Feel this," he said, thrusting his hips against her backside again. "And feel the pleasure that I give you."

She reached up, grabbing hold of the hand that was resting on her breasts, as though she was trying to get him to ease his pleasuring of her. As though it was too much. He collected that wrist, holding it in his hand like an iron manacle, and then he took hold of her other hand, bringing them around behind her and holding them fast, pinning them to her lower back as he continued to toy with her between her legs with his free hand.

She shifted her hips. "You're holding me prisoner now?"

"It seems fair. I've been held captive by you for years now."

"Luca," she breathed his name, total capitulation to what was happening between them. He worked his fingers between her legs faster, stroking her slickness over her clit before bringing his fingers down to the entrance of her body again, delving deep. The waves of her release seemed to come from deep within her, her internal muscles pulsing hard around his fingers as she found her pleasure.

He propelled her out onto the balcony, up to the edge of the bath. He tightened his grip on her stomach, lifting them both down into the water, prepared by her already. And there they were calm out under the stars again, only this time, there were no people. Nobody in a nearby ballroom to come out and discover them. No one at all.

He sat on the edge of the tub, whirling her around to face him, wrapping her legs around his waist, the slick heart of her coming into contact with his arousal.

"Out here," he said, "if you scream no one will hear you. Only the stars."

Those stars. That brightness. Her brightness.

"Then I suggest you do your part to make me scream."

He moved both hands down to cup her butt, freeing her wrists as he did. She moved her hands to his shoulders, gripping him tightly as he moved them both across the tub, the slick glide of the water over their skin adding a sharpness to the sensuality of the moment.

"You want to scream?" He moved them over to the glass edge of the tub that overlooked the sea and turned her, maneuvering her so that she was in front of him, facing the water, the reflection of the silvery moon over the waves.

"Hold on to the edge," he commanded.

She did so without arguing, though there was a hesitancy to her movements that spoke of confusion. She would not be confused for long.

He pressed one hand to her hip, and with the other, guided his erection to the entrance of her body. He pushed into her in one decisive thrust, grabbing both hips and pulling her back against him, the motion creating ripples in the water.

She gasped, leaning forward, her breasts pressed against the glass, her hands curved around the edge like claws. She bowed her head over the tub. He reached forward, grabbing hold of her dark curls and drawing her head back, none too gently, as he found her throat with his lips, kissing her, then scraping it with the edge of his teeth.

He rode her like that, one hand gripping her hip tightly, his blunt fingers digging into her skin, the other holding her hair as he thrust into her in an endless rhythm that pushed fire down his spine and sent pleasure through him like a river of molten flame.

He felt when her thighs began to quiver, when she got close to release. And he slipped his hand to her furrow again, brushing his fingers over where she was most sensitive, not stopping even as he felt her release break over her. Not stopping until she was screaming herself hoarse into the night, out over that endless ocean, up to the stars.

Into the darkness.

Into his darkness.

And when his own control reached its end he grabbed hold of her with both hands, holding her steady while he poured himself into her. His despair, his need, his release, nothing like a simple achievement of pleasure, but the sharp edge of a knife, cutting into him, making him bleed.

Reducing him. Right there in front of her. And there

was nothing that could be done about that. Nothing he could do to fight it.

He reached out, holding on to the edge of the tub, bracing himself for a moment while he caught his breath. She looked over her shoulder, those eyes connecting with his. She looked… She looked as undone as he felt, and he could not ignore the question in them. The need. To be held.

He gathered her up in his arms and carried her across the tub and they stepped out onto the balcony. There was a large, fluffy towel folded up on a shelf adjacent to the tub and he grabbed hold of it, wrapping it around her and holding her against him as he brought her back into the bedroom, depositing her onto the center of the bed.

He didn't bother to dry himself, coming down beside her completely naked as she wrapped the edges of the towel more firmly around her body.

She rolled onto her back, letting out a long, slow sigh. She had the towel pulled over her breasts, but it parted just above her belly button, revealing that delicious triangle at the apex of her thighs. He was not going to disabuse her of her illusion that she might be covered.

"Luca," she whispered. "Why do I get the feeling that it isn't the secret of Annalise that stands between us?"

CHAPTER ELEVEN

"I don't follow you."

"That's not your secret. You may not have ever told anyone about it, but I think you never told anyone because it wasn't important. I think there's something important. Something you don't talk about because of the heaviness."

She rolled to her side, looking at him, her dark gaze much more insightful than he would like. He felt… Well, he felt naked. A ridiculous thing, because he had been naked this entire time. But suddenly, he felt as though she had cut into him and peeled his skin from his bones, giving her a deep look into places that he had been so certain were hidden. And yet, she had seen. Easily and with accuracy.

"I'm not talking about this now."

"Then when? It's a wonderful thing, a beautiful thing, to have you out of control when we are together like this. But what about the rest of the time? What about what comes after? When we have to live a life together."

He growled, rolling over, pinning her to the bed, pressing his palms into her shoulders. "The dark things that live in me… It will do you no good to know about them." He felt a sick kind of shame roll over his skin like an oily film, as if he had not just been made clean by the water in the bathtub. As if he had not just been made clean by joining to her.

He realized, with a sharp sort of shock, that there was an element of fear buried in his deep reluctance to never speak of his past. Luca was an attractive man, and he well knew it. Not just physically; the women responded to his looks, to his expertly sculpted body and to his sexual prowess. But also, he was a man with money, a man with a title. It would be disingenuous for him to pretend he presented absolutely no attraction to women.

But he realized that the words his mother had spoken to him after that night had taken root deeper than he had imagined. That it would make people think things about him. That it would repulse and appall Sophia if she knew the truth. If she knew the things that had been done to his body, would she want him at all? Or would she find him damaged in some way?

It was an unacceptable weakness. To worry about these things. To care at all.

And that was the real problem. He wanted to pretend that it didn't matter. That he didn't think about it. That it only shaped him in good ways. In ways that he had chosen. But these feelings, this moment, made it impossible. An illusion he could no longer cling to. If he resented Sophia for anything, it was this, most of all.

"Do you want to know why reputation is so important to me?" The words scraped his throat raw on their exit. He didn't want to speak of this, but the very fact that it had become such a leaden weight inside him that it had become something insurmountable, meant it was time for him to speak of it. Because if there was one thing he couldn't stand more than the memory, it was giving it power.

It was acknowledging all that it meant to him.

He wanted it to be nothing. Which meant speaking of it should be nothing. But the ugly turn of that was if it meant something to Sophia… If he had to see disgust or pity in her eyes…

But suddenly, that luminous gaze of hers was far too much for him to withstand. And he thought that perhaps, as long as she wanted him in the end, a little bit of distance was not the worst thing.

"My mother had lovers," he said. "I imagine you didn't know that."

Sophia frowned. "I've never heard my mother or your father speak of his first wife."

"Yes. Well. It is not because he was mired in grief. Though I think he felt some measure of it, they were no longer in love by the time she died, if they ever were. I think…" Suddenly, a thought occurred to him that never had before. "I think your mother was his first experience of love. I think perhaps that is why the connection was so powerful there was no care given to propriety. Not when he already knew what could happen when you married someone who was supposed to be suitable."

"You… You knew that she had lovers. But you must have been…a boy."

"I was. Very young. At first, I did not question the presence of men in the palace and my father's absence. We had many people stay there at many different times. But it was clear, after a fashion, that they were…special to my mother. It could not be ignored. Mostly, they ignored me. But there was one… He often tried to speak to me. Attempted to cultivate a relationship with me. I was sixteen."

"That was just before she died," Sophia said softly.

"Yes. Giovanni was the last one. It was as if everything came to a head at that point." He hesitated. "Remember that ball I told you about?"

"The one with Annalise."

"Yes. I think perhaps the reason that my memory of her is so sharp is because… Sometimes my life feels as if it's divided into before and after. I know that many people would think I mean my mother's death. But that is not the case. Before and after the night of that ball. I was a different person then. A boy. Protected from the world. That is the function of palace walls, after all. They keep you insulated. And I was, for certain."

He didn't want Sophia to touch him while he spoke of this. Didn't want there to have been any contact between them. He rolled to the side, putting a solid expanse of bedspread between them. She seemed to understand. Because she didn't move. She stayed rooted to the spot he had pinned her in a moment ago.

"That night, after the ball ended… Giovanni had gotten me a drink. It was slightly unusual as he took pains in public to pretend he didn't know me. Why hint at a relationship with my mother? But still. I took the drink. I felt…very tired. And I remember I left early. I assume he then took advantage of the fact that people were moving around. The fact that people were walking through the halls… It was all normal. And anyone who was in attendance had certainly been vetted and approved by the royal family."

"Luca," she whispered, "what happened?" He could hear both confusion and dawning horror in her voice.

And he knew that she had not guessed, but that she felt a strong sense of disquiet. Of fear.

He took a breath, closed his eyes. "He violated me."

The words were metallic on his tongue. There were uglier words for what had happened to him. More apparent. But they were still too difficult to speak, because *victim* lay on the other side of them, and that was something he could not admit. Something he could not speak.

"He…"

He did not allow her to speak. "I think you know the answer."

She said nothing for a moment, silence settling heavy around them as flashes of memory replayed themselves in his mind. Flashes were all he had. A blessing of sorts, he supposed. A strange, surreal state brought about by whatever drug he'd been given.

"Why wasn't he arrested? Why weren't you protected?"

"It never happened again," he said gravely. No. He had gone straight to his mother. Because there had been no one else to speak to about it. How could he tell his father what had happened, at the hands of his mother's lover? To do so would mean to uncover her. But surely, she would protect her son.

She had not.

Not really.

Her version of protection had been to ensure that Giovanni didn't come to the palace anymore. She had cut off her association with him, but she did not, would not, push punishing him. For her own reputation.

"The reputation of the nation," he said, his throat tightening. "It was the most important thing."

"How can you say that? Of course it wasn't. Your

safety was the most important thing. Justice for what had been done to you."

Her lip was curled upward, an expression of disgust. Likely directed at what had been done to him, and not at him. But still, somehow it felt all the same.

"What does that mean in context with an entire nation of people?"

"You were raped," she said.

The words hit him like the lash of a whip. "And how is a nation supposed to contend with that? A future king who has been…victimized. Who was held down in his own bedchamber… It could not be. My mother explained why."

"Your mother?"

"There is no point having this discussion. She was correct. It would follow me, Sophia. It would be the story of who I was. Something like that cannot be forgotten. Admitting a weakness on that score…"

"You are not weak," she protested. "There is nothing weak about… You were drugged."

"So easy it would be to destroy the throne then. To attack the kingdom. See how vulnerable I am?"

"No," she protested.

"I don't believe that," he said. "To be clear. I was there, and I'm well aware of what I would have been able to fight and what I could not. But that would be the speculation, Sophia. And there is a reason that this does not get spoken of."

"Luca…"

"I have trusted you with it. You asked for this. You pushed for it. Don't you dare betray me."

He felt some guilt at saying that. As if she would. Of course she wouldn't. She was looking at him with the truest emotion he had ever seen. His mother certainly hadn't looked at him like that. She had been horrified, too. But not about what had been done to him half as much as what the fallout could be. The fallout for her.

He hated this. He hated thinking of it. It was best left buried deep, with the lesson carried forward. There was no point to this. Because there was nothing that could be done. It was dragging out dead bodies and beating them. And there was simply no reason for that.

You could not spend your life punching at ghosts. That much he knew.

"Am I a strong king, Sophia?"

"Yes," she said softly.

"Would I be so strong in the eyes of the people if they knew?"

"You should be," she said.

"But *would I be*? We cannot deal in what should be. If what should have happened had happened I would not have been violated. But I was. I can only deal in reality as it is. And I cannot take chances. Why do you think I did my very best to stay away from you? I have a reputation. Our country has a reputation. And what exists now? It has been built on the back of my silence. And now I've blown it all to hell."

"Luca, you cannot carry all of that. You're a man. You cannot control what people think of you. You're a good man, that's what matters. Not what people think. But what you do for the country."

"So you say. But our standing in the world would greatly be affected by the way the people perceived me. By the headlines. And when it came to my child… There was no choice. In that I would choose him."

"You should have chosen yourself," she said softly.

He bit back the fact that it was his mother who hadn't chosen him. So why the hell should he?

He had already stripped his soul bare, had already confessed to the kind of weakness and shame that made his skin crawl to even consider. The last thing he was going to do was go further into mommy issues.

"I chose San Gennaro," he said instead.

"Luca..."

He got out of bed. "I have some more work to see to."

"It's late."

"Yes," he said. "But it will not wait."

There was no work. But he needed distance. Feeling like he did, he could not allow her to touch him. He needed a chance to get distance from this moment. To forget this conversation had ever happened.

He had expected... He had expected her to pull back, and she wouldn't. Damn her. She surprised him at every turn.

He collected his clothing and pulled it on, walking out of the bedroom, ignoring Sophia's protests. He pushed his hands through his hair and paused for a moment, only just now realizing how quickly his heart was beating. But he had done it. He had spoken the words. Maybe now... Maybe now it wouldn't matter.

He walked down the hall toward his office, and when he entered the room his phone was lighting up, vibrating on his desk.

It was his stepmother. He picked up the phone. "It's late," he said.

"You need to come home," she said.

"I'm busy at the moment."

"Luca," she said, "I would not tell you to come home if it wasn't absolutely necessary. This is all getting out of hand. And you cannot simply leave the country to take care of itself."

"What about Sophia? This is for her benefit, not mine."

"Then leave her there alone. Wherever you've spirited her off to, leave her in peace while you come here to deal with the fallout of your actions."

"I assure you that your daughter has culpability in the situation."

"Oh, I have no doubt, but if your only view is to protect her, then leave her behind and come back and address your people."

"You know I can't do that. If we step out, we must do so together."

"That is likely true. But… Luca, I beg you, don't hurt Sophia. She is not from your world. No matter how long she has lived in it… It is not ingrained in her the way that it is in you. That duty must come first. For her, love will always come first."

Yes, and he knew that. Because for her, what his mother had done was unfathomable. While to him… He might resent it, but… In the end, could he truly be angry about it? What he had said to her was true. He would be defined by that experience if the world knew of it. It was difficult to be angry about the fact that he was not.

"I won't," he said.

"I wish I believed you."

"I will marry her. I will not abandon her."

"That's my concern. But you seem to think that is all that is required of you. There is so much more, Luca."

"What else is there?"

She said nothing for a moment. "Come home."

"I will ready a plane for an early morning departure."

CHAPTER TWELVE

WHEN SOPHIA AWOKE to see Luca standing at the side of the bed, wearing nothing but a pair of dark slacks, his arms crossed over his bare chest, his expression forbidding, she knew something was wrong.

"What?" She scrambled into a sitting position and pulled her sheet up to her chest.

Suddenly, last night came flooding back to her. His confession. What had happened to him at the hands of his mother's lover. He had left after that. And it had hurt that he had pulled away, but she had understood that it had been required.

Still. She wanted to hold him. She wanted to…offer him something.

She knew that he wouldn't let her.

"We need to leave," he said, his voice stern.

He walked over to the closet and took out a crisp white shirt, pulling it over his broad shoulders and beginning to button it slowly.

"Why?" She shook her head, trying to clear the webs of cotton from her brain. "I thought we were going to stay here until everything died down."

"We were. But your mother called. She convinced me otherwise." His jaw firmed, his expression like iron.

"It is not going to be easy. But she is correct. I have left the country to burn in my absence, and I cannot do that. She suggested…that I leave you here."

"I don't want to stay here. I want to go with you."

He seemed to relax slightly at that. But only slightly. "I feel it would be best for you to come with me. It would be good for us to present a united front. However…"

"There is no however," she said, pushing herself up so that she was sitting straighter. "You're right. If you return without me the rumors will only get worse. Whatever you say. I need to be there. I need to be there, speaking for myself. There is no other alternative that is acceptable."

"You are very brave, Sophia."

Was she? She had never felt particularly brave. A girl who had tried once to gain the attention of her father, only to fail. Who had then spent a life infatuated with a stepbrother who didn't even like her.

Suddenly, it all became clear, as if the clouds had rolled back, revealing a clear sky and full sun. She had spent those years infatuated with Luca to protect herself. If she had ever fancied herself in love with him, she had been wrong. Because she had not known him.

He had never even been kind to her. Had never demonstrated any softness toward her. Had taken no pains to make her feel welcome in the palace.

He had been the safest.

Until the moment he had touched her in the garden, and it all became painfully real.

But until last night, she had never really known him.

She had been attracted to the untouchable quality he had. To the safety that represented. And more than that, to his strength. The integrity that he exuded.

She had admired that, because she had known men without it. Her own father being one of them.

But that wasn't enough to be love.

Suddenly, as he stood there, putting himself back together, after making himself so vulnerable the night before, putting the king back on over the top of the wounded boy, she fully appreciated what that integrity meant. What that strength cost.

That the granite in his voice, the hardness in his eyes, the straightness in his stance, the way he held his head high, had all come with great difficulty.

Anyone who knew his public story would think he was a man who was exactly as he had been raised to be. A man who had never faced any real adversity, beyond the loss of his mother. And what famous, handsome prince these days had not experienced such a thing?

But they didn't know. Not really.

Until last night she hadn't, either.

Suddenly, it felt as if someone had reached inside her chest and grabbed hold of her heart, squeezing it hard. Feeling overwhelmed her. There was no safety here. There was no careful divide created by his disdain, no distance at all. This wasn't simple attraction, wasn't fascination. It was more. It was deeper.

It was something she had not imagined possible. Something she hadn't wanted.

Love, for her, apart from her family, had always been a simple word.

This was more. It created a seismic shift inside her, incited her to action. To open herself up and expose herself to hurt.

The very last thing that love was was a feeling. It was so many other things first.

She understood that then.

Because until then, she had not loved Luca.

But she did now. Deeply.

"I must get myself presentable," she said. And then she rose out of the bed, not covering herself at all, and walked over to the closet, where, at the moment their clothes were mingled. Would it always be like this? With their lives tangled together?

She imagined that Luca fancied a royal marriage to be something based on tradition. That they would carry out their separate lives, in their separate quarters.

But their parents hadn't done that. His father, and her mother, had shared everything. Space. Life. Breath.

That was what she wanted. She didn't want to be the wife of his duty. She wanted to be the wife of his heart.

She turned to face him, whatever words on her lips there had been dying the moment that her gaze connected with his. With the heat there. He was looking at her with a deep, ferocious hunger that made her feel… both happy and sad all at once.

Luca wanted her. There was no denying that.

But whatever else he felt…

He was perfect. A man perfectly formed, with a wonderfully symmetrical face, classically handsome features that his aristocratic air pushed over into being devastating. His physique was well muscled, his hands large and capable. So wonderful to be held by.

But he was scarred. Inside, he was destroyed.

And no one looking at him would have any clue.

She wondered…

She wondered if there was any way to reach past those scars.

Any way to touch his heart.

She turned away from him again, concentrating on dressing herself. She selected a rather somber black sheath dress, not one that would be approved by the new stylist, but one that would best suit their return back to the country. She had a feeling they would be trying to strike a tone that landed somewhere between defiance and contrition. Not an easy thing to do. But they would have to be resolute in what they had chosen, while being mindful of the position the nation was put in due to the scandal.

He was distant the entire plane ride back to San Gennaro, but she wasn't overly surprised by that. He was trying to rebuild that wall. Brick by brick. Oh, not to keep out that physical lust. Not anymore.

But that new emotional connection that had been forged last night…

He wanted badly to turn away from that. And she didn't know how to press it. She had always imagined she had lived the harder life. She was from poverty, after all. She had a father who didn't want her. She knew what it was to go to bed hungry. She'd been fortunate enough to come into a wonderful life at the palace, but it had been foreign to her. Filled with traditions and silverware that were completely unfamiliar to her.

But now she knew different.

Now she knew that incredible strength could mask unfathomable pain. The walls of a palace could not keep out predators when they had simply been let in.

When the plane descended it felt like a heavyweight was pushing them down toward the ground. Or perhaps that was just the feeling inside her chest. Heaviness.

She wished they could stay on the island. That they could stay in a world where rigorous walks on the beach and lazy lovemaking sessions in a tub were the most pressing things between them.

She had to wonder… If they had not spoken last night…would he be ready to fly back today? Would he be so dead set on their need to return home?

She wondered if he wasn't facing his duty so much as running from her.

No, that wasn't fair.

If there was one thing Luca was not, it was a coward. He would forcefully tell her he didn't want to speak of something, that was certain, but he would not run.

"Prepare yourself," he said, the first words he had spoken to her in hours as the plane door opened.

And indeed, his words were not misplaced. Their car was down there waiting for them, but it was surrounded. Bodyguards were doing their best to keep the horde at bay, but camera flashes were going off, blinding Sophia as they made their way down the stairs and toward the limousine.

Luca wrapped his arm tightly around her and guided her into the car, speaking firmly in Italian before closing the door behind them.

"We will have to speak to them, won't we?" she asked as the car attempted to maneuver its way through the throng.

"Eventually," he said. "But I will do it on my own terms. I am the king of this nation, and I will not be led around by the dictates of the press. Yes, we have answers to give. Yes, we must return and create a solid front for the country. But I will not stand on the tarmac and give an interview like some fame whore reality TV star."

She examined the hard line of his profile, shiver working its way down her spine.

Everything he believed in was crumbling in front of him, and still, he was like granite. Protecting his image had been everything, because if it wasn't…

She felt like she'd been stabbed in the chest as she realized, fully, deeply, the cost of all this to him. How it linked to the pain of his past, and the decisions that had been made then.

It made her want to fix it. To fix him. Because she had been part of this destruction. But she hadn't understood.

"Luca," she said softly.

"We don't need to talk," he said, firm and rigid. "There will be time later."

"Will there?"

"We will have to prepare a statement."

Preparing a statement was not the same as the two of them talking. But she wasn't going to correct him on that score right now.

Later, when she was installed back in her normal bedroom, alone, she wished she had pressed the issue.

But Luca had been forceful and autocratic like he could be, and he had determined that the two of them should not do anything wildly different from normal until they figured out how they were going to handle the public fallout.

She wished that she was in bed with him.

But then, maybe it was good for her to have some time alone.

She tossed and turned for a few moments, and then got out of bed. She crossed the large room, wearing only her nightgown, and padded out to the balcony. She leaned over the edge, staring out at the familiar grounds below, illuminated by the moonlight. She looked in the direction of the garden. Where all of this had started.

She wouldn't take it back. She simply wouldn't.

Not when being with him had opened the door to learning so much about herself.

To learning about love.

The discovery that she had been protecting herself all those years was a startling one, and yet, not surprising at the same time.

The breeze kicked up, and she could smell the roses coming in on the wind, tangling through her hair. She closed her eyes. And for a moment she thought she might be able to smell Luca's aftershave. His skin. That scent that had become so beloved, and so familiar.

"Here you are."

She whirled around at the sound of his voice, only to see him standing in the doorway of the balcony, looking out.

"Did you think I had jumped?"

"I rather hoped you hadn't."

"I thought we weren't going to talk tonight."

"I couldn't sleep," he said.

He pushed away from the door frame, and came out onto the balcony. He was wearing the same white button-up he'd had on earlier, the top three buttons undone. She could imagine, so easily, what his muscular chest would look like. What it would feel like if she were to push her hand beneath the edge of the shirt and touch him. His hair was disheveled as though he had been running his hands through it. Her eye was drawn to the gold wristwatch he was wearing. She didn't know why. But it was sexy. Maybe it was just because to her, he was sexy.

"I couldn't sleep, either." She frowned. "But I suppose that's self-evident."

"Perhaps."

"It's dark out here," she said, lifting her shoulder.

"What does that mean?"

"We can talk in the dark." She hadn't meant to say that. But she wondered if it was true. If this balcony could act as a confessional, like their bed had done last night.

"We can talk in the light just as well," he said, his tone stiff.

"No," she said, weary. "I'm not sure we can. At least, I think it doesn't make things easier."

"What is it you have to say?"

"I hope that you have some things to say to me. But…"

She wasn't quite in a space where she wanted to confess her undying love. But she did want him to know… She wanted him to know something. "You know," she said slowly. "After our parents were married… I saw my father. He found me. Actually, all of the press made it easy."

Luca frowned. "You were protected by guards."

"Yes. But they were hardly going to stop me from meeting with my father."

"I didn't know about it."

"Well, you wouldn't have. You were away at university by then. We saw each other for a while… Until your father refused to give him a substantial sum of money. I was so angry, Luca. I thought that your father was being cruel. Because after that my father took himself away from me. He didn't want me. He never did. But I couldn't see that. Not then. I was only thirteen, and it felt immeasurably awful to have my father taken from me simply because yours wouldn't give him what he needed."

"What a terrible thing," Luca said, his voice rough. "To be so badly used by a parent."

"But you know about that, don't you? I didn't think you did. I thought… I thought for you things were so easy. I admired you. Even when you weren't nice to me. I admired how certain you were. How steady. You were all of these things that I could never be, wearing this position like a second skin. But now I know. I know what it costs you to stand up tall. And it only makes me admire you all the more."

He ignored her, walking over to the balcony, standing beside her. He gripped the railing, and she followed suit, their hands parallel to each other but not touching. Still, she could feel him. With every breath.

"How did you come to be close with my father? After all that anger you had toward him?" Luca asked. He quite neatly changed the subject.

But she didn't mind talking about this. She wanted to tell him. She wanted to… Well, she wanted to give no less than she took.

Or, what she hoped to take.

"He proved to be the better man," she said.

"How?" He seemed hungry for that answer.

"My father quit seeing me after your father refused to pay him off. Meanwhile, I was a wretch to your father. I was rude. I was insufferable. And he never once threatened to remove himself from my life. No. He only became more determined to forge a relationship with me. He refused to quit on me. Even when I was a monster. He could have… He could have simply let us exist in the same space. There was no reason that he had to try to have a relationship with me. But he did. He proved what manner of man he was through his actions. He showed me what strength was. What loyalty was." She swallowed hard, her throat dry like sandpaper. "He demonstrated love to me. And I had certainly seen it coming from my mother. But not from anyone else. He made me feel like I was worth something."

Yes, the king had pursued her. Her affection. He had made that relationship absolutely safe for her before she had decided to give of herself. But when it came to Luca…it wasn't the same.

When it came to him, she might have to put herself out there first. And she…

That was terrifying. She wasn't sure she could.

It wasn't something she was sure she could do.

If only he would…

She bit her lip. "I was very grateful to have your father. He did a lot to repair the damage that my own father created."

"I can only hope to be half the father he was."

"Well, I hope to be as good of a mother as my own."

It was the first time they had really talked about the baby in those terms. It had all been about blood, and errors and duty. But it had been real. It had not been about being a mother and a father.

"Your mother has always been good to me," he said. "She never had a thing to prove, you know. Not a thing to hide. Not like my own mother did. She is a truly kind woman, who had many things said about her by the media. Cruel, unfair. But she held her head high. You are the same, Sophia. I know you are. You will show our child—son or daughter—how to do the same."

She ducked her head, her heart swelling. "I hope so."

"If it had to be that our child was born in scandal, there is no one I would trust better to teach him to withstand."

Suddenly, Luca released his hold on the railing and turned away from her. She felt the abandonment keenly. As if the air had grown colder. Darker.

"Wait." She held up her hand, even though he couldn't see her. But he stopped, his shoulders held rigid. "I don't… I'm not sorry. So you know. I don't regret this."

Only the slight incline of his head indicated her words had meant something to him. The pause he took.

"Good night, Sophia," he said.

She wanted to say more. The words gathered in her chest, climbed up her throat, tight in a ball like a fist. But she couldn't speak them. So instead, she issued a request. "Stay with me. Tonight."

Then he took her by the hand, and led her to bed. And he did stay, all through the night.

It was surprising how quickly a royal wedding could be put together. Certainly, the wedding that they had assembled for Erik and Sophia had come together quickly enough, but this had been accomplished in lightning speed. They had handled the press a few days earlier, making a joint statement from the grounds of the palace, that had been streamed live over the internet and television. They had spoken about their commitment to San Gennaro, and to each other. And unsurprisingly it had been met with somewhat mixed reviews. But he had expected nothing less.

There was no way they were going to have a universal buy-in from the public. Not given the state of things.

They would have to win them over through the course of time. He had a feeling the baby would help.

Babies often did.

They were to be married in two days' time, and truly, he couldn't ask for things to be going much better than they were. He had Sophia in his bed every night, in spite of his determination that they would not carry on in that regard once they were back at the palace, and everything was going as smoothly as it possibly could. In terms of his lack of control when it came to bedding her…

She was his weakness. That was the simple truth.

He was a man who hadn't afforded himself a weakness as long as he'd been a grown man. Sophia had always challenged him. Had always slipped beneath his resolve and made him question all that he knew about himself.

He didn't like it. But he rather did like sleeping skin to skin with her.

Sacrifices had to be made.

There would be a small gathering tonight, of the guests arriving for the upcoming union. Nothing large, like it would have been with more time. Like it would have been if there wasn't a cloud hanging over the top of them.

It would fade. Surely, it would fade.

And if it didn't? An interesting thought to have. He had been so wedded to his reputation, to guarding what everyone thought, the idea that he had no more control over it was…

He frowned. He wasn't even certain he cared.

Sophia was the mother of his child. She was to be his wife. There was no arguing with that. And as she had said to him just the other night…whatever people thought of him, he could rule. And he could do it well.

The rest didn't matter.

"How are you finding things?" he asked as Sophia was ushered toward him at the entrance of the dining hall.

She was wearing a dress of such a pale color that the sequins over the top of it looked as though they had been somehow fastened directly to her pale, smooth skin. It glittered with each step she took, and the top came to an artful V at her breasts, showing off those delicate curves in exquisite fashion.

She took hold of his arm, looked up at him. "Entertaining dignitaries' wives is a strange experience."

"But it is your life now," he pointed out.

She wilted somewhat at that.

"I am sorry, *cara mia*," he said, "but it cannot be ignored that being queen does carry its share of burdens. Your mother, I'm certain, knows all about that."

"Yes," she said, though somewhat hesitant.

He wondered what the caveat was, because there was one. He could hear it. Unspoken, deep down her throat. But they were walking into a dining room crowded full of people, half of whom were hoping they would be witnessing some sort of glorious meltdown, he was certain, so he was hardly going to broach the topic now.

He sat at the head of the table, and Sophia had departed from him and made her way down to the foot.

Tradition, he mused, was such a fascinating thing. Things like this… They formed from somewhere, and that demonstrated that humans could clearly create them out of thin air. On a whim. But there were certain points in history where tradition had simply been followed, and not created. As though someone else had made those rules, and human beings were bound to them. As though they could not be broken.

Tradition. Appearances.

Those things had been paramount to his mother, even while she had lived in exactly the fashion she had wanted. And he… He clung to it because it gave him a sense of purpose. Because it made him feel as if what had happened to him—and the lack of fallout after—had been unavoidable.

It was the reason that he was seated across the room from Sophia now, when he would like her at his side.

All of these fake rules.

He was a damned king, and yet there were all these rules.

The rules that kept him from receiving any sort of justice. The rules that prevented him from acting on his attraction to Sophia in the first place.

And the rules that kept him from sitting beside her now. The rules that had kept them from spending the day together.

A strange thing. All of it.

Those seated around him directly had been artfully chosen people. Selected carefully by members of his cabinet. People who would only speak highly of him, and certainly not call into question his union with his stepsister. He was certain the same could be said for those who had been seated directly around Sophia, and those in the middle could fling poison back and forth across the table to their hearts' content, for he and his bride could not hear it.

When the meal was finished he rose, nodding his head once and signaling Sophia to follow suit.

She looked up at him with slightly cautious eyes, but she followed his lead. She had watched his father and her mother do this many times. She knew that she was simply to follow his lead.

They met at the center of the table and he took her arm again, then they turned toward the doors and made their exit.

The guests would follow shortly, but they had a moment, a quiet moment there in the antechamber.

"Are you all right?"

"Yes," she said. "I do understand how these things work."

"But it's only just dawning on you that your role in them has changed. Am I correct in assuming that?"

"It's a lot of things. Marrying you. Becoming a mother. The fact that I was going to be queen was low on my list of things to deal with."

"And yet, you will be my queen. Tomorrow."

Her skin looked a bit waxen, pale, her gown and her necklace glittering in the dim light, which was helpful to her, as she herself did not glitter at all at the moment.

"It's too late to go back," he said.

She jerked her focus toward him. "I didn't say that I wanted to."

"You don't seem happy."

"I'm overwhelmed. I have been overwhelmed from the moment that you kissed me in the garden all those weeks ago. I don't know how you can expect me to feel any differently than that."

"Well, I suggest that by the time we are in the chapel tomorrow you find a way to feel slightly less overwhelmed."

She lifted a brow, her expression going totally flat. "As you command, sire."

He had no opportunity to respond to that because their guests began to depart the dining room and fill the antechamber.

"With regrets," Luca said, "I must bid you all goodnight. As must my fiancée. With the wedding tomorrow we do not wish to overextend her."

He wrapped his arm around her waist, breaking with propriety completely by engaging in such an intimate hold in public, and propelled her from the room. She was all but hissing by the time they arrived in her bedroom.

"Luca," she said. "We have guests, and I spent the entire day on my best behavior, not so that you could ruin it now."

"My apologies," he said, his tone hard. "I am ever ruining the reputations of others."

She looked ashamed at that. And he felt guilty. Because he knew that wasn't what she meant.

"Luca, I didn't mean..."

"I'm aware. I apologize for using that against you."

She didn't seem to know what to say to that. "Don't apologize to me," she said finally. "We're going to have to learn how to make this work."

She looked thoughtful at that.

"We don't have a lot of practice getting along. Not outside of bed anyway," he said.

"That is very true." She clasped her hands and folded them in front of her body. Then she let out a long, slow breath and lifted one leg slightly, towing her high heel off, before working on the other. It reduced her height by three inches, leaving her looking a small, shimmering fairy standing in the bedchamber.

"I know how they made it work," she said slowly. "I know why it was easy for them."

"Why is that?"

"They loved each other. They loved each other so very much, Luca. It wasn't a child, or the need for marriage or money that brought them together. They risked everything to be together. Not because they had to, but because they wanted to."

Her words were soft, and yet they landed in his soul like a blow. "I don't understand what you want me to do with that. I don't understand what you want me to say. You're pregnant. Your mother was not pregnant. I cannot change the circumstances of why we are marrying."

"I know," she said. "But I've found that over the past weeks my reasons for marrying you have changed." She looked up at him, her dark eyes luminous. "Luca, I imagined myself half in love with you for most of my life but it wasn't until after that night in San Paolo that I realized that wasn't true."

His stomach crawled like acid. Of course. She had realized she didn't love him after she found out that he had been such a weak victim of such a disgusting crime. That his body had been used in such a fashion. Of course she was repulsed by him. Who wouldn't be? He was repulsed by himself most of the time. Questioning a great many things about him. Questioning his attraction to Sophia herself. If it was something inside him that had been twisted and broken off beyond repair. Something that had caused him to want a thing that was forbidden to him.

"I am sorry to have destroyed your vision of me."

"No," she said. "That was when my vision of you became whole. Luca, you were a safe thing to love. I couldn't be with you. You were my stepbrother. How could it ever happen? You could never hurt me, not the way my father had done. And all the better, as long as I was obsessed with you, no one else could hurt me, either. You were a wall that I could build around myself. A thing to distract my heart with. The minute that you touched me that wall was destroyed. I didn't know you. How could I love you if I didn't know you? I admired things about you. I admired your strength. I admired what an honest man you were. But I didn't know the cost of those things, Luca, and knowing that… That was when I began to love you for real. I love you, Luca. I didn't want to say it. Because I wanted so badly to protect myself. I have been rejected before. I loved my father, and he only wanted to use what money your father could give him. I could not face being the one who tore themselves open and revealed their whole heart, only to be met with nothing. And I almost did… The other night I almost did. But I was afraid. I'm not going to be afraid anymore. I don't want to be. You deserve more than someone hiding and protecting themselves." She swallowed hard. "I love you."

Everything inside him rebelled at her claim. Utterly. Completely. There was no way it could be true. No way in heaven or hell.

"You don't love me," he said, his voice hard. "You want to make all of this a bit more palatable for you. You want to make it easier. But you don't love me."

"I do."

"Fine. Think what you wish, but that doesn't mean it's going to change anything."

"Why not? Why can't it change anything?"

"Because I don't love anything," he said. "Nothing at all."

"That can't be true, Luca. You loved your father. You care a great deal for my mother..."

"Family. Is different."

"How? Your mother was family..."

"I'm going to marry you, Sophia," he said. "I don't see why we need to get involved in an argument regarding feelings. I have committed to you. Why should you want anything else?"

"Because it's not just something else. It's everything else. Love is vital, Luca, and without it... It's the glue. It's not about lust. It's not blood. It's love."

"There we disagree. Because some days it's the promises that will be all that hold us together. That is how life works. Sometimes it's simply the things you have decided that keep you going. You cannot make decisions in desperation. You must make them with a cool head, and only then can you be certain you will act with a level of integrity."

"Fine. I can accept that you feel that way. In fact, it's one of the things I admire about you. You're a good man. You always have been. There is no doubt about that. But there has to be more. We cannot have one without the other. I don't want commitment without love, Luca. I can't."

"Why not?"

He could not understand why she couldn't let this go. Love was nothing. Love was...

Love failed. It left you bleeding on the ground. He had heard it said many times that love did not seek its own, but that was not his experience.

His mother cared only for herself.

He had been a casualty in her pursuit of pleasure, in her pursuit of protecting her own comfort.

He hadn't mattered.

Why should Sophia feel that he did? And why should she try to demand that he…?

It didn't matter. It didn't matter as long as he promised to stay with her.

"Because don't I deserve to be loved? Don't I deserve to be at the forefront of whatever action is being taken? I have been loved, richly so in my life. But… I've never been chosen. My mother loved me in spite of the fact that having me plunged her into poverty. Your father loved me because he loved my mother. My own father didn't care at all. He wanted money. And you want the baby. Is it so much to ask, Luca, that I be wanted for who I am? That I be loved for who I am?"

"I have told you a great many times that you are a sickness in my blood. If I didn't want you then we wouldn't be here at all. There would be no baby."

"Being your sickness isn't the same as being your love, Luca, and if you can't sort that out, then I'm not sure we have anything left to say to each other."

"So you'll just storm away from me?" he asked, anger rising up unreasonably inside him. "If you can't have exactly what you want the moment you want you're going to leave?" Of course she would. Why would she stay with him? That was the fundamental issue with all of this. She could profess to love him, and she might even believe it. But when it all came down, that would not be so. It couldn't be.

Because he was a man who had been used and discarded. The violation he had experienced at the hands of his mother's paramour not remotely as invasive as the one he had experienced when his mother had chosen to maintain her reputation over protecting him. Seeking justice for him.

And he had no idea how to feel about it. Because she was dead. Because he wasn't entirely certain he wanted his pain splashed all over the headlines, and had they sought legal action against the man who had harmed him, he certainly would have been in the headlines.

He didn't know what he wanted. He didn't know what he was worth.

But he knew he wasn't worth Sophia and all of the feelings she professed to have for him now.

She had tried to explain to him how her feelings for him had shifted, but she didn't truly understand. She couldn't.

"I told my mother what was done to me," he said, his voice low. "I went to her. Trusted her. I had been drugged. I had been violated. Abused. And I told her as much. That she had let that man into the palace, and that he had sought me out and harmed me in such a way. She was upset. And she was fearful. But it was not for me. It was for her own self. She could not have my father finding out she had been conducting affairs. She could not have the public finding out that she had been engaged in such a thing. And if we were to bring him before the law, then of course he would expose my mother for what she was. She couldn't have that. She didn't care for me, Sophia. Not one bit. My own mother."

"She was broken," Sophia said. "As my father is broken. You cannot possibly think that I deserve the way my father treated me, can you?"

"That's different."

"It isn't. You're just too afraid to step out from beneath this."

"Because on the other side is nothing. Nothing but the harsh, unending truth that I was nothing more than an incidental to the person who should have loved me simply because of the connection that we shared."

"Luca," she said. "I love you."

Suddenly, the emotion in his chest was like panic. Because she kept persisting even though he had told her to stop. And the monster inside him was growling louder, and he couldn't drown it out with platitudes. Nothing about promises or duty, or about standing tall in the face of an unfriendly press. About being a king and therefore being above these kinds of emotions, needing to rule with a cool head and a steady heart, rather than one given to things such as this. But he could not speak those words. He could not even feel them.

"You cannot love me," he said. "You cannot love me because I do not love myself." He gritted his teeth, despising the weakness inside him. "The man I could've been was stolen from me. I had to rebuild myself out of something, because God knows nobody was going to do it for me. I was broken open. All that I might have been poured out. And when I put myself together I did not make an effort to replace those things within me that were weak. Those things within me that had… That made me seem as though I might make a good victim."

"No," she said. "That's not fair."

"There is no fair in this. I was chosen for a reason. The boldness that it takes to do to me what that man did. Did you ever think of it that way? I was the future King of San Gennaro, and he felt as though he could take advantage of me, and he knew that he would not be punished. He knew that my mother would protect him. He knew that I would not be able to come forward and speak out against him. My hands would be tied. I refused… I refused to be remade in the same fashion that I had been born. I despise what I was, but I like the man I am now a little more. You cannot…"

He turned away from her, closing his eyes and gathering his control once again. "You cannot."

"Luca," she said, sounding broken, and he hated that, too. She deserved something else. Something different. A chance to be with a man, to want a man, to care for a man, who was not…broken in this way.

"Do you know," he said. "I have often wondered if there was something inherently sick inside me."

"You keep saying that word."

"I know. Because I wonder if it's why I've wanted you so badly for so long. Because there was something in me…"

"No. Stop trying to push me away."

"I'm not trying to push you away. I'll marry you. But I'm never going to love you in the way that you want me to. I can't. That part of myself is gone. It's dead. I had to cut it out of me so that I can survive all that I went through." He shook his head. "I will not change it for you. I cannot."

To change now would be to open himself back up to the kind of pain that he wanted gone from him forever, and he wouldn't do it.

"But you are pushing me away," she said.

"Sophia…"

She took a step away from him. "I'm sorry, Luca. I love you. And I'm not going to marry you simply because of duty. I would marry you because I loved you but I want you to marry me for the same reason. It would be so easy…" Her words came out choked, her brown eyes filling with tears. "It would be so easy to simply let this be. To take what you're offering, and be content with that. But I… I cannot. Luca, I can't. Because I think we could both have more. It doesn't have to be a sickness. It can be the cure. But only if you let it. And if I stay, and I allow you to have me without risking anything…"

His stomach tightened, turned over, and he ceased hearing her. Stopped listening. "If you don't want a man who's been raped, *cara mia*, all you have to do is say so."

"*Don't.* Don't make it about me being scared. I am scared, but I'm doing the brave thing. The hard thing. I refuse to let us live our lives as broken pieces when we can be whole together."

"What are you saying?"

"That for the second time, Princess Sophia is not going to show up to her wedding."

And with that, Sophia turned and walked out of the room, not bothering to gather her shoes. And he simply stood there, looking at them. Thinking this was the strangest interpretation of a Cinderella story he had ever heard of.

But after that came a strange pain in his chest like he couldn't remember feeling before. And he didn't even try to stop it from dropping him to his knees.

CHAPTER THIRTEEN

SOPHIA RAN UNTIL her mind was blank. Until there was nothing but her bare feet pounding down on the damp grass, the blades sticking between her toes, mud giving way and creating a slick foothold as she prayed her legs wouldn't fail her. Prayed they would carry her far away from Luca. From heartbreak.

She was still on the palace grounds, for they extended vastly, and she knew that she was going to have to stop running and get in a car. Get on a plane, to truly escape Luca. But for now she couldn't stop. For now she could do nothing but run.

She stopped when she came to the edge of the woods, and then she took a cautious step forward, the texture of the grounds changing to loose dirt and pine needles, the heavy tree cover protecting her from the pale moonlight. It was cool, almost frigid, there beneath the dark trees.

She shivered. She wrapped her arms around herself, trying to catch her breath. She took another step forward, and another, her dress shimmering in front of her, catching stolen beams of moonlight, flashing in the darkness.

She didn't know what she had just done. Didn't know what her plan was.

To walk into the forest and die?

No.

That was hardly the solution to dealing with a man not returning your affection.

She had been right, in what she had said to him. She couldn't go through with a marriage to a man who didn't love her. Not just for her own sake, but for his.

She had the feeling that many people—herself included until recently—thought love to be a beautiful, quiet thing. A force that allowed you to be yourself. And while that was true…it didn't mean the self that you projected to the world.

Real love, she fully understood now, challenged that identity. It forced you to reach down deep to your essence, and ask yourself who you were *there*. Real love was not about being comfortable. Not about being protected. Real love was about being stripped bare. Was about revealing yourself, unprotected to the other person, trusting that they would not use your tender and vulnerable places against you. That they would protect them for you, so that you didn't have to.

Real love was the difference between hiding in a darkened forest, or standing in the light.

Right now she was hiding in a forest.

She closed her eyes, a tear tracking down her face.

And it was then she realized where her feet were carrying her. She pressed on through the forest. Through and through. Until she found the paved drive that wound through the trees.

Her mother had moved into the dower house some time ago. It was an outmoded sort of thing, surely, as the palace was so large, but her mother seemed to like it. Liked having her own house rather than standing on ceremony in the massive palace.

It gave her a sense of peace. Gave her a small slice of her simple life back. Although the cottage, with its impeccably tended garden, bright pink roses climbing up the sides of the walls and exquisite furnishings was far grander than anything possessed by Sophia or her mother in their former lives.

It was dark now, the white stucco of the cottage shining a pale beacon through the dimness, the roses fluttering slightly against the wall as the breeze kicked up.

The gravel in the driveway cut into her feet, but she didn't care.

She walked up to the door and knocked.

It opened slowly, and then more quickly when her mother realized it was her.

"Sophia," she said. "What are you doing here?"

"I..." She swallowed hard. "I didn't know where else to go. I didn't even know I was coming here until... Until I realized where I was."

"What happened?"

"Luca and I fought. I... I called off the wedding."

"Come inside," her mother said, ushering her in.

There, Sophia found herself quickly wrapped in a blanket and settled on the couch, and before she knew it, a cup of tea was being firmly placed into her hand.

"Tell me."

"He doesn't wish to love me," Sophia said. "Which I feel is very different to not loving me at all. He doesn't want love. It... It frightens him." She would not reveal Luca's secrets to her mother. Because though she trusted her mother to keep confidences, they were Luca's secrets to tell. "He is very wounded by some things in his past, and he doesn't want..."

"He doesn't want to be healed?"

"Yes. Was his father like that?"

"No." Her mother shook her head. "I was. Your father hurt me deeply. Years of being shunned for being a single mother. The casual judgment I faced every day leaving the house. Collecting assistance so that I could feed you. It all left me scarred and hardened. And then I met Magnus. He charmed me. And yes, when we met, seduced me. I'm not going to dance around that, Sophia, since I know you know full well about those things."

Sophia felt her face heat. "Indeed."

"It was easy for him to tempt me into his bed, but into his life was another thing entirely. And I did my best. To work my job, to keep my liaisons with a king private. To continue to be a good mother to you. I thought I could keep all those things separate. That all of those parts of myself didn't have to be contained in one woman. That I could put walls up." She smiled softly. "But I couldn't. Not in the end. But I was hanging on very tightly to my pain. And I realized I was going to have to open my hands up and drop that pain if I was going to grab hold of what he was offering me. But when your pain has been fuel for so long, it is a difficult thing to do."

"I think that's how it is for him. I think his pain has kept him going, because without it..."

"Without it there's only despair. Anger is much easier. Do you know what else anger is preferable to?"

"What?"

"Hope. Learning to hope again is a terrifying thing. And when you have been harmed, you don't want it.

You resist it. Those little bits of light creeping back into the darkness are the most terrifying thing. You cannot hide in the light, Sophia. Darkness is a wonderful concealment. But it conceals everything. The beauty of the world. All that we can have around us. But it reveals us, too. The light. I suspect that is what Luca is resisting."

"What should I do? Should I go back to him? Love him even though he doesn't love me?"

"I can't tell you what to do. I don't want you trapped in a loveless marriage. But…"

"If I love him it isn't loveless," she said softly.

"No. It isn't." Her mother sat down on the couch next to her, clasping her hands in her lap. "The king loved me all the while when I could not love him. But he also didn't compromise. He did not want a mistress. He wanted a wife. And as far as he was concerned, if I didn't love him, even if we took vows, I might as well be a mistress."

"So he gave you an ultimatum."

"No. He just made it known he could not fully bring me into his life without love."

"Well. Luca and I can't exactly have that sort of arrangement. We are going to have a child together. And I live in the palace half the time."

Her mother laughed softly. "I'm not telling you what to do, Sophia. I feel there is the potential for heartbreak at every turn with this situation."

"That's not very encouraging."

"It isn't supposed to be encouraging. It's just the truth. I guess the question is… If he's going to break your heart either way… Would you rather be with him or be without him?"

"I don't know."

Except she did know. She wanted him. She wanted to be in his life, in his bed, but it felt like a potentially dangerous thing to do. The wrong thing. Like it would damage…

Her pride. Her defenses.

Perhaps she was more like her mother than she imagined.

Claims of love were bold, but quite empty when the action was withheld until the other person performed to your specifications.

His mother had given up on him. Had put herself before him.

Sophia realized she could not do the same.

Luca was not a man given to drink. He was not a man who indulged in anything, particularly. But he was drunk now. There was nothing else that was going to calm the pounding ache in his head. In his chest. He had sat there, for hours, on the floor of Sophia's bedroom, pain biting into him like rabid wolves. And then he had gotten up and gone back to his own quarters, and proceeded to drink the contents of his personal bar.

Now the pain was just swimming back and forth inside him, hazy and dull and no less present.

And he had even less control of his thoughts now. Chasing through his mind like rabid foxes after their own tails.

He was worthless. Worthless. A king of an entire country, worth absolutely nothing.

He did not allow himself those thoughts. He never did. But in this moment, he not only allowed them, he fed them. Like they were his pets. He allowed them to rain down on him, a black misery that coated him completely.

He embraced, wholly, his misery. His self-pity.

Sophia had spoken of how he stood tall in spite of everything. But here he was, on the floor. Prostrate to the sins that had been committed against him, and to what remained of his own soul. Black and bruised like the rest of him.

Dark.

He was a night without stars.

Sophia was the stars.

He rolled onto his back, the earth spinning on its axis.

He was worthless because he had been treated like an object. Worthless because his own mother had not cared to seek justice for him.

And yet, in the midst of those thoughts, in the midst of that darkness, there came a glimmer.

Sophia did not see him as worthless. Sophia thought he was strong.

Sophia thought he was worthy of love.

And in an instant, as though the sun had broken through storm clouds, he felt bathed in light.

Why should his mother, Giovanni, be the ones who formed his life? Why should they decide what he was?

Perhaps, in withholding what had happened to him from the media, his mother had protected him from having the public form an opinion on who he was, but within that, he had allowed her to form his opinion of his life. Of what he could be. Of what he could have.

He had escaped the press defining him by that night, but he defined himself by it. By his mother's response.

Had trained himself to believe that if he did not act

above reproach in every way at all times, that he would be as useless as he had long feared.

Sophia saw more than that. Sophia saw through to the man he might have been. She made him think that perhaps he could be that man again.

And he had sent her away, because he didn't feel worthy of that.

But she thought he was. She mattered more. She mattered more than Giovanni. She mattered more than his mother.

She mattered more than all the stars in the sky.

If Sophia could love him…

Pain burst through him, as brilliant and blinding as the light from only a moment before.

He loved her. He loved her. And he had hurt her. He had sent her away to protect himself. Which was truly no different than what his mother had done, in many ways.

Putting himself before her.

He would not.

He didn't want to marry Sophia because of the baby. He didn't want her because he was sick.

He wanted her because she was her.

Undeniably, beautifully her.

When he closed his eyes, it was her face he saw.

And then, he knew nothing else.

CHAPTER FOURTEEN

THE DAY OF the wedding, Sophia stayed in her mother's house until clothing could be sent. Then she was bundled up and whisked off to the palace, where she checked to see if anything had been canceled.

It had not been.

Perhaps it was Luca's ferocious pride not able to come to grips with the fact that she was going to defy him.

Perhaps he had a plan to try and win her back.

Or perhaps, he had simply known that in the end she wouldn't leave him to be humiliated.

Whatever the reasoning, she would find out later. With the help of her stylist, she got dressed in her wedding gown far earlier than was necessary. And then she began to make inquiries of the staff.

"Where is he?" she asked.

"The king?"

"Yes."

"In his rooms. But you know it is bad luck for the groom…"

"I already had the bad luck to fall in love with my stepbrother. I think I have reached my limit." She picked up the front of her dress and dashed across the palace, making her way to Luca's chamber.

But he wasn't there. Dejected, she began to make the journey back to her own. The halls were remarkably empty, the staff all seeing to preparations for the wedding that might not happen, it seemed to Sophia.

So she was surprised when she heard another set of footsteps in the corridor.

She looked up and saw Luca standing there. He was wearing black slacks and a white shirt that was unbuttoned at the throat. For one blinding second she could hardly fight the impulse to fling herself across the empty space between them and kiss him there. Right at his neck, right where his heart beat, strong and steady.

But she remained rooted to where she was, her breathing shallow.

"Luca," she said.

"I was searching for you," he said.

"Here I am."

He frowned. "You're wearing a wedding gown."

She swished her hips back and forth, the dress swirling around her legs. "Yes."

"You said you wouldn't marry me."

"I changed my mind."

"Well. I have decided that I changed my mind, as well."

"What?"

"I do not wish to marry you simply because you're having a baby, Sophia. You're right. That would be a terrible thing. A terrible mistake."

Sophia felt crushed. As if he had brought those strong hands down over her heart and ground it into powder.

"You don't want to marry me?" she asked.

"I do want to marry you," he said. "But I'm happy to not marry you. We can live in sin. We can have a bastard. We could create scandal the world over and forget everyone else."

Sophia was stunned. She blinked. "No. Luca, your reputation… The reputation of San Gennaro…"

"It doesn't matter. If I must court scandal to prove my feelings for you, then I will do so. It is nothing in the face of my feelings for you. My love for you. And if I have to burn all of it to the ground to prove to you that what I feel is real, believe me, Sophia. My reputation is nothing, my throne is nothing, if I don't have you. I would give all of it up. For you. That was the real sickness in my blood, my darling girl. That I wanted so badly to hold on to this thing that I believed was more important than anything. Was the only thing that gave me value. While I fought with what I really wanted on the inside. You. It was always you. But I knew that I was going to have to give up that facade of perfection that felt as if it defined my very existence if I was going to have you. Please believe me, *cara mia*, I would gladly leave it all behind for you. For this. For us."

Then Sophia did cross the space between them. She did fling her arms around his neck. And she kissed him there, where his pulse was throbbing at the base of his throat. "Luca," she whispered. "Luca, I believe you. And I want to be married to you. Because I want it to be real. I want it to be forever. We could make vows in a forest, and I know it would be just as real, but we might as well give our child legitimacy, don't you think?"

"I mean, I suppose it would make things easier. With succession and everything."

"You're a king. We could bend the rules. But I feel like perhaps we should just get married."

"I kept thinking there were more rules for me because I was a king. But all those chains were inside me. And all the darkness… It's because I refused to let the light in. I stood there, on the island, and looked up at the stars. And I marveled at them. And wished very much that I could… That I could be more than darkness. That you could be my light. The only one stopping that was me. All along. The only thing stopping it was…"

"Fear. I understand that… That hope is the most frightening thing there is."

"It is," Luca agreed. "Truly terrifying to want for more when you simply accepted all the things you would never have. When you've told yourself you don't need it."

"Luca," she said softly. "You're not broken. You are not damaged. The people who hurt you… They are the ones who are broken."

"I was broken," he whispered. He grabbed hold of her hands and lifted them, kissing her fingertips. "I was broken for a time. But not now. You put me back together."

"We put each other back together."

"I love you," he said.

"I love you, too."

"I did not think I would get my happy ending."

"You didn't?"

He shook his head. "Stepsiblings of any stripe are always evil."

"Well, then I could just as easily have been evil, too."

"Of course not," he said. "You're the princess."

"And you happen to be my Prince Charming, Luca. Stepbrother or not."

"Am I very charming?" He grinned at her, and the expression on his face made her light up inside.

"Not always," she said, smiling slightly. "But you're mine. And that's all that matters."

"That makes you mine, too."

"I choose you. I choose you over everything," she said. She pressed a kiss to his lips, and he held her for a moment.

"I choose you, too," he said. "Over everything."

And though they spoke their vows later that day, it was those vows that she knew would carry them through for the rest of their lives.

EPILOGUE

SHE WAS ABOVE him in absolutely every way. A radiant angel of light, his wife. And never had he been more certain of that than when he looked at her, holding their daughter in her arms.

He had been right about one thing, the scandal of their union had settled quickly enough once the excitement over the royal baby had overshadowed it all. A new little princess was much more interesting to the world over than how Sophia and Luca had gotten their start.

Luca knelt down by his wife's hospital bed, gazing in awe at the two most important women in his life.

"What do you think, Your Majesty?" she asked.

"I think..." He swallowed hard. "I think that with two such brilliant lights in my life I will never have to be lost in darkness again."

* * * * *

THE SHEIKH'S PREGNANCY PROPOSAL

FIONA BRAND

To the Lord.

"Our Lord showed me an inward sight of His homely loving. I saw that He is everything that is good and comforting to us. He is our clothing. In His love He wraps us and holds us. He enfolds us in love and He will never let us go.'
—The Revelations of Divine Love,
Julian of Norwich

Heartfelt thanks to Stacy Boyd for inspirational suggestions, patience and grace in editing. It's always a joy to work with you.

One

Twenty-four hours away from the deadline to sign a marriage contract…

The stark thought shoved Sheikh Kadin Gabriel ben Kadir out of a restless sleep. Tossing crisp linen sheets aside, Gabe flowed to his feet and pulled on a pair of narrow dark jeans. The cool light of a New Zealand dawn flooded his suite, a floor above the Zahiri consulate in Wellington, as he broodingly considered the concept of once more entering into the intimacy of marriage.

Marrying a wealthy heiress would solve his country's financial problems. The problem was, after the disaster of his last marriage, he had no desire to ever immerse himself in that particular hell again.

The morning air cool against his torso, he padded barefoot to the French doors and dragged aside heavy linen curtains. Dark gaze somber, he surveyed the gray rain drenching his last day of bachelor freedom. At that moment, like a fiery omen, the sun pierced the thick veil of storm clouds that hung over Wellington Harbour, illuminating a large painting of his twelfth-century ancestors, which dominated one wall of his suite.

Gabe studied the painting of the original Sheikh Kadin on whose birthday he'd had the bad luck to be born. A battle-hardened Templar Knight, Kadin's main claim to fame was that he had taken someone else's bride along with her diamond-encrusted dowry. The captured bride, Camille de Vallois, a slim redhead with dark exotic eyes, had then proceeded to entrance his ancestor to the point of obsession. Gabe's stomach tightened at the remembrance of the obsession that had haunted his own youthful marriage, although in his case the possessive intensity hadn't emanated from him.

Once they were married, Jasmine, his childhood sweetheart, had become increasingly clingy and demanding, dissolving into tears or throwing tantrums when she didn't get her way. She had resented his busy work schedule, and had become convinced he was having affairs. When he had refused to start a family until their relationship was on a more even keel she had taken that as a sign that he regretted the marriage. The guilt she had inspired in him had taken on a haunting rawness when, after a tense exchange during a boat trip, Jasmine had stormed off in the yacht's tender, overturned on rocks and drowned.

The memory of the icy salt water dashing off rocks as he had attempted to save Jasmine started a dull ache in the scar that marred one cheekbone, a permanent reminder of that day.

Legend said Gabe's ancestor had a positive outcome

to his passionate involvement with the woman he had married. Gabe's experience had been such that he would not allow a woman to have that kind of power over him again. As far as he was concerned, passion had its place, but only in short, controllable liaisons. Love was another thing entirely; he would not be drawn into that maelstrom again.

A rap at the door of his suite was a welcome distraction. Shrugging into a T-shirt, he opened the door to his longtime friend and Zahir's chief of security.

Xavier, who had just flown in from Zahir, strolled into the spacious lounge that adjoined Gabe's bedroom and handed him an envelope. "Special delivery."

Slitting the envelope, Gabe extracted the marriage contract he had discussed with his lawyers before leaving Zahir.

Xavier stared at the contract as if it were a bomb about to explode. "I don't believe it. You're actually going to go through with it."

Gabe headed for the state-of-the-art kitchenette that opened off the lounge. "There aren't a whole lot of options."

With the cold winds of bankruptcy at their backs and the remains of Camille's extraordinary wealth lost during the confusion of the Second World War, it was up to Gabe to restore the country's fortunes with another arranged marriage to an extremely wealthy woman.

Xavier shook his head to the offer of a glass of orange juice. "I would have thought that after Jasmine—"

"That it was time I moved on?"

Xavier's expression became impatient. "When you married Jasmine you were both too young. It's time you had a *real* marriage."

"The marriage to Jasmine was real enough." Gabe drained his glass of juice and set the glass down on the counter with a sharp click. As far as he was concerned, their marriage had been all too real. He could still feel the familiar coldness in his gut, the tightness in his chest every time he thought about the past and how completely he had failed his wife when she had needed him most. "This marriage won't be." It was prescribed and controlled, preventing any possibility of destructive, manipulative emotion. "Remember, it's a business arrangement."

Xavier, who was happily married, didn't bother to hide his incredulity. "You can't seriously think you can keep it that way. What woman will ever allow that?"

Gabe lifted a brow as he flipped to the back pages of the contract. It contained a short list of candidates and photographs of the pretty young women from wealthy families who had expressed an interest in the prestige and business opportunities inherent in a marriage to the future Sheikh of Zahir.

Xavier frowned at the list. "I still think you're making a big mistake, but I guess it's your funeral."

Gabe saw the moment Xavier realized the import of his final comment about a funeral. He cut off Xavier's apology with a curt word. They had grown up together. Xavier had been his best man when he'd gotten married, and when Jasmine had died, he had kept the press and hordes of well-meaning friends and relatives at bay, gifting Gabe the privacy he had needed. Through it all, their friendship had endured. "I have to marry at some point. Don't forget, aside from the money, Zahir needs an heir."

After Xavier left, Gabe grabbed fresh clothing and headed for the shower. He considered Xavier's comment that he and Jasmine had been too young to marry. He had been twenty, Jasmine eighteen. The marriage had lasted two years.

Flicking on the shower, he waited until steam rose off the tiles before stripping and stepping beneath the water. Now he was thirty, and as his father's only son he needed to marry and continue the family line. The prospect of a second marriage made his jaw clench. He could think of other ways to raise the money Zahir needed, Westernized ways that weren't presently a part of Zahir's constitution. But with his father recovering from cancer and wary about new investments, Gabe had accepted his father's old-fashioned solution.

Minutes later, dressed in a white shirt, red tie and dark suit, he stood drinking the dark, aromatic coffee he preferred as he stared out at the heavy rain sweeping the harbor. As cold and alien as the view was, thousands of miles from sunny Zahir, it was nevertheless familiar. Not only had his mother been born in New Zealand, but Wellington had been a home away from home for him because he had gone to school here.

Checking his watch, he placed his empty mug on the coffee table next to the marriage contract. Right now he had a breakfast meeting with both the Zahiri and New Zealand ministers for tourism. That would be followed by a string of business meetings, then a cocktail party and presentation on Zahir's attractions as a tourist destination at the consulate tonight.

Despite Gabe's resolve, he could think of better ways to spend his last day of freedom.

One more day—and night—as a bachelor, before he committed to the marriage of convenience that was his destiny.

* * *

She was destined to be loved, truly loved...

The chime of her alarm almost pulled Sarah Duval out of her dream, but the irresistible passion that held her in its grip was too singular and addictive to relinquish just yet. Eyes firmly closed against the notion of another day of unvarying routine in her teaching job, she groped for the alarm and hit the sleep button. Dragging a fluffy feather pillow over her head, she sank back into the dream.

The directness of the warrior's gaze was laden with the focused intent she had waited years to experience, as if he thought she was beautiful, or more—as if he was actually fascinated by her.

Strong fingers cupped her chin. Sarah dragged her gaze from the fascinating scar that sliced a jagged line across one taut cheekbone and clamped down on the automatic caution that gripped her, the disbelief that after years of being let down by men an outrageously attractive man could truly want her. The searing heat blasting off his bronzed torso, the rapid thud of his heart beneath her palms, didn't feel like a lie.

In point of fact, the warrior wasn't saying a lot, but Sarah was okay with that. After years of carefully studying body language, because she had learned she could not always trust what was said, she had learned to place a measure of trust in the vocabulary of the senses.

Throwing her normal no-nonsense practicality to the winds she lifted up on her toes, buried her fingers in the thick night-dark silk of his hair, and pressed herself firmly against the muscular warmth of his body. His mouth closed over hers and emotion, almost painful in its intensity, shuddered through her.

Dimly, she acknowledged that this was it. The long years of waiting were over. She would find out what it felt like to be truly wanted, to finally make love—

The shrill of the alarm once more shoved Sarah out of the dream, although the warrior's voice seemed to hang in the air, as declarative as his dark gaze.

"You are mine to hold."

An electrifying quiver ran the length of her spine, lifting all the fine hairs at her nape as she silenced the alarm. Blinking at the grayness of the morning, she registered the comforting ticking of the oil heater she'd dragged beside the bed to keep out the winter chill. She sucked in a breath in an effort to release the tension that banded her chest and the sharp, hot ache at the back of her throat. As if she really had been the focus of a powerful male's desire…

A soft thud drew her gaze to the leather-bound cover of the family journal she had been reading before she'd gone to sleep. It had slipped off the edge of her bed and fallen to the floor. The journal, which had been partially transcribed from Old French by an erudite cousin, relegated the dream to its true context—fantasy.

None of it had been real. At least no more real to Sarah than the dramatic contents of the personal diary of Camille de Vallois. A spinster and academic who had lived more than eight hundred years ago, Camille had been sold into marriage by her family. However, when her ship had foundered on the rocks of Zahir, she had made herself over as an adventurous femme fatale and gone after the man she discovered she wanted, a sheikh who had also been a battle-hardened Templar Knight. Camille had risked all for love, admittedly with the help of an enormous dowry, and she had succeeded.

Frowning, Sarah reviewed the vivid dream and reluctantly let the last remnants of the powerful emotions that had held her in thrall flicker and die. Camille's story had clearly formed the basis of the dream. Plus, the previous day, caught up in the romance she'd been reading in the journal, she had called at the Zahiri consulate and picked up a pamphlet about a scheduled exhibition of Zahiri artifacts and a lecture on their history and culture. While exiting the building in the middle of a rain shower, head down because she had forgotten her umbrella, she had run into a man so gorgeous that for long seconds her brain had refused to function.

By the time she had recovered the power of speech, he had picked up the pamphlets she'd dropped, handed them to her with a flashing grin and strode into the consulate. The hero of her dream, scar and all, had looked suspiciously like that man.

Her cheeks warmed at the memory of some of the graphic elements of the dream, the searing embrace and a toe-curling kiss that had practically melted her on the spot. It had definitely been the stuff of fantasies and nothing to do with her normal life as a staid history teacher.

In her ancestor's case, the dream had come true, but Sarah could never allow herself to forget that Camille's romance had been smoothed along by a great deal of cold hard cash. Love story or not, Sarah was willing to bet that Sheikh Kadin had known on which side his bread had been buttered.

Pushing upright in the cozy nest of her bed, she reached down and retrieved the journal, which included photocopied sheets of the original, written in Old French, plus the sections of the journal her cousin had so far transcribed.

A heavy gust hit the side of her cottage, rattling the windows and making the old kauri timbers groan. Pushing free of the heavy press of quilt and coverlet, Sarah inched her feet into fluffy slippers, belted a heavy robe around her waist and padded to the window to stare out at the stormy day.

The steep street she lived on was shrouded in gray. The sodium lamps still cast a murky glow on neatly trimmed hedges, white picket fences and the occasional wild tangle of an old rose. The houses, huddled together, cheek-by-jowl—some so close a person could barely walk between them—were neither graceful and old nor conveniently modern. Inhabited by solo homeowners like herself or young families, they were something much more useful: affordable.

Letting the drapes fall back into place, she walked to the kitchen to make herself a cup of tea before she showered and got ready for work. Her tiny kitchen, with its appliances fitted neatly to take up minimal space, was about as far away from the exotic isle of Zahir as she could get.

As she sipped hot tea, her reflection in the multipaned window over the counter bounced back at her and she found herself critically examining her appearance. With her hair bundled into a knot, her face bare of makeup, the thick robe making her look ten pounds heavier than she was, she looked washed-out, tired and…boring.

Frowning, chest tight at the thought that at twenty-eight she was no longer in the first flush of youth, she peered more closely at her reflection. Her eyes were blue; her skin was pale; her hair, when it was loose, was heavy, straight and dark. It was the faded robe that drained the color from her skin, and the tight way her hair was scraped back from her face that was so unflattering. She wasn't old.

Although she would be twenty-nine next month. In just over a year she would be thirty.

The pressurized feeling in her chest increased. She sucked in a breath, trying to ease the tension, but the thought of turning thirty made her heart hammer. She was abruptly aware of time passing, leaving her behind, of her failure to find someone special to love and who would love her back in return.

On the heels of those thoughts an old fear loomed out of the shadows. That her disastrous track record with men wasn't about bad luck or bad judgment, it was about *her*; she was the problem. Perhaps some aspect of her personality, maybe her academic bent and blunt manner, or more probably her old-fashioned insistence on being truly loved for herself before sex entered the equation, was the reason she would never be cherished by any man.

Grimly, she considered her two engagements, which had both fallen through. Her first fiancé, Roger, had gotten annoyed when she hadn't felt ready to sleep with him the week of their engagement, and so had called it off. Not a problem.

The second time she had chosen better, or so she had thought. Unfortunately, after months of dating a fellow teacher, Mark, who had seemed quite happy with her views on celibacy before marriage, she had discovered, on the morning of their wedding, that he had fallen in love with somebody else. A blonde and pretty somebody else with whom he had been sleeping for the past four months.

Normally, she didn't wallow in the painful details of those relationship mistakes. Burying her head in the sand and anaesthetizing herself with work had been a much more attractive option.

But reading the journal that had recently arrived from her cousin and dreaming that deeply sensual dream had changed her in some imperceptible way. Maybe what she was feeling was all tied up with the realization that her biological clock was ticking. Whatever the cause, she felt different this morning, tinglingly alive and acutely vulnerable, as if she were standing on the edge of a precipice.

And she knew what that precipice was: she was finally ready to try again. Her pulse sped up at the knowledge that after years of relationship limbo she wanted to love and be loved and this time, marriage or not, she wanted the passionate, heart-stopping sex. Adrenaline zinged through her veins at the thought of tossing her old relationship rulebook away. She was tired of waiting, of missing out. She wanted to take the risk, to find a man she could not just desire, but with whom she could fall recklessly, wildly in love.

A man like the dangerously handsome guy she had run into the day before.

Absently, she sipped her cooling tea. In the past, she had been black-and-white in her thinking. She had wanted all or nothing. She didn't understand how she had become that way. Maybe her deep need for emotional certainty had been fueled by the fact that her father had only ever been a sometime presence in her life. Or maybe it was because she was naturally passionate in her thinking. For most of her adult life "all or nothing" had been the catchphrase that had summed up her approach.

Whatever the cause, it had devastated her last two serious relationships and was already sounding the death knell for the lukewarm friendship she shared with an importer of antiquities and fellow history buff that was the closest thing to a romance on her dating horizon.

Her jaw firmed. If she was going to find someone to love, someone she could marry and have babies with, it was clear she would have to be more flexible than she had been in the past. She would have to change. She would have to bite the bullet and experiment with a casual affair.

And the clock was ticking.

Replacing the mug on the counter, she dragged her hair free of the elastic tie that held it in place. Feeling tense and a little shaky, she raked her fingers through the warm, heavy strands, trying to work some volume into her satin-smooth hair. With her hair tumbling loose to her waist, she looked younger and sexier. Relief made her feel ridiculously light-headed.

She dragged off the robe and let it drop to the floor. The nightie she was wearing didn't help matters. Made of cotton flannel in an unflattering shade of pale pink, it reminded her of the nightwear her grandmother used to wear. Great for cold nights, drinking hot chocolate and reading a book, but ultimately as sexy as a tent.

The only positive was that beneath the material she had a good figure. Her breasts were shapely, her waist narrow, her legs long and toned from all the walking she did.

Shivering at the chill, she dragged on the robe and returned to her bedroom. Flicking on a light, she flung her closet wide and began examining hangers of clothes she had bought for the honeymoon that hadn't happened.

Annoyed at how affected she still was by the canceled wedding and Mark's easy dismissal of her in favor of a woman who had been dishonest enough to sleep with an engaged man, she hauled out slinky clothes and dropped them on the bed. She needed to exorcise the past by either wearing the clothes as if they had not been bought for a special, life-changing occasion, or else give them away to a charity shop.

Sarah arrayed the collection of jewel-bright garments across her bed. With a start, she realized that almost four years had passed since Mark had jilted her.

Four years.

Jaw set at the time that had passed, she selected a red dress. The color was sensual and rich, the silk jersey warm to the touch. With three-quarter-length sleeves and a V-neck, the design was classic. Bought for the romantic honeymoon she had paid for in Paris then cancelled, it was also sexy and sophisticated.

Before she could change her mind, she stripped out of the robe and nightgown and pulled on the dress. The jersey settled against her skin, making her shiver. Strolling to her dressing table she examined the effect of the dress, which, worn without a bra and with her hair rumpled and loose, was startlingly sensual. The deep, rich color made her skin look creamy instead of pale, and turned her dark hair a rich shade of sable. She stared at the bold, definitely female image, feeling oddly electrified, like a sleeper waking up.

The woman in the mirror in no way looked boring or tired. She looked young and vibrant. *Available.*

Years had passed since Mark had ditched her practically at the altar. Years that she had wasted, and which had been her prime window in terms of finding a suitable mate. If she had been focused by now she would have met and married her Mr. Right, gotten pregnant and had at least one baby.

She had put her lack of success with relationships down to her heavy work schedule. According to her mother, Hannah, the real reason Sarah hadn't found a relationship was fear. Two engagements had fallen through and in her usual stubborn way Sarah had refused to go out on a limb a third time.

Hannah's solution had been to produce a constant supply of eligible men from among her interior-decorating business contacts, which was how Sarah had met Graham Southwell. Although, after several platonic dates, she had received the overwhelming impression that Graham was more interested in her connection to the missing de Vallois dowry than in an actual relationship.

As it happened she was meeting Graham that evening. After the revelation of the dream, she could not view tonight as just another dead-end date with a man who did not really see her. Tonight was an opportunity to effect the change that was already zinging through her.

She could not afford to wait any longer for her true love to find her; experience had taught her that might never happen. Like her ancestor Camille, she had to be bold. She had to formulate a plan.

By the time she was ready to leave for work she had settled on a strategy that was time-honored and uncannily close to Camille's plan to win her sheikh.

Sarah would dress to kill, and when she found the man of her dreams, she would seduce him.

Two

Sarah found a space in the parking lot next door to the historic old building that housed the Zahiri consulate. Situated just over the road from the waterfront, the entire block was dotted with grand Victorian and Edwardian buildings and a series of old warehouses that had been turned into bars and restaurants.

As she stepped out of the car, cold wind gusted in off the sea and spits of rain landed on her skin. Her hair, which she'd spent a good hour coaxing into trailing curls with a hot curling iron, swirled around her face. Turning up the collar of her coat and shivering a little, because the red silk jersey dress was not made for a cold Wellington night, she locked the car and started toward the consulate.

Feeling nervous and self-conscious about all the changes she'd made, especially her new makeup and a pair of black boots with heels a couple of inches higher than she normally wore, she hurried past a group of young men hanging around the covered area outside a bar.

The wind gusted again, making her coat flap open and lifting the flimsy skirt of her dress, revealing more leg than she was accustomed to showing. Her phone chimed as she clutched the lapels of her coat and dragged her hemline down. Ignoring a barrage of crude remarks and a piercing wolf whistle, she retrieved the phone and answered the call.

Graham had arrived early and was already inside on the off chance that he might actually get to meet the elusive Sheikh of Zahir, who was rumored to be in town. Since it was cold and on the verge of raining, he had decided not to hang around outside waiting for her as they had arranged.

Irritated but unsurprised by Graham's lack of consideration, Sarah walked up the steps to the consulate and strolled into the foyer, which was well lit and warm.

She was greeted by a burly man with a shaved head who was dressed in a beautifully cut suit. He checked her invitation and noted her name on a register. When he handed the invitation back, his gaze was piercing. In New Zealand it was unusual to be scrutinized so thoroughly. She was almost certain he wasn't just a consulate official. With the sheikh in residence it was more likely that the man was one of the sheikh's bodyguards. Though a Christian nation, Zahir, a Mediterranean island, was caught between the Middle East and Europe. The elderly sheikh had been kidnapped some years ago and so now was rumored to always travel with an armed escort.

She hung her coat on the rack provided. Ignoring an

attack of nerves caused by losing the cozy, protective outer layer that had mostly hidden the red dress, she walked through an elegant hallway and into a crowded reception room. It was a cocktail party and promotional evening aimed at selling Zahir, with its colorful history as a Templar outpost, as a tourist destination. Sarah had expected little black dresses and the rich exotic colors of the East to abound, but crisp business suits and black and gray dresses toned down by jackets created a subdued monochrome against which she stood out like an overbright bird of paradise.

Sarah's stomach sank. When she had read the pamphlet she hadn't seen the evening as focused on business, but if she didn't miss her guess, most of the guests were business types, probably tour operators and travel agents and no doubt a smattering of government officials.

Deciding to brazen it out, she moved to a display concerning the mysterious disappearance of the remains of Camille's dowry. Hidden by a member of the sheikh's family at the time of the evacuation during the Second World War, the location of the hiding place had been lost when the family member died in a bombing raid.

A short, balding man in a gray suit also stopped by the display, but seemed more mesmerized by the faint shadowy hollow of her cleavage. Annoyed by his rudeness, she sent him the kind of quelling glance that would have had her pupils scrambling to apply themselves to their study. As he scuttled away, she thought longingly about retrieving her coat and covering up the alluring brightness of the dress, but she refused to cut and run because she was attracting male attention. After all, that had been the whole point.

A waiter offered her a glass of wine. A little desperately, she took a glass and sipped slowly as she moved to a display of Templar weaponry. Instantly riveted by a history she found even more fascinating after immersing herself in Camille's journal, Sarah read the notes about the Templar band under the command of Sheikh Kadin. Setting her glass down on a nearby table, she stepped closer, irresistibly drawn to the largest weapon—a grim, pitted sword that had clearly seen hard use. A small label indicated the sword had belonged to the sheikh. In that moment she remembered a passage of the journal, which had outlined Camille's first meeting with Kadin.

"An overlarge warrior with a black, soaked mane, dark eyes narrowed against the wind, a workmanlike blade gripped in his battle-scarred hand."

The fascination that had gripped Sarah as she'd read Camille's account came back full force. A small sign warned against touching the displays, but the powerful compulsion to immerse herself in sensation, to touch the sword, far outweighed the officious red wording.

Breath held, her fingertips brushed the gleaming grip where the chasing etched into the bronze was worn smooth by use. The chill of the metal struck through her skin. A split second later, the bracket holding the sword came loose and the heavy weapon toppled, hitting the carpeted floor with a thud.

Mortified, Sarah reached for the sword, hoping to prop it against the display before anyone noticed. Before she could grab it, a large tanned hand closed around the bronze grip. With fluid grace, a tall, broad-shouldered man straightened, the blade in his hand, and her heart slammed once, hard, as her dream world and the present fused.

The warrior.

That seemed the only adequate description. The man was tall enough that her gaze was firmly centered on his jaw. Heart pounding, she tilted her head and stared directly into the amber gleam of eyes that, for a split second, she fully expected to be as passionately focused on her as those of the warrior who had haunted her dream.

Her breath caught in the back of her throat as she recognized the man she had run into the previous day. The curious tension that had invested the dream drew every muscle taut as she took in black hair cut crisp and short, the blade-straight nose and the intriguing scar on his cheekbone. The planes and angles of his face were mouthwateringly clean-cut, although any sense of perfection was lost in the grim line of his jaw and the lash of the scar.

His brows drew together as if he recognized her and was trying to remember from exactly where. A split second later his gaze shuttered and she had to wonder if she'd imagined that moment of intense interest.

Or, on a more practical note, if he was married. As a single woman with years of dating experience, it would not be the first time she had been checked out by a man who then suddenly recalled that he was committed elsewhere.

His gaze dropped to her hands. "Are you all right? For a moment, I thought you might have cut yourself."

The low, rough timbre of his voice, the cosmopolitan accent, was definitely European, but with a slow cadence that indicated he had spent time in the States. The accent, along with the short cut of his hair and the suit, added to the impression that had been forming, the only one that made sense—he was either an aide to the sheikh or a bodyguard. Given his muscular build, and the fact that he had arrived within seconds of her touching the sword, she would go with the security option.

She dredged up a smile and displayed her palms to show she wasn't injured. "I'm fine, just a little startled the sword wasn't secured. Especially since it belonged to Sheikh Kadin."

For another heart-pounding moment his gaze seemed riveted on her mouth. "You're right, the Wolf of Zahir would not have been so careless. I'll have a word with the staff who set up the display."

She dragged her gaze from the line of his jaw. "Oh no, really…it was completely my fault. I shouldn't have touched the sword." Shouldn't have allowed herself to be distracted by her ancestor's passionate love story when she needed to apply herself to establishing her own.

With an easy movement, he propped the weapon against the display board. As he did so an angled spotlight above gleamed over his damaged cheekbone, and cast a shadow over the inky curve of his lashes. Suddenly the dream warrior, as riveting as he had been, seemed too cosmetically perfect and lacking in personality. From memory, he had also been oddly compliant. In the way of dreams, he had done exactly what she had wanted, in contrast to this man who looked as seasoned and uncompromising as the Templar Knight who had originally wielded the sword.

To her surprise, instead of moving on, he held out his hand and introduced himself as Gabriel, Gabe for short.

Surprised at the informality and that he seemed to want to keep the conversation going, Sarah briefly gripped his hand as she supplied her name. Tingling warmth shot through her at the rough heat of his palm. "I'm a history teacher."

She caught the flash of surprise in his expression and her mood dropped like a stone. He was tall, gorgeous, *hot*—as different from Graham as a dark lion from a tabby cat. Incredibly, he also seemed to be interested in her, and she had just ruined the outward impression of sexy sophistication she'd spent hours creating. If she'd had her wits about her she would have relegated her teaching occupation to some dusty dark hole and claimed an interest in travelling to exotic places.

"I'm guessing since you're at the exhibition that it's Templar history?"

Her mood dropped even further when she realized she now had to tell him how boring and prosaic her subjects were. "I specialize in the industrial revolution and the First and Second World Wars." She let out a resigned breath, convinced they had nothing in common. "What about you?"

"Five years at Harvard. It was useful."

Hope flared anew. "Harvard. That sounds like law, or business."

"Business, I'm afraid."

He sounded almost as apologetic as she had been. Her heart beat faster. Not a bodyguard then, despite the muscle. Perhaps he was one of the sheikh's financial advisors. She was riveted by the thought that maybe all wasn't lost.

Just as she was searching for some small talk, two Arabic men in suits joined them. The taller one, carrying a screwdriver, immediately set about refixing the bracket that had held the sword. The other suit, a plump man with a tag that proclaimed he was Tarik ben Abdel, the consulate administration manager, sent her a disapproving glance. He then button-holed Gabe and launched into a tirade in a liquid tongue she recognized as Zahiri.

Gabe cut him off with a flat, soft phrase, although Sarah was distracted from the exchange. Graham had appeared just yards away, head swiveling as if he had finally remembered to search for her. His gaze passed over her then shot back to linger on the hint of cleavage at the V of her dress. When he fished in his pocket for his cell phone and turned away, an irritated look on his face, she realized that, aside from checking out her chest, he had failed to recognize her.

Tarik, with a last disapproving glance at her, marched away, the second suit trailing behind. She noticed that the sword was once again affixed to the display.

Sarah was suddenly blazingly aware that the tall dark man hadn't left as she had expected him to and that he was studying her with an enigmatic expression, as if he'd logged the exchange with Graham.

Still mortified at the fuss she'd created, she rushed to apologize. "I read the sign. I know I shouldn't have touched the sword, that artifacts can be vulnerable to skin oils and salts—"

"Tarik wasn't worried that the sword might be damaged. It survived the Third Crusade, so a fall onto soft carpet is hardly likely to cause harm. He was more concerned about the tradition that goes with the sword."

Understanding dawned. If there had been a preeminent symbol of manhood in the Middle Ages, it had been the sword, and this had been a Templar sword. "Of course, the Templar vow of chastity."

Amusement gleamed in his gaze. "And a superstition that a woman's touch would somehow disable a warrior's potency in battle."

A curious warmth hummed through her as she realized that, as nerve-racking as the exchange had started out, she was actually enjoying talking to the most dangerously attractive man she had ever met. "Sounds more like a convenient way of shifting blame for a lackluster performance on the battlefield."

"Possibly." Gabe's mouth kicked up at one corner, softening the line of his jaw and revealing the slightest hint of an indentation. "But, back then, on Zahir, if a woman handled a man's sword, it was also viewed as a declaration of intent."

Breath held, Sarah found herself waiting for the dimple to be more fully realized. "What if she was simply curious?"

His gaze locked with hers and a tension far more acute than any she had experienced in her dream flared to life. "Then the warrior might demand a forfeit. Although most of the Templars that landed on Zahir eventually gave up their vows."

"Including the sheikh, who married."

The cooling of his expression as she mentioned marriage was like a dash of cold water. For the second time she wondered if he was married. Disappointment cascaded through her at the thought. A glance at his left hand confirmed there was no ring, although that meant nothing. He could be married, with children, and never wear a ring.

A faint buzz emanated from his jacket pocket. With a frown that sent a dart of pleasure through her, because it conveyed that he didn't want to be interrupted, he excused himself and half turned away to take the call.

Unsettled and on edge because she was clearly developing an unhealthy fascination for a complete stranger,

Sarah remembered her glass of wine. As she took a steadying sip, her cell phone chimed. Setting the glass back down, she rummaged in her handbag and found the phone and another text from Graham. Although there was nothing romantic or even polite about the words. Where are you?

Annoyed at his blunt irritation, the cavalier way he hadn't bothered to meet her as they had arranged, Sarah punched the delete key. She might be a victim of the love game, but she would not be a doormat. Temper on a slow simmer, she shoved the phone back in her handbag.

Gabe terminated his call. "Are you with someone? I noticed you came in alone."

Suddenly the tension was thick enough to cut, although she couldn't invest the knowledge that he had noticed her entrance with too much importance. She was the only person dressed in red in a sea of black and gray; of course he had noticed her. "Uh, I was supposed to meet someone..."

"A man."

She crushed the urge to say she wasn't meeting another man; that would have been a lie. "Yes."

He nodded, his expression remote, but she was left with the unmistakable impression that if she had said she was alone the evening might have taken a more exciting turn than she could ever expect with Graham.

His expression suddenly neutral, Gabe checked his watch. "If you'll excuse me. I have a call to make."

Sarah squashed a plunging sense of disappointment. As he walked away, she forced herself to look around for Graham.

She spotted him across the room involved in an animated discussion with a man wearing a business suit and a kaffiyeh, the traditional Arabic headdress. She studied the Arab man, who she assumed must be the sheikh. She had read a lot about Zahir, but most of it had been history, since Zahir was a small, peaceful country that didn't normally make the news. She knew that the sheikh was on the elderly side, and that he had married a New Zealander, a woman who had originally come from Wellington, which explained Zahir's close ties with her country.

She strolled closer just as the man with the kaffiyeh moved away and finally managed to make eye contact with Graham.

The blankness of his expression changed to incredulity. *"You."*

Not for the first time Sarah looked at Graham and wondered how such a pleasantly handsome man could inspire little more in her than annoyance. "That's right, your date."

He shook his head as if he couldn't quite believe what he was seeing. "If you'd told me you were going to change your appearance—"

Her jaw locked at Graham's unflattering response, as if the act of putting on a dress, a little extra makeup and messing with her hair was some kind of disguise. "This *is* how I look."

He stared at her mouth, making her wonder if she'd been a little too heavy on the berry lip gloss. "Not usually. If you had, we might have hit it off a little better."

Sarah realized there was one very good reason she had never been able to really like Graham. Not only was he self-centered with a roving eye, he had a nasty streak. She had been looking for a prince and, as usual, had ended up dating a frog. "How about I make it easy for us both. From now on don't call and don't come around to my mother's house for dinner. A clean break would suit me."

His expression took on a shifty cast. "What about the journal? You said I could look at it."

"That was all you really wanted, wasn't it?"

"I wouldn't say that, exactly."

No, because what he really wanted was to find the lost dowry and cash in on it. Sarah drew a deep breath and let it out slowly. The first two men in her life had dumped her for other women; that she could accept. Graham preferring *a book* and the possibility of cold hard cash over her was the proverbial last straw. "Forget the journal. It's a private, family document. Hell would freeze solid before I'd give it to you."

Feeling angry and hurt, hating the fact that she had lost her temper but relieved she had finally finished with Graham, Sarah spun on her heel then froze as she spotted Gabe talking with an elderly lady. He was close enough that he had probably heard some of her conversation with Graham. His gaze locked with hers, sharp and uncomplicatedly male, and for a moment the room full of people ceased to exist. Then a waiter strolled past with a tray filled with glasses, breaking the spell.

Her stomach clenched on a sharp jab of feminine intuition, that despite knowing she had a date, after he had made his call, Gabe had come looking for her. When he'd seen her talking with Graham, he'd stopped far enough away to allow her privacy—*to allow her a choice*—but close enough to keep an eye on her.

Graham didn't find her attractive, but she was suddenly acutely aware that Gabe did. Talking to him at the sword display had been easy; there had been nothing at stake. Instinctively, she knew a second conversation meant a whole lot more. It meant she would have to make a decision. Suddenly the whole concept of abandoning her rule about no sex before commitment seemed full of holes when what she really wanted was love, not sex.

Feeling utterly out of her depth, her chest tight, she dragged her gaze away and made a beeline for the ladies' room and the chance to regroup.

Pushing the door open, she stepped into a pretty tiled bathroom. Her reflection bounced back at her, tousled hair and smoky eyes, sleek dress and black boots. Her cheeks flushed as she registered what Gabe was seeing. Graham was right. *She* barely recognized herself. The woman who stared back at her looked exotic and assured. Experienced.

She wondered if all Gabe saw was the outer package and the possibility of a night of no-strings passion. What if, like Graham, Gabe wouldn't be attracted to who she really was?

She found her lipstick and reapplied it, her fingers shaking very slightly. The knowledge that Gabe was attracted to her, that the improvement she had made to her appearance had worked, was unsettling. She hadn't expected such an instant response.

She should be buoyed by her success. Instead, she felt on edge and, for want of a better word, vulnerable. Maybe it was because in her mind Gabe had become linked with the dream that had been the catalyst for all of this change. She knew almost nothing about him, but in the moment he had picked up the sword, he had made an indelible impression; he had symbolized what she wanted.

She stopped dead as the final piece of the puzzle of

her dysfunction with men dropped neatly into place. She drew a deep breath. She felt like quietly banging her head against the nearest wall, but that would not be a good idea with all the security personnel roaming around. The reason she had not been intimate with anyone, even her fiancés, was because, hidden beneath the logic and practicality and years of academia, she was an idealist. Worse, she was a *romantic*.

Maybe all the years of burying her head in history books had changed her in some fundamental way because it was now blindingly clear why an ordinary, everyday kind of guy with a nine-to-five job had never been quite enough. Somehow, despite common sense, in her heart of hearts, she had wanted the kind of seasoned, bedrock strength and stirring romanticism that it was difficult to find in the twenty-first century.

She had wanted a knight.

When she stepped back into the reception room, despite giving herself a good talking-to about the dangers of projecting crazy romantic fantasies onto a man she barely knew, she found herself instantly looking for Gabe. When she couldn't find him, disappointment gripped her. In an adjacent room the lecture on Zahir was beginning. She strolled inside and saw him at the back, in conversation with a well-known government official.

The jolt in her stomach, the relief and the tingling heat that flooded her, should have been warning enough. In the space of an hour she had somehow fallen into a heady infatuation with a virtual stranger, but after years of emotional limbo the blood racing through her veins, the crazy cocktail of emotions, was addictive. Just as she debated what to do—brazenly approach Gabe or wimp out completely and ignore the intense emotions—an elegant young woman walked up to Gabe and flung her arms around him.

Numb with disappointment, Sarah turned on her heel, walked into the foyer and began searching for her coat. She was fiercely glad she hadn't approached Gabe, because he appeared to have a girlfriend, or, more probably, a wife.

Frowning, she flipped through the rack of coats again and pulled out a coat which looked like hers, but which wasn't. Someone had obviously left in a hurry and taken her coat by mistake. As much as she needed a coat, she drew the line at helping herself to one she knew wasn't hers. Besides, she still had her small telescopic umbrella, which fit in her handbag. In the wind, it probably wouldn't last long, but it was better than nothing.

Outside, lightning flickered and, in the distance, thunder crashed. As Murphy's Law would have it, the rain, which had been light earlier was now tropical.

Extracting the umbrella, Sarah paused by the antique double doors of the entrance, reluctant to step out into such a heavy downpour. A flicker of movement turned her head. She saw Gabe speaking to the tall, bald man who had checked her invitation.

Aware that in just a few seconds he could turn and see her standing in the foyer, watching him, she pushed open the doors and stepped outside.

As she descended the steps the wind, damp with rain and bitingly cold, sent a raw shiver through her. She came to a halt at the edge of the sheltered area. Flipping up her umbrella, she stepped into the wet and wild night.

The bottom half of her dress was almost instantly soaked. Water seeped into the soles of her boots as she threaded through cars that gleamed beneath streetlights.

The parking lot seemed farther away than when she had arrived. In the murky darkness, the garish lights from the nightclub were overbright, although the steady thud of music was now muted by the sound of the rain.

Dragging soaked hair from her eyes and glad she was wearing waterproof mascara, she fumbled in her bag, searching for keys. She depressed the key lock, suddenly wishing she hadn't parked quite so close to the night-club. The lights of her car flashed and she headed for the welcome beacon of her small hatchback. As she opened the door, she became aware of a cluster of dark shadows congregated beneath the overhang of the warehouse-size building that housed the nightclub. Slamming the door closed, she immediately locked it, just in case the youths tried something silly.

She inserted her key into the ignition. The starter motor made its familiar high-pitched whine, but the motor itself refused to fire. Feeling a little desperate, she tried again, then a third time. When the starter took on a deeper, slower sound, as if the battery was becoming drained, she immediately stopped. She was no mechanic but, at a guess, the wind had driven rain under the hood and the electronics had gotten wet. The car wouldn't start until she managed to dry the motor. If she kept using the starter she would also end up with a flat battery.

She considered ringing her mother then immediately dismissed the thought. Hannah was overseas on a buying trip for her interior-decorating business. Graham was still inside. As much as she didn't want to ask him, he would have to help her. Groaning, she tried texting. When minutes passed with no reply, she bit the bullet and rang him. The call went through to voice mail.

Deciding that it would be a whole lot simpler to just walk back into the consulate to get help, Sarah grabbed her bag and stepped out into the rain, which had thankfully eased to a fine drizzle. A tap on her shoulder made her start.

"Having trouble, darlin'?"

She stiffened at the shock of being touched by a stranger and stepped away from the powerful whiff of alcohol fumes. "Nothing I can't handle, thanks."

He grinned hazily. "I'd sure like to help you."

There was a stifled laugh somewhere behind him. With a jolt Sarah realized they had been joined by two more men, both of them like the first, darkly dressed, wearing leather and decorated with tattoos and multiple piercings.

The taller of the two grinned. "Don't keep her to yourself, Ty. We'd *all* like to help the lady."

Jaw set, Sarah debated trying to get back into the car and locking the doors, but decided against that. If she did, they could prevent her from closing the door and before she knew where she was, they would be inside the car with her and she would be in a worse position.

Rape. The horrifying thought shuddered through her. She was a virgin. She had saved herself for love and marriage. The first time she was with a man could not be because she was being forced.

Footsteps sounded across the parking lot. They were no longer alone. Thinking quickly, Sarah's fingers tightened on her umbrella. It wasn't much of a weapon, but she would use it if she had to. "I don't need help. My boyfriend's here. He'll fix the car."

"What boyfriend?" The taller man grabbed her arm as she edged away.

Jaw gritted, Sara brought the umbrella's wooden handle crashing down on the man's fingers.

"This one," a dark voice murmured, as Gabe stepped around a chunky utility vehicle into the light.

Three

Rubbing bruised knuckles, the tall guy, who now didn't seem large at all compared to Gabe, stumbled backward. "Hey, sorry, man," he mumbled. "Didn't know she was taken."

Gabe glided closer. When he stretched out his hand, it seemed the most natural thing in the world to put her fingers in his. "Even if she wasn't 'taken' you shouldn't have gone near her. But, as you said, she is taken, so don't bother her again."

Tall Guy took another step backward. The other two had already climbed into a car decorated with dents. He held one hand up in a placating gesture as he fumbled open the rear passenger door. "Yeah, man. She's yours. Totally. We won't bother her again."

He clambered into the car, which jolted into motion with a squeal of tires.

Gabe released his grip on her hand. "Are you okay?"

Sarah replaced her car keys in her bag. She was cold and her fingers were shaking, but she barely noticed because she was so focused on the fact that Gabe had come after her. She didn't know how he had located her in the dark, or why he had walked out into the rain to find her, just that he had. "I am now, thank you."

"Problem with your car?"

She blinked at the shift of topic. His gaze was still fixed on the taillights of the retreating car. The steely remoteness of his expression sent a chill down her spine. He looked more than capable of backing his flatly delivered challenge with physical force.

A fierce, oddly primitive sense of satisfaction curled through her. Gabe had not only come to her aid, but he had been prepared to physically fight for her.

When he repeated the question about the car, she realized he was deliberately distracting her from the nastiness of the encounter. Suppressing a shiver, she replaced her umbrella in her bag. "I think the electronics got wet."

Gabe, who had walked around to the front of her car, took a sleek phone out of his pocket and stabbed a short dial. "Is there still a charge in the battery?"

"I stopped before it went flat."

"Good." Gabe spoke quietly into his phone in the same liquid Zahiri she had heard him use before then slipped the cell back in his jacket pocket. "Xavier will have a look at the car. He's not a mechanic, but he spends a lot of his spare time tinkering with cars."

She hooked the strap of her bag more securely over her shoulder. It was an odd moment to register that the wind had dropped, leaving an eerie calm after the storm. With mist rising off the wet concrete, wreathing the cars and forming a halo around the street lamps, the night now seemed peaceful.

With a reflexive shiver she rubbed at her chilled arms and tried not to let her teeth chatter. Now that she was no longer buzzing with adrenaline the cold seemed to be seeping into her bones. "I suppose Xavier is one of the sheikh's bodyguards." The remark was shamelessly probing but she didn't care. She suddenly needed to know more about Gabe, what he did for a living, how long he would be in Wellington, when or *if* he was coming back—

His gaze glittered over her, making her aware of the soaked red dress clinging to her skin, her hair trailing wetly around her cheeks. "Only when the sheikh leaves Zahir."

The answer was confusing, as if the sheikh was still in Zahir when Sarah knew him to be here, in Wellington. But with Gabe walking toward her, dark trousers clinging low on narrow hips, his jacket damply molded to broad shoulders, white shirt plastered to his chest so that the bronze of his skin glowed through, it was hard to concentrate on unraveling subtleties.

He frowned. "You're cold. Have you got a coat in the car?"

"No c-coat. Someone at the consulate took mine by mistake."

A moment later, his jacket dropped around her shoulders, swamping her with warmth and filling her nostrils with the scent of clean male and an enticing hint of sandalwood. An electrifying thrill shot through her, reminding her of the sharp, visceral jolt she had felt when Gabe had said she was his.

He was briefly close enough that she felt the heat radiating off his body, and she had to resist the urge to sway a few inches closer to that delicious warmth. Her fingers closed on the fine weave of the jacket lapels, hugging the fabric closer. Despite everything, all of the warnings she was giving herself, she couldn't help loving that she was wearing his jacket, which was so large the sleeves dropped almost to her knees. After the nasty scenes with Graham and the leather-clad thugs, Gabe's chivalry—his consideration, as if she truly mattered to him—was a soothing balm.

Gabe checked his watch. "Xavier's on his way. If you'll give me your car keys, he'll take a look. In the meantime I suggest you come with me back to the consulate. There's a guest suite there, so you can dry off while you wait."

A vivid flash of the young woman flinging her arms around him made Sarah stiffen. "Won't your...girlfriend mind?'

His expression registered his surprise at the question. "I don't have a girlfriend. If you're referring to the young woman who came into the lecture, she was a cousin I haven't seen in years. She dropped in because she knew I was leaving in the morning."

The relief that the pretty girl wasn't a love interest was almost instantly replaced by the depressing confirmation that Gabe was leaving in a matter of hours.

His hand briefly cupped her elbow as he helped her step up onto the higher level of the consulate parking lot. "Is she the reason you left the lecture?"

Her mouth went dry at the bluntness of the question but after everything that had happened, somehow it didn't seem as intrusive as it should have been. It would have been easy to say she'd had a fight with Graham and was upset, but the truth was, whatever she had felt for Graham had been utterly overshadowed by her response to Gabe.

He was leaving in just a few hours.

Lifting her chin, she met his gaze. There was no point trying to hide what was already clear to him. She had been hurt and disappointed when she had thought he was committed to another woman. "Yes."

There was a moment of vibrating silence, filled by the muted sound of their footfalls on wet pavement, the distant wash of the sea and the slow drip of water splashing off a gutter. Sarah's stomach tightened as Gabe directed her to a door at the side of the consulate building and held it for her. Somehow, in the space of a little over an hour they had achieved a level of intimacy that made her stomach tighten and her pulse pound. But her time alone with him was almost up. Soon they would be joined by other people and a conversation that had become unexpectedly important would be over.

As if to underscore her thoughts, the plump administrative official, Tarik, strode down the corridor toward them, disapproval pulling his brows into a dark line. She drew a breath, but it was already too late to ask Gabe the question that was burning inside her.

He knew she was strongly attracted to him and that was why she had left the consulate so quickly. But was attraction the reason he had come looking for her?

Gabe left Sarah freshening up in the guest room that opened onto his study and strode along the hall to his suite. The moment he had seen the thug lay hands on her replayed through his mind, making him tense. When he had registered the danger, the half-formed desires and intentions that had driven him out into the stormy night had coalesced into one burning reality.

He wanted Sarah Duval.

He hadn't liked the fact that she'd had a date. He had liked it even less that the drunk thought he could simply reach out and touch her. Crazily, because Gabe barely knew her and had no interest in emotional attachments, his attraction to Sarah had coalesced into the kind of knee-jerk possessiveness he could not afford on the eve of his engagement. But, as hard as he tried to shake it, he couldn't—for one simple reason. In his mind he had already claimed her.

As he unlocked the door, Xavier stepped out of the elevator and followed Gabe into the suite. Gabe grabbed a towel from the bathroom and began blotting his hair and face. "What's the verdict on the car?"

Xavier shrugged. "We could have it going in half an hour if we put it in the consulate garage, but to get it there we'll need to tow it and none of the hire vehicles have tow bars. The best-case scenario is that I call her a taxi."

"No." Gabe unknotted his tie and peeled out of his wet shirt and tossed both in the laundry basket.

The sensible thing was to do what Xavier suggested. The last thing he needed was a complication that would make the commitment he had to make in the morning even more difficult. But ever since Sarah had walked into the reception room, glowing like a fiery beacon in red, her dark hair a sexy tousled mass, the obligation and duty of his impending marriage had seemed secondary. When she had disobeyed all instructions and laid her hand on his ancestor's sword, he had been entranced.

Somehow, the fact that she had knocked the sword,

which was practically a sacred object on Zahir, off its bracket had only made her more interesting.

She was a *history* teacher. Against all odds, he found himself grinning.

Like no history teacher he'd ever seen.

Gabe strolled into his bedroom to find a clean shirt. In the past hour something curious had happened. He felt lighter and more carefree, as if a weight had lifted off him.

Because for the first time in years when he had looked at another woman, he hadn't been haunted by thoughts of Jasmine.

He guessed the fact that Sarah was literally Jasmine's polar opposite—tall and curvy with a steady, resolute gaze and hints of a fiery temper, instead of tiny and fragile and sweetly feminine—had helped. When Sarah had toppled Kadin's sword, in some odd way the separation from his past had seemed complete. Jasmine had hated all of the old Templar relics and the violent history that went with them. Sarah had seemed fascinated. From the way she had wielded her umbrella in the parking lot, he was willing to bet she would not be averse to holding a sword.

He stared at his crisply starched shirts in the closet, looking for something that didn't belong in a boardroom. Clothing that might indicate that he had a life. "I'm taking her home."

Xavier muttered something soft and short. "I don't think that's a good idea. Neither will your father."

Gabe shrugged into a dark shirt and buttoned it. The searing attraction that had sent him walking out into the night to find Sarah settled into grim determination. Xavier's unease mirrored his own because it was a fact that Gabe didn't want to just spend time with Sarah—he wanted her. Period. But just hours out from signing his life away, he was in no mood to deny a response he thought he would never feel again. "Right now a whole lot of things are happening that are not exactly good ideas."

An outmoded financial system that did not allow for the foreign investment Gabe had been advocating for years, and the marriage that *was* Zahir's financial rescue plan.

"The marriage is just an arrangement, you could have an—"

"No." Zahir was Western, but it was also extremely conservative. And Gabe was clear on one fact: once he was married he would not dishonor his vows or his family's integrity.

Xavier looked uncomfortable. "Sometimes I forget the pressure you're under. But what do you know about this woman? She could be some hard-nosed journalist angling for a story."

"Sarah's not a journalist." Gabe shrugged into a soft black leather jacket. "And she won't go to the press."

"You can't know that. You've only just met her. You have no idea what she'll do."

Gabe went still inside as a memory flickered. Cold rain scything, a dark-haired woman, head down against the weather, stepping around a corner. As his hands had shot out to stop her caroming into him he had noticed that her hair had been scraped back and her face had been almost bare of makeup. *She* had looked like a history teacher. But it had been Sarah, her eyes that deep, pure blue, the faintly imperious nose and exquisite cheekbones, the soft, generous mouth.

Instead of tempering his attraction, the recollection had the disconcerting effect of deepening it. In that moment, Gabe recognized the quality that drew him to Sarah most of all—the fact that in the midst of all the superficiality of the social world he usually moved in she was exactly what she seemed, a refreshingly direct woman unafraid to reach out and take what she wanted. "I met her yesterday."

Xavier's brows jerked together. "That makes it even worse."

Everything Xavier was saying was true. Normally he didn't pursue women he had only just met. Because of his position, he accepted that security checks on the women he dated were a fact of life. But ever since he had woken up that morning he had been restless and in no mood to be controlled. "Relax. She doesn't know who I am."

"How is that possible?"

"I think she expected my father to be here." Gabe walked through to the sitting room and pointedly held the door for Xavier. "I don't need an escort. As of now you're off duty. Take the rest of the night off."

Gabe waited until Xavier disappeared into the elevator before walking down the corridor to check on Sarah's progress in the guest suite. He could hear the sound of the hair dryer in the bathroom, so he returned to his suite to check his laptop. There was a message from his father and one from their lawyer, Hadad. Both messages, naturally, were centered on the contract Xavier had delivered.

He replied briefly to both then, jaw set, sat down to examine the list of marriage candidates that was clipped to the back of the contract. The candidate his parents preferred was at the top of the list.

He studied the color photo of Nadia Fortier. She was

slim and beautifully dressed, with long dark hair. She had to be all of eighteen.

He checked the basic information that had been provided. He saw he had been wrong about Nadia's age; she was twenty, a whole two years older than he had thought. And a good ten years his junior.

He flipped through the rest of the candidates. There were four in all. Extremely wealthy and young, all from good families, most of them with either noble or royal connections. Girls straight from exclusive finishing schools, groomed to make very good marriages as their designated career paths.

His gaze snagged on another notation: "guaranteed pure."

His jaw tensed. He realized that the situation was probably even more stressful for the girls, but he was beginning to feel like a prize stallion being led to stud. Broodingly, he wondered what kind of description of him they had received.

Tossing the document down on the coffee table, he strolled to one of the tall sash windows that looked out over the city streets. On a personal level he would not have dated any one of those candidates purely on the grounds that they were too young. He doubted they had any interests in common on which to build a marriage. The notation about purity explained the emphasis on youth, but as perfect and beautiful as each one was, none of them inspired even the remotest flicker of desire.

Unlike Sarah.

In that moment, the urge to do the unthinkable, to bail out of the arranged marriage and immerse himself in a tangled, messy, flamboyant affair with the very interesting Ms. Duval was irresistibly, powerfully appealing.

Massaging the taut muscles at his nape, he strode into his bedroom and found the keys to the Jeep that had been rented for him while he was in New Zealand. As he did so, his gaze snagged on the portrait of Kadin and Camille. Camille was dressed in flamboyant red, her dark gaze composed and direct, and for a split second he had an inkling of the fascination that had dominated his ancestor's life. The thought was like a dash of cold water. It was an obsession Gabe was determined would not dominate him.

He had already had a taste of the manipulation that went hand in hand with emotional excess. As tempting as it would be to toss tradition and his country's need and do exactly what he wanted, he could not walk away from his responsibilities.

Exiting the suite, he walked back to the guest room, his mood once again remote. He could understand Xavier's anxiety, because Gabe's behavior was distinctly out of character. Normally he took responsibility and did the right thing, and tomorrow he would choose which candidate he would marry. He had given his word.

But right now, tonight, he didn't want to think about the future. He was determined to accept the invitation he had seen in Sarah's eyes.

He was going to spend his last few hours of freedom with his quirky, fascinating lady in red.

Sarah finished blow-drying her hair and stared at the result in the gilt-framed mirror that dominated the ivory marble bathroom. With its gold taps and step-down bath, the room was utterly decadent. Her makeup was gone, washed off in the rain, and her hair had lost all of its curl. It fell in a shiny but depressingly straight waterfall to her waist. Her dress was still damp and clinging to her skin, but thankfully the silk seemed to be drying fast.

With all the glamor and magic of the makeover gone, there was no getting past the fact that, like Cinderella at the stroke of midnight, she was once again plain-Jane Sarah Duval. Although, she no longer felt like a plain-Jane. Her cheeks were softly flushed, and her eyes had a depth and sparkle she had never noticed.

Maybe that was because, just when she had thought there was no chance with Gabe, he had walked out of the night and rescued her. Now, she had been admitted to the hushed elegance of one of the sheikh's private apartments and suddenly the scenario she had planned seemed terrifyingly possible.

Placing the fluffy oversize towel she'd used in a laundry hamper, she checked that she hadn't left anything behind, hooked the strap of her bag over her shoulder and walked out into the luxuriously furnished bedroom, which opened onto a study.

Her heart slammed hard in her chest when she spotted Gabe standing at one of the tall sash windows in the study, watching the rain, which was once again pounding down. As he turned, she caught the flare of appreciation in his gaze and at the same time noticed that he had changed into dry clothes. If he'd looked formidable and just a little remote in a suit, the dark, soft shirt and black leather jacket, narrow trousers and black boots achieved the exact opposite, making him look younger and infinitely more approachable.

He indicated the rain streaming down the window. "With this weather, there's nothing we can do about the car tonight. If you want a lift home I can drop you. Or if you'd prefer I'll call a taxi."

Her heart sped up at the offer. The sensible thing, of course, would be to call a taxi but the instant she considered that option, she knew she wasn't going to take it. "If you could drop me, I'd appreciate it."

"No problem." Gabe picked up a set of keys he must have placed on a side table.

As he opened the door, she noticed an oil painting of a man dressed in robes on the wall. "Is that the sheikh?"

He glanced at the painting, but didn't seem inclined to linger. "Yes."

The painting had obviously been done when the sheikh was a lot younger, but even so, with his clipped beard and wearing traditional robes, it was difficult to see exactly what he looked like. He didn't look a lot like the man Graham had been talking to at the reception, but with the facial hair it was hard to tell. "Are there any paintings of Sheikh Kadin?"

Gabe went very still as he held the door for her. "The first Sheikh Kadin?"

She stepped out into the corridor, distracted by the sudden curtness of his tone. "I didn't realize there was more than one."

Gabe pressed a button on a sleek, private elevator and gestured that she precede him. "The name reoccurs practically every second generation in the sheikh's family." He pressed the button for the ground floor. "The name is also popular on Zahir, mostly because it's linked with prosperity."

She frowned at the flatness of his tone. "You don't sound overly impressed by the first sheikh."

"It's ancient history."

"And an ancient love story."

The doors slid open. Gabe waited for her to exit first. "According to tradition."

Her head came up at the implication. "You don't think love was involved?"

Gabe indicated a gleaming Jeep Cherokee situated at the far end of the cavernous garage, next to the doors. "Kadin was broke, Camille was wealthy. What are the odds?"

Even though she had entertained similar thoughts about Kadin's motives, she frowned as they strolled through the dim shadows. After reading Camille's very personal revelations about how strongly she had been attracted to Kadin, she couldn't help taking his comments personally. "So I suppose you think that just because Kadin was a knight and good-looking, Camille was lucky to get him? That the money somehow made up for her defects?"

He came to a halt beside the Jeep, his expression enigmatic. "Let's just say that if Camille hadn't been traveling with approximately a metric ton of gold and jewels that history would probably have taken a different turn."

He opened the door for her, his consideration taking the sting out of his words and dampening down the knee-jerk urge to spring to her ancestor's defense. His hand cupping her elbow as she climbed into the passenger seat further distracted her. After Graham's dismissive treatment, Gabe's manners and the feeling that while she was with him she was the absolute focus of his attention were a much-needed balm.

Feeling breathless, she fastened her seat belt. As Gabe swung into the driver's seat, the cab of the Jeep seemed to shrink, suddenly claustrophobically small and disturbingly intimate.

Sarah attempted to relax as Gabe accelerated out of the garage into the murky night, but the easy camaraderie of earlier in the evening had evaporated. Bludgeoned out of existence by her usual bluntness, she thought grimly.

Minutes later, when he pulled into a parking space on the road above her rain-drenched cottage, her stomach tightened at the knowledge that whatever she and Gabe had shared would be over in a matter of seconds. "Thank you for the lift."

She fumbled at the door handle, but before she could push it wide, Gabe swung out of the cab and walked around to hold the door. Rain swirled down, shimmering in the pooling light of street lamps as she retrieved her bag.

Once she was out, Gabe closed the door with a discreet *thunk*. "I'll see you to your door." A beep and flash of lights indicated that he had locked the vehicle.

Feeling breathless and chilled after the warmth of the cab, Sarah led the way to her porch with its single glowing light. She paused in the shelter of the wide, old-fashioned porch and extracted her house key from her bag. A moment later, she pushed the door wide. The house was softly lit and comforting, with lamps burning in the sitting room. Warm air flowed out, making the night seem even colder and damper.

She glanced at Gabe, suddenly awkward. A restless part of her wished for the boldness that had arisen out of nowhere earlier in the evening. She longed to have the confidence to do what she had planned and fling herself into a wild, passionate affair, to curl her fingers into the soft lapels of his jacket, go up on her toes and kiss him. But as nice as Gabe had been in looking out for her and giving her a lift home, she was determined not to make a fool of herself by misreading the situation. "Thank you for everything. I'll collect my car in the morning."

"No problem." He produced a card from his pocket and scribbled a name and number on the back of it. "Xavier will be gone, but a receptionist will be there. She'll have your keys."

She took the card, careful not to touch his fingers, and tucked it in her bag. "You're leaving first thing?"

"I have business to attend to on Zahir."

A little desperate that he was about to leave, she searched for a reason to detain him, if only for a few seconds. The question that had consumed her earlier, resurfaced. Heart beating a rapid tattoo, she lifted her chin. "Why did you follow me when I left the lecture?"

Something flared in his gaze, the electrifying intensity she had been aware of at the reception, as if he were searching for something intangible but utterly necessary to him. As if he had found that necessary quality in *her*.

His gaze connected with hers. "I couldn't let you go."

The words sent a bolt of pure sensation through her. In that moment her mind cleared on the whole issue of risk. She had gone out tonight specifically looking for a wild fling to break herself out of the emotional rut she'd fallen into. Her mother would count it a victory if Sarah married Graham. In Sarah's mind that would be the ultimate relationship train wreck because Graham would never give her the one thing she craved: true love.

But with Gabe, on some instinctive level, she knew the opposite to be true. The connection sizzled between them. She could see it in his eyes, *feel* it with every cell of her body. There was no logic or sense to it. They barely knew each other, and yet she knew in her heart that something deep and essential was right between them.

He was edgy and utterly male, and he'd been ready to go to war for her. At times he had been grim and remote, but there had been a softness and humor she had loved. She didn't know him, and yet every instinct she possessed informed her that he was everything and more she wanted in a man.

He was perfect, and in a few minutes she was going to lose him.

She drew a swift breath. "Don't go. Not yet."

Four

Gabe said something low and soft then his mouth was on hers.

Heat and sensation seared through her, time seemed to slow and stop as she lifted up on her toes, wound her arms around his neck and fitted herself more fully against him. She logged the solid wall of muscle that was his chest, the warmth of his arms as he pulled her in close, the firm swell of his arousal.

The kiss was soft and lingering and the intimacy of it rocked her. She had been kissed before, more times than she could count, but in other kisses she had been aware of an element of recoil in the process. Either she didn't like the way her date touched her, his taste or smell, or she didn't like her date, period.

There had been times when she had wondered if she was the tiniest bit frigid, but with Gabe the details that registered were all on the plus side. He smelled clean and male and delicious and his touch and taste shivered through her senses, making her feel boneless and weak. While every other kiss she'd ever experienced had been wrong in some way, this kiss was somehow right, filling her with an absorbing, dissolving heat so that she wanted to press herself even more firmly against him.

His mouth lifted then sank again, taking her under. Dimly she was aware of the strap of her handbag slipping off one shoulder. Misty rain swirled around the enclosure of the porch, triggering disorienting flashes of the sensual dream she had experienced just that morning.

Gabe lifted his head. His gaze locked with hers. "If you want me to leave, you should say so now."

The cool separation when only moments before she had been held against the muscled heat of his body was faintly shocking. He wanted her. That thought alone was enough to anchor her, when for years she had felt rejected as a woman and intrinsically undesirable.

Now she knew that none of those past relationships had been right because she had been waiting for the deep connection she needed. It had never happened with anyone else, but through some strange alchemy it had happened with Gabe.

The knowledge filled her with dizzying relief. She had begun to think she was odd, different, that she would never marry, never have the warm family chaos, the husband and babies that were at the center of most of her friends' lives. She had begun to believe that she would never be truly loved.

It was a huge leap to go from one kiss to thinking that Gabe could be hers. Making love with him would be a risk, but *not* making love would be an even bigger risk.

She might miss her only chance to feel this way—loved and desired by the man of her choice.

Sarah touched Gabe's jaw, loving the rough feel of his five-o'clock shadow. Drawn by an impulse that had its roots in the dream, she allowed her fingers to drift over the smooth, ridged scar that marred his cheekbone.

Something flared in his eyes, gone almost as swiftly as it had appeared, then his mouth was on hers. A split second later, the world went sideways as Sarah found herself swung into his arms.

One step and they were inside her house. She heard the door slam shut then they were moving.

Gabe lifted his head. "Which way is the bedroom?"

She indicated a left turn. Moments later he carried her into the dim shadows of her room lit only by the lamplight washing down the hall and the glow of a streetlight flowing through her window. Setting her down, he shrugged out of his jacket, letting it drop to the floor. He kissed her again, drawing her against him as he slowly drew the zipper that fastened her dress down the sensitive curve of her spine. Cool air circulated against her skin as she stepped out of the dress and set to work on the buttons of Gabe's shirt, although that work was momentarily halted as Gabe dispensed with her bra and cupped her breasts.

Long dizzying seconds passed as he bent and took first one breast, then the other into his mouth, the sensation pulling every muscle tight and starting a heavy ache low in her belly. Despite the coolness of the air against her skin and the chilly sound of the rain on the windows, heat flushed her skin making her feel restless and hot.

Lifting his mouth, Gabe dispensed with the remaining buttons of his shirt and shrugged out of it, before pulling her close. Drawing in a breath at the seductive heat of skin on skin, Sarah coiled her arms around his neck and pulled his mouth to hers, the kiss deepening as he walked her backward to the bed. She felt the soft give of the mattress at the back of her knees then she sank back onto the down-filled white quilt, Gabe sprawled beside her.

He moved over her, his weight pressing her down. Little more than fifteen minutes ago she had been on the verge of saying good-night out on the porch, now they were on the verge of making love. Disorientation hit her at how fast things had moved, but the night had an odd dreamlike quality and the dizzying intensity of emotion that burst through her with every touch of his hands, his mouth, was too addictive to relinquish.

She felt his fingers tugging at her panties and shifted restlessly, helping him strip them down her legs. The faintly rough weave of his pants brushed against her sensitive skin.

Frustrated that while she was naked Gabe was still half dressed, she reached down and tugged at the fastening of his pants. She dragged the zipper down and felt the blunt, silky shape of him in her hands. He muttered something taut beneath his breath as he moved between her legs. A split second later she felt him lodged against her. Hot, irresistible sensation burst through her as she instinctively pressed against him, inviting him deeper.

He tensed and attempted to withdraw but, utterly mesmerized by a burning maelstrom of sensation, Sarah's arms coiled tighter as she pressed closer still. An agonizing second later he shoved deep and the irresistible, coiling heat shimmered and dissolved along with the night.

* * *

Long minutes later, Gabe propped himself on one elbow, his gaze in the darkened room brooding and reflective. He stroked one fingertip over her tender bottom lip in a lingering caress that sent a shiver through her. "How likely is it that you'll get pregnant?"

The question was shocking. Although it was a possibility Sarah had been turning over while she'd attempted to adjust to the intimacy of what they'd just done and the shameless way she had pressed herself against him before he'd had a chance to use a condom.

The possibility of an unplanned pregnancy. It was not a problem she had ever thought she would face. Along with the thought of a pregnancy and all that entailed, Gabe's practicality in asking the question brought her back to earth with a thump. For long minutes she had been caught up in her own very private fantasy, but with every second that passed it was becoming increasingly obvious that Gabe did not share her longings.

She swallowed against the sudden ache at the back of her throat and made an effort to dismiss the hurt. She needed to be as practical as Gabe. She had wanted to make love and they had. It had been a huge risk and, whatever the outcome, she refused to regret what had happened.

A baby. The thought that in the past few minutes they could have made a tiny human life together was stunning.

Gabe might have no interest in anything more than an interlude, *a one-night stand*, but if there was a baby, Sarah would want it. She loved kids and adored babies. She had always wanted at least one of her own, and the way things had been going she had begun to think she would never be a mother.

She drew a deep breath. Gabe's silence spoke louder than words, there was no way he wanted the complication of a baby. Since he was leaving in the morning, and he hadn't indicated that he was coming back to New Zealand, she had to assume that it was entirely possible that they would never see each other again. "Don't worry about a baby. It won't be a problem."

If she was pregnant, it was too late now; it was done. And if Gabe did not want an actual relationship with her then so be it. She would take sole responsibility for the child.

Gabe cupped her jaw, his gaze intent. What he saw in her eyes must have satisfied him. "I've never done that before, so you don't have to worry about STDs."

She suppressed the sharp hurt that Gabe was clearly used to making love with women, and the jab of guilt that he obviously thought she had taken care of contraception. "Ditto."

Something like relief flickered in his gaze. "Good."

As Gabe climbed from the bed and drew the curtains against the rain still spattering the windows, it registered that he hadn't noticed she was a virgin. That small point shouldn't have mattered, but somehow it did. Although, with the swiftness with which they'd come together, Gabe probably hadn't had time to process anything beyond the fact that they'd had unprotected sex.

As he peeled out of his boots and pants, items she hadn't given him time to fully dispense with, Sarah surreptitiously pulled back the quilt and shimmied beneath it.

Gabe, who was in the process of tearing open a foil

packet, prevented her cover up by the simple expedient of stripping back the quilt. "Don't," he said softly. "I want to remember you like this."

The finality of the words—as if they'd already said goodbye—struck her forcibly.

Despite her innate caution, while they'd been kissing, undressing, hope had formed. She and Gabe would swap numbers. He would call her from Zahir and somehow they would form a relationship. And maybe, just maybe, sometime in the misty future there would be the possibility of something real and enduring.

Tension gripped her as she watched Gabe sheath himself in the dim light. With his biceps bronzed and gleaming, chest and abs tautly muscled, he was beautiful in a fierce, completely male way and she wanted him.

But he wasn't hers. The truth was there in the faint remoteness of his gaze, a subtle distance she could feel even in the midst of passion.

As he joined her on the bed, she propped herself on one elbow and looked directly into his eyes. "Are you married?"

"No."

Relief filled her. "Good." She suspected that Gabe wasn't as free as he seemed but she didn't want to know that there was a girlfriend or significant other back on Zahir. If there was, what was between them obviously wasn't strong enough to hold Gabe. To her mind that meant it wasn't love.

Love. The concept burned through her, initiating a new tension. Everything she had felt for Gabe had been new, intense and passionate. She drew a swift breath as the reality hit home of how affected she had been by him. She didn't see how anyone could fall in love in the space of a few hours, but she had.

Her chest squeezed tight. Swallowing the impending hurt, the silly desire to cry, she leaned down and kissed Gabe, her hair sliding like a curtain around them.

The thought that she could be pregnant already made her feel even more unsettled. As his hands moved to her waist, drawing her down to him, she forced herself to forget about the possibility of a pregnancy, forget about the fact that Gabe was leaving.

If they only had one night, she was determined that it would be a night to remember.

Sarah woke to sun streaming through a gap in the curtains. Yawning, she turned over, reaching for Gabe only to find cool rumpled sheets and a pillow with an indentation. She glanced around the room. The certainty that he had gone was there in the absence of any of his clothing.

A knock at the front door had her jackknifing out of bed. Shrugging into her robe, she tightened the belt around her waist and dragged fingers through her tangled hair. Her first thought was that Gabe must have gone out for a walk, or maybe to buy some breakfast.

When she opened the door, a uniformed courier was standing on her porch with a huge bunch of dark red, perfectly formed roses.

Her mood plunging, Sarah took the flowers and set them on a side table just inside the hall while she signed an electronic pad to confirm she had received them. Closing the door, she leaned against it and stared at the beautiful, expensive bouquet. A quick check revealed there was no card.

Stomach tightening, she picked up the heavy bunch

and carried them to her small kitchen. She had received roses only twice before in her life. Roger had given her a modest bunch on her birthday, once, but they had been pink and wrapped in yellow paper with the unmistakable tag of a local supermarket. Mark had sent her one lone rose on a Valentine's Day. Neither man had thought to send her two-dozen roses that hinted at the passionate, sensual bond she now knew could exist between a man and a woman.

But then, she hadn't slept with either of them.

She found a vase large enough to hold the flowers, although a part of her didn't want to either keep them or display them just in case they did represent "goodbye."

It occurred to her then that she didn't know Gabe's full name, and she had somehow forgotten to give him her phone number. Although he knew her name and address, so it should be easy enough for him to find her.

She bent forward and inhaled the fragrance. She would stay positive, hang on to hope. All of her instincts told her that Gabe was special, that despite that touch of remoteness—a caution she well knew—he had valued their passionate hours together as much as she.

He would call; it was just a matter of time.

Gabe could not afford to contact Sarah, ever.

The thought made his mood even grimmer as he boarded his chartered flight, late.

Xavier, who had been waiting in the departure lounge, strode alongside him, his expression taut. "I thought I was going to have to come and get you."

Gabe took his seat in the small jet's luxury cabin, resignation settling in at his friend's implication. "Don't tell me, there was a GPS tracker on the Jeep."

Xavier dropped into the seat beside him. "There's always a GPS. You're the son of the sheikh, the heir apparent. If I hired vehicles that didn't have that facility, I'd be fired."

Gabe fastened his seat belt for take-off and concentrated on resisting the insane urge to disembark and drive back to the small seaside suburb where Sarah lived.

"Please tell me you won't be seeing her again."

Gabe didn't bother answering. Xavier was justifiably upset because he had been tasked with Gabe's security. He had slipped the leash and given Xavier a difficult night. But the whole point had been that Gabe had one last night to himself.

Only it had been a little more complicated than that.

He had hoped that when he made love with Sarah the attraction would lose its potency. He had been wrong. Despite the short length of time they had spent together, he still felt the force of their connection, the emotional pull, which was even more reason to leave.

As the jet leveled out, a pretty Zahiri air hostess dressed in an elegant blue uniform, her hair caught up in a glossy knot, served coffee.

Gabe set his briefcase down on the fold-down tray, flipped it open and extracted the marriage contract. Xavier pretended to be immersed in a newspaper while Gabe once again read through the list of marriage candidates. His jaw tightened as he came back to the young woman his parents had rated number one.

Dispassionately, he studied her face, which was beautiful but, to Gabe, lacking in personality. There was no hint of stormy emotions or engaging boldness. There was absolutely no evidence of the sharp, take-no-prisoners intellect that would make life interesting. It was a face he would be seeing on a daily basis once they were married.

Xavier put down his paper. "If you really are going ahead with a marriage of convenience you shouldn't have had a one-night stand with a twenty-eight year old history teacher."

"Twenty-eight?"

"Almost twenty-nine."

Controlling his irritation that Xavier had referred to the hours Gabe had spent with Sarah as a one-night stand, Gabe flipped to the legalese of the agreement. "I suppose you had to do the security check."

"I was worried. You don't normally go off the grid like that."

"Normally I'm too busy." Trying to finesse the traditional approach to finances his father clung to into a system that would bring his country out of its financial nosedive. Now their lack of solvency had reached a critical state, stopping a resort development vital for Zahir's continued prosperity in its tracks.

And yet, despite his country's problems, his mind returned to Sarah. She was almost twenty-nine. The small snippet of information was intriguing, and made sense. She had been far too interesting to be younger and yet, with her moonlight-pale skin and silky hair, her passionate intensity when they had made love, she had seemed much younger. No wonder they had clicked so instantly. Besides the college education, the fact that they were close in age was one more thing they had in common.

As the jet gathered speed, Gabe closed out an image of Sarah lying in a tumble of sheets, her hair spread out over the pillow and applied himself to reading through the fine print. He hit the clause that stipulated his bride had to be pure, which was why each of the candidates was so young. With every year that passed, logic dictated that it was more difficult to find a suitable candidate for marriage who was still a virgin. A twenty-eight-year-old virgin was an impossibility.

Or, maybe not.

Gabe's heart slammed once, hard, against the wall of his chest as the engines reached a crescendo and the jet leaped into the air. Pressed back into his seat for the ascent, he felt electrified, every nerve ending in his body on fire as the missing piece of the puzzle that was Sarah fell into place.

She had been a virgin.

Nothing else explained her unusual behavior. She had been at once bold and shy, and she hadn't employed any exotic techniques. She had simply made love to him. In all the years he had been involved in relationships, no woman he had ever been with had ever made love to him like they meant it, including his wife.

He could kick himself. He had felt the initial constriction, noted the moment of discomfort on her face but, stunned by the knowledge that he had been so caught up in her passionate response that he had failed to protect them both, the significance of those sensations had bypassed him. Given that the first time had been over almost before it had begun, maybe he could be forgiven for the oversight.

"What's wrong?" Xavier must have picked up something in his expression. "Please tell me you protected yourself."

Eventually. Although he hadn't wanted to, and that had been a first. But from the moment he had seen Sarah at the reception he had been thrown off balance. Grimly he noted that if the jet wasn't in the air, he would have done something precipitate and obsessive, like walk off the flight and refuse a marriage arrangement that, long-term, would provide the stability and the heir both his family and Zahir needed. He would have behaved emotionally—in a way that he knew from bitter experience destroyed happiness and lives.

Letting out a breath, he forced himself to once more study Nadia's profile. He knew her family, of course. Her father was a French billionaire who had made his money in shipping. No doubt those two details had appealed to Gabe's father who, with the onset of his illness, had become a little obsessed with the legend of Sheikh Kadin. No doubt he thought there was a satisfying symmetry to the idea of Gabe marrying a shipping magnate's daughter. After all, that was how Zahir had made its money in the first place.

Gabe replied to the email, accepting the preferred candidate, Nadia Fortier.

His father had decreed a short engagement to give them time to get to know one another. A few months' grace in which to get to know and accept the woman he would marry.

And to forget Sarah Duval.

Five

Four months later Sarah double-checked the results her doctor handed her.

"You're absolutely sure I'm pregnant?"

Evelyn lifted a brow. "You're not just pregnant, you're very pregnant and I think you knew that. You should have come to see me sooner."

Caught between resignation, dismay and the dizzying sense of wonder that had gripped her over the past few weeks as she'd logged the undeniable symptoms of a pregnancy, Sarah tucked the sheet of paper in her handbag.

Of course she had noticed that she had missed her first period. But, caught stubbornly in denial, she had waited another month. When her cycle missed for the second time and she had begun to feel faintly nauseous, she had begun to accept that what she had thought would never happen had happened.

She sent Evelyn an apologetic look. "Sorry. I needed some adjustment time."

To her credit, Evelyn, who was an old friend, didn't comment on the fact that Sarah was pregnant and didn't have a husband or even a boyfriend. "I presume you want to keep the baby?"

The words were discreetly put while Evelyn pretended to be busy shuffling papers and checking something on her computer screen.

"Yes." The answer was unequivocal.

"Can you supply me with any history of the father?"

Despite bracing herself for this question, Sarah's cheeks warmed. This was the part she'd been dreading. She had done some research on the whole business of having a baby and knew that sometimes details about the father, such as blood type and genetic conditions, were important. "No."

There was a small, vibrating silence. Evelyn ducked her head, her own cheeks flushed, but not before Sarah caught the flash of compassion in her friend's eyes. Evelyn knew Sarah's past, vividly. Evelyn was supposed to be Sarah's bridesmaid at the first wedding, her maid of honor at the second. Instead, Sarah had cried on Evelyn's shoulder over men, twice.

She wouldn't be crying on Evelyn's shoulder a third time because this mistake was in a whole new league.

Sarah hadn't been sedately courted by a man she and her family and friends knew well. She'd had a wildly romantic night of passion with an exotic stranger, a one-night stand, and then he had disappeared, leaving her flat.

She had committed every mistake in the book within the space of a few hours, literally picking up a guy, having unprotected sex with him and getting pregnant, and she didn't even know Gabe's full name. All she knew was that he lived thousands of miles away on an island in the Mediterranean and that he worked for the Sheikh of Zahir. Since Gabe had been careful not to supply her with any contact details, or even his full name, it was clear that he did not want further interaction with her.

Her behavior had not just been uncharacteristic, it had been dumb, and all because she'd been seduced by a romantic dream and frightened by the thought that she would end up thirty and alone.

She should have been a lot smarter than she had turned out to be. Becoming a mother was going to have a huge effect on her life. For a start, she would have to quit her full-time teaching job, because she wanted to stay home with her child. That meant she would have to find alternative employment, something she could do from home. Although she had already come up with an idea which was, crazily enough, based on Camille's journal.

Sarah forced herself to relax. There was no need to panic. She would work it all out one step at a time. "Okay, what do I do now?"

Evelyn scribbled her signature on a form and handed it to Sarah. "You'll need to have a blood test and make an appointment to come and see me in a week's time, but you've always been in great health so I don't anticipate any problems."

She opened a drawer and took out a bunch of pamphlets, selected several and slipped them across the surface of her desk. "Do some reading, don't drink alcohol and don't take any medication unless you run it by me, not even a painkiller. If you've been feeling sick, that's normal, but if it gets too bad come and see me right away."

Evelyn pulled up a file on her laptop and tapped briskly before hitting the print button. When the copy printed out, she handed it to Sarah. "It's an application for a scan. Since it looks like you're at least four months pregnant, you should have one of those. The clinic will contact you with a date and time."

Sarah took the form. A tentative, dawning delight began to spread through her. If anything could make the baby real, this was it. "Thanks."

Slipping the paperwork inside her handbag, she pushed to her feet.

Evelyn walked Sarah to the door. "If you need to stay longer and talk, I can stall the next appointment for a few minutes. And if you just want to talk, call me at home. Anytime."

Sarah pinned a smile on her face. She had been coming to Evelyn for years. Aside from the friendship that had developed between them at university, they had the perfect doctor/patient relationship. But if Sarah had to admit to Evelyn how naive she'd been, the relationship would be permanently dented. "I'll be fine, thanks. Don't forget I have a mother."

"Of course."

The relief on Evelyn's face confirmed Sarah's thoughts. Evelyn was smart, successful and married to another doctor. They had three children, a nanny and what looked like a perfectly organized life. As compassionate as Evelyn would try to be, there was no way she could understand why Sarah had slept with Gabe.

As Sarah walked out of the medical center into the warmth of a summer's day, she felt a tiny flutter, like butterfly wings, in her stomach. She froze, her hand going to her abdomen. The flutter came again and a sense of wonder spread through her. In just a few months she would be a mother.

Joy, heady and a little incredulous, hit her. For long moments she simply stood on the sidewalk, foot traffic flowing around her. She didn't have everything she wanted out of life. She didn't have a husband to love and who would love her, but she was going to have a baby, something she'd thought she would miss out on altogether.

Feeling disoriented and shaky, she took dark glasses from her bag, slid them onto the bridge of her nose and strolled to where she'd parked the car. She unlocked the driver's-side door, opened it and waited a few seconds for the heat that had built up inside to dissipate before climbing in. Instead of driving home, she drove by the Zahiri consulate.

On impulse, she pulled into the parking lot and found a space just outside the main entrance. Heart pounding at the idea that had blossomed, that she should at least think about contacting Gabe, she checked her appearance in the rearview mirror before exiting the car. Her hair was coiled in the messy knot she had perfected and her skin was positively glowing. Rummaging in her bag, she found her makeup kit, retouched around her eyes and applied fresh gloss to her mouth.

Stepping out of the car, she smoothed the loose white shirt she had teamed with a pair of camel pants, both items classic and stylish, but loose enough to fit comfortably, given that her waist had started to thicken.

A dark-haired receptionist, different from the one she had collected her car keys from the morning after she had slept with Gabe, listened to her enquiry. "We don't have anyone named Gabe working here. Do you have a surname?"

Sarah explained that Gabe had only been in the country for a short time, with the sheikh's entourage.

The woman's gaze grew oddly evasive. Sarah was almost certain she knew exactly to whom Sarah was referring.

She pushed to her feet. "Just one moment."

Frowning, Sarah watched her disappear into a side office. Moments later she reappeared with a small, plump man—Tarik. Sarah's stomach dropped.

After an unsatisfactory interview in which Tarik had first pretended not to recognize Sarah, and had then feigned confusion over which Gabe she was referring to, Sarah lost her temper. "The Gabe who picked up the sword after I dropped it at the reception. The man you appeared to know very well."

There was a small silence. "Do you have a photograph of him?"

Sarah's brows jerked together at the odd question. "No."

Tarik seemed to relax at that point, his voice turning as smooth as butter. "He doesn't work for the sheikh. He was just on…assignment."

Her fingers tightened on the strap of her bag. "What does that mean?"

Tarik fixed her with a bland stare. "It means he is not in the sheikh's employ."

"So you won't help me contact him?"

"No."

Annoyed at being treated like some kind of groupie, or worse, a stalker, Sarah turned on her heel and left the consulate, aware of two sets of eyes boring into her back. She was convinced they knew exactly who Gabe was, and where he was, and that for some unfathomable reason they were protecting him.

Grimly she decided that reason was probably that Gabe was married, even though he'd said he wasn't. Maybe her judgment in sleeping with him had been more skewed than she'd thought.

Her temper, held on a tight leash for most of the interview, boiled over again as she unlocked her car door. Lately, with the pregnancy, she had noticed a tendency toward mood swings. It no doubt had something to do with the hormones rioting through her body. Whatever the cause, her personality had definitely found another gear.

Fuming, she drove home and walked into her front room. Her plan was to find the first Zahiri ornament that came to hand and smash it in the hopes that small satisfying act of destruction would make her feel better. Instead she found Graham in her house.

Graham's head jerked up guiltily. He had a sheaf of papers in his hand. "I thought you'd be at work."

Sarah dropped her bag on a side table. "Normally I would be, and—" she checked her wristwatch "—that would have given you another good two hours to steal whatever it was you came to steal."

Graham tried for a smile. "You're looking good, Sarah, positively blooming. We should go out sometime."

She couldn't believe his nerve. She noticed Camille de Vallois's journal on a coffee table, the spine broken. "You've copied the journal." And by the looks of things, he'd been cheeky enough to use her paper and copier.

"I didn't think you'd mind—"

"You mean you hoped I'd never find out."

His cheeks reddened. He glanced at his watch as if he was suddenly in a hurry. "Uh—I need to go. I'm flying out to Zahir in a few hours, so I need to pack."

Sarah pointedly held the front door open. "Good luck finding the missing dowry. And if I ever find you in my house again, I'll call the police."

Graham's expression turned decidedly unpleasant. "I won't be back. Why would I when I've got what I wanted?"

Sarah slammed the door as Graham scuttled up the drive. She hooked the chain for good measure then walked back into her tiny sitting room, picked up the journal and sat down. She took a calming breath, then another, as she heard the whine of Graham's sports car, which must have been sneakily parked outside someone else's house, accelerate away.

The interview with Tarik, followed by the altercation with Graham, had worn her out.

She strolled through to her bedroom to put away the journal, but on the way down the hallway, something went curiously wrong with her balance. Head spinning, skin flushing with perspiration, she clung to the wall for long seconds before making a dash for the bathroom.

Minutes later, she rinsed out her mouth and staggered the rest of the way to the bedroom. Up until a few minutes ago she had felt healthy and alert and even more energetic than she normally did. But now that she had finally acknowledged the pregnancy, it seemed her body had decided to catch up on a few symptoms.

Opening her closet door, she put the journal on a shelf. As she did so, she glimpsed a flash of red on the floor of the closet. The dress she had worn the night she had made love with Gabe.

Jaw clenched against another wave of nausea, she retrieved the crumpled dress and sat on the edge of the bed as she waited for her stomach to settle. She should get rid of the dress, get rid of every last association with Gabe, but a part of her couldn't. In her heart of hearts she had been sure that there was a genuine connection between them. What she'd felt and experienced had been too real to be fake.

Annoyed with herself for mooning over the past, Sarah bundled up the red dress, strode to the kitchen and jammed it into the trash.

Another wave of dizziness hit her. She gripped the kitchen counter. She felt so washed-out. Would she really be able to do this alone?

Yes. She was determined to be positive. She loved kids and she adored babies. This baby was hers and she would love it within an inch of its life. And concentrating on being a mother rather than a wife or lover suited her perfectly, because she was definitely off men!

Three days later, Sarah went for her ultrasound and stared, hypnotized, at the tiny life growing inside her.

The nurse, a cheerful middle-aged woman, peered at the screen. "Do you want to know the sex of the baby?"

Mesmerized by the clearly discernible arms and legs, the delicate, sleepy face, Sarah instantly said, "Yes."

"You're having a girl."

Sarah's throat tightened and her chest swelled. She was no longer just having a baby; she was having a daughter. She wasn't a crier. She hated crying, but these days tears seemed to well at the drop of a hat.

Smiling, the nurse handed her a wad of tissues. "I'll bet your husband will be pleased. Or did he want a boy?"

Sarah mopped her eyes and blew her nose and tried not to imagine what Gabe might want. "I don't have a husband."

She had developed a new and far more satisfying focus in life than searching for her own personal knight in shining armor. She was determined to learn all she could about childbirth and parenting, to enjoy the changes to her body, the weird cravings and the myriad discomforts. Once the baby was born, she would then put theory into practice and do her very best as a mother.

As she stepped out of the clinic into the glaring heat, the copy of the scan tucked into her bag, a tall lean guy in a suit strolled by, caught her eye and smiled. Automatically, Sarah smiled back, although she didn't know him at all. When she turned her head, he was still watching her, his expression appreciative. With a jolt, she realized he was flirting with her.

Feeling dazed, she unlocked her car. As she slid into the driver's seat she stared at her reflection in the rear-view mirror. Her hair, piled as it was into a loose knot, looked tousled and sexy. Her eyes were a deep, pure blue and her skin had a definite glow, as if she was illuminated from within.

With a start she realized that despite the bouts of tiredness and sickness she had never looked better. She wasn't just attractive; she was beautiful. An odd sense of lightness assailed her. For the first time in years, her failed engagements didn't seem important. Gabe's defection was too recent to discount, but that disappointment was, also, no longer crushing.

She felt stronger, more confident. Maybe someday she

would meet a man she could fall for and who would actually fall for her in return, but if that didn't happen, she wasn't going to fret about it. The moment was freeing.

Fastening her seat belt, she started the car and pulled out into traffic. All that was left to resolve was the mystery that surrounded Gabe. She needed to decide whether or not she should allow him to be a part of her baby's life.

And find out what kind of man she had slept with.

Six

Gabe boarded his chartered flight out of Dubai, following his meeting with the construction CEO who had agreed to build the stalled resort complex on Zahir. With Gabe's engagement now formalized, a partial financial settlement had been made into Zahir's accounts and he had been able to transfer the funds, enabling the contractor to resume work.

Xavier was waiting for him in the small jet's luxury cabin. "I've been trying to call you."

Gabe frowned at Xavier's presence as he dropped into a seat beside him. "Cell phone coverage is sketchy in Buraimi, but then you knew that." His gaze sharpened. "What's wrong? Is my father okay?"

"He's fine. Your mother oversees every medical detail. He wouldn't dare not recover."

Gabe found himself grinning. "It's hard to say no to

Mom." The eldest of a family of eight and with a law degree, she had the kind of immovable, steely calm that was hard to mess with.

Xavier was silent for a moment. "Have you been in contact with the Duval woman?"

Gabe froze as he fastened his seat belt for takeoff. *The Duval woman.* As if Sarah was hardened and manipulative, when Gabe knew the opposite to be true.

A picture of the way Sarah had looked, asleep, as he'd quietly dressed and left her cottage in the early morning hours shimmered in his mind. Dark silky hair sliding over one flushed cheek, the outline of her body graceful beneath tangled bedclothes. Every muscle in his body tightened at the vivid memory of what it had felt like to make love with her, a memory he had worked hard to obliterate. "You know I haven't. What's wrong? Is she all right?"

"Uh—nothing's wrong. She's fine." There was a vibrating pause. "Tarik thinks she might be pregnant."

Gabe's heart slammed against the wall of his chest. "I thought we were past the point where there was a possibility of a pregnancy."

It was a thought that had consumed him for some weeks after they had made love. Despite the major complication a pregnancy would have been, a part of him had been crazily, irresistibly attracted to the idea that Sarah could be pregnant with his child. His fingers tightened on the arms of his seat. It had been another indication that, despite his efforts to distance himself from that night with Sarah, he had become entangled in the kind of obsessive emotion he had vowed to avoid.

Xavier shrugged. "I talked to Tarik a couple of hours ago. He practically had a heart attack over the phone."

Gabe dragged at his tie, loosening the knot. "What makes him think she could be pregnant now? It's been over four months."

"A few days ago she walked into the consulate looking for you. Why would she wait so long to do that?"

Gabe's pulse rate lifted a notch at the visual of Sarah confronting Tarik and trying to prise Gabe's contact details out of the man. Gabe would have liked to have seen that battle of wills. Out of nowhere a lightness he hadn't felt for a very long time—*four months and eleven days to be exact*—flooded him, dissolving the tension that had gripped him since spending a large chunk of the marriage settlement funds. Spending the money had sealed him even more completely into the agreement. Worse, it had made *him* feel bought and paid for. "Maybe she just wanted to contact me."

Xavier looked frustrated. "This is why you need a bodyguard. Sometimes, I think you and I live in different universes. The consulate receptionist agreed with Tarik. She thought Sarah *looked* pregnant. Something about a loose blouse and a glow."

"A glow isn't exactly evidence." Although he found himself suddenly ensnared by the idea of Sarah glowing.

"Tarik uncovered something else interesting. Sarah is a descendent of Camille de Vallois's family."

Gabe frowned. "There have got to be thousands of descendants of the de Vallois family. As I recall they were wealthy and prolific."

"Granted, but you don't normally sleep with one of them."

On edge and unsettled, Gabe glanced out of the jet's window as the glittering city and blue-green sea of Dubai receded. He knew what Xavier was getting at.

Maybe Sarah was somehow fascinated by the old legend. Maybe that had been her motivation for sleeping with him. The only difficulty with that scenario was that four months ago Sarah hadn't known he was a sheikh. She had thought he was an employee.

Added to that, she had made no attempt to contact him—until she had walked into the consulate and spoken to Tarik. For long moments, Gabe became lost in the riveting concept of Sarah, *pregnant with his child* and searching for him.

When the jet leveled out, he released his safety belt and retrieved his laptop. He opened the surveillance report that he had commissioned precisely so that Xavier would have no excuse to do so. Although he already knew Sarah's daily routine by heart, including the fact that she had recently joined a gym, changed her hairdresser and added a weekly visit to a beauty therapist. Although, the factual report, fascinating as it was, didn't interest him. It was the photographs attached that he wanted to examine. Snapshots of Sarah going about her normal life, which he had perused more times than he cared to count.

He studied Sarah wearing a sleek red suit and a pair of black-rimmed glasses that made her look corporate and outrageously sexy. Sarah in jeans and a tight sweater going shopping. Another shot where she was wearing a pink dress with a slit on one side that showed off long, tanned legs. He frowned at how increasingly alluring and feminine she looked as the months had gone by. Another more disturbing word popped into his mind—*available.*

He stared at an image of Sara sunbathing on the beach below her cottage, wearing an ultra-skimpy floral bikini. Annoyance gripped him that the PI who took the photo had spied on her when she was practically naked, even though Gabe had ordered it.

He sat back in his seat, jaw tight, annoyed at the whole concept of Sarah being available. Not for the first time it occurred to him that now that Sarah was sexually awakened she would feel free to sleep with other men.

Over his dead body.

Not that he had any rights over Sarah. But if she was pregnant with his child, that would change.

The primitive surge of possessiveness took him by surprise and formed a decision that settled smoothly into place. If Sarah was pregnant, they would work something out. She wouldn't be happy with him. He had left her, and the reason he'd had to do so was still in place. Even so, if there was a child involved, *his child*, he wasn't prepared to walk away.

The ramifications of becoming a father made his heart pound. "I'm going to New Zealand."

Xavier's head jerked up. "You can't. Your wedding date is set and besides, your father will have a stroke if he finds out you had a one-night stand with a twenty-eight-year-old history teacher."

"Twenty-nine," Gabe muttered absently, as he wrote a brief email to his personal assistant to arrange the flight. "She had a birthday a few weeks ago."

"You remembered her birthday?" There was another tense silence. "I knew it. You're falling for her."

Gabe's stomach tightened at the idea of falling in love again. "Love doesn't come into the equation. Sarah's birthday was on the security report."

"You're supposed to be trying to form a relationship with your fiancée. Nadia's smart, beautiful—most men would kill to spend just one night with her."

Gabe pressed the send button.

When the jet landed, Gabe gave in to an uncharacteristic surge of impatience and rang Sarah's number which had been conveniently supplied in the report. With the time and date difference, he didn't know if she would be at home or at work. Long seconds passed. Convinced that she wasn't home, he was about to terminate the call when she picked up, her voice husky and soft as if he'd woken her from sleep.

Gabe's stomach tightened at the thought of Sarah lying in bed. For a moment he felt tongue-tied and almost entirely bereft of English. "Sarah, it's Gabe."

There was an echoing moment of silence. "Gabe who?"

The phone slammed down, the noise loud enough to make him jerk his cell from his ear.

Xavier shot him a horrified look. "You just called her. You should let me deal with this. If she really is pregnant—"

"No. Go near Sarah Duval and you're fired."

"You can't afford a scandal."

Neither could he afford to lose a child.

Gabe called Sarah again. This time the line was engaged, which meant she had left the phone off the hook.

As he stepped outside into the hot Zahiri sun he replayed the all-too-brief conversation, the small silence then the husky curtness of Sarah's voice, as if she was hurt. Even though the evidence was sketchy, he was abruptly certain that Sarah was pregnant.

When he reached the palace, he confirmed his flight and travel arrangements and cleared his schedule for the next four days, including canceling a formal dinner with his fiancée and her parents. Feeling restless and on edge, he stepped onto the balcony of his private suite and paced.

Gripping the still sun-warmed balustrade, he stared at the smooth sweep of sea glimmering beneath the rising moon, buttery gold and huge on the horizon.

Sarah trying to contact him and hitting a wall would explain why she might not feel like talking to him now. In her mind, he had abandoned her. Worse, he had made sure she couldn't find him.

Once Sarah knew his situation, she would understand the need for discretion. She would understand why he'd had to leave her.

She was a mature, educated woman. He was certain they could work it out.

Sarah stared at the shadowy shape of the phone in the dark, shock and a sharp jolt of anger running through her. Dragging tumbled hair from her face, she flicked the switch on her bedside lamp and sat up in bed. Her digital clock said it was close to midnight. She had been asleep for two hours, more or less.

She should feel exhausted, but within the space of a couple of seconds any hint of exhaustion and nausea had been vaporized. She felt alert, her mind crystal clear, the heady charge of adrenaline still zinging through her veins.

On impulse, she took the phone off the hook in case Gabe tried to call again. Maybe that didn't make sense when just days ago she had tried to contact him. But lately she had been on a roller-coaster ride of emotions. One minute she wanted Gabe in her life, the next she recoiled from that particular weakness and didn't want to know. When she had slammed the phone down, it had been a knee-jerk reaction. Now that she'd hung up, she was beginning to wonder what, exactly, Gabe had wanted.

Could he possibly want *her*?

Her heart thumped hard in her chest. Somewhere deep in her abdomen the baby kicked. It was still the merest flutter, but it served to remind her that she had turned a corner with her thinking. She was no longer hurt and vulnerable, and she was over Gabe. There was a whole lot more at stake now than romance and passion.

Tossing the bedclothes aside, she headed for the kitchen. Now that the adrenaline was wearing off, her stomach was starting to turn somersaults again. Her mother had told her to munch on a supply of salty crackers. Since they went perfectly with the other things Sarah craved—pickles and cheese—she had complied.

After piling a plate and making herself a cup of weak tea, because now anything with milk made her stomach queasy, she strolled back to bed. While she worked her way through the crackers and tea she picked up the book of baby names she'd been reading before she'd fallen asleep. So far she had isolated fifty or so names and noted them on a pad on her bedside table.

Yawning, she picked up the pad and grimly ignored the way her mind kept constantly replaying Gabe's few words, the curtness of his voice, which had sent an automatic thrill through her. She began reading through the names she'd so far chosen, mentally linking each of the names with Duval because without a husband that would be her baby's surname.

Hours later, the doorbell chimed, pulling Sarah out of a restless sleep. Belting on her robe, she dragged fingers through her hair and hurried to the door. Her heart sped up at the breathless thought that it could be Gabe, that the reason he had rung was that he was back in New Zealand and wanted to see her again.

Flinging open the door she was met by an enormous basket of fragrant red roses that matched the other bunches filling her porch. A short, bald deliveryman stared at her with undisguised curiosity as he requested her signature for the flowers.

Feeling dazed, confused and angry—because the dark red, deeply fragrant tea roses sent from the same expensive florist that had delivered the last lot, had to be from Gabe—Sarah scribbled her name. When the deliveryman had driven away, she lugged the flowers inside. After a brief search, she found a note attached to the enormous basket filled with roses and boxes of expensive chocolates. When she opened the note she stared blankly at Gabe's full name, which was unexpectedly long, and a number.

A red mist obscured her vision for long seconds. She was finally over him and *now* he decided to provide his phone number? When the mist cleared she found herself out on her deck, the myriad shreds of paper that had once been the note whipping away in the wind.

Legs suddenly weak, she walked back inside and sat down. Her skin kept going hot then cold. Her heart was beating way too fast. Rage, she decided, was definitely not good for the baby. Taking a deep breath, Sarah stared at the small fortune in roses and chocolates. She felt stunned that after all this time Gabe had decided not only to contact her, but apparently, to woo her.

Squashing the weak, wimpy kernel of hope that was unfurling irresistibly inside her, she decided that if Gabe had wanted to send her roses, he was too late.

Just like he was way late sending his contact details.

If he had genuinely cared for her and valued her, he would have given her his number months ago, or showed up at her door. Neither of those things had happened. He hadn't even bothered to check to see if she had gotten pregnant.

She went still inside. Or maybe he finally had.

That would explain the flowers and the sudden desire to be in contact, which, now that she was thinking straight, smacked of damage control.

Mood plummeting, she unconsciously cradled her abdomen, protecting the small life inside. She frowned at the thought that Tarik had seen through her visit to the consulate, that he had been suspicious enough to contact Gabe. The scenario seemed a likely explanation for both the call and the roses, given Gabe's unreliable behavior in disappearing so completely after their one night together.

Pushing to her feet, she decided that under those circumstances she didn't want the roses Gabe had deliberately chosen to remind her of the night they had spent together.

She began ferrying the roses back out onto the porch. She would give them to the pretty little church down the road, and the chocolates could go to the rest home near her school. If Gabe thought he could charm her and buy her off so she wouldn't make trouble, he could think again.

The following morning, just as she'd finished dressing for work, a knock at the door made Sarah tense. Assailed by a curious sense of déjà vu, as if she would find the same deliveryman with a new consignment of flowers, she opened the door. When she saw Gabe, she froze, too shocked to speak.

Before she could slam the door, he jammed his foot in place and planted one large palm flat on the door, holding it open. "I just need a few minutes of your time."

Chest tight, heart pounding, she did her best not to be mesmerized by his amber gaze or his fascinating scar. She was fiercely glad she had made an effort with her hair, which was wound up in a sexy knot that showed off the new caramel streaks her hairdresser had insisted she try. She was also wearing a high-waisted pale turquoise dress that was not only short enough to show off her legs, but also cleverly disguised the thickening at her waist. "You sound like a salesman."

"Technically, I'm an accountant, not a salesman."

The freely given fact about his life startled her enough that she almost weakened and let him in before she remembered that was one of the ways he had gotten her before. He had told her he had gone to Harvard to study business and she had been silly enough to think that with the prosaic nature of both of their occupations they had something in common. Determined to ignore the fascination of a man who looked like a battle-hardened warrior but had an affinity for figures—*and who had been a breathtaking lover*—she kept a firm grip on the door. "Why are you here?"

His gaze locked with hers for a burning moment that transported her back to a pitch-black night, rain pounding on her window, a breathless tangle of sheets and the heat of his skin against hers…

"I had to see you."

For a split second she was startled enough by the flat, declarative timbre of his voice that she almost weakened.

It almost seemed as if he had missed her and really had desperately needed to see her.

He frowned at her stubborn lack of response. "Did you get my roses?"

"I did."

"Let me guess, you gave them away."

"They were not exactly a happy reminder, since you left without saying goodbye and haven't bothered to keep in touch."

"But you knew I had to leave."

And she'd known that there were no promises made, on either side. Avoiding his gaze and concentrating instead on a point somewhere to the right of one mouthwatering cheekbone, she tried to nurture the fiery anger that flared whenever she considered just how much time had passed. But it was a fact that the night had been what it was: two people recognizing a mutual attraction and agreeing to sleep together. The only problem was she had been emotionally involved from the beginning.

"Thanks for reminding me." She glanced at her watch, which had a pretty turquoise band to match her dress. She tried to look as if she really was in a hurry even though the school term had ended days ago, and all she needed to do for the day was prep work for next term. "Now if that's all you have to say, I think you should go. I need to leave for work in just a few minutes." Besides that, she was beginning to feel nauseous and dizzy all over again.

Gabe's gaze seemed to pierce her, pinning her in place. "You're still working?"

His voice sounded oddly muffled, as if it were coming from a distance, although the thing that concerned her most was that something weird was happening to her vision. Vaguely, she realized she had lost her grip on the door and that Gabe had taken advantage of that fact by swinging it wide-open. Stumbling slightly, she reached for the solidity of the wall. "Why wouldn't I be?"

"I checked with your school. The receptionist said the school holidays had started."

Outrage that he had been sneaking around, poking into her life was tempered by a scary delight that he had wanted to do so. Suddenly, Gabe was close enough that she could feel the warmth of his body. It seemed the most natural thing in the world to clutch at one shoulder in a bid to stay upright. "This doesn't mean I've forgiven you." She tried to be crisp and stern, but the words sounded muffled.

His arm came around her waist. Just as everything faded to black she heard him mutter, "Damn, you are pregnant with my child."

When she came around she was lying on her couch in the sitting room and Gabe was in her house.

Tense and on edge that he had slipped past all of her defenses she cautiously levered into a sitting position. Apparently the sluggish maneuver had been way too fast, because her head started to spin again.

Gabe handed her a glass of water, which she would have refused on principle if she wasn't so thirsty all the time, and right now her mouth was as dry as a desert. Draining the glass, she set it down on the coffee table and glared at him. She was suddenly glad she had gotten rid of the roses, and hadn't allowed herself to weaken and keep any. "I don't remember inviting you into my house."

"That would be because you were too busy fainting." He loomed over her, the dark jeans and loose shirt he wore making him look lean and muscular and vital, while she felt limp and rung out. "I found your doctor's number by the phone and made an appointment." He consulted his watch. "If we leave now we might just make it."

"I don't need a doctor, there's nothing wrong with me—"

"You're pregnant."

She crossed her arms over her chest, which successfully minimized her tiny bump. "What makes you think I'm pregnant?"

Gabe dragged distracted fingers through his hair, making him look disheveled, younger and infinitely cuter. "Tarik."

Sarah's jaw tightened. That little man. It was a further confirmation she should never have gone near the consulate.

Gabe's gaze flashed broodingly over her. "Are you pregnant?"

Heat filled her cheeks. She couldn't lie. No matter how much she wanted to conceal the truth and keep the baby her secret. "Yes."

Seven

Forty minutes later Sarah was sitting in Evelyn's office while Gabe stood at a window, staring out at a slice of suburban Kilbirnie.

Evelyn strolled back into the room, throwing Gabe a glance filled with thinly veiled curiosity. Despite the fact that Sarah was still unhappy with Gabe and the way he had bulldozed her into seeing Evelyn, she couldn't help but feel a tiny glow of satisfaction that he was with her. If nothing else, it proved to Evelyn that while Sarah might have had bad luck with men in the past, at least this time she had chosen one who was certifiably gorgeous.

Evelyn handed Sarah a slip of paper with the results of her urine test. "It's not the best news. Your blood sugar is high, which makes you pre-diabetic. That accounts for the dizzy spells. It happens to some women in pregnancy."

Sarah stared at the test result. "That would also explain the thirst."

Evelyn gave Sarah a sharp look. "From now on you need to call me about anything unusual that happens. You'll need to manage your diet and I want you to have regular blood tests." Rummaging in her desk she found a diet sheet, which Gabe commandeered.

Gabe sent her a narrow-eyed glance then began asking Evelyn rapid-fire questions that indicated he had studied up on pregnancy. Evelyn crossed one elegant leg over the other and sat back in her chair, visibly preening as she smoothly answered his every question. Beginning to feel sidelined, even though she was the patient, Sarah pointedly got to her feet.

Evelyn stopped midsentence and blushed. Gabe instantly rose and cupped Sarah's elbow, in case she needed steadying. She didn't, she felt fine now, but it wasn't such a bad thing for Evelyn to understand that Gabe was here for her. Although the fact that Sarah should want to make any kind of statement at all was ridiculous because it smacked of jealousy.

When they reached Gabe's Jeep, he helped her up into the passenger seat. "You don't need to be jealous."

Sarah busied herself fastening her seat belt to disguise the fact that she was blushing furiously. "Why on earth would I be jealous?"

There was an odd, tense silence then Gabe closed her door with a soft *thunk*, walked around the bonnet and slid behind the wheel.

Enclosed in the intimacy of the Jeep the one burning question she hadn't had time to ask pushed to the fore. Jaw taut, she stared at Gabe's faintly hawkish profile as he turned into traffic. "Why are you here?"

He had already said he'd suspected she was pregnant, but she would have thought that news would make him run, not come back to her.

"If you're pregnant with my child that changes things."

"What things, exactly?"

He braked for a set of traffic lights. "I'm engaged to be married."

Fury channeled through her. If she could have found something to break in that moment, she would have broken it. Her reaction upset her. This unstable, passionate creature she seemed to be turning into wasn't her. She was normally calm and collected; she thought things through. She did not fly into rages. "I knew it. Although my guess was that you were married."

His brows jerked together. "I do not have affairs."

"But you cheated on your fiancée."

"I wasn't engaged at the time."

Her heart pounded even harder. What Gabe had said should have made the situation better, so why did it feel worse? "Let me get this right. You had sex with me then you went back to Zahir and got engaged. At least that explains why you never bothered to call."

He'd had more exciting options than a twenty-eight-year-old history teacher.

Her jaw set. "If you got engaged so quickly, you must have known your fiancée already."

Gabe pulled into her driveway. "No. It was an arranged marriage."

Horror transfixed her. "So that's why you slept with me. It was a last fling." She dragged at her seat belt, trying to unfasten it, but the mechanism wouldn't cooperate.

Gabe half turned in his seat, frowning, which only made him look more gorgeous. "It wasn't like that."

She fought against the lure of his fierce, warrior's gaze. "How was it then?"

There was a vibrating silence. "You know exactly how it was between us."

He tried to help her with the seat belt. Incensed, she pushed his hands away. "I can do this. I'm used to doing things on my own."

"You're not on your own any longer."

Even though she didn't want to feel anything at all for Gabe, his flat statement sent a dangerous hope spiraling through her. He had used the word *was* with his marriage, as if it was in the past tense. Added to that fact, he *could* have stayed on Zahir and simply ignored her. Instead he was here, *because* she was pregnant, taking charge, getting involved.

She stared at him, feeling crazily emotional, still angry but also on the verge of tears. "So how was it, exactly, between us?"

"Like this." Gabe cupped her jaw and out of nowhere the humming, tingling attraction she'd fought to suppress burst into fiery life.

He lowered his mouth, and foolishly she tossed away any thoughts of being sensible and controlled and let him kiss her.

Gabe closed Sarah's front door behind him and followed her into her sitting room. The heat that had surged through him at the kiss was still pulling every muscle in his body taut. But, aware of how badly he had mishandled things so far, he grimly controlled the need that had hit him.

As she opened French doors to let a cooling breeze in, he noticed a pad on the coffee table. Picking it up, he examined a list of names. "Tiffany, Tanesha, Tempeste..." He glanced at Sarah as she strolled out of the kitchen with two glasses of water in her hands. "Are these names for the baby?"

Setting the water down, she snatched the pad from his fingers. "They're just ideas."

"Any favorites so far?"

She snapped the pad closed. "It's just at the formulation stage. Names are important. You can't just choose any old thing."

While Sarah jammed the pad into the drawer of an antique sideboard, Gabe strolled to the French doors that opened onto a tiny deck and stared at the view over Wellington's harbor and hills. The fact that he was going to be a father hit him again, even more strongly than when Sarah had fainted. The situation was unbelievably complicated because it involved his commitment to Nadia and his country. But Sarah carrying his child changed everything.

He desperately needed to order his thoughts, to think like a Sheikh of Zahir and control the dangerous, possessive emotions that surged through him.

He needed to provide for Sarah and the baby, therefore the only possible solution was marriage. In order to marry Sarah, he would have to end his current engagement and solve Zahir's financial problems another way.

Given that his father would finally be a grandfather, and with the possibility of a future male heir to the sheikhdom in the pipeline, Gabe did not foresee that his father would hold to his stance against foreign investment.

His mind made up, Gabe turned from the view. Sarah was busy plumping cushions and tidying magazines. As she straightened, sexy tendrils of dark hair clung to her flushed cheeks, making her look both gorgeous and vulnerable. The light fabric of her dress swung against her abdomen, giving him his first real glimpse of the gentle swell of her belly. Another surge of fierce possessiveness hit him, and he frowned. Zahir's financial situation, tricky as it was, would not be a problem, but if he wasn't vigilant, what he was feeling could be. Marriage was a solution, but it could not be an unstable, emotionally based, marriage. Like the arrangement with Nadia Fortier, this too would be a marriage of convenience.

"So," he said carefully, "you're having a girl."

Sarah took a deep breath, repressing an uncharacteristic flash of temper that Gabe was extracting information from her about the baby before she was quite ready to tell him. "That's what showed up on the scan."

A curious emotion darkened his expression. Was it disappointment? Instantly she was up in arms on behalf of her child, a female baby who no doubt, in his country, was not as celebrated as a male child.

"Evelyn said you have a copy of the ultrasound. I'd like to see it."

He watched the video file through without a word then almost immediately replayed it again.

He closed her laptop. "The baby changes things. We need to make arrangements."

Her heart pounded out of control at his words, because in that moment she realized he was going to suggest the one thing she had wanted from him over four months ago: a relationship.

Although she wasn't sure how she felt about any of that now. Half of her was melting inside, teetering on the brink of hope, the other half still blazing mad that he had left her alone for so long. "What did you have in mind?"

He extracted a platinum card from his pocket.

The temper she had been trying to keep a lid on spilled out. "If you think you're going to start paying my bills, you can think again."

Before he could stop her, she grabbed the card, marched out on the deck and threw it over the side, down onto the lawn below. "I don't want your money, so you can forget it. Forget me—"

"I can't." With a swift movement, he pulled her toward him so that she found herself plastered against his chest.

His mouth came down on hers. She could have ducked her head or pulled away, but her precarious mood had taken another swing, from fury straight to desire. She didn't like what was happening. She didn't want his money. But after the sweet, tender moments in his Jeep, which had spun back the clock, with every cell in her body she wanted him to kiss her again.

Long, dizzying minutes later, she pulled free. Her mouth tingled; her body was on fire. She loved that he still wanted her, but they had been in this place once before. That time she had gotten pregnant. Before anything else life-changing happened, she had to be clear about whether or not they had a chance at the one thing that was important to her in a relationship: love. "Where, exactly, are you in this scenario?"

She finally identified the glimpse of emotion in his eyes that had baffled her from the moment she'd first seen him at her door—not quite cool detachment, but wariness. "I'm proposing marriage."

Her legs went weak at his blunt statement. "What about your fiancée?"

"First I'll need to go back to Zahir and terminate the agreement with Nadia."

The word *terminate* sent a chill through her. Had he not felt anything for his fiancée? At the name Nadia, alarm bells rang. Sarah walked back inside and sat down, her legs feeling wobbly. She had read something about an engagement in Zahir online. Suddenly the way Tarik and the consulate receptionist had behaved in protecting Gabe began to make perfect sense.

Gabe had said he was an accountant. It was possible he simply worked for the sheikh as part of his business team, but she was beginning to think Gabe was something more than that.

She remembered the piece of paper with Gabe's full name on it, which she had ripped up and tossed away before she'd read it properly. She thought she might have glimpsed the name Kadin somewhere. Her stomach plunged as a wild notion occurred to her, a notion that made sense of all the cloak-and-dagger behavior surrounding Gabe's identity and whereabouts. "Who are you, exactly?"

"My full name is Sheikh Kadin Gabriel ben Kadir. I'm not the ruling sheikh. That's my father, but I will rule one day."

Eight

Gabe, *Sheikh Kadin Gabriel ben Kadir*, insisted he take her to lunch while they talked over the situation. Too shocked by his announcement to refuse, Sarah found herself courteously helped into a gleaming Jeep. As Gabe pulled away from the curb, she took better note of the vehicle, which was brand-new and luxurious. Now, too late, all the subtle clues about him registered, like the way he had spoken to Tarik—not as a subordinate, but as someone in command. The fact that he'd had accommodations at the consulate, and that he'd gone to Harvard. Of course he was a member of Zahir's ruling family.

His gaze touched on hers. "How do you feel?"

"I'll feel fine when you explain why you didn't let me know who you are."

She noticed they were heading away from the city into the wilder hill country.

Gabe stopped for an intersection. "The same way you didn't let me know you're an ancestor of Camille's?"

She flushed at the quiet statement, although it wasn't as if she had concealed *her* identity. "How did you find that out? No, wait, let me take a wild guess. The son of a sheikh, with bodyguards and an impenetrable security force field around you? I'm betting you had me investigated."

"We had unprotected sex—"

"So you had to find out exactly who you had gotten entangled with." A horrified thought occurred to her. "I suppose you thought I was some kind of adventurer, maybe even a journalist."

He turned into a very beautiful, secluded drive that, from the signage, led to an exclusive private resort. "I didn't tell you I was a sheikh because I thought all we would share was the one night. And I knew you were exactly what you said, a history teacher, but the investigative process went ahead because security protocols still needed to be satisfied."

"And you were worried about a pregnancy." Her fingers tightened on the strap of her handbag as he parked beneath a shaded portico and a uniformed valet opened her door. "If you had left me your contact details, you could have saved yourself the trouble. I would have told you."

There was an uncomfortable silence as she climbed out of the Jeep. Gabe handed the keys to the valet. They were shown to a restaurant with a fabulous cliff-top view of the ocean. As he took a seat opposite her, she glanced around at the other diners. They were without exception beautiful, very well-groomed people with perfect tans. Most of them, even the men, were dressed in shades of white and cool pastels. Dressed as she was in vibrant turquoise, with her hair wisping damply around her face, all of the elegant restraint made her feel overly bright. It shouldn't have mattered, but the restaurant suddenly made her see the gulf in lifestyles that existed between her and Gabe.

"What's wrong?"

She frowned, hating that she was actually allowing herself to be stressed-out by surroundings that were formal and just a little pretentious. "I can't relax in this place. What if I need to be sick?" Just the thought made her feel queasy.

His gaze sharpened. "Do you feel unwell?"

"A little. It comes on suddenly."

The waiter who was delivering beautiful leather-bound, gold-embossed menus, blanched. Within minutes Gabe had canceled their reservation and the valet had delivered the Jeep to the portico. Gabe opened the passenger-side door, but instead of simply helping her up, he clasped her waist and boosted her into her seat.

Breathlessly, she released her hold on his shoulders. "I could have gotten in by myself."

"Since we're engaged, I thought we should start getting used to the idea of being a couple."

She blinked at the subtle way he was trying to bulldoze her into agreeing to marry him. "I haven't said yes yet."

He released her, but there was a curious relief in his gaze as if he liked that she wasn't jumping at his proposal. Although, she wasn't so sure *she* liked the idea that if they were to marry he would be happy with a certain distance in their relationship.

When Gabe slid behind the wheel, she directed him to

a small beachside café in Lyall Bay that was casual and cheerful, with enough background noise that they could have a conversation without being overheard.

Gabe shrugged out of his jacket and dragged off his tie. With the sea breeze ruffling his hair, he looked breathtakingly handsome. While they ate he asked questions about her family and supplied details about his. It shouldn't have surprised her that he knew her cousin, Laine—who had sent Sarah the journal—and who was married to the Sheikh of Jahir, a distant relative of Gabe's. But the fact that he was close to that branch of her family was reassuring. As big a leap as it was, it somehow made it easier to imagine being married to the next Sheikh of Zahir.

Marriage to Gabe. For a split second, her heart pounded out of control. Her last two attempts at getting married had both ended in disaster and she couldn't quite believe that this one would work out.

When they'd finished, Gabe suggested they take a walk on the beach. When he clasped her hand in a loose hold, a dangerous thrill went through her because even if Gabe didn't feel the romance of what they were doing, she did, and she was afraid of being too happy. Her experience of happiness was that once you thought you had it in your grasp, it was snatched away. "Are you certain you want marriage?" Taking a breath, she offered him an alternative that would dispense with the need for a relationship altogether. "Sharing custody is an option."

Gabe stopped and pulled her into a loose hold, his gaze oddly fierce. He hooked a loose strand of hair behind one ear, the small possessive gesture sending another sharp little thrill through her. "We're both mature, educated people. There's no reason we can't have a… successful marriage."

Sarah frowned at the way Gabe framed marriage, as if it was something one had to be qualified for, even while his measured response reassured. After all, with a baby on the way, if she was going to marry, she needed her husband to be responsible and trustworthy.

When Gabe dipped his head, she allowed the kiss and tried not to love it too much. Reluctantly, she planted her palms on his chest and kept her gaze fixed on the pulse jumping along the side of his jaw, because if she looked at his mouth or into his eyes, she would kiss him again. "We can't make love until…things are settled."

"Until you've agreed to marry me."

Her chin came up and this time she met his gaze. "Yes."

It was a fact that they couldn't get engaged until Gabe had ended his current arrangement. And Sarah knew better than anyone, a lot could go wrong between an engagement and the altar.

Two weeks later, Sarah, finding her state of relationship limbo a little too lonely after Gabe had gone back to Zahir went online to indulge her new favorite hobby, searching out news about Zahir and the ruling family.

During the two days they had spent together, they had eaten out and gone for walks. Gabe had sketched in brief details of his life, including the startling fact that he was a widower. When he'd flown out they'd agreed to stay in contact by phone. However, he hadn't called for a whole week now, and the silence after the long, cozy calls had her worried even though he had mentioned the possibility of sketchy cell phone coverage. With time passing she was beginning to have flashbacks to the silent, empty months that had followed the one night they had spent together.

Worse, she was beginning to think she had been foolishly optimistic in trusting that Gabe would choose her over Nadia Fortier. She needed to know more about his engagement, even if it was just internet gossip. And she needed to know more about the wife he had lost.

Her mother, who made a habit of dropping in unexpectedly, walked through the door, just as Sarah found a reference site. Hannah, who was naturally suspicious of Gabe, paused beside the screen, which was currently displaying a dated story about Gabe's engagement. "If you were having a boy, he would have put a ring on your finger immediately."

Sarah blinked at the flamboyant outfit her mother was wearing. A saffron-yellow dress over blue leggings. Cobalt-blue earrings made her short, spiked blond hair look even more startling. "What makes you say that?"

Hannah fished in her bag and placed cold cups of fresh fruit smoothies on the table. "Stands to reason. The sheikhdom is patriarchal, so only male children can rule, specifically the first male child. If the baby was a boy, he would be the next sheikh."

Sarah picked up her smoothie, took a sip and decided she would have to tell her mother the truth. "Gabe proposed. I'm the one who hasn't agreed, yet."

Hannah stared at her as if she'd just landed from Mars. "I thought you wanted to marry him?"

"I do." But only if Gabe truly valued her and their baby girl. Only if there was the possibility of love.

Hannah dug two salad rolls out from the depths of her bag and plunked them down on the table. "You've wanted to get married for years. Now you're dangling one of the most eligible, *hot* men on the planet?" she sat down and peeled plastic wrap off a roll. "Sometimes I don't know you."

With difficulty Sarah refrained from pointing out that her mother had just expressed two conflicting views about Gabriel. "Is it such a bad thing to not want to make another mistake?"

Too irritable to eat, she searched a site she normally never bothered with, because it was full of the kind of magazine articles and sensationalized gossip that normally didn't interest her. Moments later she found a short article posted just two days ago. She stared at a photo of Nadia Fortier in a skimpy bikini lying on a dazzling beach, a glass of champagne in one hand.

Nadia was accompanied by a broad-shouldered, dark-haired man who had his back to the camera. Sarah's heart stuttered to a halt in her chest. It looked like Gabe, and the text confirmed it. Apparently, Gabe and Nadia were spending some quality alone-time at a secret hideaway in Tuscany before the wedding.

Sarah pushed to her feet so fast the chair went flying. So much for angsting about Gabe's dead wife, when it was the gorgeous young fiancée she should have been worrying about.

At the periphery of her vision she was aware of her mother, staring at her with a frown. Sarah righted the chair, too focused on Gabe's blatant betrayal to try to appear normal or calm.

She had begun to trust him again. She had liked his phone calls, especially when he'd called late at night and she'd been snuggled up in bed.

His behavior during their two days together had made

her think he would be a wonderful father. She had seen it in his absorption with all the aspects of her pregnancy. She had loved it when he had fussed over her when she'd felt tired and ordered takeout. The next day he had insisted on stocking her pantry with healthy low-fat food.

But it had all been a smokescreen. He had lied. He hadn't gone back to Zahir to make any kind of arrangement that would benefit her and the baby. He was spending his time wining and dining his beautiful, slim fiancée at some swanky Italian *castello*.

And in that moment Sarah knew why she had been both ecstatic and miserable for the past two weeks. It wasn't just that her hormones had been running riot. She had been busy falling head over heels in love with Gabe all over again—the father of her child and a man who would be marrying someone else in three months' time.

Her mind was spinning. She could scarcely believe how completely Gabe had deceived her. Although this kind of betrayal had happened to her before.

Sarah glared at the grainy, blurred photo, which had obviously been taken with a telephoto lens, and clicked on the mouse to close the site. Caught between fierce anger and utter misery, she walked out onto her small deck, barely registering the humid grayness of the day, which was a whole lot different from the arching blue sky and blistering heat of Tuscany. A brisk wind laced with spits of rain flattened her dress against her body and sent her hair flying. So much for her improbable daydreams of moving to Zahir, of Gabe really and truly falling for her once they had time to spend together.

Trying to stay calm, she walked back into her sitting room, which was cluttered with baby paraphernalia: a pretty white bassinet and piles of bright fluffy toys. She picked up a pink bear Gabe had sent, and which was so ridiculously large it occupied its own chair. Fury boiling over, she marched the bear through to the spare room and jammed it in the closet, out of sight.

Slamming the door, she leaned against it, breathing hard.

Hannah, who had been making tea in the kitchen poked her head around the corner, looking concerned. "Are you all right?"

"Yes." No. "Eat your lunch, I'll be out soon. Promise."

Maybe the photo and the article hadn't portrayed the absolute truth. She had to stop reacting emotionally and start operating on the facts. The only way she could reliably gather facts was to go to Zahir.

Returning to the computer, she found a travel site and searched for fares. Once she had made bookings, she felt shaky but glad she had acted. She had lost two potential husbands because she had not cared enough to actively claim her man. But this time was different. Her heart and her baby's future happiness were both at stake.

She was over sitting quietly at home. Whether Gabe liked it or not, she was joining him on Zahir.

In just two days' time she would no longer be Sheik Kadin Gabriel ben Kadir's guilty secret.

Nine

Gabe walked into Gerald Fortier's office in Paris flanked by Xavier and Hasim, Gabe's personal assistant, just ten minutes short of midnight. They were all wearing the formal business attire of Zahir: well-cut suits, white shirts with ties and white kaffiyeh headdresses fastened with black rope *agals.* Kadin's *agal* was differentiated by the badge of his family, a lion rampant.

This was a meeting he had demanded ten days ago, after he'd received information that Nadia was not staying with an aunt in the South of France as her family had claimed but instead was shacked up with an Italian count in Tuscany. Fortier, clearly aware that Gabe could declare the marriage contract null and void on the basis of it, had ducked the meeting until now.

Gabe presented his ID to a doorman who seemed mesmerized by his scar, the headdress and the entourage.

Seconds later, they stepped into the elevator to the penthouse suite. When they emerged, Fortier was standing at a large plate-glass window, staring out at the spectacular view of Paris at night and the glittering landmark of the Eiffel Tower.

Fortier turned to face Gabe. As always the older man's expression was smooth and urbane, although when he noted the kaffiyehs, something usually reserved for formal or ceremonial occasions, his dark gaze became wary. He consulted his wristwatch, as if he were in a hurry to leave despite the late hour. "You're lucky you caught me, I have a plane to catch."

"To Tuscany?"

Fortier's expression paled as he indicated they should sit down on the comfortable black leather chairs grouped around a coffee table.

Gabe ignored the offer of a seat. He produced a photocopy of a snippet from a French newspaper where Fortier had stated Gabe was holidaying in Tuscany with his daughter. "You know very well I've been in New York and the United Arab Emirates for the past few days."

Fortier placed the page on the coffee table. "It was a solution. Damage control."

"Only if I still wished to marry your daughter."

Fortier stiffened. "There's no reason our agreement can't stand, especially since a substantial partial payment has been made. The agreement is sealed."

"Not any longer."

Fortier plowed on as if Gabe hadn't spoken. "Of course I can compensate you for a certain…breach of the conditions."

The breach being that Nadia was no longer a virgin and, according to the report Gabe had received, hadn't been for quite some time. Gabe also happened to know that Gerald Fortier had been well aware of that fact when he'd signed the marriage agreement.

Until Gabe had spent that one night with Sarah he hadn't realized just how much integrity in his relationships mattered. "I'm afraid," he said softly, "that part of the agreement is nonnegotiable."

There was a small, tense silence. Fortier's gaze flickered over Xavier and Hasim, who were flanking Gabe in an unmistakably military fashion. Fortier jerked at his tie. "In that case I will require immediate and full repayment of the funds you've received."

Gabe kept his expression neutral. With the small constitutional change Gabe's father had made, repaying Fortier would not be a problem. "You'll have the money as soon as the finance I've arranged with a New York bank is approved. In return I'll make certain that the information that Nadia is having an affair is not leaked to the press."

Fortier's face went dead white then flushed bright red. "Thank you."

The man's momentary loss of control informed Gabe that, for all his faults, Fortier cared about his daughter's reputation.

Turning on his heel, Gabe led the way to the elevator. Within an hour he was back on the small jet he had chartered. The engagement was now null and void, although he couldn't allow himself to celebrate just yet.

His mother was quietly over the moon that Gabe wanted to marry a New Zealand girl and that there was a grandchild already on the way. Breaking the news to the general populace of Zahir, however, would be a more delicate issue.

Preparations for the wedding were almost complete. Invitations had been sent and hotels had been booked out. The cancellation was a matter that would have to be handled by the public relations experts. Although Gabe was certain that once the tourism minister got hold of the fact that Sarah was a descendent of Camille de Vallois, he would leverage the information into a wave of public approval that would smooth over the fact that he was changing brides.

Grinning at the thought that finally there was a practical application for the romantic story of Kadin and Camille, he dropped into a leather seat. Taking out his cell he logged the string of missed calls from Sarah and tried to call her before the jet taxied onto the runway. It was something he hadn't been able to do while in the remote hill country of Buraimi.

When the call went to voice mail and Sarah didn't respond on her cell, he checked his messages. There were two from Sarah. He listened to the cool, low register of her voice as she requested that he contact her. The last message had been left four days ago.

Grimly, he tried calling Sarah again. When there was no reply, he turned his cell off. If there was an issue with the pregnancy, Sarah would have said so in one of the two messages she'd left, and which he hadn't been able to pick up because there was no cell phone service in Buraimi.

Xavier, who had been talking to the pilot, dropped into the seat beside him. "A problem?"

"Nothing I can't handle."

He'd been away from Sarah for two weeks. Two weeks too long. He had missed her.

His jaw tightened at just how much, because a part

of him didn't want to be subject to the whims of desire and the havoc it could wreak.

While the other part of him couldn't wait to have her back in his arms.

Zahir glittered beneath the scorching noonday sun as Sarah paid the bellhop who had delivered her bags then strolled through the cool, spacious hotel suite she had reserved for the next ten days.

After changing into a white cotton dress, she collected her camera and a notebook and took the elevator to the ground floor. Evelyn had reluctantly given her the all-clear to travel after her blood test had been much improved. Now that Sarah had moderated her diet the dizzy spells had abated and she was feeling much more energetic.

She strolled out onto one of Zahir's narrow, quirky streets, loving the heat and the quaint lime-washed buildings clinging to the hills and cliffs that rimmed most of the bay. Zahir was also home to a cluster of beautiful resorts, all owned by the sheikh. The resorts had all been built to blend with the historic old city and looked more like ancient villas and palaces than actual hotels.

Lifting her camera, she took several shots to catch the panoramic view then started down the steep hill to the main street, which ran along the shoreline and was famous for its cafes and souks. As she strolled, she frowned at the sight of a sign in Zahiri and English congratulating Sheikh Kadin on his upcoming marriage. Festive ribbons and lights strung across the streets and huge planters spilled richly scented flowers in celebration. Her mood dropping, she lifted her camera and snapped a photo. If she had wanted confirmation that the wedding had not been called off, this was it.

The zeal she'd had to gather information then fling it at Gabe when next he contacted her abruptly flatlined. It was all very well playing detective, but it didn't feel so good when the results seemed to confirm her worst fears. Feeling deflated, she stopped to buy a cold drink at a small bustling café.

The pretty English waitress who served her was breezy and chatty and happy enough to answer the few halting questions Sarah asked.

She set a cool drink in front of Sarah. "Almost no one's actually seen Nadia. I think her family are keeping her under wraps until the day, you know? Although, if you go online you'll find a few photos. She's young and drop-dead gorgeous. Apparently she used to be on social media until the engagement was set in concrete, then—" she made a slicing gesture across her throat "—nothing."

Sarah took a desultory sip of her drink, which was a delicious sweet-sour concoction of plum and lemon, laden with ice. "I guess Gabe—the sheikh, can be controlling."

The waitress gave her a disbelieving look. "I was talking about Nadia's father. Kadin is a whole different kettle of fish, a total babe. A lot of women have tried to entice him into marriage, but since he lost his wife, he hasn't been interested." She shrugged, her gaze turning soft and a little dreamy. "I guess he must have really loved her. Rumor is that's why he agreed to an arranged marriage this time around. He can't have Jasmine, but he needs an heir. Oh, and of course, the Fortiers are rich. I'm guessing that helps."

Sarah set her glass down, suddenly losing any desire

for the drink or the conversation that had gone with it. The pipe dream that she could have a marriage, maybe even true and lasting love, with Gabe was receding fast. She had thought Nadia Fortier was the only problem but, according to the waitress, Nadia came in a bad second because he was still in love with a first wife that he'd almost never mentioned!

Tired and on edge after the night flight from Paris, Gabe negotiated Zahir's main street traffic, his temper on a tight rein as he noted the displays of ribbons and strings of colored lights, and the congratulatory messages that were appearing despite the wedding date being weeks away. His phone vibrated. He took the call while he waited at a traffic light.

Xavier, who had been met by his wife when they'd landed, sounded weary. "An Italian tabloid has gotten hold of the story that you're supposed to be holed up in a *castello* in Tuscany with Nadia. What do you want me to do?"

"What we always do, nothing." With any luck the fact that he had openly spent two days in New York and the past week in Dubai would discredit the gossip. "Any luck getting hold of Sarah?"

"Same luck you had. She's not answering her phone. Tarik went around. She wasn't home."

The sense of unease that had gripped him when he hadn't been able to get hold of Sarah before the flight from Paris returned full force. He tensed at the thought that she might have had another fainting episode. Maybe the diabetes had worsened and she'd been admitted to the hospital. He had thought she was okay now that her diet was under control. But it was always possible she had suffered some other complication.

Suddenly the distance between them, a distance he had thought he needed in order to control his own emotions—was a barrier he was no longer prepared to tolerate. As soon as he could locate Sarah, he would make arrangements to have her fly out to Zahir. Jaw taut, he instructed Xavier to keep trying to locate Sarah, including checking the hospitals.

A thought occurred. Sarah had told him the man she'd dated the night she and Gabe met at the consulate, Southwell, had once broken into her house. It was possible he'd come back to harass her again. "And check on Southwell."

Even though Sarah had finished with him, Gabe couldn't rule out the fact that Southwell might try to make another move on Sarah. "One more thing, ask Tarik to check the airport manifests just in case Sarah has left the country."

Gabe hung up as the light changed. He inched forward in the heavy traffic. He was probably overreacting. It was possible Sarah had gone away for a few days, although that didn't explain why she hadn't called or answered her phone. Wherever she was, she would still have a cell phone, which meant she was choosing to be out of contact with him.

He frowned at that thought. Usually, Sarah was more than happy to talk for as long as he wanted to stay on the phone. For her to close off all communication meant something had happened. His fingers tightened on the wheel. At a guess, she had picked up on the scandal brewing around Nadia.

The fact that Sarah had reacted by closing him out,

the kind of manipulative tactic Jasmine had often used, should have had him backing off from the relationship. Instead, he thought grimly, it was having the opposite effect and for good reason. Even though he was certain Sarah was emotionally involved with him, she had also made it crystal clear that vulnerability was optional: she could get along without him.

Gabe braked as a truck pulled out from the curb and brooded on the prospect that Sarah might have made the kind of bold, declarative decision she seemed prone to make and ditched him. Caught in traffic, surrounded by the hubbub of a hot Zahiri day, Gerald Fortier's manipulation still leaving a bad taste, it was an odd moment for Gabe to reach a point of absolute clarity about the future.

He had made a mistake in leaving Sarah alone for so long. It was a mistake he would not make again. Now that he had terminated the agreement with Fortier, he was going to insist he and Sarah get engaged immediately.

Gabe had almost reached the palace when Xavier rang with the news that Sarah had left New Zealand and landed in Zahir that morning.

Fierce satisfaction curled through Gabe. Sarah hadn't run from him, she was here, on his island. And there could be only one reason: she had come after him.

She loved him, he was suddenly certain of it. Nothing else explained why she had let him make love to her in the first place and then been willing to take him back, even after he had left her flat.

The thought that Sarah was committed enough to come to Zahir in search of him should have sounded alarm bells, but the relief that she had done so somehow canceled out any recoil he should feel. He had dreaded Jasmine's brand of intense, cloying love, but he found he did not feel the same way about Sarah. If Sarah was in love with him then, as far as he was concerned, that provided a counterbalance to her strong will and a measure of certainty he needed. The desire to consolidate their relationship with marriage settled even more firmly into place. He registered that Xavier was still talking.

"Uh—as it happens Southwell is also on Zahir, but they're not staying at the same hotel and they didn't travel together."

Frowning at the irritating specter of Southwell, Gabe did a U-turn and headed for the hotel. He braked for a stream of pedestrians crossing to a waterfront souk. A woman dressed in white with dark, caramel-streaked hair arranged in a sexy knot caught his eye. He couldn't see her face, but something about the confident feminine stride spun him back to a stormy night in Wellington.

Traffic moved at a snail's pace as the woman in white paused at the entrance to the souk. Hitching the strap of her handbag a little higher on her shoulder, she checked her watch. Gabe's heart slammed against the wall of his chest. He would recognize the elegant shape of her cheekbones, the smoky slant of her eyes and that delicate, faintly imperious nose anywhere. It was Sarah.

There was no place to park on the congested street, so he backed up a few feet, waited on traffic then turned down a narrow lane that ran down one side of the souk. There was no official parking, just dedicated loading bays for the stallholders. He found a space at the back of a diamond merchant's shop and parked.

As he locked the car, the security guard for the merchant, a tall heavyset man dressed in a suit, stepped into the loading bay. His grim expression changed when he noted Gabe's signature kaffiyeh and *agal*. Moments later, the security guard was joined by the owner, who assured Gabe he could leave his car for as long as he wanted. The effusive offer was followed by a sales pitch on a line of diamond earrings that would make Gabe's future bride melt with desire.

Gabe assured the owner of the souk that if he required diamonds, he would be sure to consider him. It was a fact that now that the way was clear to marry Sarah, he would need a ring. It would seal the engagement and be a tangible sign that Sarah was his.

He found himself wondering what kind of diamond Sarah would like. It was not the kind of question that had ever consumed him before. Jasmine had insisted on choosing her own ring, and he had never known what Nadia liked; the ring she had received had been chosen by Hasim. But Gabe had an intimate knowledge of Sarah's tastes: fresh flowers and spicy food; old-fashioned, mismatched dinner plates; colorful, funky kids' clothes. *His* kid's clothes.

Stepping out into the main thoroughfare, Gabe skimmed the press of shoppers that flowed like colorful flotsam through the streets. Most were Western tourists, drawn here by a media campaign that had been formulated by Zahir's young and aggressive minister of tourism. A Harvard graduate Gabe had met while he was studying, Faruq Malik was intent on selling Zahir as an island of romance, history and mysticism.

Faruq had left no stone unturned in his attempt to resurrect the mystery of Camille's lost bridal dowry and the first Sheikh Kadin's ancient romance. He had even invented new aspects to the story, claiming that the moon had been full the night of the wedding and that the vows had been exchanged at midnight.

Gabe glimpsed a cool flash of white in a sea of vibrant reds, blues, oranges and glaring pinks. He made his way through eager streams of shoppers, all avid for gold and silks, jewel-bright rugs and exotic spices, until he reached the silk merchant's shop that Sarah had entered.

A group of Japanese tourists were clustered around the counter. Sarah half turned as he entered the shop, a sumptuous drift of berry-red silk held draped against her body. For a split second, Gabe was riveted. The sensual richness of the cloth seemed to make her skin glow and her eyes seem even darker and more exotic.

Red. It was her color.

Sarah's gaze passed blithely over him then zapped back. *"You."*

The fiery glare spun him back to the conversation in his Jeep when Sarah had discovered he had gotten engaged straight after they had made love. She had been angry and then she had kissed him.

A purely masculine satisfaction filled him. If Sarah had been disconnected and indifferent, he would be worried, but she wasn't. She was mad, her glare pointed and highly personal as if everything that was wrong was his fault. Which, if she had read the gutter-press story claiming that he was holed up with Nadia in Italy, was understandable.

In the heat of that glare, he found himself feeling oddly at home, as if they had just picked up on a half-finished conversation. In that moment he realized how much he'd missed the long phone calls and the electrical connection that seemed to hum between them. Crazily, putting distance between them had done nothing to lessen what he felt for her.

"Sarah. What a surprise to find you on Zahir."

Ten

Unwillingly arrested by the traditional kaffiyeh and *agal*, which had distracted her from recognizing that it was Gabe filling the shop doorway, Sarah dumped the red cloth back in a bin filled with colored silks. The low timbre of his voice shivered through her, but she refused to be seduced by it. Been there, done that, she thought grimly. Didn't want the T-shirt.

She dredged up a cool smile. "I'd hate to miss your wedding."

In the dim interior of the shop, dressed in a dark suit with the kaffiyeh, his jaw stubbled as if he hadn't had time to shave, his amber eyes gleaming in the shadows, he looked exotic and even larger and edgier than she remembered.

Her anger and hurt that he had not canceled his wedding and had spent the past couple of weeks at some

Italian *castello* with Nadia dropped to a slow simmer as Sarah registered how utterly out of place Gabe was in a silk merchant's shop. That could only mean that he had seen her and followed her into the shop. The thought instigated a flicker of pleasure that she could not allow to make headway, given that Gabe had betrayed both her and their baby and from all accounts had enjoyed every moment of it.

Her anger bolstered by that thought, she lifted her chin another notch and decided she had nothing to lose by the direct approach. "Where's Nadia?"

A deathly silence descended on the shop.

Gabe glanced at the number of women filling the shop. "We need to talk…elsewhere."

Dimly, Sarah realized there seemed to be a lot of women holding cell phones. Cell phones equaled photographs, social media, maybe even a video of the conversation. She imagined it was the kind of situation that had happened to him in Tuscany.

When she didn't immediately follow his order, Gabe gave her the kind of irritated look that made her feel like *she* had betrayed *him.* A split second later she found herself hustled out into blazing sunlight.

Gabe gave her a searing glance as he threaded his way through a stream of shoppers and into a shaded alleyway between merchants' shops. "I haven't been with Nadia. I've been in the Emirates negotiating with a building contractor for most of the past week. Finding cell phone coverage is difficult. Does that answer your question?"

She dug in her heels, halting them both and tried not to notice that with the snowy-white kaffiyeh framing the masculine planes of his face, Gabe looked almost fiercely beautiful and completely at home in the sun-drenched souk. “So that wasn’t you at the *castello* in Tuscany?”

He said something curt beneath his breath. She was fairly certain it was one of his swear words. “Since I’ve never been to Tuscany, no, it wasn’t.”

He hadn’t been with Nadia. Relief surged through Sarah, making her feel faintly dizzy. Silly, emotional tears pricked at the backs of her eyes.

Blinking furiously, she searched in her bag and found a tissue. “Who was it, then?”

“Raoul Fabrizio. Some Italian count.” Gabe ducked down and peered into her eyes. “Damn, you’re crying.”

As she dabbed her eyes and blew her nose, she found herself eased into a loose embrace. The deep rumble of his voice and the steady thud of his heart were oddly soothing. She drew a shallow breath, and the clean scent of his skin laced with the irresistible whiff of sandalwood that she had worked so hard to forget made her tense. After days of stress and fury it was hard to adjust to the fact that he wasn’t the villain she’d been building up in her mind.

Sniffing, she blew her nose again. “I never cry. It must be the pregnancy.”

When she searched for a second tissue, he handed her a beautifully folded handkerchief. “How have you been? Have you put on weight?”

She stared at the monogramed handkerchief, which was too beautiful to use, and tried not to be seduced by the deep, velvety timbre of his voice. She glared at him. “Do you really care?”

A couple of tourists strolling in the direction of the beach, towels slung over their shoulders, glanced at them curiously.

Gabe frowned. "We can't talk here. If you'll come with me now, I know a place where we can be private."

Sarah checked her wristwatch and tried to look like she was on a schedule and wasn't quite sure if she could fit Gabe in. "Will it take long?"

"You've got other appointments?"

A fresh wave of hurt and anger fountained up at the note of incredulity in Gabe's voice, as if pregnant, abandoned history teachers did not have appointments. "I'm not on Zahir for a holiday. Now that I've got a child to support, I'm starting a new career as a travel writer."

His brows jerked together. "You don't need a job. I'll support you and the baby."

She pulled free of his hold, fire shooting from her eyes. "I will not be dependent on you."

"I didn't ask you to be."

The calm timbre of his voice somehow defused the anger that kept trying to erupt, conversely leaving her feeling vulnerable and unsure. Sarah decided she preferred the anger.

Gabe indicated they should follow the couple with the towels. Aware of him close behind her, a few steps later Sarah found herself in a service lane lined with vans and small trucks.

The sidelights of a sleek black sedan with darkly tinted windows flashed as Gabe unlocked the vehicle. Sarah stopped in her tracks. "You said we would talk somewhere in private, not that you wanted to put me in a car and drive me somewhere."

He looked momentarily arrested as he held the passenger-side door. "It's not that sinister. All I want to do is find somewhere private to talk where we won't be overheard. I've got a beach house five minutes away. If you don't want to go there, we could go to your hotel."

Her eyes widened. "You know where I'm staying?"

Frustration burned in his gaze. "Zahir's not exactly a big country—"

"So you sicced some kind of Zahiri secret service on me."

"It wasn't that high-tech. Xavier called the airport."

Sarah climbed into the luxurious Audi and tried not to like the chill of air-conditioned air and the smell of new leather. "Your henchman. I should have known."

Gabe closed the door then walked around and slid behind the wheel. "Xavier's not a henchman. We decided not to have those a few years back. He's head of palace security. Mostly he checks locks and alarm systems. Occasionally he checks out people who are close to the family."

She fastened her seat belt and tried not to love the sexy quirk to Gabe's mouth as he took off the *kaffiyeh* and *agal* and tossed them on the backseat. Instead she needed to remember how easy he found it to forget about her.

His comment about people close to the family got her attention. "But your family doesn't actually know about me."

His gaze dropped to her mouth, making her heart pound. "Of course they know about you and the baby."

Feeling mollified and altogether calmer now that she knew he had actually told his parents about her, she relaxed back into the cloud-like seat. Deliciously cool air washed over her as Gabe accelerated into traffic. He stopped for a stream of pedestrians heading for the souks and Sarah stiffened as her cell phone chimed. Aware of

Gabe's proximity and that he would hear every word she spoke, she picked up the call from her mother.

The conversation was brief. Hannah wanted to know how Sarah was and if she'd checked into her hotel. She also wanted to let her know that she had heard from a mutual acquaintance that Graham was on Zahir.

Sarah frowned at the mention of Graham, who must still be on his wild-goose hunt for the missing dowry. After their last meeting when he had broken into her home, she had no interest in seeing him ever again. Luckily, with all the holidaymakers on Zahir, the chances that she and Graham would actually cross paths were slim.

Gabe turned down a narrow driveway that flowed beneath a shady grove of ancient olives. He brought the car to a halt outside a villa built on a small rise overlooking a tiny, jewel-like bay. "Was that Southwell?"

Sarah grasped the door handle. It would be a simple matter to say it was her mother, but after the past week of turmoil and uncertainty, she still felt ruffled and hurt. "I don't think that's any of your business."

Leaning across, he pulled the door shut, trapping her in place. "I don't want you seeing Southwell."

For a moment she was close enough that she could see the faint shadows under his eyes, as if he hadn't gotten a lot of sleep, and the intriguing roughness of his five-o'clock shadow. "I wouldn't see Graham Southwell if he was the last man on earth."

He let go of his hold on the door. "Who were you talking to, then?"

She wanted to stick to her resolve to leave Gabe in the dark about her personal life, and let him experience a little uncertainty. But with Gabe close enough that she could feel the heat blasting off his body and breathe in his clean masculine scent it was difficult to think straight. Unfortunately, she was also seduced by the dizzying notion that Gabe was jealous. If he was jealous, that meant he did care for her. "It was my mother."

His gaze dropped to her mouth, sending a sharp tingle of heat through her. "My apologies," he said curtly. "But I was worried about you. Southwell is on Zahir, too."

She tried not to stare into his irises, which really were a mesmerizing hue of amber, striped with chocolate brown. "Graham comes here a lot. Besides being an importer, he's obsessed with finding Camille's dowry."

He *was* jealous. A dizzying surge of pleasure flowed through her, warming her from the inside out so that she was practically purring. "Did Xavier make a call to find out where Graham is?"

Gabe's gaze narrowed, signaling that she was playing with fire, but she didn't care. As wary as she was about what he might feel for her, she loved him. He was the father of her child and he'd been gone for over two weeks, and in that time she had *missed* him. Added to that, she had thought she was on the brink of losing him to a woman she was certain he did not love. As far as she was concerned she had a right to the truth.

"To be strictly accurate, Xavier asked an investigative firm to confirm Southwell's movements."

But Gabe had paid for the report. She had to suppress the sappy desire to grin. "Isn't that a bit paranoid?"

"Not from where I'm standing. I needed to know that he wouldn't come near you."

He *was* jealous.

Feeling suddenly giddy that not only had Gabe not slept with Nadia, but that in the time he'd been absent, he had actually worried about her, she pushed the door wide and stepped out onto a pristine white shell drive.

Gabe gestured at a path that led to a shady patio overlooking the sea. He unlocked and opened a set of French doors. She stepped into a sitting room shaded by shutters. Tiled floors were strewn with bright Zahiri rugs and low, comfortable couches were strategically placed to make the most of the stunning view.

Gabe walked through to a sleek kitchen that opened off the sitting room. "Would you like a drink?"

The polite request distracted her from checking out the beautiful house that was obviously not Gabe's primary residence since it had been shut up for some time. "Water will be fine."

She heard the opening of the refrigerator, the chink of ice. Gabe indicated she should take a seat. When she did so, she found herself staring at a vivid oil painting of a woman seated in an enclosed garden, wearing a vivid flame red dress.

"Camille." Gabe handed Sarah a frosted glass then strolled to the open doors to stare out at the view.

Gaze drawn to the broad width of his shoulders emphasized by the snug fit of his suit jacket, Sarah sipped a mouthful of water. Unable to bear the silence, she asked, "What did you want to talk about?"

He turned, his expression oddly neutral. "Us. As of last night I'm no longer obligated to marry Nadia. I'm proposing that we should get married next month."

Eleven

For long moments, Sarah thought she had heard wrong. She set her glass down on the beautiful ebony table, careful not to spill any water on what looked like a precious antique. "You really mean it, you want to marry me?"

Gabe's expression was still curiously neutral. She realized the descriptive she should be using was "guarded."

Given his worry over Graham, she knew Gabe had feelings for her. But she was also aware that his approach to marriage was just a little too businesslike. He hadn't said he loved her, and he very probably didn't at this stage. Her stomach dipped when she realized he almost never mentioned his first wife.

The reality was that for now the pregnancy was dictating what happened next, but Sarah had hoped for something more, a glimpse of the warmth and love they could share once they were living together.

Despite her efforts to stay just as guarded as he, her heart swelled with emotion. The problem was, she thought a little desperately, that she loved him and she wanted to marry him—even if he didn't feel the same right now. "Next month?"

He mentioned a date and her stomach plunged. She knew that date. It was engraved in fiery letters on her heart. Despite her effort to stay calm, she found herself on her feet, too upset to sit. "I presume you mean the same date you were going to marry Nadia?"

"Yes."

The cautious joy that he did still want to marry her was swamped by annoyance. "Let me guess, the wedding venue is booked, the guests are invited and there's no wedding without a bride?" She knew how that went, since she'd had to cancel wedding plans, twice.

"I know it's not ideal, but it's a fact that we need to get married soon, and the wedding, which is important for Zahir, has been arranged."

"I understand the practicalities." But it was hard to feel cherished and special when the proposal sounded as forced as Gabe's last engagement, and when she was being offered a second-hand wedding.

Still caught in the curious ambivalence of receiving the proposal she wanted from Gabe but in a way that sounded more like a transaction than a relationship, Sarah paced to the portrait of Camille.

A small heated tingle shot down her spine as she registered Gabe close behind her. Determined to control her response to him, she concentrated on the painting. "She had style."

"She was a woman who knew what she wanted."

Sarah couldn't help wondering if that was how Gabe

viewed her. "Is there anything wrong with knowing what you want?"

"Not as long as it means you'll say yes and marry me."

She swung around, his words sending a bittersweet pang through her. She had thought he hadn't noticed that she hadn't actually agreed to marry him yet. They had made plans back in New Zealand, but all of that had been tentative, knowing he had to end things with Nadia first.

Sarah wanted marriage, but only because she truly believed he might fall for her over time. She guessed she had hoped he might view their relationship as more than just a solution. "Do you want to marry me?"

His expression closed up and she wondered if she'd said something wrong, then his hands curved around her upper arms, seductively warm against her skin.

"We're good together. We like one another. We're going to have a child."

And the lovemaking had been off the register. Two weeks ago it had seemed almost enough. "What about the money?"

"Money is no longer an issue for Zahir." Gabe's fingers meshed with her's, pulling her close. "I want you, Sarah, and I think you know that. I have spent weeks making and breaking deals to have you. Will you marry me?"

Time seemed to slow, stop. She had wanted to change her life, to take risks, and she had. Now there was no way she could go back to the flat and endless routine of her old life. This version of life might be hurtful, but at least she knew she was alive.

Above all, she had to think about the baby. If there was a chance for them to be a real family, she had to take it. "Yes."

Relief flared in his gaze. He bent and touched his mouth to hers.

The slow, lingering kiss sent a hot pang all the way to her toes. Before she could stop herself, she clutched his shoulders, lifted up and deepened the kiss. This was what she had wanted, what she had longed for even when trying to be cautious.

Gabe's arms closed around her, fitting her even more closely against him. Relief flooded her as she felt the firm shape of his arousal pressing against her hip. His blunt, masculine response was a reassurance that, in the wake of the article claiming that he was with Nadia, she badly needed.

When he lifted his head, she boldly wound her arms around his neck and instigated another lingering kiss. When Gabe dragged pins from her hair so that it cascaded around her shoulders then lifted her against him so that her feet left the ground, the eroticism of it sent a flush of heat through her.

When he lowered her to the floor, she felt the cool leather of a couch at the backs of her knees. With a tingle of excitement, she realized he had carried her there while they'd kissed.

He tangled his fingers in her hair, his gaze burned into hers. "Are you well enough to make love?"

Heat burned through her at the question. "I'm fine, never better."

He kissed her again. They were going to make love. The reality of it, when an hour ago she was in the depths of despair, was faintly shocking.

With fingers that fumbled slightly, she unknotted his silk tie then started on the buttons of his shirt. Irresistible flashes of the last time they'd made love kept making her heart pound out of control. There were a lot of things about their relationship that needed working on, but she couldn't help thinking that this part was absolutely perfect.

Minutes later, with her dress lying puddled on the floor, Gabe lowered her to the leather couch. He had already dispensed with his jacket and shirt, and now eased out of his pants. As he tossed stretchy gray boxers on the floor, she drank in the sight of him, naked. In her bedroom, at night, he had been beautiful. In full daylight, the hot Zahiri sunlight making him look bronzed and sleek and muscular, he was breathtaking.

He joined her on the couch, his weight pressing her down. Automatically, she moved to accommodate him. His gaze locked with hers and a faint tension assailed her as she felt him lodged against her. Now that marriage and a baby were part of their equation, she was worried that she might disappoint him in some way. After all, she was not a glamorous jet-setter like Nadia, or a fragile beauty like his first wife.

A split second later the worry ceased to be important as she held her breath against the exquisite moment of their joining. He kissed her then pulled her closer still, holding her tight against him as if he needed her, as if she truly mattered to him, as they moved together and the afternoon dissolved in a blinding shimmer of heat.

Much later, after they'd both showered and dressed, Gabe found his cell and pressed a speed dial. "Hasim will take care of the change to the invitations. Meantime, I'll need you to stay on in your hotel and keep our engagement under wraps until the palace issues a press release."

Still caught in the rosy aftermath of lovemaking, the

sudden switch to the "business" of the wedding was a little jarring. Sarah picked up her handbag and adjusted the strap over one shoulder. "Stay in the hotel, as in lay low?"

Gabe's gaze settled on her mouth and lingered. Not quite all business, then, she thought with relief.

"It would be expedient. Once the press get hold of this they'll go crazy—"

Whoever Gabe was calling picked up. He half turned away while he spoke in rapid Zahiri. A few minutes later, he hung up and slipped the phone back in his shirt pocket. "That was Faruq, the minister of tourism. He'll take care of the press release. Once the announcement is made, we can move you into the palace."

Gabe drove Sarah back to her hotel, taking the time to question her about her and the baby's health, wanting verbatim accounts of exactly what Evelyn had said. Sarah couldn't help basking in his concern. To her mind, like the beautiful, off-the-register lovemaking, it was a sign that he was falling for her.

Feeling bemused and a little dreamy after the hours they'd spent making love, Sarah strolled into the deep shade of the hotel's portico. Graham's sudden appearance as he popped up from a café table caught her completely off guard.

His gaze swept her with that hint of disbelief she still found irritating. As if updating her look had somehow changed her beyond all recognition. Still intensely annoyed with Graham for breaking into her house and copying the journal, she fixed him with a flat glare. "What do you want?"

"Do I have to want something?"

When he opened his arms as if they were actually going to hug, Sarah stepped back, neatly avoiding the fake intimacy. “In my experience, yes. Although I thought you’d already gotten what you wanted.”

Unfazed, Graham fell into step beside her as she strolled into the gorgeous mosaic tile lobby.

“Mostly. I think I’m finally onto something, I just need you to decipher the piece of the journal that’s still written in Old French—”

“No.” Sarah stepped into an elevator. As the doors slid closed, Graham’s expression was red-faced and belligerent, but she didn’t care. She was too absorbed with Gabe to pay attention to Graham.

The elevator doors opened on her floor and she found herself staring blankly at a pair of probable honeymooners, their eyes starry, skin tanned, bright new wedding rings gleaming on their fingers.

As she strolled to her suite, she checked her watch, dazed at how little time had passed. Just over three hours since she had left. And yet in that time Gabe had found her, proved their attraction was still fiery and tingling with life. They had made love and the engagement had been confirmed.

Pulse speeding up at the memory of their lovemaking, she stepped into her suite and caught a glimpse of her reflection in the mirror by the door. She touched a red mark on the side of her neck. She remembered Gabe’s jaw scraping her tender skin, the ripple of sensation that had gone through her at the utterly sensual caress, as if he couldn’t get enough of her.

She drew a deep breath as it sank in just how much she had changed.

She was no longer the dry, low-key history teacher who had stayed in Friday, Saturday…let’s face it, *every night.* She was the kind of risk-taking woman who attracted a sheikh and who, after one wildly passionate night, was carrying his child.

Gabe had made love to her as if she was desirable, as if he couldn't resist her. As if she belonged to him.

Just as she knew that Gabe was hers.

A little startled by the clear, bold thought, she set her bag down and strolled to the refrigerator to get herself a cold drink. Carrying the ice water back to the sitting room, she sat down on the sofa and booted up her tablet. After the conversation with the waitress in the café, she was even more curious about Gabe's first marriage. Maybe she should have asked him about it, but she hadn't quite been able to broach the subject because she had wanted him to confide in her.

Minutes later, she had turned up an old tabloid report that seemed to confirm everything she'd heard. Gabe and Jasmine had been childhood sweethearts and married young. She had died tragically in a boating accident.

Another search turned up a series of photographs of Jasmine, fragile and breathtakingly pretty, an enormous diamond solitaire sparkled on her finger.

A ring. It was a small detail and something Sarah and Gabe hadn't spoken about, something they hadn't had time for, yet.

The phone rang. When Graham's voice registered, she slammed the receiver down then took the phone off the hook. For good measure she also turned her cell off then went back to her tablet.

A couple of hours later, a rap on the door woke her from a nap. She checked the peephole in case it was Graham. It was Gabe.

Still feeling on edge about Gabe's almost complete

silence about his first wife, she opened the door. Gabe was obviously freshly showered and looked utterly gorgeous in dark pants and a light, gauzy shirt. "I didn't expect to see you so soon."

His gaze narrowed as he picked up on the coolness in her voice. "I tried to ring but your cell seems to be turned off, and the hotel phone is off the hook. There's been a change of plan. I've arranged a house for you to move into. It was originally a fortress, so it's more secure than the hotel. If you can collect your things I'll take you out now, then I thought we might go out for dinner."

She stiffened at the calm way he was making arrangements, as if he'd smoothly moved past the minor glitch of almost losing her. Before she could stop herself, the question she'd promised herself she would not ask burst out of her. "Why don't you ever talk about your first wife?"

His expression turned bleak. "The marriage ended years ago."

Her fingers tightened on the doorknob. "But you haven't forgotten her."

"My wife died, that's not something I'm likely to forget."

Instantly, she felt guilty and contrite that she'd stirred up painful memories. Although that didn't stop her wondering if the reason Gabe wasn't falling for her was because he was still in love with his dead wife.

A group of cleaners, one pushing a trolley filled with cleaning products, strolled past, their expressions openly curious.

Gabe kept his gaze firmly fixed on her. "Why did you turn your phones off?"

Her brows jerked together at the probing question. She had only had her phones off for a couple of hours, while Gabe had been incommunicado for a whole week. "I bumped into Graham in the foyer. He tried to follow me to my room, then he started calling."

"Southwell." Gabe straightened, a grim fire burning in his gaze. "That's why I've arranged the shift to the old fortress."

He glanced at the cleaners who had stopped a short distance away and who seemed fascinated by their conversation. "We can't discuss this in the corridor. Are you going to let me in?"

A little thrill shooting down her spine, she stepped back as Gabe stalked into her suite.

Closing the door, he crossed his arms over his chest. "What did Southwell want?"

"He wanted me to translate some Old French from the journal."

Gabe looked briefly arrested. "You know Old French?"

"I did a couple of papers in historical linguistics." She shrugged. "I'm not as good as Laine."

He shook his head, the grimness morphing into an expression that made her heart race, as if he liked her quirky, oddball education, more, as if he liked *her*.

He shook his head slightly. "Damn," he muttered. "Back to Southwell. If he ever comes near you again, call me immediately. And if you're thinking of arguing about the move out to the house, you can forget it. I need you safe."

Another small thrill shot down her spine at the flat series of commands, most especially the last statement, that Gabe needed her safe, as if her safety was personally important to him. And in that moment she knew that Gabe's feelings toward her were neither neutral nor businesslike.

She had a sudden flashback to the night of the cocktail party at the Zahiri consulate, the moment when Gabe had walked out of the stormy night to rescue her.

The gloom that had enshrouded her when she had been focused on Gabe's wife, Jasmine, dissipated. She had been concentrating on the past, but what was happening right now was significant. Gabe had gone out on a limb for her. He had changed his country's constitution, brokered deals and canceled his marriage contract. He wanted her—enough that he'd made her pregnant. Now he wanted to put her in a fortress to keep her safe.

They were not the actions of a businessman wanting a marriage of convenience; they were the actions of a warrior with a passionate heart. A heart that had *not* been buried with his wife.

Twelve

The drive out to the house, which was situated on a cliff above Salamander Bay, took fifteen minutes along a narrow, winding road. The house itself stole Sarah's breath, because although it had been extensively remodeled it was clear that the original structure had once been a cliff-top fortress.

Gabe introduced her to the resident housekeeper and gardener, Marie and Carlos.

She chose a room that had white walls and dark floorboards strewn with jewel-bright rugs, and which contained a huge four-poster bed draped with a filmy mosquito net. Light and airy French doors opened onto a stone balcony, and like many of the rooms she'd glimpsed, there was a spectacular view of the sea.

Sarah quickly unpacked then dressed for dinner in a softly draped red chiffon dress that floated off her shoulders and clung in all the right places. When she walked downstairs, Gabe strolled in from the terrace, which opened off a large sitting room that seemed filled with antique furniture and artwork.

Her interest piqued, she examined the carving on a chest that inhabited one corner of the room. "This must be a twelfth-century piece if it's a day. Looks like it came off a ship."

"It came off Camille's ship, the *Salamander*. It's one of the few objects that survived the wreck." He nodded in the direction of the terrace. "If you want to see the remains of the *Salamander*, the outline of the hull, which is mostly buried, is still visible."

Sarah followed Gabe out onto the windswept terrace.

Gabe leaned on the parapet, as he pointed out the shadowy outline of her ancestor's ship, still visible where it had foundered in the rocky shallows of Salamander Bay.

Once she had seen the wreck, he hurried her back inside. "We need to discuss meeting my parents and we need to do it fast, because they're on their way here."

The sharp chiming of the doorbell sounded in the distance.

Gabe's expression turned rueful. "Too late. They've already arrived."

Moments later Sarah heard the click of high heels on ancient flagstones as Maria showed the Sheikh of Zahir and Gabe's mother into the great room.

The sheikh was tall and lean with a dark, penetrating gaze. Forty years on, Gabe would look exactly like him. Gabe's mother was slim and medium height. Despite being in her fifties, with her dark blond hair smoothed into a stylish short cut, she looked a good ten years younger than her husband.

The instant Hilary Kadir saw Sarah her face softened, and Sarah knew it was going to be all right.

Hilary gave Sarah a hug. "Your name's Sarah?" Sarah barely had time to nod before Hilary continued. "Are you all right? Is he treating you okay?" She shot Gabe a faintly accusing look then smiled apologetically before introducing herself and her husband.

The sheikh was kind, but formal. From the paleness of his skin, Sarah guessed he was still unwell, so she hurried to offer him a seat then blushed because she'd been here less than an hour, and the house belonged to the Kadir family.

Hilary smiled. "We're sorry for the ambush, but when I heard you were pregnant I couldn't stay away. Since Jasmine—"

"Mom."

Hilary frowned at Gabe and sent Sarah an apologetic look. "If we'd known there was a baby, we would have been in contact a whole lot sooner."

Marie arrived with a tea tray.

Broodingly, Gabe watched as Sarah fielded his mother's questions. Until that moment he hadn't realized how on edge he had been about this particular meeting.

The turnaround in his thinking was immense and complete. He had gone from an organized, convenient marriage to marrying a woman he wanted. It was the exact opposite of the situation he had planned.

Gabe's father was understandably cautious about the relationship, even with a baby on the way. Gabe knew that the biggest obstacle for his father right now was accepting the money situation, but he had finally handed the financial reins over to Gabe with his blessing.

His gaze rested on Sarah as she talked with his mother, who was a talented linguist. Whimsically, he wondered what his mother would think when she found out that, like her, Sarah could read Old French. Sarah reached up and adjusted a pin in her hair, and the memory of what it had felt like to have those strands cascade over his hands in a silky mass made him tense.

Dispassionately, he examined why he was so attracted to Sarah. Possibly it was because, with her double degree and forthright manner, she was as unlike Jasmine as it was possible to be. Although that wasn't the whole of it, and the way he reacted to Southwell was a case in point.

Gabe considered the thought that he was jealous and dismissed it. Sarah was pregnant with his child, she was going to be his wife and Southwell was an unsavory character. There would be something wrong with him if he didn't react possessively.

Hilary smiled at Sarah, her gaze narrowed shrewdly as she and her husband got ready to leave. "You love him, don't you? I can tell."

Sarah felt heat rise up in her cheeks. "Yes."

She let out a breath, gripped by the thought that it was really that simple. She loved Gabe and she had from the first. A lot of things had happened that should have killed that love, but through all the reversals and the stinging betrayal of finding out he was engaged to Nadia, she hadn't let go. Somehow her emotions were stubbornly anchored. She couldn't imagine losing interest in Gabe; everything about him fascinated and drew her. She even loved his occasional bad temper because when it came down to it she would rather fight with Gabe than spend time with anyone else.

Although she had to be careful not to let him know that.

"He likes you," Hilary said quietly. "And I think he's over the moon that you're pregnant. A lot of marriages have started with less."

Gabe took Sarah to a small restaurant down on the waterfront, which had a private room. Seated on a balcony right over the water, the setting couldn't have been more romantic. Although the dinner had a practical aspect. While they ate, Gabe filled her in on more family information, including the names of about twenty cousins, most of them female, and a raft of children.

"After meeting my mother you'll understand why you need to know this stuff. She's big on family."

"I like your mother." They'd chatted for ages, and Sarah had hemorrhaged most of her life story, including the two failed engagements. As appalled as she'd been over spilling those kinds of details, in the end she hadn't minded because there had been a genuinely compassionate streak to Hilary Kadir.

After dinner, Gabe took her for a walk along the waterfront. The romanticism of the moonlit walk was somewhat marred by the fact that a very large bodyguard trailed them all the way.

She glanced at the guard, who was trying to look inconspicuous, but at six feet eight inches, with huge shoulders, that was difficult. "Do you always have a bodyguard?" Offhand she couldn't remember seeing one in New Zealand.

Gabe looped his arm around her shoulders, drawing her close. “It depends. Sometimes I slip the leash.”

Half an hour later, Gabe dropped her off at the fortress house. He hadn’t suggested they sleep together, which had been obsessing her through the evening, because after what had happened at the beach house that afternoon she had assumed they would continue to sleep together. When his fingers tangled with hers when she opened the door, relief made her feel a little shaky and she found herself inviting him in.

The house was dark except for a couple of lamps left burning in the sitting room. Sarah automatically gravitated to the balcony, with its view. Gabe’s arms came around her and it seemed the most natural thing in the world to turn and kiss him. Long minutes later, he pulled her inside with him.

The perfumed warmth of the night air flowed around them as they undressed in her room. Somehow the more leisurely pace, so different from the fierce interlude in the beach house that afternoon, seemed even more intimate. Breathlessly she realized that this time they had all night.

With easy strength, Gabe swung her into his arms, lowered her to the bed and came down beside her. He cupped the small mound of her stomach then one rounded breast and she logged his curiosity.

“These are different.”

“They changed almost immediately.”

He bent his head and kissed each breast. The sensations low in her stomach coiled, tightened.

He lifted his head. “Do you want me to use a condom?”

The roughness of his voice and the jolting practicality of his question registered, but somehow couldn't mar the magic of the night. He hadn't asked the question when they'd made love earlier. She ran her hand down his chest, loving the heated feel of his skin. "Why use one when we don't need it?"

He went very still. "Are you sure?"

Her breath suddenly locked in her throat. "Unless there's a reason that you should use one."

"There isn't. I haven't been with anyone since you."

Out of nowhere joy hit her. His words weren't a declaration of love, but they were significant. She touched the scar on his cheekbone, running the tips of her fingers gently across the smooth tissue. He captured her hand, deliberately possessive as he bent and kissed her again. She clutched at Gabe's shoulders, drawing him close, lifting against him. This time their lovemaking was quieter, deeper, and as the night slowly unraveled around them she felt that something precious and right had flared to life between them.

She woke to gray morning light and the sound of Gabe in her shower. He dressed in the clothing he'd worn the previous night and dropped a kiss on her cheek. Since he didn't have any clothes at the house he had to return to his apartment at the palace to change. Feeling sleepy and bemused, Sarah agreed to meet him for lunch.

Gabe made a quick call to the guard who had looked after them last night, arranging for him to pick her up around eleven.

After Gabe had gone, Sarah had a leisurely breakfast out on the terrace then checked the palace's events online, noting that there was an open day today. It was part of the tourism promotion around the wedding, so the palace was bound to be crowded. Some spin doctor called Faruq seemed to be running everything.

Since it was now supposed to be her wedding, she decided to take a risk and join a tour, despite Gabe's warning to stay out of sight for now. A tour of the palace as an anonymous tourist would fill in time before lunch, and provide more background information about Gabe's family before she became an official part of it.

After changing into an ice-blue dress that looked fabulous with her new tan and a pair of sexy heels that were comfortable for walking she strolled downstairs, talked to Maria about the car in the garage and managed to get the keys.

The sun burned down on the acres of perfectly manicured grounds and the elaborate wings and towers of the palace. The building itself was impossibly beautiful and romantic. To imagine that she would live there one day soon seemed a dream.

Humming beneath her breath, Sarah took the tour, journal in hand. Despite seeing photos, the palace took her breath away with its vaulted ceilings, marble columns and mosaic floors. Most of the tour seemed concentrated in the reception rooms that would be used for the wedding, and those rooms were filled with a buzz of activity as exquisite furniture was polished, fresh paint applied to paneling and the gilding on the high, ornately plastered ceilings was retouched.

As she lingered in a hallway that resembled an art gallery, a slender young woman, accompanied by two large men in suits with the unmistakable look of bodyguards, strolled by.

Shock reverberated through Sarah as she recognized

Nadia. With her hair trailing in loose, sexy tendrils, a gold-and-diamond pendant hanging suspended in the faint shadow of her cleavage, her wrists coiled with elegant bracelets, she looked more like a fashion model than the young heiress portrayed in her engagement photo.

Sarah's stomach lurched. There could only be one reason for her to be here; Nadia was trying to get Gabe back.

After all Sarah and Gabe had shared yesterday and last night, she shouldn't worry about Nadia's machinations. Yet she couldn't help but wonder—was this why Gabe hadn't wanted Sarah to come to the palace?

Thirteen

Frowning, Sarah watched where Nadia went as the tour trailed into a formal library that was in use by the family. Sarah glanced into a room that opened off the library and caught a glimpse of a familiar set of broad shoulders.

A small shock went through her. She hadn't expected to see Gabe. He had told her he would be in meetings all morning. Although of course, he hadn't said with *whom* he was meeting. Adrenaline zinged through her as Nadia strolled into view and it became obvious that Gabe was meeting with his ex-fiancée. In that moment the door to what must be Gabe's office closed, blocking Sarah's view.

Feeling ruffled and upset, because she had thought Nadia was out of the picture completely, she found herself marching toward the closed door. Popping it open, she breezed inside as if she was expected.

Gabe, who was leaning against a gleaming mahogany desk, turned his head, his gaze clashing with hers. Nadia stared at Sarah, clearly annoyed at the interruption.

Sarah plastered a steely smile on her face and kept her gaze on Gabe. "Darling, I hope I'm not interrupting anything important. I just wanted to check what time we were going to buy the engagement ring, before lunch or after?"

Marching up to Gabe, who looked taut and sleekly urban in a dark suit and pristine white shirt, a royal-blue tie at his throat, she went up on her toes. Curling her fingers into the lapels of his jacket, she kissed him on the mouth, noting the glint of amusement in his gaze.

His arm curled around her waist, holding her close. "How about before lunch?"

"Good, I'll just go and finish the…research I was doing next door." Kissing him one more time for good measure, Sarah made a beeline for the door.

Gabe's voice stopped her in her tracks. "How long will the research take?"

"I'll be researching until you're finished in here."

"That's what I thought."

Nadia started speaking in low, rapid French. Sarah, who spoke French fluently, understood fighting words when she heard them, then the door swung closed behind her, cutting off Gabe's reply.

Adrenaline pumping, Sarah walked straight into the tour group again, but she was no longer interested in the architectural and interior wonders of the palace. Peeling off, she practically jogged through the large library toward a set of French doors that opened onto a courtyard. Since the library was next to Gabe's office, if she walked outside, she should be able to hear what was going on between him and Nadia.

Tiptoeing over the paved courtyard outside, she sidled through a thick tropical shrub and peered into Gabe's office. Frustrated when she couldn't see anything, and wondering if somehow she had gotten the wrong office, she circumnavigated a tub of flowers and a trellis festooned with a dark, glossy creeper, to peer into the window.

"See anything interesting?"

The rough timbre of Gabe's voice spun Sarah around. When the heel of one shoe caught in the gap between pavers, she grabbed at a bunch of foliage to keep herself upright. "Not yet."

Gabe pulled her out of the shrubbery and picked a leaf out of her hair. "I thought we agreed you wouldn't come to the palace—"

"Because I'd find out you're meeting with your fiancée?"

"Ex-fiancée."

Sarah extracted herself from his hold. "It didn't look that way a few minutes ago."

"What you just saw was Gerald Fortier sending his daughter in to apply pressure. Apparently, he thought if I received a little 'encouragement' and an extra financial carrot, I'd go ahead with the marriage."

She stared at Gabe's stubbled jaw and an intriguing mark on the side of his neck. She could feel herself blushing at the memory of just how he had gotten that mark. "And were you encouraged?"

He cupped her nape, drawing her close. Dipping his head, he touched his mouth to hers, the kiss tingling all the way to her toes. He lifted his head. "If I was 'encouraged' do you think I'd be out here with you?"

She clutched at the lapels of his jacket again, using them as a convenient anchor. "I'm not going to apologize for making a scene." She had lost her last fiancée to another woman; she would not risk losing Gabe.

"Nadia Fortier's gone. Xavier's taken her back to her hotel. He's putting her on a chartered flight back to Paris this afternoon."

Gabe ushered her back through the library and into his office. "Now that you're here, I have something for you. I was going to give it to you at lunch, but with the damage Fortier's caused with leaked photos and documents, it needs to happen now. Faruq has set up a press conference straight after lunch, and I'd like you to attend it with me."

"You're going to officially announce our engagement?"

Gabe opened a wall safe and extracted a set of keys. In succinct tones he outlined the information that would be given to the media. In light of the fact that both he and Nadia had discovered they were not as compatible as they had first thought, they had ended their engagement. But, after the deepening of a relationship with a previous flame, a descendent of the de Vallois family, the wedding would proceed, just with a different bride. "We won't announce the pregnancy straight off. We can do that a few days before the wedding."

Sarah stiffened at the sanitized version of how the whole tangled situation had unfolded. There was nothing untruthful in the statement, but it was definitely constructed to distract attention away from the more scandalous aspects of the story.

Indicating that she should precede him, Sarah stepped out into the beautiful, echoing hall. Closing the door behind him, Gabe's hand dropped to the small of her back. A small tingle of pleasure went through her at his casual possessiveness as they strolled past tourists and palace staff who now stared at her with open curiosity.

A man in a suit acknowledged Gabe with a lift of his hand and fell into step behind them and the reality of her situation struck home. As Gabe's wife she would have to get used to security.

Gabe opened a heavy wooden slab of a door and they descended an ancient stone stairwell, leaving the brightness of day for the hard glow of artificial lighting. The dry coolness grew, enough to raise gooseflesh on her arms.

Gabe glanced at her, shrugged out of his jacket and dropped it around her shoulders. "I forget how cold it gets down here."

The jacket instantly swamped her with heat, sending a reflexive shiver through her. They stopped at another door, this one smaller in size and alarmed.

When Gabe had disarmed the door, she followed him into a room that had probably once been a cellar. He halted at a steel door that was utterly twenty-first century high-tech, unmistakably a vault, and tapped in a code. Depressing the handle, he pushed open the thick door.

The small room was lit with halogen bulbs and lined with metal shelves containing glass-fronted cabinets filled with ancient books, scrolls and archives that instantly piqued Sarah's interest. As an historian she loved examining original documents, although she seldom got the chance since most ancient texts were too fragile to be handled. There was also a series of locked steel cabinets and boxes. "Is this where the dowry used to be kept?"

Gabe checked through the ring of keys and found the one he wanted. "It was kept here, but in those days the security was primitive, just two locked doors and old-fashioned iron keys, which was why the dowry needed moving when the island was evacuated."

Gabe chose a cabinet, unlocked it then withdrew two midnight blue velvet cases. Setting them down on a sleek metal table that occupied the center of the vault, he opened the smallest. Already prepared for the fact that he was probably going to give her a ring because they were in the palace vault and she would be presented as Gabe's fiancée that afternoon, Sarah was still stunned.

The ring wasn't the old family jewel she had expected, borrowed for convenience. Made by a staggeringly exclusive jeweler, the oval-shaped sapphire rimmed with diamonds was modern and breathtakingly gorgeous.

Extracting the ring, Gabe picked up her left hand. "May I?"

Sarah blinked back ridiculously sentimental tears as he slipped the ring onto her third finger. It was a moment she had experienced twice before but which had never been more important or filled with emotion. "It's beautiful." And it fitted perfectly.

He opened the other flat velvet box, which contained equally gorgeous drop earrings and a pendant. "You'll need these, as well. After lunch, Faruq's arranged for one of the designer boutiques to outfit you for the press conference."

Still feeling a little misty, the businesslike necessity of the press conference grounded her. Sarah tucked the velvet boxes in her bag and minutes later they walked out of the dim lower rooms and back into the airy lightness and clamor of the palace.

In the end, lunch with Gabe was canceled because Faruq, a small quick man who looked more like an accountant than a marketing genius, insisted Sarah not only needed an outfit, but that she must have her hair, nails and makeup done. Hilary Kadir, who had joined them, agreed to take Sarah to her stylist. Surrounded by palace staff, suddenly the responsibility Gabe carried hit home. It explained his calm, measured manner, the lack of outward emotion that sometimes felt like coldness. She knew for a fact that he was neither cold nor emotionless, but with cameras constantly pointed at him and literally thousands of people dependent on him, he would have learned early on to maintain that steely self-control.

Two hours of relentless pampering later, wearing a slim-fitting royal blue jacket and skirt that deepened the color of her eyes, her hair smoothed into a glossy, thick swathe and tucked behind her ears to show off the earrings, Sarah walked into the press conference with Gabe. Already warned about the hot lights and the camera flashes, and prepped on what she should and should not say, she did her best to keep her expression serene.

The questions came thick and fast, although Gabe blocked most of them with a flat "No comment."

Thanks to the genius of Faruq, who had also briefed the press beforehand and had plied them with champagne and canapés, the sticky territory of their fling before Gabe had gotten engaged to Nadia was barely touched upon. Apparently, Nadia was now old news. The story everyone wanted was the love affair between the sheikh and the schoolteacher, a mismatch that carried echoes of Zahir's romantic past.

Annoyed by the idea that they were a mismatch, but bolstered by the positive atmosphere, Sarah allowed the beautiful ring to be photographed. When one of the journalists asked Gabe if he had finally gotten over Jasmine, and wanted to know what it felt like to be getting married again, Gabe pushed to his feet, pulling her with him. Thanking the press, his expression cold, he propelled her from the room.

A security guard fell into step behind them. When they reached Gabe's study, he took a call. His already grim expression turned icy. He glanced at Sarah, but seemed to barely see her. Curtly, he informed her that something urgent had come up then instructed the guard to see Sarah back to the cliff-top house.

As Sarah followed the guard out of the palace, the fact that Gabe had some emergency to cope with took second place to the question that was burned into her mind. The one that had abruptly ended the press conference and which she had hoped she had put behind her.

Was Gabe over Jasmine?

Fourteen

Sarah glanced in the rearview mirror as a sleek black sedan nosed out of the parking lot behind her. Feeling more and more upset as the minutes ticked by, Sarah pulled into the parking lot of the cliff house. She needed some air, without her guard, the six foot eight, Yusuf.

Changing into light jeans and a cotton camisole with a tight white cardigan buttoned over top, she checked to see where Yusuf had gone. When she heard his voice in the kitchen, she picked up her camera and bag and sneaked out a side door. When she reached the car, still in the clear, she turned the key in the ignition and pointed it down the drive. In her rearview mirror, she saw Yusuf race out onto the drive.

Adrenaline pumping, she turned onto the coast road. Her phone rang, but she didn't answer. Once she got to the bottom of the cliff, she would text the number he had given her before she had left the palace and let him know she would be an hour at most. A second turn and she was winding down the hill to the parking lot at the beach.

She drew a swift breath as Salamander Bay came into view, wild and beautiful and still almost devoid of habitation. As she brought the car to a halt in a parking lot occupied by half a dozen vehicles, she climbed from the car, feeling miserable, but consoled by the wildness of the spectacularly beautiful white sand beach with its high rock promontory that ran like a dark finger out to sea.

After texting Yusuf, she took a photo of the beach, which was occupied by sporadic bathers and the occasional bright umbrella. Turning, she took a shot of the rock promontory, which was brooding and spectacular, then she walked down onto the sand. She took a couple of snaps of the dark, brooding cliff face crowned by the fortress, which occupied the highest point in the bay, a square set against the onslaught of the wind with a sole crenellated tower.

Still feeling terminally unsettled because she was worried that Gabe was still in love with Jasmine, and that he wasn't willing to trust Sarah with that truth, she walked out along the rock promontory. The extra height gave her a better view of the beach and the place that was the wreck site of the *Salamander*. Sunlight glittering off polished metal caught her attention. A black sedan had just pulled into the parking lot.

She couldn't believe it when Graham emerged from the car and had the nerve to wave at her. She pretended not to see him and continued taking photos.

Irritated beyond belief that he seemed to find ways to insert himself into her life, she walked a little farther along the rocks. A wave, larger than any she'd yet seen, almost completely submerged the rocks ahead. Spray exploded, close enough to wet her. Suddenly aware of the danger and kicking herself for not being more careful, she tucked the camera in its the bag and started for shore.

Her stomach tightened as a flash of movement alerted her to the fact that someone was walking toward her. A curious sense of inevitability gripped her as she turned to see Gabe, still dressed in his formal suit. "Let me guess. Yusuf called you."

"You weren't supposed to leave the house without him." His gaze was trained steadily seaward. "Didn't you read the sign?"

"What sign?"

The sound of another large wave hitting rock spun her around, cold spray drenched her.

Gabe's arm snaked around her waist, steadying her. "The sign that said don't go out on the rocks." There was small, bleak silence. "This is where Jasmine died when her boat overturned."

The shock of his statement—of his finally mentioning Jasmine—was canceled out as the next wave flowed toward them, this one even larger. Fingers laced with hers, he pulled her onto a higher shelf of rock and back toward shore.

Breathless, Sarah worked to keep up with Gabe's smooth, gliding stride, glad that she was wearing sneakers and that she had kept up her walking during the pregnancy and was still reasonably fit. "I suppose people get swept off."

The wave broke sending more spray flying. The distraction took her attention from the uneven rock surface for a split second, making her wobble.

Gabe said something hard and sharp beneath his

breath as he reeled her in close again then swung her into his arms. "Not today."

Coiling her arms around his neck, she held on tight, worried that she had provided another painful reminder of Jasmine, but loving that Gabe had come to her rescue. Water dripped from his hair and clung to his lashes. His gaze rested on hers for a moment, the glint of masculine satisfaction sending a warm surge through her. She was soaked, they both were, but suddenly she didn't care. For a few moments they were alone, and like the hours they'd spent together last night, he was *hers*. "I'm sorry. I should have kept a better watch out. Graham arrived at the beach and I got a bit creeped out. I thought he would try and follow me."

Gabe's expression turned grim. "Don't worry about Southwell. Xavier has him under surveillance."

Resting her head in the curve of his neck and shoulder, she breathed in his warm scent. "I suppose that's how you found me? I ran into your secret service?"

She felt his smile rather than saw it. "What did you expect when you gave Yusuf the slip? Tell me, *kalila*, are you always this difficult?"

She was startled by his rueful expression, the softness of his gaze, as if he liked it that she was giving him such a hard time. "Only when I get engaged."

"And when you're pulling swords off displays, assaulting thugs with your umbrella and giving Tarik a hard time."

She blinked at the picture of herself. "Maybe I am difficult."

A curious expression crossed his face. "Don't change, I like it." Bending, he kissed her.

Her heart thumped at the kiss and the tone of his voice. "What does *kalila* mean?"

Stopping at the edge of the rock promontory where it flowed into the smooth, broad curve of the beach, he set her on her feet. "It's an endearment. On Zahir we use it much as you would honey or darling."

Feeling suddenly self-conscious, she smoothed wet straggling hair back from her cheeks. When his gaze flickered to her chest she glanced down and realized that her thin white cardigan and camisole were wet. Luckily, she had a bikini top beneath, so she could afford to ignore the wet T-shirt effect.

Gabe glanced along the cliff face. Graham was still there somewhere because his car was in the parking lot, although he was nowhere to be seen. At a guess he had disappeared into the warren of caves that riddled the rock.

When Gabe spoke his voice was terse. "I'm moving you into the palace tonight."

Gabe arranged for all of their belongings to be transferred to the palace.

Night was falling with a pretty sickle moon, the sky studded with brilliant stars as he drove into a cavernous garage beneath the palace.

He gave her a quick tour of the residential area, which used to be the old harem quarters and which had been remodeled into a series of family apartments. He pointed out where his parents stayed and two other empty apartments. "There are also a whole bunch of single and double rooms, but those are mostly empty unless family or guests come to stay."

He opened the door to their apartment and a warm

glow suffused her as she walked into the main sitting room, which was filled with comfortable leather couches and low coffee tables. A dining table was positioned in an alcove next to a gleaming kitchen. The dining table was set, candles lit, giving the room a welcoming elegance while the warm aromas of the meal that had been kept hot in silver chafing dishes drifted on the air.

Gabe gave her a quick tour. The next room, which Gabe indicated as they walked past, looked like a beautifully appointed guest room. That was followed by a large bathroom tiled in cream marble with a tub big enough to swim in.

She examined the large walk-in shower and the supply of fluffy white towels. "We'll have to block off the bathroom once the baby starts walking."

"Good point." He stared at the marble bath, which had steps that would be slippery when wet. "Even better, we'll get a house. This place is a death trap for kids."

The casual comment about getting a house made her heart glow with happiness. More and more they were starting to feel like a regular couple. She stepped inside what looked like the master bedroom, since it had its own bathroom and dressing room opening off it. This was confirmed by the masculine bedspread, the faint scent of Gabe's cologne and one of his shirts slung over the back of a chair.

Sarah checked out the dressing room, a faint tension she hadn't realized was there dissipating when she saw her suitcase. "I take it I'm staying in this room."

Gabe was leaning against the doorjamb watching her. "That's right, with me. Although, you can have the guest room if you want."

She strolled toward him and when he didn't move

aside she took another half step, which brought her up against him. She wound her fingers in the smooth silk of his tie. "I choose this room."

"I was hoping you were going to say that."

His phone hummed. Looking frustrated, he took the phone from his pocket, checked the screen and frowned. "I need to take this."

"No problem." While Gabe sat at a desk in a small study that opened off the lounge and took a series of calls, Sarah unpacked then had a quick shower to remove the salty residue from that afternoon. Toweling herself dry, she put on fresh underwear. Instead of dressing in the cotton shift she'd chosen, she decided to wear an exquisite rose-pink silk kaftan she had bought in the souk the morning Gabe had found her. The kaftan was gossamer fine and flowing but when belted with a silk sash became a gorgeous Eastern dress.

She combed out her hair and used the blow-dryer. When her hair was mostly dry and trailing down her back, she quickly applied a little eye makeup. Now that she finally knew how the makeup should look and what products to buy, she was determined not to go back to dashing on a bit of dark brown eyeliner and rose-pink lip gloss, both of which usually faded into invisibility within an hour.

Rummaging through her suitcase she found the pashmina that went with the outfit, an exquisitely fine woven cashmere stole in rich hues of purple and pink with splashes of deep red that added a sensual grace to the pretty kaftan. She examined the effect in the bathroom mirror. The outfit was more modest than the red dress she'd worn the night she'd met Gabe, there was only the barest hint of shadowy cleavage, yet somehow it was infinitely more feminine and mysterious.

With her hair dropping around her shoulders in a dark curtain, her eyes taking on a smoky, exotic slant courtesy of the eye shadow and mascara, she didn't look remotely like a sensible history teacher, neither did she feel like one anymore. The clothing seemed to underline the inner change that had taken place, almost without her being aware of it.

When she walked out into the lounge, Gabe was dishing up food. He must have had a shower in the other bathroom because his hair was damp and he'd changed into a pair of dark pants and a polo shirt. His gaze met hers as he set the plate he'd just filled on the table. Her pulse sped up at the intensity of his gaze as he took in the softly sensual outfit. "Are you hungry?"

"Starved."

They ate, although as delicious as the food was, Sarah could barely concentrate because she was so aware of Gabe.

When she was finished, he took her plate and set it in the sink in the kitchen, his expression taut. "Would you like dessert?"

She followed him and placed an empty salad bowl on the counter. "Not really."

"Me neither." With a grin, he picked her up and carried her through to the bedroom. "When you walked out of the bedroom like that, I didn't think I'd make it through dinner."

He set her on her feet. The Pashmina slid to the floor as she reached up to kiss him. One kiss followed another. She felt the silk sash loosen then slip off her shoulders and puddle at her feet. Two steps back and they were on the bed and somehow, this time, she was on top, her hair sliding silkily around them. Long drugging minutes later she was naked and so was Gabe.

Tension gripped her as she studied Gabe in the wash of light from the hall. For the first time, she was actually beginning to believe that he could be hers.

Cupping his face, she looked directly into his eyes. "I love you." The words were bald and declarative, leaving her nowhere to hide.

Instead of the words she wanted in return, she felt his instant tension and knew she shouldn't have made the declaration, shouldn't have pushed him. Even if he had mentioned Jasmine today, it was still too soon. A split second later, he kissed her and, determined not to fret, she relaxed into the kiss and let the warmth and heat of lovemaking encompass them both.

A phone call in the early hours brought Sarah out of a deep, dreamless sleep. Rolling over in bed, she slipped an arm around Gabe's taut waist as he lay, propped on one elbow, speaking in rapid Zahiri. When he hung up, the gray light of dawn illuminated the grim expression on his face. "That was Xavier. They've been keeping Southwell under surveillance. Apparently, he's found the lost dowry, which was sealed in a side cave in Salamander Bay. That's what he was doing there today, repacking the caskets and getting ready to transport them to the loading docks at the port where he has an export container waiting." Expression taut, Gabe set the phone down. "Damn Southwell and the dowry. Why did he have to find it *now*?"

Climbing out of bed, Gabe dressed and was gone within minutes.

Unable to go back to sleep, Sarah belted on the beautiful silk kaftan, freshened up in the bathroom then walked through to the sitting room. Gabe's words kept echoing through her mind.

Damn Southwell and the dowry. Why did he have to find it now?

As if Gabe had wished the dowry had been found some other time. Probably months ago, a year ago, so he would never have given way to the pressure of an arranged marriage in the first place. Because if that hadn't happened, he would never have spent a dangerous night of passion with her that had resulted in a pregnancy, and what could only be termed a marriage of convenience.

Dragging fingers through her tangled hair, she paced through the huge apartment, strolling through moonlit rooms only to find herself in Gabe's study, the one room she hadn't seen on their tour. Curious, she flicked on a light and strolled to tall French doors and looked out onto a beautiful patio. When she turned, she noted a rich leather photograph album on top of a polished mahogany desk.

Knowing that she shouldn't, she flipped the album open. The first section had Gabe and Jasmine's engagement photos. Lavish wedding shots followed and the final section was filled with romantic honeymoon photos. Feeling a little sick, because Jasmine looked glowingly happy in every photo, her arms either draped around Gabe's neck or his waist, as if she couldn't bear not to touch him.

She closed the album with a snap. As she did so, she noticed a folder beside it, carrying her name.

Feeling like an automaton, she picked up the file and opened it. Fifteen minutes later, feeling sick, she set the file back in its place. She had known that Gabe had had her investigated, but this file was a detailed *surveillance* record that Gabe had ordered after their first night together. He had expressly stated that he wanted her watched in case she was pregnant.

Seeing the truth about how Gabe had viewed her, in stark contrast to his romantic, loving relationship with Jasmine, was hard to take. It *hurt*.

She guessed that, given he was a sheikh's son and the future ruler of Zahir, she could understand his approach. But that didn't change the fact that she had given up everything for Gabe, including her heart, and he had given up very little for her. He still hadn't shared even the bare facts about his marriage.

Feeling numb, she replaced the file. As understanding as she had tried to be, she wasn't stupid, she had limits, and her limits had just been breached.

She had taken a risk in loving Gabe, moving in with him and agreeing to marriage. She knew he'd been hurt in the past, but even so she had believed there was a possibility that he would come to love her someday.

But she couldn't stomach marriage on such compromised terms, with someone who had seen her as predatory. It underlined the fact that if she hadn't gotten pregnant and forced his hand, she would never have seen Gabe again.

Face burning at the humiliation of seeing the basis of their relationship laid bare, of having her life sifted through, *by the man she loved*, she left the study and found her way back to the bedroom. Their bedroom, but not any longer.

Lamplight pooled like liquid gold, casting a soft glow on the beautiful plastered walls and delicate frescoes.

Chest tight, she opened a set of doors and stepped onto the balcony, staring out over the moonlit city to the sea. It was all unspeakably beautiful and she loved it, but she was going to have to leave.

She finally understood why Gabe had agreed to a marriage of convenience to Nadia and why he'd never confided in her about his past with Jasmine. It was because he didn't want the one thing she craved: intimacy.

The moment was defining. She had said she would marry Gabe, but how could she when his heart wasn't in it? When his heart might *never* be in it?

She knew what it felt like to be second best, to be passed over. It hadn't been a good feeling, but she had gotten over it. She didn't think she could get over Gabe, but neither would she be second best for him.

She had always thought she was lacking in passion, but when Gabe had entered her life she had discovered that she was passionate and volatile. She wanted a real love with Gabe with a fierceness that shimmered and burned and made her want to cry.

Knowing now that she would never have his love, she had to act. When she had the baby Gabe would love their daughter and want to be a father to her, but that was a scenario with a modern solution. He might not like the idea, but the only sensible thing to do was to share custody.

Working quickly, she retrieved her bags from the closet. She didn't know how much time she had before Gabe returned, so she simply stuffed clothing into them. She found her engagement ring, which she'd left on the bedside table, and replaced it in its velvet case. She put the case along with the second case containing the pendant and earrings on the dressing table. On impulse, she walked through to Gabe's study, found the photo album and the surveillance report and placed them beside the jewelry boxes.

She checked her watch. An hour had flown by. She needed to leave before she weakened and changed her mind.

Gabe would hate it that she'd walked out on him. He was an alpha male. But the very strengths that made him such a good leader were the qualities that would push them apart in the end. He would continue to sacrifice his free choice, and perhaps his happiness, and she couldn't bear that.

Walking through to the bathroom, she splashed cold water on her face. Feeling chilled despite the balmy warmth, she used her cell to call a local taxi firm and arranged to meet the cab in the residential street that backed onto the palace grounds.

Fumbling slightly in her haste, she changed into cotton jeans and a sweater and pulled on sneakers. She found a scarf and on impulse used it to cover her hair, tying it under her chin. After all the media coverage she was now recognizable on Zahir. It wasn't much of a disguise, but it would have to do.

She carried the luggage downstairs and outside to the street, leaving it in the shadow of a huge flowering rhododendron. Walking back to the apartment, she did a last check of the rooms, picked up her handbag, hooked the strap over her shoulder and walked out onto the landing. Headlights beamed up the driveway. Heart in her mouth, feeling sick to her stomach at what she was doing, Sarah walked quickly down the stairs.

Fifteen

Gabe locked the car and headed for the stairs. Now that the situation with Southwell and the dowry was resolved, with Southwell in custody and the dowry in safekeeping, all Gabe wanted was to go back to bed with Sarah and preserve what time they had before the major news companies picked up on the story and all hell broke loose.

Faruq was coordinating the press releases. With any luck, he would finesse the timing of the discovery of the ancient treasure as a "sign" that the marriage to Sarah was propitious for Zahir. The romantic tale of his ancestor's love affair with Camille de Vallois would do the rest.

As Gabe stepped inside the apartment, the curious quality of the silence made him frown. Somewhere outside he heard a car door close, the sound of an engine. On edge he walked into the bedroom. Moonlight slanted over the rumpled bed, which was empty. Stomach tight, he checked the bathroom, which was also empty.

Out of the corner of his eye he saw the two velvet cases on the dresser and the photograph album and surveillance report he had left on his desk with the intention of destroying them that morning.

He went cold inside. For the album and the file to be where they were, Sarah had clearly found and perused them. A quick glance in the spare room confirmed that Sarah hadn't just moved out of his bedroom. She had left him.

For long moments he couldn't think. Then he remembered the slamming of the car door out in the street. Sarah must have called a taxi.

Heart slamming against the wall of his chest, he picked up the phone, called Xavier and arranged to detain her at the airport.

With distaste, he forced himself to look at one of Jasmine's last gifts to him, an album filled with photos that portrayed a love story that had grown to be cloying and unhealthy.

Jaw taut, he opened the surveillance file and skimmed the damning evidence of his letter requesting a watch on Sarah in case she was pregnant. The report included an extensive back history on Sarah's life because for some reason Tarik had gotten a little overzealous and had requested the private investigator dig back several years.

Reading through the bare facts, Sarah had looked like a woman who had amassed a certain experience with men, but Gabe knew the truth. The reason none of the relationships had stuck was because she had refused to sleep with them. But she had slept with him, after little more than a few hours.

Because she had fallen in love with him.

Grimly, he remembered her saying the words to him tonight, his complete lack of response because, even then, in a sheer knee-jerk reaction he had automatically closed himself off.

She loved him.

He felt like he'd been kicked in the chest. Sarah wasn't like Jasmine, wavering with every breeze, clinging and resenting at the same time and wanting to be spoiled and cosseted. She was independent and fierce. Used to making her own way through life, for years she had refused to give in to relationship pressure and have sex. She had waited and chosen, and she had chosen him.

Once she had found she was pregnant, she hadn't panicked. She had gone in search of him, not to coerce him into a relationship, but to ascertain whether she should include him in her life. Those were the actions of a rational, independent woman who had fallen in love.

Tossing the report down on the desk, he found his keys and headed for his car. He felt electrified, every nerve ending in his body on fire. Sarah had told him, but now he knew in his gut—and his heart—exactly why she had agreed to marry him, and why she had left. She loved him but she had given up on the hope that he could love her back.

And suddenly he realized what he had done to himself, and to Sarah. After Jasmine had died he had spent years consumed by guilt, not because he had failed to save her life, but because he had never been able to *love her.*

He and Jasmine had been wrong together and that tension had reverberated through their marriage, ending in a tragedy that he had allowed to color the rest of his life.

Panic gripped him. He felt as if the scales had just been ripped from his eyes. Too late, he now realized that he did love Sarah. And now he had lost her.

He was partway to the airport when he knew it was the wrong destination. Sarah was smart. She would have known how easy it would be for him to stop her flying.

Turning the car around, he headed for the ferry terminal, the only other way off Zahir other than chartering a yacht or boarding a cruise ship. There were no cruise ships leaving today, and chartering a yacht was a lengthy process because it involved customs declarations. Boarding a ferry to the neighboring island of Al Jahir was a much simpler option.

His stomach churned at the thought that she had chosen the sea as a way to escape him. *Jasmine's choice.*

As he drove he went through every nuance of their last conversation, which had been about the dowry. He knew that, like him, Sarah placed no stock in money or possessions. Southwell had chased the treasure for its own sake, but Sarah, who should have been more interested in it than most with her family background, had barely shown a flicker of interest.

From memory the only thing about the past that had interested her had been whether or not his ancestor had loved hers.

His fingers tightened on the wheel as he turned down the street that led to the docks. Jaw tight, he found a space and slammed out of the car. Sarah was simple and declarative. She had told him she loved him, but he had failed to reciprocate. He had taken the easy way out, *the cowardly way out*, because then he didn't have to expose his own emotions. He didn't have to take any risks.

That would have to change; he couldn't lose her.

Gabe faced the raw depth of emotions that in the past had caused him more pain than happiness.

He wouldn't let Sarah go without a fight.

Sarah boarded the early-morning ferry to Al Jahir.

Stepping inside the lower deck cabin, which was already half-filled with passengers drinking coffee and watching TV, Sarah made a beeline for a seat near a window. She stopped when she noticed a large TV was on and that the coverage riveting most of the passengers was a news story on the crates of gold and jewels that Graham had tried to steal.

In no mood to listen to the story she was on the point of walking out onto the ferry deck when Gabe's deep voice kept her riveted to the screen. She recognized footage of an earlier interview that had been linked with the segment about the dowry, but even so, when Gabe was asked about his impending marriage his curt "no comment" stung.

The reporter smoothed over the awkwardness of the moment by stating that in Zahir any marriage by the ruling family was necessarily an affair of state.

Shivering slightly and hugging her cotton jersey closer against her skin, she walked to the upper deck and ducked inside out of the brisk wind. She stared through one of the large windows at the palace, which gleamed in the first golden touches of morning light, and the terraced jumble of streets and villas that gave Zahir such charm. Feeling miserable, she forced herself to look in the direction of Al Jahir, a misty lump on the horizon. She had made the right decision, even if it made her feel ill.

She was tired, so she bought a cup of tea from the

small cafeteria. She guessed she should eat something, but her stomach was still churning and unsettled, and the faint wallow of the sea swell wasn't helping.

She chose a seat that overlooked the docks, just in case Gabe arrived before the ferry left. She hoped he wouldn't come after her because if he did she didn't know if she'd have the strength to resist him.

Gabe walked inside the ferry building. He had missed the sailing by about twenty minutes. He could still see the ferry in the distance. He asked to see the manifest. His jaw tightened when he spotted Sarah's name.

Thanking the clerk, he left the building and made a call. Al Jahir was ruled by his cousin several times removed, Kalil. The relationship was distant, but that didn't matter. They were family. A second call and he had arranged a helicopter.

Half an hour later he landed on the docks of Al Jahir. When the ferry anchored just offshore, embargoed from landing until he had retrieved Sarah, Gabe took the launch Kalil had provided and climbed on board.

When Sarah saw him, her stricken expression gave him a small measure of hope. Although, he had mishandled their relationship so badly he had to wonder if he had finally destroyed her love.

Ignoring the disgruntled crowd of ferry passengers, he concentrated on Sarah. "Will you come with me?"

She shot to her feet, clutching her handbag. "Why?"

"Because you belong on Zahir, with me."

The sleepy-eyed tourist next to her muttered, "Last I heard slavery went out of fashion a few years back."

Someone else grunted agreement and added, "*And* piracy. Honey, if you need backup just say the word."

Jaw locked, Gabe kept his focus on Sarah. "You're free to leave anytime. But I need you to hear me out, in private."

Minutes later, caught halfway between misery and delight that Gabe had come after her, Sarah allowed Gabe to hand her down into the launch.

A short helicopter ride and they landed on the roof of the palace, which had a helipad.

As Sarah walked back into the familiarity of Gabe's apartment, her stomach tightened. "I left because I didn't want you to feel you had to marry me just to have access to the baby." She lifted her chin. "You're her father, so it's only right that you should have a part in her upbringing. We just need to reach agreement on how that will work."

Gabe shrugged out of his jacket and tossed it over the back of a chair. He ran lean fingers through his hair, looking suddenly unutterably weary. "Zahir is an old-fashioned country. The only agreement that will work here is marriage, and that's what I want."

She blinked at the intensity of his gaze. "I found the surveillance report."

His expression turned raw. "It was something I had to do, because I knew I couldn't afford to contact you again unless there was a child. If I hadn't instigated the report, Xavier would have. At least that way I could make sure the information came only to me and ensure your privacy."

The tension when she had discovered the report relaxed a little. She still hated that she'd been spied upon, but viewed that way, Gabe's actions had a protective element. "I thought you hated it that you were being forced to marry at all. If the dowry had been found months ago—"

"I would never have gotten engaged to Nadia. And since I was always going to New Zealand for the promotional tour our relationship would probably have followed a more normal path."

She stared at a pulse jumping along the side of his jaw. "But, when Graham found the dowry—"

"I was annoyed because I'd finally gotten you to myself, and then Southwell put himself in the frame again." He grimaced. "In case you hadn't noticed the dowry is a media circus. I knew I'd be out for hours."

Sarah took a deep breath. She was starting to feel happy, but she couldn't allow herself to relax just yet. "What about Jasmine?"

"I married Jasmine because I thought I loved her, but that was years ago."

The words *thought I loved her* seemed to reverberate. Her throat closed up so that when she spoke the words came out in a husky croak. "Do you still love her?"

Something cleared in his expression. "She was a childhood sweetheart. The media blew it up into a big love affair, but the marriage was a mistake. Jasmine was stuck on Zahir while I traveled. She hated it."

In terse, halting words he supplied a brief outline of the day Jasmine had drowned. He'd been spending more and more time away on business, tired of the fights and Jasmine's unhappiness. When Jasmine had insisted on accompanying him on a diving trip he had let her and when another fiery argument had ensued, he had suggested they end the marriage. Jasmine had lost her temper and in desperation had clung to him. Tired of her manipulative tactics and the clinging, he had gone below to study the navigation maps. When he had come back on deck, Jasmine, who had never handled a boat in her life, had taken the small dinghy, determined to row to shore. The dinghy had been swept onto a rock shelf and the boat had capsized on top of her. Gabe had dove down to search for her.

Sarah touched his cheek. "And that's how you got this."

His hand covered hers, holding it against the scar. "I had to get her off the rocks."

And the scar had become a permanent reminder that he hadn't been able to save his wife—more, that he had no longer loved her. It was no wonder he hadn't wanted anything to do with love again. "You can't believe it was your fault."

"I shouldn't have argued with her on the boat."

"And she shouldn't have taken the dinghy." Sarah unlocked her jaw. "I'm sorry she died, but it's a fact that she endangered your life as well as her own."

By the startled acknowledgment in his eyes she knew he hadn't considered that angle, preferring to take all the blame on his own shoulders. The only problem was that the guilt had morphed into an aversion toward emotional commitment that had almost destroyed their chance at love.

He threaded his fingers through hers, pulling her closer. "When it came to you, I knew I was in trouble, but I tried to channel the emotion into a purely sexual connection. It didn't work."

"Then I got pregnant." And he had attempted to transfer the "safe" relationship model he had settled on to her, and that hadn't worked either.

She cupped his jaw, suddenly seeing him, his tenderness and depth. "Even though I was a lot of trouble, you didn't let me go." She tried to breathe deeply, but her chest felt banded and tight. "Why?"

His hands closed around her arms, his palms warm through the cotton pullover. "That would be because I'm in love with you."

Happiness flared deep inside. Not just love, but *in love*. "Since when?"

"Since the moment I saw you completely ignore the don't-touch sign and knock my ancestor's sword to the floor." He pulled her snug against him. "I suppose you think because I'm a guy I'm incapable of that kind of depth."

She spread her palms over the warm solidity of his chest, loving the steady beat of his heart, the heat and strength of him. "It was a fact that I was a last fling before you got engaged." Flickers of the old hurt came back to haunt her at the words.

"I was on the point of getting engaged. It was an arrangement that had taken months to negotiate then I blew it by sleeping with you. That should tell you something."

She went still inside. Somewhere in all of this she realized she had lost the ability to stand back and look at the big picture, or to read between the lines. The one thing she had learned about Gabe was that for most of his adult life he had put Zahir ahead of his own wants and desires. The only times he had departed from that pattern were when he had married Jasmine, then again when he had slept with Sarah.

She stared at the clean, strong planes and angles of his face, the steadiness of his gaze. "You really did fall for me."

He cupped her face, his thumbs drifting over her

cheekbones, giving her goose bumps. "Like a ton of bricks."

"The way I fell for you."

His gaze connected with hers in a poignant moment of recognition.

She coiled her arms around his neck, holding him tight, loving the rock-solid quality that had frustrated her so often but which carried its own assurance. She knew without doubt that she and their daughter could trust Gabe with their hearts.

They had finally come home.

Sixteen

They didn't delay the wedding, even though Gabe was happy to do so. Sarah, now secure in his love, decided she had to do her bit for Zahir, and upsetting the travel plans of hundreds of people wasn't a good way to start.

The next day Gabe ushered Sarah into his study, where Faruq was impatiently waiting to find out just how the new wedding would affect his promotional efforts.

He was visibly relieved when Sarah informed him she was prepared to accept the current wedding date. She fixed him with the calm, level look she used in the classroom. "But I'm not getting married in the dead of night, like it's some kind of secret—"

"It's hardly a secret with four hundred guests."

Sarah frowned at the interruption. "—since it's my wedding." She softened the statement with a blinding smile that, to Gabe's mind, seemed to light up the room.

"Also," she continued, "I want my cousin Laine's son to be a page and her three daughters to be flower girls. Since they're family, and on the next island, that should happen."

Sarah kept her attention on Faruq as he took notes. "I'm thinking one o'clock is a good time for the ceremony. Midnight might have suited Nadia, but it doesn't suit me or my nephew or nieces. Laine's youngest has only just started to sleep through the night. You can't expect us to upset that pattern when it's taken so long to put in place."

Faruq looked suitably chastened. "Uh—of course not—"

"Good." She sent him an affirming smile. "It's also crucially important that people should understand that Gabe is not being *forced* to marry me."

Gabe hid a grin.

"Um—I don't think Sheikh Kadin was being forced as such, it was more of a service to the country."

"With a financial benefit." Sarah favored Faruq with another brilliant smile. "My point exactly. Gabe is not marrying me for money. He's marrying me because—"

"You're irresistible to him." Gabe thought he would just toss that one in.

Sarah's gaze locked with his. "Irresistible?"

Gabe pulled her into his arms. "Absolutely."

When she went up on her toes and rewarded him with a kiss, he heard the door close softly as Faruq let himself out. The meeting had ended a little precipitately, but it didn't matter. Faruq was a creative genius and he was already excited about the promotional potential in Gabe's marriage to a descendant of Camille, especially when combined with the recovery of the ancient dowry.

According to Faruq those two aspects could only enhance Zahir's new image as a destination for romantic getaways, and would make it relatively easy to gloss over the small detail that Gabe and Sarah had already made a start on a family. For Zahir the formula was win-win, but for Gabe those two elements held little importance to him when he finally had what he wanted—the gorgeous, fascinating love of his life and their first child together.

The day of the wedding dawned fine and clear. The ceremony was held in the ancient stone church next door to the palace. Golden sunlight poured through the rose window at the western end. Jewel-bright colors illuminated thick flagstones and the gleam of dark oak pews. The church overflowed with guests, so seats had been placed outside along with two very modern screens with speakers.

A restive murmur ran through the guests as Gabe's parents arrived and took their places. His father looked tanned and relaxed after a recent holiday and was no longer walking with the aid of a cane. His mother looked elegant and happier than he had seen her for years. She sent Gabe a beaming smile and a small thumbs-up.

Although Gabe couldn't quite relax until Sarah arrived. It was an insecurity that shouldn't have existed after the days and nights they'd spent together, but he couldn't quite forget the stark moment when he'd found out she'd left him just weeks ago.

Xavier checked his watch and frowned. "She's late."

"Tradition." Gabe's gaze was drawn to the priest, robed in white, as he also checked his watch. "Probably caught up in traffic."

The noise level outside increased. An usher at the front doors gave Gabe a nod. He let out a breath and relaxed. She was here.

Sarah stepped into the church, a little frazzled after the frustration of sitting in the back of a limousine that seemed to spend large amounts of time stuck in heavy traffic or at a standstill because of the crush of pedestrians. All wanting to get to *her* wedding.

A liltingly beautiful wedding march started, and the hum of conversation died. Gabe turned, looking tall and handsome in a gray morning suit and wearing the traditional *kaffiyeh* and *agal*. His gaze connected with hers through the drift of her veil. The quiet joy that he was hers seemed to swell inside her, forming an ache at the back of her throat.

Gripping the elegant bouquet that matched the simple lines of her designer gown, she began the slow, measured walk toward her husband-to-be.

With every step memories flickered. Gabe straightening with the sword in his hand at the reception in Wellington, the rescue in the parking lot, their first kiss, the first night they had spent together.

Blinking back tears, she halted at the ancient altar, which had seen the flow of centuries, bowed her head, made the sign of the cross and turned to her husband-to-be.

Sheikh Kadin Gabriel ben Kadir, heir to the Sheikhdom of Zahir.

For a moment, her composure wobbled, but when he lifted the veil from her face and took her hands in his, the warmth of his gaze held her steady.

The hush of the church, the beauty of the words of the

ceremony, filled her with an emotion that was piercing. When Gabe slipped the simple gold band on her finger, tears finally spilled.

His mouth brushed hers; his hands at her waist burned through the silk of her gown. Beeswax candles guttered in the faint breeze that blew through windows and suddenly the air was filled with the wild sweet scents of honey and thyme.

Sarah's head spun dizzily as she went up on her toes to kiss him back.

She finally had it all, more than she had ever dreamed—the father of her child and the love she had waited for, the husband of her heart.

* * * * *

SHOCK HEIR FOR THE KING

CLARE CONNELLY

For romance readers everywhere, and especially my Advance readers, who are some of the best champions and friends a writer could hope for.

PROLOGUE

THERE WERE THREE things Matthias Vasilliás loved in life. The glow of the sky as the sun dipped into the horizon, bathing the world in streaks of gold and peach; the country he was one week away from ruling; and women—but never the same woman for long, and never with any expectation of more than this: sex.

The wind blew in across the hotel room, draping the gauzy fabric of the curtain towards him, and for a moment he looked at it, his mind caught by the beauty, the brevity, of such a fragile material—the brevity of this moment.

In the morning he'd be gone, she'd be a memory—a ghost of this life. In the morning he would fly back to Tolmirós and step into his future.

He hadn't come to New York for this. He hadn't intended to meet her. He hadn't intended to seduce a virgin—that wasn't his usual *modus operandi.* Not when he couldn't offer any degree of permanence in exchange for such a gift.

No, Matthias preferred experienced women.

Lovers who were *au fait* with the ways of the world, who understood that a man like Matthias had no heart to offer, no future he could provide.

One day he would marry, but his bride would be a political choice, a queen to equal him as King, a ruler to sit beside him and oversee his kingdom.

Until then, though, there was this: there was Frankie, and this night.

She ran her fingertips over his back, her nails digging into him, and he lost himself to her completely, plunging inside her, taking the sweetness she offered as she cried out into the balmy New York evening.

'Matt.' She used the shortened version of his name—it had been such a novelty to meet a woman who didn't know who he was, didn't know he was the heir to the throne of a powerful European country, that he was richer than Croesus and about to be King. Matt was simple, Matt was easy, and soon this would be over.

For ruling Tolmirós meant he would have to abandon his love of women, his love of sex and all that he was, outside the requirements of being King. His life would change completely in seven days' time.

Seven days and he would be King.

In seven days he would be back in Tolmirós, the country before him. But for now he was here, with a woman who knew nothing of his life, his people, his duties.

'This is perfect,' she groaned, arching her back so two pert breasts pushed skyward and he shoved his guilt at this deception aside, his guilt at having taken an innocent young woman to bed for his own pleasure, to slake his own needs, knowing it could never be more than this.

She didn't want complications either. They'd been clear on that score. It was this weekend and nothing more. But he was using her, of that he had no doubt. He was using her to rebel, one last time. Using her to avoid the inevitable truth of his life, for one night longer. Using her because right here, in this moment, sleeping with Frankie made him feel human—only human—and not even an inch royal.

He took one of her breasts in his mouth and rolled his tongue over the tight nipple. It budded in his mouth, desperate for his touch, his possession, and he thrust into her depths, wondering if any woman had ever been so perfectly made for a man?

His fingers fisted in her long, silky blonde hair and he pushed her head up to meet his, claiming her lips, kissing her until she whimpered beneath him and the whole of her body was at his command.

Power surged through him at the way this felt, but it was nothing to the power that awaited him, the duty that would soon be at his feet.

For his country and his people, he would turn his back on pleasures such as this, on women such as Frankie, and he would be King.

But not quite yet.

For a few more hours he would simply be Matt, and Frankie would be his…

CHAPTER ONE

Three years later

NEW YORK SPARKLED like a beautiful diorama, all high-rises, bright lights and muted subway noise. He stared down at the glittering city from the balcony of his Manhattan penthouse, breathing in the activity and forcing himself not to remember the last time he'd been in this exact position.

Forcing his eyes to stay trained in the opposite direction of the School of Art, and definitely not allowing himself to remember the woman who had bewitched him and charmed him.

The woman who had given him her innocence, given him her body, and imprinted something of herself in his mind.

Inwardly he groaned, her name just a whisper in his body, a curse too, because he had no business so much as thinking of her, let alone remembering everything about her.

Not when his engagement would be made formal within a month. Not when his future awaited—and duty to his country called to him as loudly as ever. Then, he'd been one week away from assuming the throne, and now he was weeks away from making a marriage commitment.

All of Tolmirós was waiting for its King to finally wed and beget an heir. An heir that would promise stability and the safekeeping of the prosperous nation: all of that was on Matthias's shoulders, as much now as it had been then. He'd run from this fate for as long as he could. His family had died when he was only a teenager and the idea of marrying, having his own children, as though you could so easily recreate what had been lost, pressed against his chest like a weight of stone.

But it was needed; it was necessary. His country required its King to beget an heir, and he needed a wife. A suitable wife, like one of the women his assistant had vetted for him. A woman who would be cultured, polished and appropriate.

His eyes shut and there she was: Frankie. Frankie as she'd been that afternoon they'd met, her clothes paint-splattered, her hair scraped back into a ponytail, her smile contagious. His gut clenched.

His wife—his Queen—would be nothing like Frankie.

What they'd shared went beyond logic and reason—it had been an affair that had rocked him to his core because, after only a matter of hours, he'd known he was in danger of forgetting everything he owed to his people if it meant more time with the woman—she had been like some kind of siren, rising out of the sea, drawing him towards danger unknowingly.

And so he'd done what he was best at: he'd drawn his heart closed, he'd pushed his emotions deep inside, and he'd walked out on her without a backwards glance.

But now, back in New York, he found himself thinking of her in a way he'd trained himself not to. His dreams he could not control, but his waking mind was as disciplined as the man himself, and he saw no point in dwelling on the past, and particularly not on such a brief event.

Only she was everywhere he looked in this city—the lights that sparkled like the depths of her eyes, the elegance of the high-rises that were tall where she had been short, the nimble alertness, the vivid brightness—and he wondered what it would be like to see her once more. Call it idle curiosity, or simply scratching an itch.

He was a king now, not the man he'd been when they'd first slept together. But his needs were the same. His desires. He stared out at the city and the idea grew.

What harm could come from dipping into the past, just for a night?

'The lighting is beyond perfect,' Frankie enthused, glancing her trained artist's eye over the walls of the midtown gallery. The showing was scheduled for the following day; this was her last chance to make sure everything was absolutely as she wanted it to be.

A *frisson* of excitement ran down her spine.

For years she'd been struggling. Establishing oneself as an artist was no mean feat, and every spare penny she made was funnelled into trying to keep a roof over their heads. It was one thing to be a starving artist when you were footloose and fancy-free—there was even a degree of romance to the notion.

The reality was a lot less enjoyable, particularly with a rapidly growing two-and-a-half-year-old to care for and a mountain of bills that seemed to go on for ever.

But this show…

It could be the game-changer she'd been waiting for.

Two broadsheet newspapers had already sent reviewers to have a pre-show viewing, and the opening night had been advertised across the city. Her fingers, her toes and the hairs on her head remained crossed that she might finally catch her big break into the competitive New York art scene.

'I did think of using small spotlights here.' Charles nodded towards some of her favourite landscapes—sun rising over oceans, but all in abstract oils—gashes of colour scratched over the paper to create the impression of day's dawn. Each picture would be interpreted differently by the spectator, and Frankie liked that. It was her take on each day being what you made of it.

'I like the overheads you've chosen,' she demurred, another shiver running down her spine. Her whole body was a tangle of nerves—and she told herself it was because of the exposure. Not the media exposure—the exposure of herself. Every thought, lost dream, wish, fear, feeling had been captured on these canvases. Even the paintings of Leo, with his stunning crop of black curls, intense grey eyes, so shimmery they were almost silver, lashes that curled precociously and wild. He was her little love, her heart and soul, and his image now hung on the walls of this gallery, waiting to be seen by thousands, she hoped, of viewers.

'The door,' Charles murmured apologetically, in response to a sound that Frankie hadn't even noticed. She was moving closer to the painting she'd done of Leo last fall.

He'd been laughing, collecting dropped leaves from the sidewalk and tossing them into the air with all the enthusiasm a two-year-old boy could muster, and as they'd fallen back to earth he'd watched their progress before crouching down and crunching a new selection into his chubby grip.

His joy had been so euphoric she'd had to capture it. So she'd snapped hundreds of photos from different angles, committing the light to her memory, and then she'd worked late into the night.

And she'd done what she did best: she'd taken a mood, a slice of one of life's moments, and locked it onto a canvas. She'd created a visual secret for the viewer to share in, but only for as long as they looked at her work. It was a moment in time, a moment of her life, and now it was art.

'The opening is tomorrow night, sir, but if you'd like to take a brief look at the collection…'

'I would.'

Two words, so deep, and from a voice so instantly familiar.

A shiver ran down Frankie's spine of a different nature now. It wasn't a shiver of anxiety, nor joyous anticipation, it was one of instant recognition, a tremble of remembrance and a dull thudding ache of loss.

She turned slowly, as if that could somehow unstitch the reality she knew she'd found herself in. But when she looked at Charles, and then the man beside him, all her worlds came crashing down at once.

Matt.

It was him.

And everything came rushing back to her—the way she'd awoken to find him gone, no evidence he'd even slept in the same bed as her, no note, nothing. No way of contacting him, nothing to remember him by except the strange sensation of her body having been made love to, and a desire to feel that sensation again and again.

'Hello, Frances,' he said, his eyes just exactly as she remembered, just exactly like Leo's. How many dreams had she spent painting those eyes? Mixing exactly the right shades of silver, grey and flecks of white to flick, close to the iris? The lashes, with their luxuriant black curls, had occupied much of her artist's mind. How to transpose them onto canvas without looking heavy-handed? They were so thick and glossy that no one would actually believe they really existed.

It had been three years since Frankie had seen this man but, courtesy of her dreams, she remembered him as vividly as if they'd met only the day before.

Oh, how she wanted to drag her eyes down his body, to luxuriate in every inch of him, to remember the strength in his frame, the contradictory gentleness he'd shown when he'd taken possession of her body that first time, when he'd held her in his arms and removed the vestiges of her innocence. How she wanted to give into the temptation to hungrily devour him with her gaze.

With the greatest of efforts, she crossed her arms over her chest and maintained her attention on his face. A face that was watching her with just as much intensity as she was him.

'Matt,' she murmured, proud beyond description when her voice came out steady and cool. 'Are you looking for a piece of art?'

Something seemed to throb between them. A power source that was all its own, that Frankie pushed aside. It wasn't welcome.

'Would you show me your work?' he responded, and it wasn't an answer. It was an invitation, one that was fraught with danger. Belatedly, she recollected that the wall of paintings behind her was of their son and if he looked a little to the left or right he'd see clearly for himself the proof of their weekend together.

'Fine,' she agreed, a little rushed, moving deeper into the gallery, towards another annex. 'But I only have a few minutes.'

At this, she saw Charles frown in her peripheral vision. No wonder he was confused. Without knowing anything about Matt, it was clear that he had enough money to buy everything in the place, probably a million times over. From the fit of his suit to the gleam of his shoes, this was a man who obviously lived very, very comfortably. In normal circumstances, she wouldn't dream of rejecting a potential investor in her work.

But Matt?

Matt who'd crashed into her world, seduced her effortlessly, triumphed over her and gone away again, just as quickly? He was danger, and not for anything would she spend more time with him than she had to.

He's your son's father. Her conscience flared to life and she almost stopped walking, so intense was the realisation, the moral impetus that stabbed into her sides.

'I will take over when Miss Preston leaves.' Charles's offer came from just behind them.

Matt stopped walking, turning to face the other man. 'Miss Preston's company will be sufficient.'

Frankie saw pink bloom in the gallery owner's face and sympathy swelled in her. Charles La Nough's gallery was renowned in New York, and he was used to being met with respect, if not a degree of awe.

To be dismissed in such a way was obviously a new experience.

'I'll call if we need you,' Frankie offered, to soften the blow.

'Very well.' Charles sniffed, turning and disappearing in the direction of the rooms that would eventually lead to the front door.

'You didn't have to be so rude,' she responded, only this time the words were breathy and her pulse was rushing inside her. They were close—just a few feet apart—and she could smell him, she could feel his warmth and her skin was pricking with goosebumps.

Responses she had long since thought dead were stirring to life and demanding indulgence. But she ignored them—such feelings had no place here, or anywhere any more. She tilted her chin defiantly and stared at him. 'And now that he's gone you can tell me exactly what you're doing here. Because I know it's not to buy one of my paintings.'

He regarded her through shuttered eyes. Memory was a funny thing. He'd recollected her in intimate detail over the years, but there were a thousand minute differences now that he stood toe to toe with Frankie Preston. Things his mind hadn't properly written into his memory banks, so that he wanted to hold her still and just *look*.

She remained the most distractingly intriguing woman he'd ever seen, and yet there was no one thing in particular he could ascribe that to. It was *everything* about her—from eyes that were feline in shape and just as green as he remembered, to a nose that had a tiny ski jump at its end and a flurry of pale freckles rushing over its bridge, and lips—*Dio*, those lips.

Pink and pillowy, soft, so that when he'd crushed his mouth to them three years earlier they'd parted on a husky sigh, surrendering to him, welcoming him. His body tightened at the recollection.

Then, she'd been coming home from an art class, carrying a rolled-up canvas in a bag, wearing a pair of paint-splattered jeans and a simple white singlet top, also marked with the signs of her artistic labour. And she'd been so distracted in her own thoughts that she'd walked right into him, smearing a healthy dose of what he'd later discovered to be Cerulean Blue on his suit.

He'd liked her in those clothes—so casual and relaxed.

Now, she wore a dress, black with puffy sleeves that just covered her shoulders and a neckline that dipped frustratingly close to her cleavage without revealing even a hint of the generous curves beneath. It fell to her ankles, and she'd teamed it with leather sandals and a bright yellow necklace. It was a more elegant ensemble, but still so very Frankie.

As she was in his mind, anyway.

But wasn't it more than likely that the woman he'd slept with three years earlier was more a creation of his than a real-life, flesh-and-blood woman? Wasn't it more than likely he'd created a fantasy? How well could he have really known her, given that they'd spent so little time together?

'How do you know,' he drawled, considering her question, 'that I am not here to make a purchase?'

She blotted her lips together; they were painted the most fascinating shade of dark pink—as if she'd been feasting on sun-warmed cherries and the natural pigments had stained her mouth.

'Because you're not interested in my art.'

He thought of the piece in his office, the piece he'd bought through a dealer to keep his acquisition at arm's length—the painting Frankie had been working on the day they'd met—and frowned slightly. 'Why would you say that?'

A hint of pink bloomed in her cheeks. 'Well, I remember clearly how well you played me. Pretending interest in my work is how you fooled me then. I won't be so stupid this time around. So what is it that brings you to the gallery, Matt?'

Her use of that name filled him with a confusing rush of emotions. Shame at having given her only the diminutive of his full name, because surely it proved that he'd set out to deceive her, even from that first moment? Pleasure at the memories it invoked—no other woman had called him that; it was *their* name, it belonged to that weekend, and he would hear it on her lips for ever, calling out to him at the height of her passion.

He wanted her.

Even now, after three years, after walking away from her, he congratulated himself on doing the right thing. He'd been strong in the face of incomprehensible temptation, and he'd done it for his kingdom.

But…

Oh, yes. He wanted her.

Moving slightly closer, just enough to be able to catch a hint of her vanilla perfume, he spoke, his eyes intent when they met hers.

'I am to marry. Soon.'

* * *

His words seemed to come to her from a long way away, as though he were shouting from atop a high-rise, and the floor of the gallery lifted in one corner like a rug being shaken, threatening to tip her off the sides of the earth.

I am to marry.

Her stomach rolled with what she told herself must be relief. Because his impending marriage meant she was safe—safe from the flashes of desire that were warming her insides, safe from an insane need to revisit the past even though it was so obviously better left there. How dare she feel like that, when he'd walked out on her without having the decency to leave so much as a note?

'That's nice,' she said, the words not quite as clear and calm as she'd have liked. 'So perhaps you are after a painting after all? A wedding present for your wife?' She spun on her heel, moving deeper into the gallery. 'I have some lovely landscapes I painted out in Massachusetts. Very pretty. Romantic. Floaty.' She was babbling but she couldn't help it.

I am to marry. Soon. His words were running around and around in her mind, ricocheting off the edges of her consciousness.

'Perhaps this piece.' She gestured to a painting of a lake, surrounded by trees on the cusp of losing their leaves, orange and bright, against a beautiful blue sky. Her heart panged as she remembered the day, that slice of life, when she'd taken Leo on their first vacation and they'd toured Paxton and its surroundings.

'Frankie…' His voice was deep and, though he spoke softly, it was with a natural command, a low, throbbing urgency that had her spinning to face him and—damn him—remembering too much of their time together, the way he'd groaned her name as he'd buried his lips at her neck, then lower, teasing her nipples with his tongue.

Only he was so much closer than she'd realised, his large frame right behind her, so when she turned their bodies brushed and it was as though a thousand volts of electricity were being dumped into her system.

She swallowed hard then took a step backwards, but not far enough. It gave her only an inch or so of breathing space and when she inhaled he was there, filling her senses. *He's getting married!*

'What are you doing here?' She didn't bother to hide the emotion in the question. He was a part of her past that hadn't been good. Oh, the weekend itself, sure, but waking up to discover he'd literally walked out on her? To find herself pregnant and have no way of contacting him? The embarrassment of having to hire a detective who even then could discover no trace of this man?

'I…' The word trailed off as he echoed her movement, taking a step forward, closing the distance between them. His expression was tense; his face wore a mask of discontent. Frustration and impatience radiated off him in waves. 'I wished to see you again. Before my wedding.'

She took a moment, letting his statement settle into her mind, and she examined it from all angles. But it made no sense. 'Why?'

His nostrils flared, his eyes narrowed with intent. 'Do you ever think about our time together?'

And the penny dropped and fury lashed at her spine, powerful and fierce, so she jerked her head away from him and bit back a curse her adoptive mother certainly wouldn't have approved of.

'Are you kidding me with this, Matt? You're getting *married* and you're here to walk down memory lane?' She moved away from him, further into the room, her pulse hammering, her heart rushing.

He was watching her with an intensity that almost

robbed her of breath. Only she was angry too, angry that he thought he could show up after all this time and ask about that damned weekend…

'Or did you want to do more than walk down memory lane? Tell me you didn't come here for another roll in the hay?' she demanded, crossing her arms over her chest, then wishing she hadn't when his eyes dropped to the swell of her cleavage. Indignation made her go on the attack. 'You can't be so hard up for sex that you're resorting to trawling through lovers from years ago?'

A muscle throbbed low in his jaw as her insult hit its mark. Matt Whatever-his-last-name-was was clearly all macho alpha pride. Her suggestion had riled him. Well, so what? She couldn't care less.

'And no, I *don't* think about that weekend!' she snapped before he could interject. 'So far as I'm concerned, you're just some blip in my rear-view mirror—and if I could take what happened between us back, I would,' she lied, her stomach rolling at the betrayal of their son.

'Oh, really?' he asked softly, words that were dangerous and seductive all at once, his husky accent as spicy and tempting as it had been three years earlier.

'Yes, really.' She glared at him to underscore her point.

'So you don't think about the way it felt when I kissed you here?' She was completely unprepared for his touch—the feather-light caress of a single finger against her jaw, the pulse-point there moving into frantic overdrive as butterflies stormed through her chest.

'No.' The word was slightly uneven.

'Or the way you liked me to touch you here?' and he drew his finger lower, to her décolletage, and then lower still, to the gentle curve of her breast.

Heaven help her, memories were threatening to pull her

under, to drown her with their perfection, even when the truth of their situation was disastrous.

Just for a second, she wanted to surrender to those recollections. She wanted to pretend they didn't have a son together and that they were back in time, in that hotel room, just him and her, no consciousness of the outside world.

But it would be an exercise in futility.

'Don't.' She batted his hand away and stepped away from him, anger almost a match for her desire. She rammed her hands against her hips, breathing in hard, wishing there was even the slightest hint of his having been as affected by those needs as she had been. 'It was three years ago,' she whispered. 'You can't just show up after all this time, after disappearing into thin air...'

He watched her from a face that was carefully blanked of emotion, his expression mask-like. 'I had to see you.'

Her heart twisted at those words, at the sense that perhaps he'd found it impossible to forget their night together. Except he'd done exactly that. He'd walked away without a backwards glance. He could have called her at any time in the past three years, but he hadn't. Nothing. Not a blip.

'Well, you've *seen* me,' she said firmly. 'And now I think you should go.'

'You're angry with me.'

'Yes.' She held his gaze, her eyes showing hurt and betrayal. 'I woke up and you were *gone*! You don't think I have a right to be angry?'

A muscle twisted at the base of his firm, square jaw. 'We agreed we would just spend the weekend together.'

'Yes, but that wasn't tacit approval for you to slink out in the middle of the night.'

His eyes narrowed. 'I did *not* slink.' And then, as if bringing himself back to the point, he was calm again, his arrogant face blanked of any emotion once more. 'And it was best for both of us that I left when I did.'

It was strange, really, how she'd been pulling her temper back into place, easing it into the box in which it lived, only to have it explode out of her, writhing free of her grip with a blinding intensity. 'How? How was you disappearing into thin air *best* for me?' she demanded, her voice raised, her face pale.

He sighed as though she were a recalcitrant toddler and his impatience at fraying point. 'My life is complicated.' He spoke without apology, words that were cool and firm and offered no hint of what had truly motivated his departure. 'That weekend was an aberration. In retrospect, I shouldn't have let it happen. I had no business getting involved with someone like you.'

'Someone like me?' she repeated, the words deceptively soft when inside her cells were screeching with indignation. 'But it was fine to sleep with someone like me?'

'You misunderstand my meaning,' he said with a shake of his head. 'And that is my fault.'

'So what is your meaning?'

He spoke slowly, carefully, as though she might not comprehend. 'I wanted you the minute I saw you, Frankie, but I knew it could *never* be more than that weekend. I believe I was upfront about that; I apologise if you expected more from me.' He went to move closer but she bristled, and he stilled. 'There are expectations upon me, expectations as to who I will marry, and you are not the kind of bride I would ever be able to choose.'

She spluttered her interruption. 'I didn't want to *marry* you! I just wanted the courtesy of a goodbye from the man I lost my virginity to. When you crept out of that hotel suite, did you stop to think about what I would think?'

She had the very slight satisfaction of seeing something

like remorse briefly glance across his stony features. 'I had to leave. I'm sorry if that hurt you—'

'Hurt me?' She glared at him and shook her head. It had damned near killed her, but she wasn't going to tell him that. 'What *hurts* is your stupidity! Your lack of decency and moral fibre.'

He jerked his face as though she'd slapped him, but she didn't stop.

'You were my first lover.' She lowered her voice. 'Sleeping with you *meant* something to me! And you just left.'

'What would you have had me do, Frankie? Stay and cook you breakfast? Break it to you over scrambled eggs and salmon that I was going to go back to Tolmirós to forget all about you?'

Her stare was withering. 'Only you haven't forgotten me, have you?'

She held her breath, waiting for him to answer, her lips parted.

'No,' he agreed finally. 'But I left because I knew I needed to. I left because I knew what was expected of me.' He expelled a harsh breath, then another, slowly regaining control of himself. 'I didn't come here to upset you, Frankie. I'll go away again.'

And at that, true, dark anger beat in her breast because it simply underscored their power imbalance. He'd come to her and so she was seeing him again, and he'd touched her as though desire was still a current in the room—it was all on his terms. All his timeline, his power, his control. He thought he could leave when it suited him and have that be the end of it.

Well, damn him, he had no right! 'Did you even think about the consequences of that night, Matt? Did you so much as give even a second thought to whether or not I would be able to walk away from what we shared as easily as you did?'

CHAPTER TWO

For the briefest of moments he misunderstood. Surely, he'd misunderstood.

As the heir to the throne of Tolmirós, Matthias had *never* taken any risks with sex. That weekend had been no different. He'd employed protective measures. He'd been careful, as always.

'I knew there would be no consequences,' he said, shrugging, as though his heart hadn't skidded to a dramatic halt seconds earlier. 'And I truly believed a clean break would be better for you.'

And for himself. He hadn't trusted his willpower to so much as call her, to explain who he was and his reasons for needing to disappear from her life.

'*How* did you know that?'

His frown was infinitesimal. 'Are you saying there was a consequence?'

'A consequence?' she repeated with an arched brow. But her fingers were shaking, a small gesture but one he noted with growing attention. 'Why are we speaking in euphemisms? Ask what you really mean.'

She spoke to him in a way no one in his life had ever dared, and it was thrilling and dangerous and his whole body resonated with a need to argue with her, just like this. Passions were stirring inside him but he shoved them aside, focusing everything on whatever the hell she was trying to say.

'You are the one who is insinuating there was a complication from our night together.'

'I'm *telling* you your arrogant presumption that you took sufficient measures to protect me from the ramifications of our sleeping together is wrong.'

He narrowed his eyes and her words sprayed around them like fine blades, slicing through the artwork on the walls.

'Are you saying you fell pregnant?' he demanded, his ears screeching with the sound of frantically racing blood. The world stood still; time stopped.

For a moment he imagined that—his child, growing in her belly—and his chest swelled with pride and his heart soared, but pain was right behind, because surely it wasn't possible. His forehead broke out in perspiration at the very idea of his baby. He knew it was inevitable and necessary, but he still needed time to brace himself for that reality—for the idea of another person who shared his blood, a person who could be taken from him at any time.

Rejection was in every line of his body. 'We were careful. *I* was careful. I took precautions, as I always do.'

'Charming!' She crossed her arms over her chest. 'Tell me more about the other women you've had sex with, please.'

He ground his teeth together. He hadn't meant that, and yet it was true. Sexual responsibility was ingrained in Matthias. Anyone in his position would take that seriously.

'What the hell are you saying?' he demanded, all the command his position conferred upon him in those words.

She sucked in a deep breath as though she was steadying herself. 'Fine. Yes. I fell pregnant.' Her words hit him right in the solar plexus, each with the speed and strength of a thousand bullets.

'What?' For the first time in his life, Matthias was utterly lost for words.

When his family had died and a nation in mourning had looked to him, a fifteen-year-old who'd lost his parents and brother, who'd been trapped in a car with them as life had left their bodies, he had known what was expected of him. He'd received the news and wrapped his grief into a small compartment for indulgence at a later date, and he'd shown himself to be strong and reliable: a perfect king-in-waiting.

She lifted her fingertips to the side of her head, rubbing her temples, and fixed him with her ocean-green stare. Her anguish was unmistakable.

'I found out about a month after you left.'

His world was a place that made no sense. There were sharp edges everywhere, and nothing fitted together. 'You were pregnant?'

She pulled a face. 'I just said that.'

His eyes swept shut, his blood raced. 'You should have told me.'

'I *tried*! You were literally impossible to find.'

'No one is impossible to find.'

'Believe me, *you* are. "Matt". That's all I had to go on. The hotel wouldn't give me any information about who'd booked the suite. I had your name and the fact you're from Tolmirós. That's it. I *wanted* to tell you. But trying to find you was like looking for a needle in an enormous haystack.'

And hadn't he planned for it to be this way? A night without complications—that was what they'd shared. Only everything about Frankie had been complicated, including the way she'd cleaved her way into his soul.

'So you made a decision like this on your own?' he fired back, the pain of what he'd lost, what his kingdom had lost, the most important thing in the conversation.

'Decision?' She paled. 'It was hardly a decision.'

'You had an abortion and took from me any chance to even know my child,' he said thickly, his chest tight, his organs squeezing inside him.

She sucked in a loud breath. 'What makes you think I had an abortion?'

He stared at her, the question hanging between them, everything sharp and uncertain now. When he was nine years old he'd run the entire way around the palace, without pausing for even a moment. Up steps, along narrow precipices with frightening glimpses of the city far beneath him, he'd run and he'd run, and when he'd finished he'd collapsed onto the grass and stared at the clouds. His lungs had burned and he'd been conscious of the sting of every cell in his body, as though he was somehow supersonic. He felt that now.

'You're saying…' He stared at her, trying to make sense of this, looking for an explanation and arriving at only one. 'You didn't have an abortion?'

'Of course I didn't.'

Matthias had a rapier-sharp mind, yet he struggled to process her words, to make sense of what she was saying. 'You did not have an abortion?'

'No.'

And something fired inside his mind, a memory, a small recollection that had been unimportant at the time. He spun away from her and stalked through the gallery, through the smaller display spaces that curved towards a larger central room. And he stared at the wall that had framed Frankie when he'd first walked in. He'd been so blindsided by the vision of her initially that he hadn't properly understood the significance of what he was seeing. But now he looked at the paintings—ten of them in total, all of the same little boy—and his blood turned into lava in his veins.

He stared at the paintings and a primal sense of pride and

possession firmed inside him. Something else too. Something that made his chest scream and his brow heat—something that made acid coat his insides, as he stared at the boy who was so familiar to him.

Spiro.

He was looking at a version not only of his younger self, but also of his brother. Eyes that had held his, pain and anguish filling them, as life ebbed from him. Eyes that had begged him to help. Eyes that had eventually clouded and died as Matthias watched, helpless, powerless.

For a moment he looked towards the ground, his chest heaving, his pulse like an avalanche, and he breathed in, waiting for the familiar panic to subside.

'This is my son.' More than his son—this was his kin, his blood, his.

He didn't have to turn around to know she was right behind him.

'He's two and a half,' Frankie murmured, the words husky. She cleared her throat audibly. 'His name is Leo.'

Matthias's eyes swept shut as he absorbed this information. Leo. Two and a half. Spiro had been nine when he'd died, the vestiges of his boyish face still in evidence. Cheeks that were rounded like this, and dimpled when he smiled, eyes that sparkled with all his secrets and amusements.

He pushed the memories away, refusing to give into them like this. Only in the middle of the night, when time seemed to slip past the veil of living, when ancient stars with their wisdom and experience whispered that they would listen, did he let his mind remember, did he let his heart hurt.

He turned his attention to the paintings, giving each one in turn the full power of his inspection. Several of the artworks depicted Leo—his son—in a state of play. Laughing as he tossed leaves overhead, his sense of joy and vitality communicated through the paint by Frankie's talented hand. Other paintings were a study of portraiture.

It was the final picture that held him utterly in its thrall.

Leo was staring out of the canvas, his expression frozen in time, arresting a moment of query. One brow was lifted, his lips were turned into a half-smile. His eyes were grey, like Matthias's—in fact, much of his face was a carbon copy of Matthias's own bearing. But the freckles that ran haphazardly across the bridge of his nose were all Frankie's, as was the defiant amusement that stirred in the boy's features.

Emotions welled inside Matthias, for his own face was only borrowed—first from his father, King Stavros, and it had now been passed onto his own son. What other features and qualities were held by this boy, this small human who was of his own flesh and blood?

His own flesh and blood! An heir! An heir his country was desperate for, an heir he had been poised to marry in order to beget—an heir, already living! An heir, two years old, who he knew nothing about!

'Where is he?' The question was gravelled.

He felt her stiffen—he felt everything in that moment, as though the universe was a series of strings and fibres connected through his body to hers. He turned around, pinning her with a gaze that shimmered like liquid metal.

'Where.' The word was a slowly flying bullet. 'Is.' He took a step closer to her. 'He?'

All the myths upon which he'd been raised, the beliefs of his people as to the power and strength that ran through his veins, a power that was now in his son's veins, propelled him forward. But it was not purely a question of royal lineage and the discovery of an heir. This was an ancient, soul-deep need to meet his son—as a man, as a father.

Alarm resonated from Frankie and until that moment he'd never understood what the term 'mother bear' had been coined for. She was tiny and slight but she looked more than capable of murdering him with her bare hands if he did anything to threaten their child.

'He's outside the city,' she said evasively, her eyes shifting towards the door. Through it was the foyer, and somewhere there the man who ran this gallery. Her fear was evident, and it served little purpose. He was no threat to her, nor their son.

With the discipline he was famed for, Matthias brought his emotions tightly under control. They didn't serve him in that moment. Just like his grief had needed to be contained when his family had been killed, so too did his feelings need to be now.

His whole world had shifted off its axis, and he had to find a way to fix that. To redefine the parameters of his being. An heir was driving his need for marriage and here, it turned out, an heir already existed! There was no option for Matthias but to bring that child home to Tolmirós.

His future shifted before his eyes, and this woman was in it, and their son. All the reasons he'd had for walking away from her still stood, except for this heir. It changed everything.

'I had no idea you were pregnant.'

'Of course you didn't. How could you? You probably walked out as soon as I fell asleep.'

No, he'd waited longer than that. He'd watched her sleep for a while, and thought of his kingdom, the expectations that he would return to Tolmirós and take up his title and all the responsibilities that went with that. Frankie had been a diversion—a distraction. She'd been an indulgence when he'd known he was on the cusp of the life he'd been destined to lead.

Only she'd also been quicksand, and a fast escape had seemed the only solution. The longer he'd lingered, the deeper he'd risked sinking, until escape had no longer been guaranteed.

Besides, he'd comforted himself at the time, he'd made her no promises. He'd told her he was only in the States for the weekend. There were no expectations beyond that. He hadn't broken his word.

'If you'd left your number, I would have called. But you just vanished into thin air. Not even the detective I hired could find you.'

'You hired a detective?' The admission sent sparks through him—sparks of relief and gratitude. Because she hadn't intentionally kept their son a secret. She'd wanted him to be a part of the boy's life. And if he'd known of the child back then? If he'd discovered Frankie's pregnancy?

He would have married her. Her lack of suitability as a royal bride would have been beside the point: his people cared most for the delivery of an heir.

And now he had one.

Every possibility and desire narrowed into one finite realisation. There was only one way forward and the sooner he could convince Frankie of that, the better.

'Yes.' She looked away from him and swallowed visibly, her throat chording before his eyes and his gut clenched as he remembered kissing her there, feeling the fluttering of her racing pulse beneath her fine, soft skin. 'I felt you should know.'

'Indeed.' He dipped his head forward and then, appealing to the sense of justice he knew ran through her passionate veins, 'Will you come for dinner with me?'

Her refusal was imminent but he shook his head to forestall her. 'To discuss our son. You must see how important that is?'

She was tense, her face rigid, her eyes untrusting. But finally she nodded. A tight shift of her head and an even tighter grimace of those cherry-stained lips. 'Fine. But just a quick meal. I told Becky I'd be home by nine.'

'Becky?'

'My downstairs neighbour. She helps out with Leo when I'm working.'

He filed this detail away, and the image it created, of the mother of his child, the mother of the heir to the throne of Tolmirós, a child worth billions of euros, being minded by some random woman in the suburbs of New York.

'A quick meal, then,' he said, giving no indication he was second-guessing her child-minding arrangements.

'Well?' The owner of the gallery appeared from behind the desk, his eyes travelling from Frankie to Matthias. 'Isn't she talented?'

'Exceptionally,' Matthias agreed, and he'd always known that to be the case. 'I will take all of the artworks against that wall.' He gestured through the doorway, to the display that housed the portraits of his son.

'You'll what?' Frankie startled as she looked up at him, though he couldn't tell if she was surprised or annoyed.

He removed a card from his wallet. 'If you call the number on this card, my valet will arrange payment and delivery.' He nodded curtly and then put a hand in the small of Frankie's back, guiding her towards the front door.

Shock, apparently, held her quiet. But once they emerged onto the Manhattan street, a sultry summer breeze warming the evening, she stopped walking, jerking out of his reach and spinning to face him.

'Why did you do that?'

'You think it strange that I should want paintings of my son?'

She bristled and he understood—she had yet to come to terms with the fact that he was also the boy's parent, that she now had to share their son.

Not only that—he couldn't have paintings of his child, the heir to his throne, for sale in some gallery in New York. It wasn't how things were done.

'No,' she admitted grudgingly, and the emotion of this situation was taking its toll on her. The strength and defiance she carried in her eyes were draining from her. Wariness took their place.

'Come on.' He gestured towards the jet-black SUV that was parked in front of the gallery. Darkly tinted windows concealed his driver and security detail from sight but, as they approached, Zeno stepped out, opening the rear doors with a low bow.

Frankie caught it, her eyes narrowing at the gesture of deference. It was so much a part of Matthias's day that he barely noticed the respect with which he was treated. Seeing it through Frankie's eyes though, he understood. It was confronting and unusual.

'You know, I never even had your surname,' she murmured as she slid into the white leather interior of the car—her skin was so pale now it matched the seats.

There was so much he wanted to ask about that. Would she have given their child his name if she'd known it? The idea of his son being raised as anything other than a Vasilliás filled him with a dark frustration.

He wanted to ask her this, and so much more, but not even in front of his most trusted servants would he yet broach the subject of his heir.

With a single finger lifted to his mouth, he signalled silence and then settled back into the car himself, brooding over this turn of events and what they would mean for the marriage he had intended to make.

'I presumed you meant dinner at a restaurant,' she said as the car pulled up to a steel monolith on United Nations

Plaza. The drive had been conducted in absolute silence, except for when the car drew to a stop and he'd spoken to his driver in that language of his, all husky and deep, so her pulse had fired up and her stomach had churned and feelings that deserved to stay buried deep in the past flashed in her gut, making her nerve-endings quiver and her pulse fire chaotically against the fine walls of her veins.

'Restaurants are not private enough.'

'You can't speak quietly in a restaurant?'

'Believe me, Frankie, this is better.' His look was loaded with intensity and there was a plea in the depth of his gaze as well, begging her to simply agree with him on this occasion. There was a part of her, a childish, silly part, that wanted to refuse—to tell him it didn't suit her. He'd disappeared into thin air and she'd tried so hard to find him, to tell him he was a father. And now? Everything was on his terms. She wanted to rebel against that, but loyalty to their son kept her quiet. All along, she'd wanted what was best for Leo. She'd spent all her life feeling rejected and unwanted by her biological parents, and she had wept for any idea that Leo might feel the same! That Leo might grow up believing his father hadn't wanted him.

'Fine,' she agreed heavily. 'But I really can't stay long.'

'This is not a conversation to be rushed.' He stepped out of the car and she followed. He placed a hand on her elbow, guiding her through the building's sliding glass doors. The lifts were waiting, a security guard to one side.

She hadn't noticed this degree of staff with him back then. There hadn't been anyone except a driver, and she'd never really questioned that. It was obvious that he had money—but this was a whole new degree of wealth.

'Have you had some kind of death threat or something?' she muttered as the doors of the lift snapped closed behind them.

The look he sent her was half-rueful, half-impatient; he said nothing. But when the lift doors opened into the foyer of what could only be described as a sky palace, he urged her into the space and then held a hand up to still the guard.

More words, spoken in his own tongue, and then the guard bowed low and slipped back into the lift, leaving them alone.

She swallowed at that thought—being alone with him—distracting herself by studying the over-the-top luxury of this penthouse. It wasn't just the polished timber floors, double height ceilings, expensive designer furnishings and crystal chandeliers that created the impression of total glamour. It was the views of the Manhattan skyline—the Chrysler Building, the Empire State, Central Park—it all spread before her like a pop-up book of New York city.

Large sliding glass doors opened out onto a deck, beyond which there was a pool, set against a glass rail. She imagined swimming in it would feel a little like floating, high above the city.

The contrasts between her own modest apartment in Queens and this insanely beautiful penthouse were too ridiculous to enumerate.

'Matt,' she sighed, turning to face him, not even sure what she wanted to say. He was watching her with a look of dark concentration.

'My name,' he said quietly, 'is Matthias Vasilliás.'

It was perfect for this man—as soon as he gave her the full version of his name it resonated inside her, like the banging of a drum. *Matt* was too pedestrian for someone like him. He was exotic and unusual.

'Fine.' She nodded curtly, pleased when the word sounded vaguely dismissive. 'Matthias.'

At this, his eyes flashed with something she couldn't comprehend. 'You have not heard of me?'

Something like an alarm bell began to ring inside Frankie's mind. 'Should I have?'

His lips twisted in a sardonic smile. 'No.'

But it sounded like judgement rather than offence, and she bristled. 'So? What gives?' Her frown deepened. 'What's with all the security?'

He sighed heavily. 'This is a light protection detail.' He shrugged. 'At home, there are many more guards.'

'Why? I don't get it. Are you some kind of celebrity or something?'

'You could say that.'

He moved into the kitchen and pulled out a bottle of wine. Her stomach rolled at the memories of the wine they'd shared that night—only a few sips, but it had been the nicest she'd ever tasted. He poured her a glass and walked around to her; she took it on autopilot.

'What's going on, Matt—Matthias?'

His eyes narrowed and she wondered if the sound of his full name on her lips was as strange for him as it was for her. Matt had suited him, but Matthias suited him better. She liked the taste of those exotic syllables on the tip of her tongue.

'My family was killed in an accident many years ago. When I was a boy of fifteen.' He spoke matter-of-factly, so it was impossible for Frankie to know how those deaths had affected him. She could imagine, though.

'I'm sorry,' she murmured crisply, wishing she didn't feel sympathy for him. Wishing she didn't feel *anything* for him.

His lips twisted in acknowledgement. 'It was a long time ago.'

'I'm sure it still hurts.'

'I have become used to being alone.' He brushed her concern aside. 'My father's brother took on many of the responsibilities of my father. At fifteen, I was too young.'

'What responsibilities?' she asked.

'Shortly after their deaths, it was decided that on my thirtieth birthday I would assume my role.' He pinpointed her with his gaze, but he was obviously back in time, reflecting on the past. 'One week before I turned thirty, I met you. I was only in New York for the weekend. One of my last chances to travel as myself, without this degree of… company.' His expression shifted.

'What did your parents do?'

But this wasn't a conversation with questions and answers. It was a monologue. An unburdening of himself, and it was an explanation she'd wanted for such a long time that she didn't even particularly mind.

'I shouldn't have got involved with you, but you were so… I cannot explain it. I saw you, and I wanted you.' He stared at her, his eyes glinting like steel, and her heart was ice in her chest. It had been that simple for him. He'd seen her. He'd wanted her. And so he'd had her.

'I knew it would only ever be a brief affair.'

Her throat constricted with those words, damning what they'd been to such a cynical seduction. 'Yet you did it anyway?'

He was quiet.

'Did you think about how I'd feel?'

'No.' He swept his eyes shut. 'I told myself you were just like me—looking for a weekend of pleasure. Casual, easy sex.'

'I think the term "casual sex" is oxymoronic,' she said stiffly, turning away from him so she didn't see the way his expression shifted, the way a fierce blade of possession pressed into him.

'If I had known you were a virgin…'

'I didn't lie to you intentionally,' she muttered. 'I just got caught up in how I felt. It was all so overwhelming.'

He dipped his head forward in silent concession. 'It is in the past,' he said. 'What I'm interested in dealing with is our future.'

And here it was. The custody discussion she'd been dreading. And as the days had turned into months and her status as a single mother had been firmly established, she'd come to accept that it was a conversation she'd never need to have. Now, though, faced with the father of her baby, she had no interest in denying him his right to see their child. To be a part of his life. Even when his admission that he'd gone into their affair expecting it to be 'casual sex' had cut her deep inside.

'After I left you, I went back to Tolmirós and took up the position that was my birthright.'

She frowned. 'Just what kind of family business are you in?'

His smile was more like a grimace. 'It is not a business, Frankie. My name is Matthias Vasilliás and I am the King of Tolmirós.'

CHAPTER THREE

'I'M SORRY.' SHE blinked slowly. 'I thought you just said you were…' She laughed, a brittle sound of disbelief. 'I mean, is this some kind of joke?'

But she looked around the penthouse with new eyes, seeing the degree of luxury and wealth as if for the first time, understanding how uniquely positioned a person would have to be to enjoy this kind of residence. And it wasn't just this ludicrously expensive apartment—how much would something like this even cost? More than she could imagine, that was for sure. And she saw *everything* through the veil of his words and her stomach dropped and her knees shook. Because it was *so* obvious now.

Even then, staying at a hotel, he'd been so *different* to anyone she'd ever known. He'd spoken to her of ancient myths and he'd weaved magic into her being.

He'd been totally unique. A king.

'It's no joke. That weekend with you was my way of trying to ignore the reality of how my life was about to change, of pretending I wasn't about to take the throne and the mantle of King. But I do not believe in hiding, Frankie. And so I left you in order to return to my country, my people, and my role as ruler.'

His words came to her from very far away.

He was a king.

Which meant… Oh, God. She reached behind her for

the sofa, dropping down into it with a thud and drinking her wine as though it were a lifeline.

'Yes,' he agreed, moving closer to her, the word drawn from deep in his throat. 'Our son is my heir. He is a prince, Frankie.'

'But…he's not… We weren't married.' She clutched at straws desperately. 'So doesn't that mean he can't be your heir?'

His expression darkened and he took a moment to answer. 'It complicates matters,' he agreed eventually, with a shrug. 'But nothing changes the fact he is the future of my people.'

She swallowed, his certainty formidable.

'Do you remember the Myth of Elektus?'

She swayed a little, the words he'd spoken that night burned into her memories. 'No,' she lied huskily, staring out at New York.

'My family has ruled Tolmirós for over a millennium. Our line remains unbroken. Wars and famines consumed neighbouring countries but, within the borders of Tolmirós, life has been prosperous and stable. The myth of our First Ruler is one my people hold in their hearts, even now. It is believed that my family's lineage is at the root of Tolmirós's wealth and happiness. Leo is *not* simply a boy—he is the fulfilment of a myth and ruling Tolmirós is his destiny, as much as it was mine.'

The magic he'd wound around her heart was weaving into her soul once more, and her beautiful child, who *was* so kingly, even as a child, began to pull away from her as she saw him as a figure of the fabric of this faraway country.

But he wasn't only the heir to Tolmirós's throne: he was her son. A child she had grown in her belly and nursed through fevers and helped to take his first step. He was a child she'd read to every night of his life, played ball with, lain beside when night terrors had caused him to cry out.

'My people need him to come home, Frankie. He is part of that myth—he is our future.'

Her eyes swept shut on a wave of desolation. 'You speak of your people, and you speak of his destiny. These are the words of a king, not a father.' She turned to face him. 'How can you not care about him as your son? He is a little boy and for two and a half years he has existed and all you care about is his destiny to rule a country he hasn't even heard of. You haven't asked me a single thing about him!'

His eyes glittered at the truth of her accusation. 'You think I am not burning to know *every single detail* about my son? You think I am not desperate to meet him and hold him to me, and look into his face and understand him? Of course I am. But first I must secure your understanding for what will happen next. We must move quickly if we are to control this.'

'Control what?'

He expelled an impatient breath and his nostrils flared. 'Our marriage.'

'Marriage?' She paled visibly. 'I'm not marrying *you*!'

'With respect, Frankie, that decision was taken out of our hands the minute you conceived Leo.'

'That's not how I see it.'

'Then let me be clear: there is no reality where I will not be raising my son as my son and heir.'

'Fine. Be his father. Even let him be the heir to your damned country—'

Matthias's expression darkened.

'But don't think you can show up after three years and try to take over our lives. Whatever we shared that night, it was fleeting. Meaningless. Just like you said. And it's over. You're just some guy I frankly wish I'd never met.'

His cheekbones were slashed a dark red. 'That may be the case, but we *did* meet. We slept together and now we have a son. And I cannot ignore that. We must marry, Frankie. Surely you can see it's the only way?'

She drew in a shaking breath at the finality of that, and fear trembled inside her breast.

'No.'

'No?' he repeated, and then laughed, a harsh sound of disbelief. 'You cannot simply say "no" to me.'

'Because you're a king?'

His eyes narrowed watchfully. 'Because I am his father, and I will fight you with every breath in my body to bring him home.'

'He *is* home!'

'He is the heir of Tolmirós and he belongs in the palace.'

'With you?'

'And you. You'll be my wife, the Queen of a prosperous, happy country. It's not like I'm asking you to give him up. Nor to move somewhere unpleasant. You wouldn't even have to live with me—I have many palaces; you could choose which you wanted to reside in. Your life will be significantly improved.'

'How can you say that? I'd be married to you.'

'And?'

'I hardly even know you!' The words flew from her mouth and her body immediately contradicted them. Her body knew his well. So well. Even now, dressed as he was, she saw him naked. She saw his broad, muscular chest, his swarthy tan, his wide shoulders, and her insides slicked with moist heat as—out of nowhere—she remembered the way he'd possessed her utterly and completely.

'We will get to know each other enough.' He shrugged. 'Enough to raise a family together, enough to be a good King and Queen.'

He spoke dispassionately, calmly, but the words he spoke, the images they made, filled her with a warm, tingling sense in her gut. 'It's that easy for you?'

'I've never expected any differently.'

'Wait a second. You told me tonight that you're engaged. So what's your fiancée going to say about this?'

'There is no such person. I haven't yet selected a bride.'

Frankie felt as if her head was about to explode. '"Selected" a bride?' She rolled her eyes. 'You make it sound like shuffling a deck of cards and drawing one at random.'

'It is far from a random process,' he said with a shake of his head. 'Each of the women have been shortlisted because of their suitability to be my wife.'

'So go back to your damned country and marry one of them.'

He swept his heated gaze over her body, and goosebumps spread where his eyes moved.

'Think it through,' he said finally. 'What happens if I do as you say—if I return to Tolmirós and marry another woman. She becomes my Queen, and Leo is still my son. *Our* son, mine and my wife's. I will fight for custody of him and, Frankie, I will win.' A shiver ran down her spine at his certainty, because she knew he was right. She knew the danger here, for her. 'I will win, and I will raise him. Wouldn't you prefer to avoid an ugly custody dispute, a public battle that you would surely lose? Wouldn't you prefer to accept this and simply agree to marry me?'

'Simply?' There was nothing simple about it. 'I would *prefer* you to go right away again.'

He made a small sound—it might have been a laugh, but there was absolutely no humour in it. 'No matter what we might wish, this is the reality we find ourselves in. I have a son. An heir. And I must bring him home. Surely you can see that?'

The city twinkled like a thousand gems against black velvet. She swallowed, her eyes running frantically over the vista as her brain tried to fumble its way to an alternative. 'But marriage is so…'

'Yes?'

'It's so much. Too much.' She spun back to face him, and her heart thudded in her chest. Marriage to this man? Impossible. He had embodied so many fantasies in her mind but, over time, the lust which might have become love, given the proper treatment, had instead turned to resentment.

He'd disappeared into thin air, and she'd made her peace with that.

Now? To expect her just to marry him?

'Why? People do it all the time,' he said simply, moving across the room and pouring a generous amount of Scotch into two tumblers. He carried one over to her and, despite the fact she didn't drink often and the wine had already made her brain fuzzy, she took it as if on autopilot.

'Do what all the time?' Her mind was still fumbling for something to offer that might appease him.

'Get married because it makes sense.'

Now it was Frankie's turn to make a strangled sound. Not a laugh, not a sob—just a noise driven by emotions emanating from deep in her throat. 'People get married because they are in love,' she contradicted forcefully. 'Because they can't bear to spend their lives apart. People get married because they are full of optimism and hope, because they have met the one person on earth whom they can't live without.'

She spoke the words with passion, from deep within her soul; they were words that meant the world to her. Words by which she lived. But each word seemed to have the effect of making Matthias withdraw from her. His handsome face tightened until his features were stern and his eyes flinted like coal.

'A fantasist's notion,' he said at length. 'And not what I'm offering.'

It was such an insult that she let out a sigh of impatience. 'It's not what I'm asking for—not from you, anyway.' She ignored the strange thumping in the region of her heart. 'I'm explaining that marriage *means* something.'

'Why?' He took a step closer to her, his eyes so focused on her they were like a force, holding her to the spot.

She frowned. 'What do you mean?'

'Why can it not just be that it makes sense?'

'Making sense,' Frankie said with a shake of her head, trying to break free of the power his gaze had over her ability to think straight, 'would be us working out how we're going to do this.' It hurt to think of sharing Leo, but she pushed those feelings aside. This was about Leo, not her. 'You *are* his father, and it was always my wish that you'd be involved in his life. I can bring him to Tolmirós for a visit, to start with, and we can allow him to gradually adjust to the idea of being the heir to your throne. Over time, he might even choose to spend more time over there, with you. And of course you can see him when you're in New York.' Yes. That all made perfect sense. She nodded somewhat stiffly, as though she'd ordered a box neatly into shape. 'There's definitely no need for us to get married.'

'I say there is a need,' he contradicted almost instantly. His voice was calm but there was an intensity in his gaze. 'And within the month.'

'A month?' Her jaw dropped, her stomach swooped and spun.

'Or sooner, if possible. We must act swiftly. There is much you need to learn on the ways of my people. Much Leo will have to learn too.'

'Hang on.' She lifted her hand, pressing it into the air between them as though it might put an end to this ridiculous conversation. 'You can't talk like it's a foregone conclusion that I'll marry you! You've suggested it and I've said, "Absolutely not". You can't just ride roughshod over me.'

His eyes narrowed almost imperceptibly. 'Do you think not?'

'*Definitely* not. Unless you think I'm not a sentient person, capable of making my own decisions?'

'On the contrary. I think you are very capable of that—which is why I'll expect you to make the right one. But be assured, Frankie, regardless of what you think and feel, I have no intention of leaving this country without my son. It is obviously better for everyone if you come with him as my fiancée.'

She sucked in a breath as the truth of what he was saying settled around her. 'You're actually threatening to take him away from me?'

'I'm asking you to marry me.'

Her eyes swept shut. 'Telling me, more like.' When she blinked her eyes open he was closer, so close her palm was almost touching his chest.

'I'm asking you,' he insisted, almost gentle, almost as though he understood her fear and wanted to ease it. 'I'm asking you to see sense. I'm asking you not to put me in a position where I have to fight you for our child.'

Fear lanced her breast because she didn't doubt the sincerity of his words, nor that he had the ability to follow through. She had some savings, but not a lot. Her adoptive parents were comfortable but by no means wealthy. Not in a million years would she be able to afford a lawyer of the calibre necessary to stave off this man's determination. Would he even need a lawyer? Or would he have some kind of diplomatic privilege, given he was King?

'You're such a bastard,' she said, stepping backwards. It was a mistake; the window was behind her. Ice-cold against her back, and rather like a vice clamping her to the spot.

'I am the father to a two-year-old. A little boy I didn't know about even three hours ago. Do you think wanting to raise him is truly unreasonable?'

'Raise him, no. Marry me? Yes.'

'I want this as little as you do, Frankie.' He expelled a sigh and shook his head. 'That is not completely true, in fact. I still want you. I came here tonight because I was thinking of our weekend together and I wished to take you to bed once more.'

She bit down on her tongue to stop a curse from flying from her lips. 'How dare you?' The words were numbed by shock. 'After all these years? After the way you slept with me and then disappeared into thin air? You thought you could just turn up and have me fall at your feet?'

'You did once before,' he pointed out with insufferable arrogance.

Her fingertips itched with a violent impulse to slap him. 'I didn't know you then!'

'And you don't know me now,' he continued, moving closer, speaking with a softness that was imbued with reasonable, rational intent. It was like a magic spell being cast. His proximity was enough to make her pulse thready and her cheeks glow pink.

But she hated him for the ease with which he could affect her and she did her best to hide any sign that she so much as noticed his proximity.

'You don't know that I am a man who has won almost every battle he's fought. You don't know, perhaps, that I am a man accustomed to getting everything I want, when I want it. You do not know that I have the might of ten armies at my back, the wealth of a nation at my feet, and the heart of a warrior in my body.'

Another step closer and his fingertips lifted to press lightly against her cheek. His eyes held hers, like granite locking her to the window.

'You think I don't know you get what you want?' she returned, pleased when the words came out cool and almost derisive. 'You wanted me that weekend and look how that turned out.'

It was the wrong thing to say. Memories of their sensual, delicious time together punctuated the present, and she was falling into the past. With his body so close, so hard and broad, a random impulse to push onto her tiptoes and find his earlobe with her lips, to wobble it between her teeth before moving to his stubbled jaw and finally those wide, curving lips, made breathing almost impossible.

They were perfect lips, she thought distractedly, her artist's mind working overtime as they studied the sculptured feature.

'You are not seeing anyone else.' It was a statement rather than a question, and his certainty was an insult.

'Why do you say that?' she asked, a little less steadily now.

There was something enigmatic and dangerous in his gaze, something that spoke of promises and need. Something that stilled her heart and warmed her skin. 'You do not react to me like a woman who's in love with another man.'

She sucked in a breath; it didn't reach her lungs. 'What's that supposed to mean?'

His smile was sardonic. 'You look at me with eyes that are hungry for what we shared. You tremble now because I am close to you.' He dropped his fingertips to the pulse point at the base of her neck and she cursed her body's traitorous reaction. 'You do not wish to marry me, Frankie, but you want to be with me again, almost more than you want your next breath.'

Oh, God, it was true, but it was wrong! And there was a difference between animal instincts and intelligent consideration—there was no way she'd be stupid enough to fall prey to his virile, sensual pull. Not again. Only she was already falling, wasn't she? Being drawn into his seductive, tantalising web…

'No,' she denied flatly, moving sideways, proud of herself for putting distance between them, for dismissing him with such apparent ease. If only her knees weren't weak and her nipples weren't throbbing against the lace of her bra. 'And the fact I'm single doesn't mean I'm up for this stupid idea. I'm not marrying you.'

He turned his back on her. His spine was rigid, his shoulders tight in his muscular frame. He paced across the room, reminding her of a prowling animal, some kind of Saharan beast, all lean and strong.

She watched him, her body shivering, her mind struggling to make sense of anything.

'What choice do we have?' He kept his back to her and thrust his hands into his pockets. He was looking out at the city, staring at the view, and his voice had a bleakness to it that reached inside her and filled Frankie with despair.

She followed his gaze; nothing seemed to shine now.

'What choice do I have?' he repeated. 'I have a son. He is a prince, and the fate of my country is on his shoulders. I must bring him home. I owe it… I owe it to my people,' he said firmly. He moved one hand from his pocket to his head, driving his fingers through his dark hair, then turning to face her again. 'And you owe it to Leo, Frankie.' His eyes held hers and there was earnestness and honesty in his expression. 'You want to raise him with me, don't you?'

Her chest tightened because he was right. 'I want to

raise a son who is happy and well-adjusted,' she said finally. 'Who has two parents who love him. That doesn't mean we have to marry...'

'When we were together, back then, you told me of your upbringing,' he said with a soft strength in his voice. 'You told me of weekends spent hiking in the summer and playing board games in the winter, reading around the fire, cooking together. You told me how you'd longed for a sister or brother because you wanted a bigger family—lots of noise and happiness. You told me your family meant everything to you. Would you deprive our son of that?'

She stared at him, aghast and hurting, because, damn him, he was right. Everything he'd repeated was exactly as she felt, as she'd always felt, ever since she'd known the first sting of rejection. Since she'd understood that adoption often went hand in hand with abandonment—for the two parents who had chosen to raise her, there were two who had chosen to lose her, to give her away.

She'd seen everything through a prism of that abandonment, never taking family time for granted, seeing it with gratitude because she had feared her adoptive parents' love, once given, might also be taken away again.

Her eyes swept shut and, instead of speaking, she made a strangled noise, deep in her throat.

His eyes swept over her beautiful face and, seeing her surrender, he pushed home his advantage. 'Marry me because our son deserves that of us. You and I slept together, we made a baby together. From the moment of his conception, this stopped being about you and me, and what we both want. We have an obligation to act in his best interests.'

More sense. More words that she agreed with, and suddenly the pull towards marriage was an inevitable force. She knew she would agree—she had to—but she wasn't ready to show him that just yet.

'It's too much,' she whispered, lifting her eyelids and staring at him with confusion and uncertainty. 'Marrying you, even if you were just a normal man, would be... ridiculous. But you're a king and I'm the last person on earth who wants to be...who's suitable to be... I wouldn't be any good at it.'

'First and foremost, you will be my wife, and the mother to my children. Your duties as Queen will not need to be onerous.' He softened his expression. 'In any event, I think you are underselling yourself.'

But she heard nothing after one simple word. 'Children? As in, plural?'

'Of course. One is not enough.' The words were staccato, like little nails being slammed into her sides. Something deep rumbled in his features, a worry that seemed to arrest him deep inside.

But she shook her head, unable to imagine having more children with this man. 'I don't want more children.'

'You do not like being a mother?' he prompted.

'Of course I do. I love Leo. And if I could lay an egg and have four more children, then I would. But, unfortunately, to give you more precious *heirs* I'd need to...we'd need to...'

'Yes?' he drawled, and she had the distinct impression he was enjoying her discomfort.

'Oh, shut up,' she snapped, lifting her fingertips to her temples and massaging them.

'We are getting married,' he said, and apparently her acquiescence was now a point of fact. 'Do you think the question of sex is one we won't need to address?'

His ability to be so calm in the face of such an intimate conversation infuriated her.

'*If* I were to marry you,' she snapped, resenting his confidence as to her agreement, 'sex wouldn't be a part of our arrangement.'

He laughed. 'Oh, really?'

'Yes, really. And it's not funny! Sex should *mean* something, just like marriage should *mean* something. You're laughing like I'm saying something stupid and I'm not—the way I feel is perfectly normal.'

'You are naïve,' he said with a shake of his head. 'Like the innocent virgin you were three years ago. Sex is a biological function—two bodies enjoying one another: pleasure for pleasure's sake. Marriage is an alliance—a mutually beneficial arrangement. Even those who dress it up as "soulmates" and "love" know it for what it really is, deep down.'

'And what's that?' she demanded.

'Convenience. Companionship. Sex.'

Her cheeks flamed pink. 'How in the hell did you get to be so cynical?' she demanded.

'I am more realist than cynic.' He shrugged insouciantly. 'You will grow up and see things as they really are one day, Frankie.'

'I hope not.'

'Don't be so glum,' he cautioned and, without her realising it, he'd crossed the room and was standing right in front of her. His eyes bored into hers and everything in the room seemed to slow down, to stammer to a stop. She stared up at him, her heart racing, her mouth dry, her eyes roaming his face hungrily. 'You will enjoy certain aspects of being my wife.'

She swallowed in an attempt to bring moisture back to her mouth. 'You're wrong.'

He laughed, a dry sound, and swooped his head down, to claim her mouth with his. 'When it comes to women and sex, Frankie, I'm never wrong.'

Her pulse hammered in her ears and her body went into overdrive, her nerve-endings tingling, her heart throbbing.

She wanted to resist him. God, she wanted to make a point. She wanted to push him away. But with her dying breath, with every fibre of her being, she wanted this more. She lifted her hands, burying them in his shirt, her senses noting everything about him—his warmth, his strength, his masculine fragrance, his closeness, his hardness, his very *him*-ness. Memories of how it had been before flashed through her and she whimpered, low in her throat, when one of his hands moved behind her, cupping her bottom and pulling her forward, pressing her to his arousal until she made a groaning sound, tilting her head back to give him better access to her mouth.

And he dominated her with his kiss, his mouth making a mockery of her objections, his lips showing her how completely he could force her surrender, how quickly he could crumble all her reserves, how quickly he could turn her into trembling putty in his arms.

How little, in that moment, she minded.

He lifted his head, pulling away from her, his breathing roughened by passion, as her own was. 'I have no intention of making your life difficult or unpleasant, Frankie. Through the days, you'll barely know I exist.'

Her pulse was still hammering inside her and her body was weak with desire. When she spoke, the words were faint, breathy. 'And at night?'

'At night,' he promised, lifting his hand and stroking his thumb across her cheek, 'you won't be able to exist without me.'

Matthias stared at his child and inside him it felt as if an anvil were colliding with his ribcage.

The little boy was the spitting image of Spiro, just as the painting had made him appear.

'Hello.' He crouched down so he could look into Leo's face. 'You must be Leo.'

Leo nodded thoughtfully. 'Yes. I am Leo.'

Matthias couldn't smile. He felt only pain, like acid gushing through his veins. How much of this boy's life had he missed? How much was there about him he didn't know?

'We are going to go on an adventure,' he said, standing, glaring at Frankie with all the rage he felt in that moment. The night before, he'd wanted to make love to her until she was incoherent, crying his name at the top of her voice. Now? He felt nothing but rage. Rage at what she'd denied him. Rage at what she'd enjoyed while he'd been none the wiser.

'Come, Leo,' he said, the words carefully muted of harsh inflection even when his eyes conveyed his mood just fine. 'We are going on an adventure together.'

CHAPTER FOUR

HER STOMACH SWOOPED as the plane came in low over the Mediterranean, but Frankie knew it had less to do with the private jet's descent and more to do with the man sitting opposite her. In the incredible luxury of this plane, surrounded by white leather furniture, chandeliers, servants dressed in white and gold uniforms, Matthias still stood out. He was imposing.

Regal.

Grand.

Intimidating.

And he was to be her husband.

Thoughts of their kiss, with her back pressed against a wall literally and metaphorically, flooded her mind and her temperature spiked as remembered pleasures deepened inside her.

The ocean glistened beneath them like a beautiful mirage, dark blue from up here, and dozens of little islands dotted in the middle of it. Each was surrounded by a ring of turquoise water and an edge of crisp white sand.

'That is Tolmirós,' he said conversationally, and it was the first he'd spoken to her all flight. The silence had been deafening, but Frankie had been preoccupied enough wondering just how the hell she'd found herself being spirited away to this man's kingdom—having agreed, at last, to be his wife!

'Which one?'

He eyed her thoughtfully for a moment and her heart rate notched up a gear. 'All of them. Tolmirós is made up of forty-two islands. Some are small, some are large. Like Epikanas,' he said, reaching across and pointing to an island in the distance.

She looked in the direction he was indicating, trying to ignore the fact that he was so close to her now, so close she could breathe in his woody masculine fragrance. When he'd kissed her, it had been as though nothing else mattered. Not the past, not the future—nothing.

'Epikanas,' she repeated.

'Good.' He nodded his approval and the smile that spread across his face warmed her from the inside out. 'You pronounced that perfectly. You will have a language tutor to help you learn how to speak our language.' He sat back in his seat and she told herself she was glad. The plane moved lower, bumping a little as it pushed through some turbulence. 'Epikanas is the main island—my palace is there, my government centre, the main business hub, our largest city. It is where we will live, most of the time.'

She nodded distractedly, turning in her seat to face him, then wishing she hadn't when she found him watching her intently. She skidded her eyes away again, to the seat across the aisle. It had been put into full recline, forming a bed, and Leo was fast asleep, sprawled lengthways.

She watched him sleep and her heart clenched because she knew, risky though this was for her, she was doing the right thing for Leo. If there was any way she could give her son the security of a family, she was going to do it. Her eyes swept shut for a moment as the single memory she possessed of her birth mother filtered to the top of her mind. It was vague. An impression of a faded yellow armchair, sunlight streaming in through a window, curtains blowing in the slight breeze, and the sound of tapping. Her mother had lifted her, hugged her, smelling like lemons and soap.

Then the memory was gone again, like the parents who hadn't wanted her. No matter how hard she tried to catch it, to unpick it and see more of her early childhood, there was nothing.

Determination fired through her spine.

Leo would never feel like she had; he'd never know that sting of rejection. He'd never know the burden of that loss. Unknowingly, she tilted her chin in a gesture of defiance, her eyes glinting with determination. For her son, she would make this work.

'This,' he said, as if following the direction of her thoughts, 'that we are flying over now is Port Kalamathi,' he said. 'The island used to be an important stronghold in our naval operations. Now, it is home to the best school in Tolmirós. It is here that Leo will go, when he is old enough.'

She looked out of her window at the island that was just a swirling mix of green and turquoise. In the centre there were buildings—ancient-looking, with lots of gardens and lawns. She supposed that, so far as schools went, the location was excellent. But wasn't it too far from the palace?

She gnawed on her lower lip and pushed that question aside. Their son was two years old: they could cross that bridge when they came to it. It would be years away. She had more immediate concerns to address.

'What happens next?' she asked, sitting back in her seat, clasping her hands in her lap in a gesture that she hoped made her look calm and confident.

He nodded, apparently relieved she was prepared to discuss things rationally. 'My security has kept the press away from the airport. Usually there are photographers on hand when my plane comes in,' he said.

'But not now?'

'No, not now.' He stared into her eyes and her mouth was drier than the Arizona desert. 'Now, there will be just my drivers and security personnel.'

'Do you have security personnel with you often?'

'Always,' he agreed.

'You didn't that weekend.'

'That weekend, I was still a prince.' His look was one of self-derision. 'I was still a boy, running from my destiny.'

She regarded him thoughtfully. 'You said your uncle was King until you turned thirty?'

'Not King, no.' He shook his head. 'Ancient rules govern the line of succession. My uncle was a *prosorinós*. A sort of caretaker for the throne.'

'What if you'd died too?' she asked, and then heat flushed her face as she realised how insensitive the question sounded.

He didn't seem to mind though. He considered it carefully. 'Then, yes, my uncle would have been King.'

She tilted her head to the side. 'I'm sure I heard once that the legal guardian of an heir couldn't assume that heir's title—lest self-interest lead them to murderous deeds.'

He arched a brow. 'True. And it is the same in Tolmirós. My uncle was not my legal guardian. In fact, I was prevented from seeing him more than once or twice a year during that time.'

She absorbed these words, turning them over in her mind before saying with a small frown, 'But he was your only surviving family? No cousins? Aunt?'

'No. He never married.' His expression shifted.

'And you didn't get to see him?'

He shrugged, as though it barely mattered. 'It is the way it had to be.'

She was inwardly appalled. 'Then who raised you?'

'I was fifteen when my family died,' he said dismissively. 'I had already been "raised".'

'You think you were a grown man at that age?' Her heart hurt for the teenager he'd been.

'I was in school, at Port Kalamathi,' he said, his eyes shifting to the window. 'I went back to school and stayed there until I was eighteen.'

'Boarding school?'

He nodded.

'And then what?' She wished she didn't feel this curiosity, but how could she not wish to understand?

'I joined the military.'

This didn't surprise her. From the first moment she'd seen him, she'd felt he was some kind of real-life warrior. A Trojan, brought back to life.

'And did you enjoy it?'

He paused, apparently analysing that question before answering. 'Yes.'

'Why?'

His smile was tight. 'Tolmirós is a peaceful country. We do not fight wars. Our military training is the best in the world, yet we rarely have cause to require our soldiers.' He shrugged. 'I learned discipline and self-reliance.'

'I can't help thinking these are qualities you already had in spades.'

He shrugged. 'Perhaps.'

There was silence, except for the whirr of the engines as the pilot brought the plane lower and lower, over the dozens of small islands, including the one they were to land on.

'How do you get from one island to the next?' she asked.

'We have a huge ferry network. Look.' He pointed and now she saw dozens of boats moving in the water. 'See the way the islands seem to shimmer?' he asked rhetorically. 'Tolmirós is referred to as the Diamond Kingdom. Each island is like a gem in the midst of the sea.'

She nodded, the magic of that description settling against her chest. The plane dropped lower and lower and it almost felt as though it might land in the ocean. But then land emerged from the depths of the sea and, beyond it, a runway, pale grey, lined with bright red flowers. The plane touched down with a soft thud and instinctively she looked to Leo. He lay where he was, fast asleep, and her heart gave a little tug.

Matthias was watching her; she could feel his gaze and it dragged on her like a tangible force. Slowly, of their own volition, her eyes raised to his.

Her breath locked in her throat; her body was frozen. Her very soul was arrested by the sight of this man she'd lost her head to three years earlier, a man who was so much more than that. He was a king, a ruler of a country, and all that implied.

Hadn't she detected that latent power in him, even when they'd been together back then? Hadn't she known he was someone to whom command came easily?

There was an intensity in his expression, a look of hungry determination, and her pulse raced hard and fast, her heart struggling to keep up with her blood's demands. When he spoke, it was with a contained sense of strength.

'Did you really attempt to find me?'

The question was so quiet she almost didn't hear it, like catching a swirling ribbon on a hazy night.

'It was impossible,' she murmured.

'I intended it to be so.'

The words were sharp in her sides. 'You had an easier job of forgetting me than I did you,' she said simply.

He looked as though he was about to say something, his

expression taut, but then he turned away from her, his eyes roaming towards Leo.

The little boy was waking now, twisting his chubby, robust body against the flat chair, starfishing his legs out so that Frankie smiled unknowingly.

'Mama?' The plane was still moving forward but they'd landed, and Frankie unbuckled her belt and stood, crossing the aisle and undoing his seat belt. He wriggled into a sitting position, from which she plucked him onto her hip. 'Where we?'

'In an aeroplane. Do you remember?' He'd been half asleep when they'd boarded the flight. He still wore his little emoji-themed pyjamas, a gift from her parents at Christmas.

'No.' He shook his head and she smiled softly. 'Who's that?' Leo pointed a finger at Matthias.

'A friend of Mummy's,' she said quickly, earning a swift look of rebuke from Matthias.

'I'm your father, Leo,' he said over the top of her, and now it was Frankie's turn to volley back an expression of outright rage. Her lips compressed and her eyes held a warning.

'Father?' Leo blinked from Frankie to Matthias.

'Your daddy.' The words were said softly but when Matthias looked at Frankie she felt a sharp dagger of judgement. Of anger. She held his gaze, determined to show him she wasn't going to back down from this fight—or any.

'Daddy?' Leo's eyes went huge. 'You say Daddy so kind!' Leo enthused, and Frankie's heart clenched in her chest. She had told Leo that, and many other things. She'd invented a father for Leo that he could be proud of, needing her son to believe a wonderful man had been a part of his creation, even when he couldn't be a part of his life.

'We're going to stay with Daddy for a while,' Frankie

said gently, ignoring the way Matthias's eyes were resting on her with startling intensity. 'Would you like that?'

Leo's lower lip stuck out and he shook his head stubbornly. Frankie dipped her head forward and hid a smile in her son's curls. Let King Matthias, who 'always got what he wanted' suck on that!

'Are you sure?' he asked teasingly, as though he wasn't remotely bothered by Leo's rejection. 'Because I happen to have a swimming pool right outside my bedroom,' he said. 'And you may use it any time.'

'A pool?' Leo tilted his head to one side in a gesture that was so reminiscent of Matthias that Frankie's chest throbbed. 'What a "pool"?'

'What's a pool?' Matthias's gaze lifted to Frankie's, subtle accusation in his eyes. 'How can you not know this? It's like the biggest bath tub you can imagine,' he said, not looking away from Frankie. 'The water is warm and salty, and you can kick and splash to your heart's content.'

'Mummy says no splashing in the bath!' Leo was dubious.

Matthias's eyes held Frankie's for a moment longer and she fought an instinct to defend herself, to defend her parenting, before dropping her gaze to Leo's. She breathed out, not having realised she'd been holding her breath until then. 'In a pool you may splash.'

Leo jumped up and down on Frankie's lap, his excitement at this relaxation in the usual rules apparent.

'Do you know what else?' Matthias leaned forward, smiling in a way that caused Frankie's breath to catch once more. 'We are very near the beach. You can go swimming whenever you like.'

Leo gleefully clapped his little hands together.

'What else do you like to do?'

That was it. Leo began to speak as best he was able, and

Matthias listened and nodded along, even when Frankie was certain he couldn't understand half of what the toddler was offering.

The plane drew to a stop and the cabin crew opened the door—sultry heat immediately blew in, replacing the climate-controlled cool of the aircraft. There was sunshine on the breeze and Frankie sucked it in, deep inside her lungs, pressing her head back against the seat for a moment, letting the air stir through her body, praying it would bring a sense of calm and acceptance to her.

She had no choice but to marry him. She could even see the sense of what he'd suggested. He wasn't just a mere man—a mortal amongst mortals. He was a king, and she'd been foolish enough to sleep with a stranger—she hadn't cared who he was; she hadn't wanted or needed to know anything about him, besides the fact that she'd wanted him with an intensity that had refused to be quelled. And so they'd found themselves in bed—he'd been so experienced and charming that what little instinct she might have had to pause, to wait, had completely evaporated.

She let out a small sigh of impatience. Why bother analysing the past? It had happened, and she couldn't even say with any honesty that she wished it hadn't. Sleeping with Matthias had given her Leo, and not for all the gold in the world would she wish him away.

Nor, if she were completely honest, would she wish she hadn't slept with Matthias. He hadn't deserved her, he sure as heck hadn't deserved her innocence, but he remained, to this day, one of the best experiences of her life.

An experience she wanted to repeat?

For a second she allowed herself to imagine that future, to imagine Matthias making love to her, the nights long with passion, rent with the noise of her pleasure and delirious need, her insides slicked with moist heat.

Foreign voices filled the plane and she looked up to find Matthias watching her, even as Leo chattered to him. Heat burned her cheeks, the direction of her thoughts warming her, and she was sure he knew, and understood; she was sure he was watching her with the same sense of heated arousal.

Frankie forced herself to look past him, to the cabin crew who were making their way into the plane. A woman was at the front and she held a garment bag in her hands. No, several, Frankie noted with disinterest.

Matthias stood and spoke to his servants in his native tongue. Their deference was fascinating to observe. All bowed low and, though they spoke in their own language, she could hear the awe with which they held him.

'This is Marina.' Matthias turned to Frankie, his expression unreadable. 'She's going to help you get ready.'

'Ready for what?'

'Arriving at the palace.'

'But… I am ready.'

He looked at her long and hard, his dark gaze moving from her hair to her face and then to her clothes and, though she was wearing one of her favourite dresses, the way he looked at her made her feel as though she were dressed in a potato sack.

'What?' she asked defiantly, tilting her chin and glaring at him as though his scrutiny hadn't affected her in the slightest degree.

'You are my fiancée,' he reminded her. 'The future Queen of Tolmirós. You will feel more comfortable dressed for that role.'

She bit down on her lip and if they'd been alone she might have had a few choice phrases to utter. Instead, she stood up, keeping Leo pinned to her hip.

'I'm sorry if I don't meet your high standards, Your Majesty,' she said jerkily, panic rising inside her at the enormity of what she was going to do.

'My standards are beside the point,' he said quietly, with all the reasonableness she had failed to muster. 'This is about what will be expected of you. And Leo.' As though their child was an afterthought, he gestured to an old woman in the huddle of staff.

Her smile was kind, her face lined in a way Frankie found instantly appealing. She looked like a woman who laughed a lot.

'This is Liana,' Matthias said, his expression unchanging as he nodded at the older woman. Emotion stirred in Liana's green eyes though, feelings Frankie couldn't begin to comprehend. The older woman's smile dropped—just for a fraction of a second. Then her attention homed in on Leo and it was as though a firework had been set off beneath her.

'Liana was my nanny, as a boy,' Matthias explained, watching as Liana moved between them and began making clacking noises at Leo. He grinned in response and then clapped his hands together. Liana did likewise and laughed, rocking back on her heels so her slender frame arched.

'May I?' she asked, a cackled question, presumably directed at Frankie, though Liana didn't take her eyes off Leo.

'I...' Frankie didn't want to hand Leo over, though. On some instinctive level, she ached to hold him close, to keep him near her.

She stared at Matthias and perhaps a hint of her panic showed itself in her eyes because his expression tightened and a pulse jerked at the base of his jaw. 'Liana will help Leo change into more suitable clothes,' Matthias reassured her, everything about him kind, as if he were trying to calm a horse on the brink of bolting. 'While you are doing likewise.'

It was a simple suggestion, and one that made sense, but the more he made sense, the more Frankie wanted to rebel.

'I really don't see the point in changing,' she said. 'You told me there wouldn't be any photographers...'

'True—' he shrugged '—but there will be staff. Hundreds of them, all looking to see the woman who will become their Queen. Would you not feel happier wearing clothes made for a princess?'

'I'm fine,' she said curtly, dismissively. Then, for Liana's benefit, 'I'd rather stay with Leo.'

He looked as if he wanted to argue with her, as if he wanted to insist. His eyes locked onto hers, he watched her thoughtfully and then he shrugged. 'It is your decision, of course.'

As soon as they arrived at the palace, she wished she hadn't been so stubborn and short-sighted. She was wearing a nice enough dress—but it was nothing compared to the grandeur of this place.

From the outside, it looked ancient. A huge, imposing castle, with the city on one side and the ocean on the other. It formed a square, and his limousine had driven under a large archway and into a central courtyard. The walls ran on all sides and when the car stopped there was a vibrant blue carpet rolled out, leading to glass double doors that had been thrown open. Servants stood on either side. The men were in suits and the women wore dresses. Most also wore white gloves to their elbows. Many had white aprons around their waists.

All looked somehow more formally attired than Frankie. Even little Leo was a resplendent king-in-waiting. A pair of grey shorts had been teamed with knee-high blue socks, shiny black shoes and a crisp white shirt with short sleeves and round buttons that glowed like pearls. His unruly hair had been combed and tamed, parted on one side, and was sitting neatly on his head with the exception of one disobedient curl that flopped into the middle of his forehead.

The three of them sat in the back of the car—a family, yet not. Matthias regarded her carefully. When he'd held his body above hers and entered her and, upon discovering for himself that she was a virgin, he'd looked into her eyes and murmured words in his language that had taken away any pain and replaced it instead with pleasure and need, so that she'd called his name over and over, an incantation, as surely as if she were a witch.

He looked at her with the desire that had rushed his bloodstream anew two nights earlier—desire that had made him want to shelve any conversation of marriage, bloodlines and their future and simply give in to his hunger for this woman. An insatiable hunger, he suspected, even when he had every intention of spending quite some time trying to satiate it.

'Well, Frankie.' He rolled her name around his mouth, tasting it, imagining kissing it against her throat, the sensitive flesh of her décolletage, down to breasts that he longed to lavish with attention. He was hard for her, ready for her already, hungry for her always. He cleared his throat, focusing on her face, forcing himself to be patient. 'Are you ready?'

Her smile lacked warmth. 'If I say "no", will it make a difference?'

His lips twisted in a grimace of sorts and he understood then what he'd failed to see on the plane. She was nervous. She was fighting with him because she was about to step off a cliff, and she had no idea what would catch her. He leaned forward so that his face was close to hers and saw the way her breath hitched in her throat, saw the way she looked at him with a quick flash of desire that she fought to cover with a tightening of her features.

'We have to do this,' he said, wishing in that moment that it wasn't the case. That Frankie didn't have to endure a marriage she clearly hated the idea of. Wishing she was free to live her life. Wishing she was free to marry a man who loved her, just as she'd insisted marriage should be.

'Then why ask the question?' Her words were snapped out but he understood now, and he frowned, wanting to relieve her tension and knowing only one way to do so.

Leo looked from one to the other and Frankie dredged up a smile for his benefit but it was weak, watery.

'Okay?' Leo asked, his little hand curving on top of Frankie's. Matthias watched the gesture with a heart that was strangely heavy.

'Fine,' she said, her smile for their child's benefit.

The door was pulled open and Matthias sat for another beat of time, looking at the woman who would be his wife, and his child. She was nervous, but there was nothing for it. They had to do this. 'Let's go then.'

Three simple words but oh, how much they meant! Because it wasn't as simple as stepping out of a car—this was like crossing an invisible border, one which she could never cross back. When she stepped out of the car, she'd cease to be a private individual. She would no longer be an up-and-coming artist on the New York scene. She'd be a royal fiancée, Matthias's bride, the up-and-coming Queen, the mother of the royal heir. She would belong to this life, to Matthias, and so would Leo.

There was nothing for it though. He'd described himself as a realist, and Frankie had a degree of realism deep in her as well. Or perhaps it was better described as fatalism, she thought, watching as Matthias stepped from the car. His staff stood still, none looking at him. He reached into the car, his arms extended, and she understood what he wanted.

Leo.

Her mouth was dry, her throat parched, her pulse racing. There was no sense in refusing him—it would be easier for her to step out of the car if she weren't holding a heavy toddler in her arms. Besides, with Matthias holding their baby, no one would be looking at her, would they?

'Go with Matthias—Daddy,' she said stiffly, kissing Leo's curls before passing him towards the door. Matthias's hands curved around Leo's midsection and then Frankie shuffled closer. Curious glances slid sideways. The servants were, perhaps, not supposed to look, and yet how could they resist?

This was their future King, arriving home as a two-year-old boy. Curiosity was only natural.

'Mama?'

'I'm coming. I'm right behind you,' she promised. And she was—she had to be. There was no way on earth Matthias would ever let Leo go. She could see that as clearly as she could the brilliant blue of the sky overhead. If she wanted to be a part of her son's life, she had to accept Matthias as a part of hers.

With nerves that were jangling in her body, schooling her features into a mask of what she hoped would pass as calm, she stepped from the vehicle.

Eyes that had been resolutely focused ahead all turned now, and it was like being in the glare of a thousand spotlights. Everyone looked at her, everyone saw her, and she knew what they must be thinking.

Why her?

With a sinking heart and regret that she'd refused to allow herself to be restyled as some sort of queen-in-waiting, she brazened it out. Shoulders squared, smile on her face, as though this was a happy day for her. As though she wasn't absolutely terrified.

His arm around her waist caught her off guard and for a second—a brief second—her smile dropped. Her gaze flew to his face and she saw a warning there. A warning, and a look of triumph. 'Welcome home, *deliciae*.'

Home.

She had only a second to process the word. A second to wonder what the lovely-sounding *deliciae* might mean. And then his head dropped and his lips pressed to hers, and she was dropping out of that present moment and crashing into the past, when she had—briefly—lived for this exact feeling. When his kisses alone had been her reason for breathing.

It was too much—her nerves were already stretched to breaking point and his kiss was a torture and a relief, an agony and an ecstasy.

Her body, of its own accord, swayed towards him as though drunk, demanding more contact, more closeness, more everything. It was a brief kiss—chaste in comparison to how they had kissed in the past, and yet it was enough. *More* than enough to rekindle everything. Flames that she had hoped extinguished flared to life and she had no idea how to put them out again this time.

Damn him all to heck.

He lifted his head, his eyes mocking when they met hers. Embarrassment warmed her cheeks.

'Why did you do that?' she demanded, lifting shaking fingertips to her lips, feeling the strength of his passion even now, seconds after he'd ended it.

His laugh was soft and sent electric shocks down her spine.

'Because you were nervous,' he said quietly. 'And I could think of only one way to calm you down.'

Her stomach swooped with his insightfulness, but the ease with which he could turn her blood to lava spiked her pride. With a hint of insurgency, she murmured quietly, so only he could hear, 'And what if I don't want you to kiss me?'

He laughed softly.

'Why is that funny?'

'You shouldn't issue challenges you don't wish to lose.'

'What does that even mean?'

'It means—' he leaned forward once more, his intent obvious, and yet she still didn't step back, even when she had ample opportunity to put some space between them '—I'm going to enjoy making you eat those words.' And he crushed his mouth to hers once again, his kiss a possession and a promise. A promise she knew she should fight and somehow, frustratingly, wasn't sure she wanted to…

CHAPTER FIVE

'AND THIS IS the private residence, madam.' A middle-aged man dipped his head deferentially, allowing Frankie to walk past. Her mind was already spinning, and she'd only been in the palace an hour. Exhaustion had begun to sink into her skin, making thought and attention almost impossible. Where Leo had slept on the plane, she hadn't—not a jot—and she couldn't even do the maths in that moment to work out what time it was in New York.

Late, though. Or early in the morning. No wonder she felt so wrecked.

The Private Residence was, in fact, more like a penthouse apartment. Where the rest of the palace was steeped in a sense of ancient tradition, with historic balustrades, paintings, old tapestries and glorious wallpaper giving it a sense of living history, this apartment felt completely modern.

'It was redecorated at the turn of the century,' the servant said. 'All of the wiring was renewed in this suite.' He moved deeper into the apartment. 'Would you like a tour, madam?'

'Oh, no, thank you.' What Frankie wanted more than anything was a strong coffee and to be left alone. To soften her refusal, she smiled. 'I'll find my way around just fine, I'm sure.'

'Certainly. There has not been time to properly complete Master Leo's rooms, but a start has been made,' the servant offered, gesturing down the hallway. Frankie moved in that direction as if being pulled by magic, her trained artist's eye making note of small details as she went. Here the walls were crisp white, but not perfect white—there was a warmth to them, almost as though they'd been mixed with gold or pearl. Flower arrangements were modern and fragrant, pictures were simple black and white, portraits and photographs. Artistic and interesting.

Undoubtedly the work of some palace designer or other, she thought with a twist of her lips.

'The blue door, madam,' the servant offered.

With a frown, Frankie curved her fingers around the brass door knob and turned it, pushing the door inwards. The room opened up before her and her heart sank.

How could she have contemplated turning Matthias down for even a moment? This room was every little boy's fantasy, she thought, stepping inside and turning a full circle. Leo followed behind her and he was as struck dumb at the scene as she was.

'Mine?'

Frankie couldn't form a response. She looked at him then back to the room, doubt and certainty warring inside her. 'Yes,' she acknowledged finally, moving to the small bed. Like something out of a movie, it was a pale cream, glossy, with sumptuous blue bedding, big European pillows—almost the size of Leo—and toy-soldier cushions, as if brought to life from *The Nutcracker*. A bay window overlooked a beautiful garden—'The chef's *potager*,' the servant advised with more than a touch of pride in his tone.

Though the room was filled with toys and books, they were all good quality: wooden, old-fashioned, simple. Frankie surveyed them, begrudgingly approving of their selection, their appropriateness for Leo's age and stage indisputable.

'Mine?' he asked again, lifting a set of blocks off the shelf.

'Yes,' she agreed once more.

'There you are.'

The heavily accented voice had Frankie turning and when she saw Liana smiling as she approached, it was natural for Frankie to return the gesture. She liked this woman, though she knew so little about her. There was a warmth and openness that Frankie needed—an ally in the midst of all that was new and frightening. Not to mention the fact she'd kicked off her shoes at some stage and now wore bright pink socks beneath sensible trousers—high recommendation indeed.

''Ello, Frankie.' Liana nodded, and Frankie liked her even more for using her name rather than any silly title or 'madam'. 'You like his room?'

'Oh, yes, it's perfect,' she said. 'I don't know how but someone's managed to fill it with all of the things Leo would have chosen himself, if given half a chance.'

'Ah, it is not so long since Matthias and Spiro were boys. I remember.' She tapped a knobbly finger to the side of her head and nodded sagely.

Frankie's curiosity was stirred to life. 'Spiro?'

Liana's eyes narrowed but she didn't answer. 'You go, you go,' she said. 'I get to know.' She pointed to Leo and when he looked at her she clapped her hands together and held them out to him.

To Frankie's surprise, rather than ignoring Liana and staying with the shelves of new toys and distractions, Leo pushed to his sturdy little legs and padded over to Liana. He smiled up at the older woman, dimples dug deep in both cheeks.

'He likes you,' Frankie said, the words punctuated with the heaviness of her heart.

'And I like him.' She grinned. 'We are going to be great friends, little master Leo. No?'

'Yeah.' He nodded enthusiastically.

Liana turned back to Frankie. 'You go, relax. I keep him happy.'

Frankie was torn between a desire never to let Leo out of her sight again and a need to be alone, to have a bath, to get to grips with all that had happened. In the end, it was seeing Liana and Leo playing happily together, walking around the room and exploring it, holding hands, that made Frankie's decision for her. She turned to leave, but at the door spun back.

'Liana?' The nanny looked up, her face patient. 'Thank you. For this.' She nodded towards Leo. 'And for this,' and she gestured around the room.

'It is my pleasure,' Liana promised after a beat of silence had passed. 'It is good to have a child in the palace again, *vasillisa*.'

The servant who'd brought her to the apartment had left, so Frankie was free to explore on her own. She did so quickly, perfunctorily, looking upon the rooms as she might appraise a new subject she was painting. It helped her not to focus on the disparity in her own private situation and this degree of wealth and privilege if she saw it as an outsider rather than as one who'd been suddenly and unceremoniously sucked into these lofty ranks.

There was the small anteroom, into which they'd entered. The corridor that came this way branched off into Leo's bedroom, and another room beside it, with sofas, a small dining table and glass doors that led to a small balcony. A children's sitting room, she surmised, the décor clearly childlike yet lovely.

Another door showed a lovely bathroom—white tiles, deep tub, a separate shower and two toilets: one regular size and one lower to the ground. The last door revealed a separate bedroom and at first she thought it would be just perfect for her—and to hell with whatever form Matthias thought their marriage would take! But a longer look showed Liana's shoes tucked neatly under the bed and her jacket hung on a hook near the door.

So this was to be the nanny's accommodation?

At least that meant they wouldn't be alone in this residence! Feeling ridiculously smug, given Matthias had no doubt approved the arrangements himself, Frankie moved down the corridor and into another sitting room, this one incredibly grand. Burgundy and gold damask sofas and armchairs formed a set for six, with a marble coffee table between them, and the dining table could easily accommodate ten. It was walnut, polished, imposing, and dark. There was a bar in the corner, beside heavy oak bookshelves, and glass doors led to yet another balcony.

She moved through the room quickly, feeling out of place, like an interloper. It was impossible to imagine she'd ever feel 'at home' here.

The next room offered some improvement. A study, with modern computers, paperback books and an armchair that at least looked as if it had been made this century.

The following room was another improvement! A kitchen and an adjoining sitting room, this was far more homely, despite the large glass doors that showed an exquisite pool beyond. She imagined Matthias swimming in it, his body on display as he powerfully pulled through the water, and her throat was dry.

She swallowed, trying to push away the image, and moved into the kitchen. She almost cheered when she saw a familiar coffee machine. She searched drawers and doors until she located coffee grinds, loaded them into the basket and pressed the button. The aroma filled the room at once and she stood very still, allowing the fragrance to permeate her soul, to reassure her and relax her as only coffee could.

The pretty cup filled, she wrapped both palms around it and continued her tour. Early afternoon sunlight filtered in through the windows as she moved to the next room, and the light was so dazzling, so perfectly a mix of milk and Naples Yellow, translucent and fragile. She stood in the light for a moment, her eyes sweeping shut, before a jolt of recognition had her opening them anew.

The bed was enormous, and it sat right in the middle of the far wall. Where the wall itself was white, the bed-linen was steel-grey, with fluffy pillows and bedside tables that were devoid of anything personal. No photographs, no books, not even a newspaper.

Her heart in her throat, she moved around the bed, giving it a wide berth, heading for another door. Hoping it might lead to a bedroom, she pushed the door inwards and saw only a bathroom—this one more palatial than Leo's, with an enormous spa pressed against windows that seemed to overlook a fruit grove. No doubt if her friendly servant was nearby, he'd be able to tell her what fruit was growing there—she couldn't see from a distance.

The shower was one of those large walk-in scenarios, with two shower heads overhead and several on the walls. The controls looked like something out of a spaceship.

She backed out of the bathroom as though she'd been stung, slamming her shoulder on the way and wincing from the pain. The last remaining door showed a wardrobe—as big as her bedroom back in Queens, but only half-filled. Suits, dozens of them, all undoubtedly hand-stitched to measure, hung neatly, arranged one by one. Then shirts, crisply ironed, many still with tags attached. There were casual clothes too, and they made her stomach clench because she could imagine Matthias as he'd been *then*. Before. In New York, when he'd been simply Matt.

She sighed, propping her hips against the piece of furniture in the middle of the room. What even was it? Square-shaped, with drawer upon drawer. She pressed one out of curiosity and it sprung open. Watches! At least ten, and all very expensive-looking. She shook her head in disbelief and pushed it closed once more.

The hint of a smile danced on her lips as she imagined for a moment the ludicrousness of her clothing in this imposing space, the look of her costume jewellery next to his couture, and a laugh at that absurdity bubbled from deep inside. And if she'd been about to wonder how the heck she was even going to get her clothes, the answer presented itself in the form of a rather stylish-looking woman who introduced herself as Mathilde.

'I take your measurements,' she said, her accent French. 'And organise your wardrobe.'

'My wardrobe?'

'You will need things very quickly, but this is not your worry. I know people.'

Frankie thought longingly of the coffee she'd placed down in the immaculate bedroom next door, and the quiet time she'd been fantasising about disappeared. For, not long after Mathilde's arrival, came Angelique and Sienna, hairdresser and beautician, who set up a beauty salon in the palatial bathroom. One worked on taming Frankie's 'mom' hair, removing all traces of playdough and neglect while still managing to keep the length and natural blonde colour in place. The other waxed Frankie's brows and did her nails—fingers and toes—both tasks Frankie had neglected for far too long.

'I'm an artist,' she found herself explaining apologetically as Sienna tried her hardest to buff a splash of oil paint from Frankie's big toe nail. 'And I like to paint barefoot,' she added for good measure.

Sienna's smile was dubious and Frankie understood. How could she ever live up to this country's expectations of its Queen?

It took hours but when Frankie was at last alone once more she had to admit that the three women had worked some kind of miracle. She stared at herself in the reflection, unable to believe how...regal...she looked. Still dressed in the same clothes as New York, it no longer mattered. Her hair sat like a blonde cloud around her shoulders and she glistened all over.

Exhaustion was a tidal wave coming towards her. She showered in an attempt to stave it off and was just in the process of pulling the same dress back in place when there was a knock at the bathroom door. With a little gasp, she grabbed the dress and simply held it across her front.

'Don't come in!' she cautioned, her heart already racing into overdrive at the very idea that Matthias might stride in and pull her naked, shower-wet body into his arms.

'Of course not, madam.' Mathilde's soft accent came through with a hint of indignation. 'Only I tell you there are some things in your wardrobe now. Not a lot, but enough to start.'

'Oh.' Disappointment fired inside her; how she resented it! 'Thank you.'

'You're welcome, madam.'

Frankie reached for one of the sumptuous robes and wrapped it around herself, luxuriating for a moment in its glamorous softness before moving out of the bathroom. This side of the apartment was empty but still she moved quickly, lest another interruption came to pass and she gave into temptation, pressing her body to Matthias's and begging him to… She pushed the thought out of her mind determinedly, slipping into the wardrobe.

One side was filled with his clothes. She cast a guilty look towards the door before moving to his clothes and running her hand over them, feeling their fabric, imagining them on his body, remembering the warmth and strength of his physique. A deep need opened up inside her gut—she feared there was only one solution.

When she emerged a few moments later, Matthias was in the kitchen, the living invocation of her fantasies. Awareness jerked inside her, desire heavy, the pulse between her legs running riot at the sight of him like this. It was strange, but it was the first moment it truly hit Frankie that this was *their* home. That they would live here, side by side. For how long?

Her pulse ratcheted up a notch.

'You've toured the residence?' he prompted, lifting his head and pinning her with those intelligent grey eyes of his.

'Yeah.' It was croaky and faint; she cleared her throat. 'Yes.' Balling up her courage, she walked towards him, pleased with herself for at least remembering how to walk calmly. 'There only seems to be one bedroom spare,' she murmured.

He looked at her, a smile playing about his lips. 'Was that a question?'

Damn him! 'You can't expect me to…'

'Share your husband's bedroom?'

She fidgeted with her fingers, and then stopped when she realised what a betraying gesture it was. 'Yes.' She forced her eyes to hold his.

'Are we back to pretending you don't feel the same desire I do?'

She opened her mouth and closed it again. How could

she deny her desire, after the kiss they'd shared earlier? Surely he'd tasted her response, felt her need.

'No,' she said softly, her eyes locked onto his with a defiance that gave her some kind of courage. 'But feeling something and acting on it are two different concepts.'

His eyes flared, perhaps showing his surprise at her admission. 'So they are.' He leaned a little closer and her stomach swirled. 'You do not need to worry, Frankie. When we sleep together it will be because you beg me to make love to you, not because I cannot control myself while we happen to be sharing a mattress. *Bene?*'

'I...'

'It is just a bed,' he said, making her feel naïve and childish. 'And I am away often.'

'I...'

He lifted a finger, placing it softly against her lips. 'If you do not adjust to me in your life, then I will have a new room made for you,' he said, and though the offer should have pleased her, it didn't. If she'd felt childish before, she felt babyish now—and like a complainer too. 'Just try it my way.'

It was so reasonable. So measured. 'I just presumed we'd have separate rooms,' she explained, forcing a smile to her lips.

He nodded once, his eyes latched to hers. 'Gossip spreads like wildfire. I don't need servants talking about our marriage before there's even been a marriage. Nor do I want it splashed over the tabloids that my convenient wife and heir are all for show.'

'But we are,' she said with a tilt of her head, relieved to say the words, to remind herself as much as anything.

'He is my heir,' Matthias murmured. 'And you will be my wife. There is nothing dishonest in that.'

She bit back whatever she'd been about to say, nodding

instead. He was right. She'd agreed to this, and she'd known what his terms were. There was no sense demeaning herself by arguing over such a trivial point.

'You'll meet your valet tomorrow,' he said, changing the subject. 'She'll help you with anything you require.'

'Valet?'

'Your point-of-contact servant. The head of your house.'

'I… I don't need that.'

He sent her a look of sardonic amusement. 'You will receive over a thousand invitations every year to social events. Then there's the dozens and dozens of requests for you to serve as a spokesperson for charities, to fundraise on their behalf and raise their profile. Each of these will require a response, and it will be impossible for you—on your own—to know which are worthy of your consideration and which are not.'

Frankie was struck dumb momentarily. 'But why would so many people want…? I mean…'

'You will be Queen—and people will presume you have the ear of the King. There is power in your position, and it is natural that many will want to use that to their advantage.'

'But I won't have the ear of the King,' she said, shaking her head and walking towards the enormous windows that looked over the mysterious fruit grove.

'Nobody will be aware of that. To the outside, our marriage will appear to be a love match—it's natural people will presume I listen to your counsel.'

Bitterness twisted inside her, and loss too—a deep and profound sense of grief at the picture he'd so easily painted. The kind of marriage she'd always dreamed she might one day be a part of. The true sense of belonging she'd sought all her life. The thoughts were dark, depressing. She stamped them out, focusing on the business at hand. 'And my valet will manage all that for me?'

'Your secretary will.'

She frowned, not taking her eyes off the trees below. 'We were talking about a valet.'

'I said the valet is the head of your house. There will be around ten members of staff—not including your security detail—who report to your valet.'

At that she turned to face him, but wished she hadn't. The sight of him, one hip propped against the kitchen counter, watching her thoughtfully, jolted her heart painfully, as though she'd been shocked with electricity. 'Matt—' she used the diminutive form of his name without thinking '—I don't want this.'

His eyes narrowed thoughtfully. 'Why not?'

'It's just strange. I can't see that I'll need that many people working for me.'

'You wish to fire someone then?'

She opened her mouth to say something and then slammed it shut; he had her jammed into a tight corner there and undoubtedly knew it. She shook her head. 'No, I just…'

'Relax, Frankie. You will adapt to all this, I promise.'

'That's easy for you to say. You grew up with this; it's normal for you.'

He shrugged. 'And it will become normal for you.' He stood up straighter and walked towards her, opening the large glass doors. Warmth billowed in from the sunny afternoon beyond. He gestured for her to precede him onto the balcony and, curious, she did. The terracotta tiles were warm beneath her feet. Out here, the fruit trees had a delightful fragrance. She breathed in deeply, letting the smell roll all the way down to her toes.

She was in a foreign country with a man she hadn't seen

in years, a man she'd slept with and then lost all contact with, a man who had fathered her son, and yet, ridiculously, standing beneath that milky sun with the citrusy fragrance like a cloud around her, the colours all green and blue with splashes of bold red where geraniums were growing, she felt completely and utterly at ease.

'My valet will coordinate with yours with regard to the wedding plans. The date has been set for two weeks' time.'

The sense of relaxation evaporated. 'Two weeks?' She jerked her head towards his. He was watching her, those eyes imprinted on her brain like ghosts.

He appeared to misunderstand her. 'This is the soonest it can be. No sooner,' he explained. 'It is necessary to give people time to travel—foreign dignitaries, royals, diplomats.'

'But…what's the rush?'

His lips were a tight line in his face. 'I have a two-year-old who, at this moment, is illegitimate and has no claim on my throne. If I were to die tomorrow, the country would not have an heir. Yet here he is, a living, breathing child of mine—you cannot see that there is a rush to marry and legally make him mine?'

Frankie bit down on her lower lip, nodding even as she tried to make sense of that. 'But you're his father—there's no doubt of that. Surely you could adopt him or—'

'Adopt *my own son*?' There was a look of cold rejection on his face, as though adopting Leo would be the worst thing in the world.

Frankie's stomach swooped and for a moment the wounds of her childhood were flayed open. 'I only meant there must be another way to legally empower him as your heir,' she said, so softly the words were almost swallowed on the breeze.

'If there was, do you think I would have been so insistent on marrying you?'

* * *

He'd gone too far. He could see it in the way all the colour had drained from her face. No, from her whole body! She was as white as the sand of Makalini Beach, her eyes green and awash with hurt.

Damn it!

But he was in shock, still trying to make sense of this, trying to see the best way forward for both of them. The last thing he wanted was to argue with Frankie. None of this was her fault, and he admired her courage and strength in taking her place beside him.

He exhaled softly, turning the words over in his heart before speaking them to her. 'I hate knowing that he was out there for two and a half years and I knew nothing of him.'

She made a strangled noise; he took it to be one of understanding.

'The laws of succession are archaic and unchangeable. Even the fact he is born out of wedlock will require a DNA test to satisfy my country's parliament. They must ratify his legitimacy and—'

'Wait—just a second,' she interrupted urgently. 'You're actually going to get our child paternity tested?'

He turned to her, confused now by the anger that had surged into her face. Relieved too, as it made her cheeks glow pink once more. 'It is necessary,' he said.

'No way.'

Her refusal intrigued him and alarmed him in equal measure. 'Why not?' He bit the words out from teeth that were suddenly clenched tight. Was it possible she'd lied about Leo's paternity?

But why would she?

'Because he's your son! He can't be anyone else's, unless it was an immaculate conception,' she said with quiet insistence. 'And because I don't want him to think he had to have a blood test to prove to his own father what's blatantly obvious when you look at the two of you together.'

He relaxed once more—because, of course, she was right. Leo was a carbon copy of not only himself, but of Spiro too. As quickly as his brain absorbed that fact, it moved onto another she'd revealed. 'You're saying you haven't slept with anyone since me?'

'I…' She swept her eyes shut and shook her head. When she looked at him again a moment later she was calm—cool and somehow dismissive. She was excellent at doing that—at submerging whatever she was feeling beneath a mask of unconcern. He'd seen her do it numerous times and on each occasion he felt overwhelmed by a desire to work out exactly how he could shake that mask loose. He knew one way, of course. One very tempting, very distracting way…

'I'm saying you're the only person who could be his father.'

'Is that not the same thing?'

'No.'

His gut clenched and a dark sensation speared through him. It wasn't jealousy exactly—it was…possession. Primal, ancient, animalistic possession. He didn't want to think of her sleeping with any other man—ever.

'Have there been other men?' he asked, the question direct, and he had the satisfaction of seeing her mask slip for a second.

'Why do you care?'

'Because I like thinking I'm the only man who's known the pleasure of your body,' he said simply, unapologetically.

Heat stained her cheeks and he could resist no longer. He moved to where she stood on the balcony, bracing a hand on either side of her. 'That's kind of chauvinistic.'

His lips twisted in a smile. 'Yes.'

And then, to his surprise, she smiled, a genuine smile

that made the corners of her eyes crinkle and it felt as if the sun was forcing its way into his chest. He stared at her, his own face unknowingly tense, rigid, frozen by the radiance of her expression. 'At least you admit it.'

He continued to stare, drinking in her beauty, but the smile dropped almost immediately and an air of seriousness surrounded them.

'You told him about me?'

She swallowed, her eyes half-closed, shielding herself from him. 'Yes.'

'You told him I was kind?' he prompted, remembering the remark their son had made on the flight over.

She was defensive. 'I wanted him to believe his father was a good man. I wanted him to be proud of you.'

Matthias's breathing was shallow. 'Why?'

She toyed with her fingers in front of her, weaving them together. 'One day, he'll be old enough to ask about you. I didn't want him to fill in the gaps in the meantime. I didn't want him to think…'

Her words trailed into nothingness.

'Go on,' he urged desperately.

'I didn't want him to think he wasn't wanted.' She cleared her throat. 'I told him you were good and kind and funny but that you live far away from us, but that…'

'Yes?' The word was quick to escape from him, an impatient hiss.

'That you think of us often. That you look into the stars and think about the stars above us.' There was defiance in her tone now. 'It's for him, not you.'

His chest felt heavy. She'd created a myth for their son, a myth of him as a good, kind, decent man—she'd done the opposite of what he might have imagined a woman in her shoes doing: she'd praised him and spoken of him in a way that would make their son want to know his father.

It was impossible not to look at her with growing respect, with appreciation. He wasn't sure he'd deserved any of that.

'I don't want him to have a paternity test,' she said quietly, but with a strength that called to him. 'I don't want him to think…'

'To think what, Frankie?' he pushed when her words trailed off into the air.

'To think he wasn't wanted.' She lifted her gaze to his and there was a haunted quality to her expression, a hurt he couldn't comprehend. 'I don't want him to think he had to have a blood test before you'd let him into your life.'

He expelled a breath, his nostrils flaring as he instinctively rejected her take on the situation. 'It is merely a formality.'

'It's unnecessary.' Again, he felt her tender insistence deep in his gut and a protective instinct surged inside him—though what he was wanting to protect her from, he couldn't have said.

'He's your son,' she continued quietly, lifting one hand to his chest and pressing it just above his heart.

And emotions flooded him—paternal pride, completeness, rightness—relief that it was this woman who'd borne him a son and heir. His words were thick with all his feelings when he dredged them from deep within his soul. 'And soon the whole world will know it.'

CHAPTER SIX

MATTHIAS COULDN'T REMEMBER when he'd last slept for longer than an hour or two. He was bone-weary, exhausted to the depths of his soul, but the sight of Frankie fast asleep in his bed arrested him and energised him all at once and he found his feet reluctant to move.

The way she'd smiled at him earlier that day had stayed with him all afternoon, replaying in his mind, so that he had rushed through his commitments, hoping to see her again, to see if he could make her smile once more. Not that he could say what he'd done to change her mood—it wasn't like in New York, three years earlier, when they'd both smiled often and freely.

He'd wanted to see her again, but events had conspired to keep him from dining with her—a problem at the embassy in Rome—and so now she was fast asleep.

Her long blonde hair was drawn around her shoulder like a skein of gold and her breathing was slow and rhythmic. Her lips, parted and pink, were so perfect, and he remembered instantly how they'd felt when she'd kissed him in New York, years earlier.

Tentatively at first, and then with the madness that had overtaken them. He remembered how she'd felt in his arms downstairs earlier today, when he'd taken her by surprise and kissed her, and he remembered the moment when she'd become pliant in his arms. He could identify the exact moment when she'd lost a part of herself to this madness. He'd known he could have deepened the kiss, that he could have taunted her with their desire and turned her into a jumble of nerves and responses in his arms, but he hadn't.

He'd stemmed his own needs, respecting her boundaries, knowing deep down how overwhelmed she must be. Not just by his position as King, and her son's place in the country's order of succession, not even by her future as Queen. But by this, them, whatever they felt. He was a man of far greater experience, of greater years, and yet he still found their chemistry explosive and somehow awe-inspiring.

Even as he stood by the bed, watching her gentle exhalations, desire flooded his system and he wondered how she'd respond if he reached for her. If he strode to the bed, put a hand on her shoulder and stirred her to wakefulness, if he pressed his lips to the soft flesh at the base of her throat that had always driven her wild…

And as though his thoughts had pushed into hers, she moved in her sleep, her eyes blinking open and landing straight on him. Breath that had been slow suddenly stopped altogether as she stared at him.

It was just after midnight, and magic was thick in the air—magic with the power to bring the past into the present.

'Matt?' She blinked, frowning, pushing up so that the sheet dropped to reveal the soft swell of her cleavage. There was nothing sexy about the singlet she was wearing or at least it shouldn't have been. But somehow it was, and he was groaning with side-splitting need.

He swallowed—hard—and he was hard all over, his body wound tighter than a spring.

'I was… You were just…' In the soft milky moonlight he saw her cheeks flush pink and he took a step deeper into the room despite every bone in his body telling him it was wrong.

'Yes?' The word came out thick and gravelled. He cleared his throat, watching her intently.

'I thought I was dreaming.'

His body fired. Desires he'd already been battling surged inside him. 'Was it a good dream?' he asked, taking the rest of the steps necessary to bring him level with the bed. His own side yawned empty and cold. Duty and responsibility were on his side of the bed, but temptation lay here, and he was oh, so tempted.

'I…' She frowned and lifted a hand to the strap of her top. His eyes followed the action and at the sight of the outline of her nipples, straining hard against the fabric of her shirt, he suppressed a groan.

There was the right thing to do, and there was what they both wanted and needed.

Ignoring common sense, he caught her hand on her shoulder, holding it low, and then, his eyes locked onto hers, loaded with challenge, he oh-so-slowly traced his fingertips over her flesh, easing the strap lower, not higher. Her skin lifted with fine goosebumps and her breath stalled in her throat. Her eyes were pleading and he watched her, challenge in every line of his face.

'What did you dream?' he asked, his other hand reaching for the strap that still sat on her shoulder. He didn't push it downwards though. He simply looped his fingers beneath it, his eyes on her face, waiting, still, frozen in time, impatient to know what she was going to say.

'I dreamed… I was… It was years ago,' she said huskily, her beautiful face clouded with uncertainty.

'And do you dream of me often?'

Her slender throat moved visibly as she swallowed and her eyes swept shut, perhaps in an attempt to block him from seeing her thoughts in that expressive face of hers. 'No,' she whispered.

'Liar.' His laugh was without humour. 'I think you dream of me frequently. Perhaps every night, even.'

At her harsh intake of breath he bent lower and, knowing he should stop this madness, he crushed his lips to hers, swallowing the little moan she made, tasting her sweetness, and memories and feelings rushed back at him because she tasted, she *felt* exactly as she had done then and his whole body rejoiced at that familiarity and rightness.

Her mouth was parted and he slipped his tongue inside, duelling with hers, reminding her of this need, and she whimpered into the kiss before her hands lifted and her fingers tangled in the hair at the nape of his neck, just as she had then. Her body lifted, her breasts crushed to his chest and he swore in his own language as impatience threatened to burst him wide open.

'Tell me you dreamed of this,' he demanded, his fingers pushing the straps down now, so her breasts were free of the flimsy garment, and he cupped them greedily in his palms, feeling their weight, their generous roundness tightening his body so his arousal strained against his pants and his whole body ached for her in a way that defied sense and reason.

She had! Oh, she'd dreamed of this again and again and in the groggy half-awake state she was in it was almost impossible to believe this wasn't just a dream. But his hands on her were real—everything about this was real. She arched her back hungrily and pulled him with her hands, pulling him down on top of her, ignoring the voice in her head that was shouting at her to see reason and make this stop.

It was the witching hour and she was bewitched. He was strong, and big, and though she pulled him he came at his own pace, slowly easing his body weight on top of hers then rolling his hips so his arousal pressed to her womanhood.

A sharp dagger of need perforated her senses. It was achingly, perfectly familiar. She needed him.

'Please,' she whimpered, knowing she was stranded on this wave of desire, that she was stranded on an island of sexual craving from which there was no other relief.

He rolled his hips again and his body, so hard and heavy, pressed to her feminine core, stoking her pulse, her needs, her wants. Pleasure was a cloud carrying her away, but reality was gravity, dragging her back to earth.

It had all been so easy for him that weekend three years ago. He'd looked at her and wanted her and she'd fallen into bed with him, despite having intended to save her virginity for the man she was going to marry. She'd had no defences for someone like him, no experience with men at all, really.

And now? She was falling for it again, letting desire make a mockery of all her good intentions.

Was she really going to be this woman? A woman who let passion control her actions and dictate her life. Was she really going to fall into the habit of sleeping with someone she desired even when love wasn't a part of the equation?

'We can't do this.' She shook her head, pulling away from his kiss, and now his body on hers felt like a crushing weight from which she needed to be free. She pressed her palms to his chest and felt the brief impression of his fast-racing heart before she shoved him bodily off herself and rolled out of bed.

'I can't,' she repeated, though he hadn't said a single word. He was simply watching her with the same intensity with which he'd been kissing her a moment earlier.

'I'm not going to do that.' She pulled her straps back into place, her fingers shaking so much she had to curve them into fists and hold them by her side.

He was still watching her, saying nothing, just staring,

and though she was now fully dressed she felt more naked and exposed than ever before. She'd put a stop to whatever had been about to happen—but the inevitably of their coming together was still heavy in the room.

He watched her for a long time, as if seeing all the pieces of her soul. 'How come you were still a virgin, Frankie?'

The question pricked something in the region of her heart. She knew her expectations were out of step with most people's reality, but they were her feelings, her resolves. 'I…just was.'

'No.' He propped up on one elbow, apparently completely relaxed. 'I don't believe it was a matter of you having simply not slept with anyone.'

'Why not?' She challenged, her eyes sparking with his.

'Because you're a flesh and blood woman,' he murmured throatily. 'And I know for myself how sensual you are. How hungry your appetite…'

Her pulse sped up and with his eyes digging into hers she found she didn't want to lie to him. What was the point? 'I wanted to save myself for my husband.' She slid her gaze sideways, aware of how juvenile the assertion must have sounded. She focused her eyes on the wall and didn't see the look of intense concentration that overtook his features.

'Why?' A single word, rough and husky.

'I've told you: sex should mean something.' She frowned. 'I *thought* it should mean something. I was… I think sex and love should go hand in hand and when I eventually fell in love, and someone loved me, I wanted it to be something I shared with them.' When had she first started to align sex with love? She wasn't sure she'd ever know. When had she inextricably bound the two, sentiment and act, together? 'And then I met you.'

There was a self-mocking tilt to his beautiful lips. 'A man who thinks sex is for fun and love is a construct.'

Her heart stammered at the coldness of that assessment. 'A man I couldn't resist.' She shook her head, clearing the vestiges of the past from her mind. 'But that was years ago and I'm not the same person any more.' Certainty strengthened inside her. 'I guess you could say I learned my lesson.'

'We have already discussed this. I need another child, another heir...'

She ignored the cold, callous conclusion to that sentence—*in case anything happens to Leo.* 'That's an entirely separate proposition to what we were just about to do. Sleeping together because we aren't strong enough to listen to common sense, to do the right thing, is simply a matter of poor judgement.'

'You are cutting off your nose to spite your face,' he observed dryly.

His comment was utterly accurate. In putting a halt to their sensual pull she was only hurting herself because she wanted him with all of herself. She needed him. And yet she was resisting him because her pride demanded it of her. Not just her pride—her heart. Her heart, that could have so easily been his; her heart that had been hurt and ignored too many times to easily trust. 'I'm not. I'm just... I'm someone who always wanted the fairy tale,' she said quietly.

But often the most quietly voiced sentiments carried the most resonance.

'There's no such thing as fairy tales,' he said after several beats of silence had passed, and he stared at her for a long moment, his expression a mask of intensity. 'And even if there were, I could not give it to you.'

She sucked in an unsteady breath, lost for words.

'You can get back in bed, Frankie. Relax. I won't touch

you unless you ask me to.' And he turned onto his side, his back to her.

Silence fell. She stood there, watching him for a moment, and when his breathing was rhythmic and steady she climbed into bed, turning her own back on him and hugging the edge of the mattress.

It was a recurrent nightmare but that didn't change the fact that it flooded Matthias with adrenalin as if it was all happening for the first time. He was back in the limousine. The smell of petrol and burning flesh filling his nostrils, his body trapped, his eyes open. His parents were dead but Spiro, beside him, was still alive.

His cries were like nothing Matthias could put into words.

'I'm coming,' he promised, pushing at the metal that was heavy on his chest. 'Just keep your eyes open.'

The driver was dead too. He couldn't see the security agent who had been travelling in the same car as them.

'I can't, Matt,' Spiro groaned, and his dark eyes were covered with tears.

'You must.' Matthias, a teenager, swore darkly into the limousine and Spiro winced. He had to get free. He had to save them.

'I'll be there in a second. Hold my hand.' He reached out and the pain was like nothing he'd ever known before. His arm was broken. He grunted, extending it as best he was able. It was just far enough. Spiro put his smaller hand in Matthias's, and Matthias looked at them; their flesh was the same colour, their hands the same shape. But Spiro's was cold. Ice-cold, like nothing Matthias had ever known.

'Listen to me.' Matthias spoke urgently. 'I can hear sirens in the distance. Can you?' There was a bleating—from far away. 'They're coming to help you, Spiro. They're going to cut you out of this car and take you to hospital. I'll be beating you again in basketball in weeks.'

Spiro smiled—his teeth were covered in blood. Matthias's chest ached. His younger brother's eyes were heavy.

'Damn it—stay awake,' Matthias commanded, pushing at the metal once more. It budged, but only by a tiny amount. 'Damn it!' he shouted again.

'Matt…' Spiro dropped his hand and Matthias jerked his head towards his brother. Stars danced in his eyes and for a second he blacked out. When he came to the sirens were louder, and Spiro was sleeping. At least he looked like he was sleeping.

'Spiro!' Matthias pushed at the metal—it must have weighed a ton. Nothing moved. His own body was broken. Hysteria groaned inside him. 'Spiro!'

He turned towards the front of the car and wished he hadn't, when the sight of his parents' mangled bodies filled his vision. He closed his eyes and prayed, then swore, then reached for Spiro with an arm that didn't seem to want to obey his brain's commands.

He needed to get free so he could save his brother. There was no water—the car had swerved to avoid a boulder in the middle of the road. It had flipped over into a valley and landed on its roof. But in Matthias's dream they were always on the edge of water, and slowly it seeped into the car. Not transparent like the water that surrounded his palace, but a sludgy black, then burgundy, like blood.

Spiro died and Matthias could do little more than reach for his hand.

At fifteen, he lost everyone he'd ever loved.

It would be two hours before the rescue teams could free him. Two hours in which he stared at his brother and tried not to look towards his parents. Two hours in which his heart, though still beating, ceased to feel.

* * *

'Matt?' She pushed at his shoulder; it was damp with perspiration. 'Matthias? Wake up.'

He made a noise and then sat bolt upright, so his head came close to banging hers. His eyes were wide open and when they swung to face hers they were huge and dark. The sun was not yet up but the sky had taken on a dawn tinge—gold and pink warred with silver-grey, bathing the room in a warm glow.

His breathing was rushed, but not in a good way. Not in the way hers had been the night before. He stared at her as though he was drowning and she could save him; he stared at her as though he expected her to say or do something, but she couldn't fathom what.

'Are you okay?' she asked, as slowly his face assumed its normal handsome appearance. His lips closed, his eyes shuttered, his colour returned to normal.

'I'm fine.' He swung his powerful legs off the side of the bed and cradled his head in his hands for a moment. His back was turned to her yet again, but this time she resented that.

'You had a bad dream.'

He made a guttural sound.

'Want to talk about it?'

Another grunt, then he pushed to standing and strolled towards the French windows that led to the balcony.

'I'll take that as a no,' she murmured, more to herself than him.

He heard though and turned back to face her. He was wearing boxer shorts, but it still took a monumental effort for Frankie to keep her attention trained on his face. 'It's nothing.' He pushed the window open and stepped outside. The pale curtain billowed in after him.

Not understanding why, she followed him, knowing he

was seeking privacy and that she should let him have that, knowing she had no reason to go after him. Understanding he wouldn't welcome the intrusion but going anyway. She padded across the room, swallowing a yawn as she went, and emerging on the balcony.

He was staring at the ocean. She followed the direction of his gaze, unable to ignore the appreciative gasp that was a natural response to the sheer beauty before her. In the early morning light the sea shimmered silver and flashes of pre-dawn sunlight made the ripples appear to glisten like diamonds and topaz. The sky itself was a work of art she could never replicate—colours that didn't appear in any manmade palette, and the combination of which, if she'd pushed them into service, would be almost garish.

'He was only nine years old.' Matthias surprised her by speaking. She drew her attention back to his face and something in her chest skidded to a halt. His expression was the most sombre she'd ever seen—not just on Matthias, but on any human being.

'Who?'

He looked at her then, but as though he didn't really see her. His expression didn't shift. 'My brother. Spiro.'

Liana had mentioned Spiro, and now it made sense. Her heart broke for him.

'He was nine when he died.'

Grief clutched at Frankie's chest. 'How?'

'A car accident.'

'I'm so sorry.'

It was the wrong thing to say. He withdrew from her visibly, shrinking into his hard-edged shell.

'It is what it is.'

'Don't do that,' she murmured, shaking her head. An early morning breeze came from the ocean, carrying with it the tang of sea salt and ruffling Frankie's hair. She caught it with her fingertips and held it over one shoulder. 'Don't act like it doesn't matter. You're talking about your brother's death. It's okay to say you're upset.'

If anything, his features tightened. 'What good can come from being upset?' he asked, the words flat, turning away from her, showing he didn't expect an answer.

'Plenty.' She gave one anyway. 'Being upset, talking about how you feel, helps you move on. Helps you process…'

He shook his head. 'Why should I get to move on when Spiro has died?' He gripped the railing and leaned over it a little, staring at the ground beneath. 'Sometimes I think that if I can just reach for him in my dream, it won't have happened. That I will wake up and he will be here. Sometimes I think the accident was the nightmare, only I don't know how to rouse myself from it.'

Frankie made a small sound of sympathy.

'There is no processing this.' His eyes were hollow when he turned to her. 'There is no moving on from it. And I don't *want* to move on. Spiro is a part of me—his life, and his death. I live for both of us.'

Her fingertips ached to touch him, to comfort him, only the memory of how incendiary contact with this man could be was still alive in her gut, fresh in her mind, and so with great determination she kept her hands at her sides.

'Your parents died in the accident as well?' she murmured gently.

His response was a curt nod but the pain in his eyes was palpable, his emotions strong and fierce.

'Oh, Matt,' she murmured, and determination gave way to sympathy and an innate need to comfort him, to ease his suffering. She lifted her fingertips to his shoulder and gently traced his flesh. He was still so warm. A kaleidoscope of butterflies launched in her belly. The sun rose higher; gold slanted across her face. 'I can't imagine what that was like for you.'

'An adjustment,' he grunted, his nostrils flaring, his eyes pinning her to the spot.

She looked at him with obvious disbelief. 'Stop acting like you're too tough to care. No one can go through something like that and not have it change them. You must have been…'

'It changed me,' he stated, interrupting her with a voice that was weighted down by his feelings. 'It changed me a great deal. At fifteen I still believed my parents were infallible, that my sovereignty was guaranteed and that Spiro would spend his life driving me crazy with annoying questions and demands for attention. At fifteen I believed that I was the future King and would one day have the power to do and fix and make just about anything. I truly thought I was omnipotent.'

She nodded slowly, unconsciously bringing her body closer to his. 'I think most teenagers feel that—royal or not.'

'Maybe so.' He didn't smile but his eyes dropped to her lips, tracing their soft roundness with visible distraction. 'By the time I turned sixteen I saw the world for what it is.'

Silence throbbed around them, emotional and weary.

'And what's that?' she prompted after a moment.

'Transient. Untrustworthy.'

She shook her head and the hand that had been tentatively stroking his shoulder curved around it now, so only her thumb swept across his warm flesh. When he still didn't look at her, she lifted the other hand to his shoulder, needing more contact, as though through her touch alone she could reassure him and somehow fix this.

'What happened to you is a terrible tragedy,' she said quietly. 'But you can't let it rob you of your own happiness. Your parents wouldn't want that. Your brother wouldn't either. You say you're living for Spiro, but how can you be when you take such a dim view of all there is out there?'

'I am a realist, remember?' he said, breathing in deep, so his chest moved forward and brushed against her front. Her nipples tingled at the unintentional contact.

'A realist? I don't know, Matt. Sometimes I think you're nudging into pessimist territory.'

His eyes held hers and the air between them was thick, like the clouds before a storm. 'Is that so bad?'

'I…' Her mind was finding it hard to keep up. She looked at him, shaking her head, but why?

'Maybe, over time, you'll change me,' he said and then his smile was cynical and the air returned to normal. She blinked, like waking up from her own dream.

'I'm not sure people really change so easily.'

He stepped out of her reach and nodded curtly. 'Nor am I.'

CHAPTER SEVEN

'JUST A LITTLE this way, please, madam,' the photographer urged, holding a slender tanned arm in the air.

Frankie followed his instructions, but the smile she had pinned to her face earlier was starting to feel as if it was held in place via glue.

'Perfect. Just a few more—over near the balcony.'

The afternoon sun was streaming in like arrows of gold, no less dazzling than it had been earlier that day, when they'd stood on a different balcony and watched the dawn crest over the ocean. But then he'd been wearing only boxer shorts and the trauma of his dream had clung to him like a dark cloak she'd needed to break him free of. Now, Matthias looked every inch the handsome King. A dark suit with a cream tie, his eyes glinted in his tanned face. Black hair had been styled back from his brow, and it was all she could do not to simply stare at him.

Mathilde had presented Frankie with a cream dress for the formal engagement announcement photo session—it was long and had a ruffle across one shoulder that fell to her waist before swishing out into a narrow skirt, all the way to her ankles. Teamed with a pair of heels, she at least had a small advantage on her usual height, so she didn't feel so small when standing beside Matthias.

'It has been forty minutes,' Matthias bit out, lifting his gold wristwatch and staring at the time. 'Surely you have enough?'

The photographer, busy looking at the digital screen on the back of the camera, glanced up and blinked, then nodded. 'Almost, Your Majesty,' he promised. 'Just five more minutes.'

Frankie risked a glance at Matthias's face; it was forbidding and oh, so regal. These engagement portraits were going to make them look as if they were on their way to a funeral rather than a wedding.

'Do you need a break, *deliciae*?' Matthias looked directly at her and her heart thumped in her chest.

She shook her head. 'I'm fine. You?'

He grimaced in response. 'Hardly my preferred way to spend time.'

'Just against the railing, please, sir. Madam.'

Matthias assumed a nonchalant, bored pose and Frankie stood beside him. The photographer shook his head. 'Lean into him a bit more. Like this—' The photographer tilted his head and smiled.

Frankie compressed her lips and looked up at Matthias before moving. He was watching her, his expression sardonic.

With a small sigh, Frankie did as the photographer had suggested, but it was like being exposed to flames. Her head rested on his pectoral muscle; she could hear his heart, feel his warmth. Her smile was barely there, a whisper on her face—how could she smile when standing upright was such an effort? Matthias's hand curved around her back and his fingers splayed wide, moving ever so slightly up and down, up and down, so heat and warmth radiated from where he touched her.

'Smile!' the photographer reminded her. Frankie tried, but all of her was tied up in that moment in simply feeling. Sensations were overriding anything else. The desire she was trying to fight with all her being surged inside her, making her nerve-endings quiver, making her want to burst from the room and drag Matthias to bed, to reclaim what she knew they could mean to one another.

Matthias dipped his head forward and said *sotto voce*, 'You are trembling like a little leaf, *mikró*.'

She looked up at him, for a moment forgetting they weren't alone. Their eyes latched and nothing—no one—existed. They were alone on the balcony, the ancient ocean rolling in the background as it had for millennia. Grey eyes held green, and she lost herself in their depths. She lost herself in the ocean of his eyes, she fell to the bottom, she drowned on the seafloor, wrapped in sand and shells, and she cared not—she forgot everything.

His head dropped slowly, as if on a time lapse, though of course it hadn't really been so slow. To Frankie, though, it was the work of minutes: long, agonising, tense moments when her lips were tingling and her eyes were holding his and she could think of nothing else but a need to sink into his kiss. It was just a brush of his lips to hers, the lightest, most frustrating contact.

He kissed her, the photographer clicked, and her body snapped to life. The moan that escaped her lips was involuntary, just a small husky sound, and then Matthias lifted his head, his eyes not leaving Frankie's passion-ravaged face. 'It is enough,' he said and his words had a cool tone.

'Yes, sir, definitely. That's plenty. Thank you, sir.'

Matthias turned to Frankie and extended a hand, and ridiculously she almost didn't take it. Fear dogged her every move. Fear of this—what she was fighting, the certainty that this passion could subsume her every good intention and intellectual certainty that Matthias was not someone she could trust with her heart, her life, her love.

How absurd. She was overthinking it!

She took his hand, purely because the photographer was there and to refuse would have seemed churlish and strange, and walked with him through the gallery they'd been posing in earlier. At the door she let go, pulling her hand back softly and rubbing her palms together.

'So the engagement will be announced when?'

'Tomorrow.'

They continued to walk down a wide beautiful corridor, lined with enormous floral arrangements. They were fragrant and stunning.

'I need to tell my parents. They're going to be…blindsided.'

Matthias tilted a look at her. 'Why?'

Frankie pulled a face. 'Well, I'm getting married, to a man they've never even heard of. A king, no less!'

'You're marrying your son's father,' he said laconically.

'A man they don't know from Adam.'

'Who's Adam?'

She shook her head. 'It's an expression. I mean, you're just some guy who…'

'Yes?'

She flicked her gaze to him and then looked away again. Ridiculously, she felt uncomfortable addressing the truth of what had happened between them. 'Who got me pregnant and disappeared into thin air.'

She wasn't looking at him, so didn't see the way his features tightened as though he'd been slapped. She didn't see the way a muscle jerked in his jaw and his eyes focused more intently on her face. 'I presume they think the worst of me.'

She shrugged. 'Can you blame them?'

'No.' The forcefulness of his word had her looking at him once more. 'If we had a daughter and this was her fate—'

'My fate wasn't so bad,' she said with a small grimace. 'I got Leo, remember?'

Matthias didn't acknowledge her comment. 'If I had known there was even the slightest chance of you having conceived that night, things would have been very different.'

'Different how?'

'I wouldn't have missed a moment of his life,' he said, the words rich with emotion. Foolish hurt dipped in Frankie's gut—hurt that it was Leo alone he would have wished to see and support. Hurt that a desire to spend more time with her didn't enter into it, when she had pined for his touch, for his smile, for months.

'We can't change the past,' she said softly.

'Nor can we secure the future. But here, in this moment, I promise you, Frankie, this is not how I would have wanted things to be. You shouldn't have had to do this alone. If I could miraculously turn time backwards and change this, I would. With all of myself, I would…'

She swallowed, looking up at him, and she could feel the truth of his regret, his remorse, his desire to have been a part of this from the beginning.

'I know.'

He stared at her, long and hard, and though he didn't speak it was as though his gaze was asking a question of her: did she really understand that? Did she really believe that he was not the kind of man to abandon a young, pregnant woman? Did she know how deeply abhorrent that was to him?

And then, as though he saw her answer, he saw her acceptance of his innocence, he nodded. As though a switch had been flicked, he became a man of action. A king. A ruler. A man without doubt and self-recriminations. 'I will call your parents and explain.'

Frankie let out a laugh. 'You've never even met my parents!'

His eyes glowed with intent. 'I am the man you're going to marry, the man who fathered their grandson, even if I haven't been any kind of a father to him. I owe it to them to explain my absence, and how I intend to remedy that.'

'Hang on.' She laughed again and was surprised to find true amusement spinning through her. His eyes clung to her smile and her heart turned over, sobering her. 'You're not…this isn't…you're not a character in a Jane Austen novel. Nor am I, for that matter. I don't need you to go to my dad and ask for permission.'

His eyes narrowed imperceptibly. 'It is a mark of respect.'

'Respect *me*,' she said, 'and my wishes, and my parents will be okay.'

'I owe them an explanation…'

'You owe *me* an explanation, not them, and you've given me one. I understand. I forgive you. They're nothing to do with this.'

'It is important to me that your parents understand I had no idea you were pregnant.'

'They know that,' she said quietly. 'What do you think I said to them?'

At this, he was very still, as though it hadn't occurred to him that she might have painted a picture of him to her family at all. 'I have no idea.'

'I told them you were an amazing man, who I couldn't contact. I told them we didn't plan to see each other again, and that it wasn't your fault I couldn't find you. I told them I'd tried—they knew about the investigator—but, ultimately, they just feel sorry for you. For what you've missed. My parents are…' She swept her eyes shut for a moment, her childhood and reality hitting her hard in that moment.

'Being parents meant everything to them. The fact you were deprived of that privilege through life's circumstances is something they were saddened by. Not angry about.'

His expression showed scepticism, but she barely registered it.

She forced a smile to her face. 'Besides, they got to be grandparents to Leo, and believe me when I tell you: no child has ever been more spoiled nor adored. No baby has ever been so hugged and kissed.'

His frown deepened. 'Yet they left you living in poverty?'

'Poverty?' She rolled her eyes now and gestured down the corridor. 'My apartment might not have been a palace, but it was hardly a slum either, Matthias. Don't be such a snob.'

His laugh was involuntary—no one had called Matthias a snob in his life.

'Mum and Dad aren't wealthy,' she said softly, a warm smile touching her lips. 'They helped when they could, but my dad has needed a heap of operations for his back and that didn't come cheap.'

Matthias's brow wrinkled.

'Insurance wouldn't cover it.' She recalled the way her father had delayed the necessary procedures, insisting he could manage, when his body gradually betrayed him. 'The last thing I wanted was for them to worry about Leo and me.'

'But you have found it difficult?'

'Financially?'

He nodded.

'Yes. But that was my choice, my business. I knew being an artist would be hard. I have had to do things I didn't particularly like, just to get by, to support Leo. It's why I need the art show to be a success. I wanted my career to be able to support us, but in reality, who knows if that would ever have been possible.'

'What things?' he prompted, homing in on the detail she'd revealed.

'Oh, nothing terrible. I just mean I've worked at school fairs doing sketch portraits, or markets, I've waitressed and bussed tables, doing whatever I can to earn money, so that I can keep doing what I really love.'

'Which is painting.'

She nodded slowly. 'But I've always known I'd probably have to grow up and get a real job some day.'

'Your talent is rare. You shouldn't abandon your art.' The praise, so casually given, made her stomach roll.

'Thank you. But, talented or not, it's not an easy world to break into.'

He seemed to take her statement and mull on it, thinking it over for a moment, before nodding, almost dismissively. 'I must insist on calling your parents for myself, Frankie.'

'But…why?'

He expelled slowly and his breath fanned her temple, so her blonde hair shifted a little. His eyes lifted to the motion. 'Because there is no excuse for having left you. You were pregnant. Alone. And I should have been there.'

'You didn't know—'

He pressed a finger to her lips, his eyes beseeching her for silence. 'I am not a man to run from his responsibilities.' He was so strong, so big, she felt his insistence and understood it. 'I failed you. I failed Leo. And your parents deserve to hear that from me.'

Frankie was utterly struck dumb. His admission was almost an apology, one she had never expected from him.

'You had no idea about Leo,' she said quietly in an attempt to relieve him of his burden of guilt. 'I know you would have helped me if you had.'

'We would have married,' he agreed with complete confidence, never mind what Frankie might have thought of that. 'And you would never have known a day of worry in your life.'

She silently disagreed with that. Perhaps not financial worry, but emotional? Oh, yes. This marriage was going to be fraught with stress for Frankie.

CHAPTER EIGHT

AFTER A BAKING-HOT DAY, it was bliss to sink into the cool water of the swimming pool and stare out at the glistening sea. Bliss to be alone, with her hair in a simple braid, her face wiped of make-up, her space clear of servants. Leo had thrown a tantrum in the afternoon and though Liana had remained calm and helped Frankie remember that two-year-olds threw tantrums, that there was nothing abnormal about that behaviour, especially in strong-willed little boys, Frankie was nonetheless drained. And it had less to do with Leo and more to do with Matthias than Frankie wanted to admit. Every encounter with the man who would become her husband required so much effort. So much self-control. It was becoming increasingly difficult to remember why she wanted to keep him at arm's length. Or to care.

In the face of her desire for Matthias, sex for sex's sake was a palatable option, even when she'd always believed otherwise. Her need to control this seemed futile and absurd given that they would marry. Wasn't she only fighting to delay the inevitable? Why not just succumb? Why not enjoy what he was offering?

She duck-dived beneath the water's surface and swam a lap, holding her breath until her lungs were stinging, then pushing up off the tiled bottom and resting her elbows on the sun-warmed terracotta tiles.

Frustration gnawed at her—she pushed it aside with effort, focusing on the vista before her. She couldn't imagine a better view from anywhere in the world.

A moment later, she did another lap, then another, then switched to freestyle on the water's surface. She'd been a strong swimmer through school, and she'd always enjoyed it. But nothing was as nice as this. The water in the pool was salty, the twilight sun had the perfect degree of warmth and after the trials of staying calm in the face of Leo's belligerence it was a delight to expend some energy in this way.

Three more laps, and she emerged to find that she was no longer alone. Matthias had slipped into the pool unannounced and, though he stood on the opposite side, he was watching her, and he might as well have reached out and touched her, for how her body reacted to his presence.

'Matt…' she cleared her throat '… I didn't know you were here.'

'I just arrived.'

How did he have the ability to unsettle her with a single look? Her nerves struggled to find harmony in her body.

'I spoke to your father.'

Frankie's eyes flew wide. 'Already?'

He nodded. 'I saw no point in delay.'

'No, of course not. I mean, we're getting married so soon. I just hadn't expected…' She was babbling. She clamped her lips together and made an effort to focus. 'What did he say?'

'He was pleased for us. I wondered if you might wish to ask them to remain for some time after the wedding, at least to help with Leo while we take our honeymoon.'

'Honeymoon!' The word slid over her back like warmed caramel. She almost groaned at the image it conjured of the two of them, tangled in sheets, warm, passionate, limbs entwined…

'You know, that thing that usually follows a wedding?'

Her cheeks flushed pink. 'But this marriage isn't… I mean… It's not like we need that. Surely you have too much work. Wouldn't it just be an inconvenience?'

'Do you not wish to see more of this country you are to be Queen of?'

She bit down on her lip. 'I just don't think a *honeymoon* is called for.'

'Why do you make the distinction?'

'Honestly? A honeymoon makes me think of beds strewn with rose petals and baths filled with champagne. That's not us.'

'No,' he agreed, moving through the water easily, his long legs carrying him into the deepest part without more than half his chest being submerged. 'But it does not mean we can't have fun.'

Her mouth was dry and every breath of air seemed to make her nerves quiver. 'I think we have different ideas of fun.'

He laughed. 'Do we?'

She flushed and nodded, but her heart was racing, her pulse throbbing. 'I've told you, I'm not interested in casual sex.'

'There's nothing casual about marriage,' he said logically. 'And I think you're very interested in sex with me.'

Her chest squeezed. He closed the distance between them completely and, beneath the water, his long fingers found the edge of her bikini bottoms. With his eyes holding hers, he pulled her close to him. And, damn it, she went, with no resistance whatsoever. As though she were an iron filing and he her magnetic pole.

'Matt,' she murmured as his other hand curved into the bikini bottoms. He was taunting her, his eyes daring her to say something. To tell him to stop. And, though she knew she should, the word wouldn't come out. In fact, nothing came out except a small husky sound of surrender.

'Listen to me,' he said softly, swimming through the water and pulling her with him. He eased her onto one of the steps at the corner of the pool and stood between her legs. 'I want you, and I believe you want me. This—' he gestured from her chest to his '—is like a live wire.'

Her eyes flared at the description; it was exactly how she felt.

Beneath the water, his fingers toyed with the elastic sides of her bikini bottoms, sliding down and curving around her buttocks so she held her breath at the unfamiliar but undeniably welcome contact. She was a fool, she knew—she had to stop this—but oh, it felt so good. Just another minute, she promised herself.

Using his hands to guide her, he brought her body forward a little, so she could feel the strength of his rock-hard arousal, the desire that was there for her, and she whimpered low in her throat. Memories of how he'd felt, moving inside her, made her crazy with longing.

'I am the only man who's ever made love to you. Yes?'

Her cheeks flushed and she shuttered her eyes, unable to meet the scrutiny of his gaze.

'Tell me,' he demanded, kissing her neck so her breath came fast and hard inside her. 'That your only experience of sex is with me.'

A strangled noise escaped her throat. 'Why does it matter?'

'Because if this is so, then you have so much to learn,' he said.

One of his hands moved from her rear, coming over her leg and buzzing the sensitive flesh of her inner thigh, before nudging the flimsy material of her costume aside. She held her breath, her mind no longer able to concentrate on what he'd been saying. He watched her intently as his fingers brushed over her womanhood, his eyes holding hers as he slid a finger into her moist, tight core.

'You have so much to learn about your body and its pleasures, and I want to teach you that.' He swirled his finger around and she arched her back, her eyes fixing on the sunset overhead, on the colours that were only enhanced by the sheer perfection of his touch. 'I want you.' His mouth dropped to the flesh at the base of her throat and he kissed her, slow and long, and she moaned again, wrapping her legs around his waist and surrendering to the bliss of this moment, surrendering to an inevitability she'd been fighting since he'd walked into her gallery and her body had started to feel fully alive for the first time in three years.

'I know you want to fight me—' he rolled his hips and she moaned, his words stoking her like flames in a fire '—but can you not see how good our marriage can be? Neither of us wanted this, but that doesn't mean it can't be everything we want now, Frankie.' Her name on his lips was a seduction, his promise a temptation that was almost impossible to resist. Because he was right. He was so right.

Frankie didn't believe in casual sex, but this wasn't casual. This wasn't even just sex. There was so much more between them; there always had been. At least, for Frankie. He wasn't just some man she'd rushed into bed with. She'd met him and on some level had tripped headlong into love. She'd given all of herself to Matthias that night, not just her virginity. Not just her body.

And he'd walked away with such ease.

Oh, he'd had to—duty had called him. But he'd stayed away and her heart had been breaking.

Could she really lose herself to him again? Could she really be so stupid?

'Tell me you want me,' he said, and he stood out of the

pool, removing his hand from her only so he could reach down and lift her, carrying her against his chest as though she weighed nothing.

'I...can't,' she whispered as her hands reached up and tangled in the hair at his nape, as her body stayed wet and cleaved to his. He carried her to a pool lounger, laying her down and disposing of her bikini bottoms swiftly, staring at her naked sex with eyes that were so hungry they robbed her of breath.

'You can't admit to this?' He arched, kneeling on the ground at the foot of the lounger, parting her thighs with strong, broad hands. His mouth on her was a sensual, terrifying possession and she cried out as pleasure, sharp and visceral, broke through her.

He didn't speak—he didn't need to. His actions made a mockery of her determination not to want him. His tongue ran over her, tasting her sweetness, and his fingers held her legs wide; she was all his. All of her.

She cried out as he moved faster, and then slid a finger deep into her core, tormenting her sensitive nerve-endings with his possession and absolute mastery of her body.

She was so close to breaking point, pleasure within arm's reach, and he lifted his head, his eyes staring at her, his expression impossible to decipher. 'Beg me,' he said simply.

Heat coloured Frankie's mind, cheeks and thoughts.

'Beg me,' he said again, dropping his mouth and lashing her with his tongue once more, his touch like heaven.

'I can't,' she cried, but then his name was dropping from her lips again and again and again, rent with desperate need. She called him Matthias, because here, in this kingdom, beneath the skies of Tolmirós, he was Matthias. Not Matt, who she'd fallen in love with—she could see that now, looking back through time, and knowing who she'd been then.

At twenty-one, she'd met Matt and fallen in love. But

she'd been a girl who believed in fantasies then, who thought sex and love went hand in hand. And now she saw that sex on its own could be enough.

'Beg for me and I will make you come,' he promised, lifting up and taking one of her breasts into his mouth, while his finger stayed inside her, tormenting her with memories and promises.

'Why are you doing this?' she asked, digging her nails into his shoulders as thought became impossible, as pleasure crashed over her. *Surrender*, her body begged, her heart implored. *Surrender and accept that this is enough!*

Of course it was—for some people.

But not for Frankie.

Her body was on fire, her pulse racing, her heart thumping, and she knew that satisfaction was within reach. All she had to do was beg him, to say the word *please* that she was swallowing inside her throat, and he would drive her over the edge; he would make her feel almost whole.

Almost.

But it would never be enough for the girl who'd wanted real love all her life.

'I can't,' she said, her breathing so rushed, dragged from so deep within her lungs it hurt. 'Don't make me beg.'

Surprise covered his features when he pulled up to look at her.

'Don't use what I feel to demean me,' she said, lying flat on the lounger, staring up at the evening streaked sky.

'Demean you?' he repeated, the word ragged. 'Frankie, by getting you to accept what you want, I am empowering you. Empowering you to enjoy sex, to enjoy this thing between us that is purely good. I have no interest in demeaning you. I want you to be brave, to face up to what you're feeling. Stop hiding from me.' And his eyes held hers for a long moment as his mouth dropped closer to her sex. She held her breath, propping up on elbows to watch him.

'Let us try it another way,' he said, the words deep and husky. 'Let me beg you. Let me beg you to let me do this,' and he flicked his tongue out, teasing her flesh so she made a keening sound of pleasure. 'Let me beg and you say, simply, "Yes".'

Yes.

The word was heavy in her throat, bouncing over and over, begging to be said, begging her to agree, so she could be put out of her misery.

'Just say yes,' he repeated, and his mouth moved faster and her pleasure built until her eyes were filled with a bright white light and she was no longer conscious of anything but this.

'Say yes,' he demanded, pulling her body closer so he could go deeper, his mouth possessing her in a way that was so intimate, so personal, so perfect. His hand scooped under her bottom, lifting her up, and she heard herself crying out, over and over and over, giving away a part of her soul that she had thought she would be able to keep locked up: 'Yes, Matthias, please. Please!'

He stared at the painting, his lips a grim slash on his face. *Don't use what I feel to demean me.*

Her words, issued in the heat of a sensual moment of passion, had stuck with him, chasing themselves around his head until he could barely think, until he couldn't fathom what he'd been thinking.

Don't use what I feel to demean me.

Had he been doing that?

Since she'd arrived in Tolmirós, he'd been intent on seducing her, on forcing her to stop hiding from the magnitude of their desire.

Matthias, with his experience of women and sex and attraction, knew what he shared with Frankie was rare. So rare that even three years after their first encounter he hadn't been able to put her from his mind. Three years later and he'd never met anyone who held the same appeal for him. This passion was rare and it deserved to be explored.

But at the cost of her self-esteem?

He swore under his breath, pacing to the windows that overlooked the ocean. It had all seemed so simple when first they'd arrived. Sex was a simple transaction. A conversion of lust to satiation.

Whatever his attitudes were to it, Frankie's were not the same.

And yet he'd driven his tongue over her, tasting her release, delighting in her complete surrender even when he now suspected he should have stopped. He'd thought he would feel triumph with her surrender; he'd thought he'd revel in her total acceptance of the tug of their mutual need.

He hadn't.

He'd felt only something very close to blinding panic. He'd tasted her as she'd fallen apart, and his own body had been begging him to bury his length inside her soft, welcoming core, yet he hadn't. He'd pulled away from her even when her desire had burst around them, and her willingness to succumb to pleasure had been palpable.

He'd been as beholden to passion as she, in the end, but it didn't matter. Because she'd been right. He'd been determined to get her to face what they felt for one another.

But why?

Why did he care so damned much that she should surrender to this desire?

Because he wanted her. He wanted her with the strength of a thousand stars, and he knew she felt the same. But her determination and willpower were many times stronger than his. Why? What did she want? Not just from him, but in general?

The damned fairy tale? He couldn't offer that. He didn't have it within his power to give Frankie the dream of love and happily ever after. But he could give her more than sex. He could give her enough, surely, to make her truly happy—not just in bed but as his wife?

And he wanted her to be happy, he admitted to himself now. He needed her to be happy, to smile at him as she had on those few rare occasions since coming to Tolmirós. He wanted to win her trust, to *earn* her trust, and the rest, surely, would follow.

Maybe it wouldn't. But Frankie deserved more than to have a husband who wanted only her body. She deserved as much of the dream as he could offer—surely some of her fantasy would be better than none?

'You look like a little prince,' Frankie enthused, tears sparkling on her lashes as she studied her son. He'd undergone a similar makeover to her own: a haircut, new clothes, and he looked utterly divine.

''E is so handsome. Just like his father,' Liana cooed, her eyes wrinkling at the corners as she bent down and picked Leo up. He didn't arch his back with Liana in the way he'd taken to doing with Frankie, she noticed with a wry grimace. Liana always got hugs and kisses and yeses straight away. But Frankie couldn't be cross about that—not when Liana had helped make Leo's transition to life in Tolmirós so easy.

A whisper of guilt flicked through her because there were only days to go until the wedding and though Frankie had spent her days ensuring Leo was settling well and making sure this private residence of the palace felt like home, she was distracted almost all the time.

When she'd first agreed to this, he'd told her two things. *Through the days, you'll barely know I exist. At night, you won't be able to exist without me.*

The latter was true. Since the afternoon in the pool, when she had surrendered herself to his mouth and given up her determination to resist the passion that flared between them, he'd made no effort to touch her. He'd come to bed late and lay on his side until he'd fallen asleep, and she'd lifted her head up and watched him, and flopped onto her back and wondered what he'd say if she gave into all her body's urges and straddled him, and begged him to forget what she'd said: to make love to her.

As for the days, she more than knew he existed then too.

He was everywhere she looked in this palace. He was in their son's face, Liana's pride, his servants' obedience, the kingdom's prosperity. He was in the enormous canary diamond and white gold ring he'd slid onto her finger two nights earlier, his eyes locked onto hers as he told her it reminded him of the yellow she'd painted the sunlight in the painting she'd been working on the weekend they'd met. And though it was a meaningless, throwaway comment, it had made her chest feel as if it were exploding with delirious joy, with pleasure and disbelief. With perfection.

He was everywhere, even when he'd said he wouldn't be, even when he made no effort to seduce her. Their conversations were polite, cordial, and lacking any indication that he even wanted her. Perhaps he didn't. Perhaps it was as simple as an impulse for him—she'd told him 'no' and he'd accepted that. If only Frankie had found it so easy to put him from her mind!

'Thank you for getting him ready for tonight, Liana, and for agreeing to come.'

'Of course! My place is with him at these functions—as much as you would like me to be,' she added tactfully.

'Royal parties are not much fun for children. They tire so quickly of being polite and well-behaved.' She looked at Leo with a wink and then reached into her pocket, pulling out a small round chocolate. 'And Leo knows there will be a treat at the end of the night, for his very good behaviour.'

Leo nodded sagely, and Frankie laughed. 'Is this his prince face?' she suggested, pride bursting through her.

'He has been practising.'

'Well, Leo, you've absolutely mastered it.'

Liana turned to face Frankie and, for the first time, looked at her properly. 'You are very beautiful, Frankie. Like a princess yourself, no?'

'Oh, no, but thank you,' she demurred, feeling more like someone going to a dressing up party. 'Ball gowns aren't really my caper.'

'Caper?' Liana frowned.

'Thing. They're not really my thing.' She ran her hands down the dress, a turquoise colour, it had a sweetheart neckline and was fitted to her waist, then fell into a flouncy skirt that made a beautiful swishing sound as she walked. It was a true Cinderella dress and the diamond tiara that had been styled into her hair completed the look. 'The dress is very beautiful, though.'

'It does suit you,' Liana complimented.

'Well, that's good, because I get the feeling I'm going to need to go to a few more of these things in my lifetime.' She shrugged her slender shoulders, her tan golden. She'd taken to spending time by the pool as well. Helping Leo swim, and swimming with him, lying in the sun while he napped, remembering how Matthias had felt in the water, how warm and cool had contrasted so sensually against her flesh.

Her cheeks flushed pink as the memories pushed into

her mind and then, as if she'd somehow miraculously dredged him up from fantasy to reality, Matthias strode into the room.

If she looked like a princess, then he was King Charming come to life.

The suit was jet black, his shirt whiter than white, a white tie at his neck completed the look. But he wore across his middle a burgundy sash, military style medals were pinned to his chest, and at his waist there was a gold weapon, a blade, long and sharp. He was far more handsome than any man had a right to be.

'Sword!' Leo pointed delightedly and he jumped up off his little bottom and held his hands out, so Matthias smiled at Liana and then took his son into his arms, tousling hair that had, a moment ago, been perfectly neat.

She didn't notice the way Matthias's eyes lingered on Leo's face with a hint of something other than happiness; she didn't see the way his expression flashed with regret and—oh, so briefly—fear.

'Sword,' Leo said again and Matthias relaxed, smiling as he nodded.

'Yes.'

'For me?'

Liana laughed, and Matthias pulled a face. 'Not yet. But soon.'

Leo pouted. 'I see?'

Matthias put their son down on the ground and then removed the clip from his waist. He held the sword—in its gold ceremonial sheath—so that Leo could run his fingertips over the blunted end.

'Look, Mama. Pictures.'

At this, Matthias glanced up, his eyes locking onto Frankie's, holding hers, and a look of searing heat flashed between them—a look that had the ability to blank anyone else from their presence. Her fingers fidgeted at her sides and then she smiled curtly, tightly, in a way that didn't feel natural and dragged her eyes down to the sword.

But desire stayed lodged in her chest, desperate, hungry, craving indulgence. Out of nowhere, she remembered the way his mouth had felt between her legs and her knees almost buckled with the sensual heat of her recollection.

'I see,' she murmured, moving closer.

'It's very old,' Matthias said, turning his attention back to the weapon. 'It was my great-great-great-great-great-grandfather's, said to have slain the king of a neighbouring country when war threatened at our doorstep.'

'War?' Leo was fascinated by this.

'A long time ago,' Frankie jumped in, sending a warning look to Matthias. He smiled at her and a dimple formed in his cheek that made her fingers itch to paint him. She had in her mind, so many times.

He stood, unfurling his body length and ruffling Leo's dark hair at the same time. 'You look beautiful.' The words were quietly spoken, intended purely for her ears.

'Thank you,' she said, able to take the compliment when she felt her appearance was really the result of couture and hair stylists.

'But not complete yet.'

She looked down at the dress and lifted a hand to the diamond choker she wore. 'What have I forgotten?'

His smile was enigmatic as he reached into his pocket and pulled out a rectangular velvet box.

'Would you do me the honour of wearing this tonight, Frankie?' He popped it open to reveal an award similar to those he wore—a thick piece of purple fabric to which a small gold pendant was attached. In the centre of the pendant there was a star, with an arrow striking through it.

'What is it?' she asked, watching as he pulled it from the

box. His fingers were deft and confident, and her mouth was suddenly dry.

'The Star of Aranathi,' he said. 'An award that was given to my mother—one of my country's highest.'

The meaningfulness of the gesture touched something in Frankie's stomach, and it set in place a chain reaction. Butterflies stirred to life, slowly at first, then faster, until a whole kaleidoscope was beating against her insides. She was oblivious to the watchful eyes of Liana, who'd moved Leo away and distracted him with a juice carton.

'What's it for?' she murmured. He lifted the ribbon to the top of her dress, his fingers almost clinical as they held the fabric taut enough to thread the pin through and latch it into place.

'Humanitarian efforts.'

'I don't…' Frankie frowned, studying Matthias up close. She studied him not as a woman who wanted a man, but as an artist evaluating a subject. She measured his features and imagined creating him from the nothingness of canvas and pigment. She imagined how she might mix her colours together to shade the cleft of his chin dimple and the very faint darkness beneath his eyes. It was his lashes, though, that fascinated her. They were black and curling, soft like silk and so thick, as though they were a curtain for his eyes. What of his face had been gifted by his mother, and what by his father?

When she looked at Leo, she saw so much of Matthias. But was some of the Queen there too? The Queen to whom this medal had once belonged?

'I don't know anything about her,' Frankie finished after a moment. 'But I'd like to.'

His expression shifted with pride first, and then surprise. 'Why?'

Frankie tilted her head consideringly. 'Because she was

your mother. And Leo's grandmother. And it strikes me that I should know something about your family, beyond the fact…' The sentence trailed off into nothingness as she realised what she'd been about to say.

'That they're dead,' he finished for her, his expression unchanged. She threw a scant look in Leo's direction; the boy wasn't listening. Nonetheless, Frankie's brows knitted together when she regarded Matthias. She'd prefer to handle that conversation sensitively, when it came time for Leo to learn of his father's family's deaths.

'What did your mother do to receive this award?'

'Many things.'

'War!' Frankie startled as Leo seemed to jolt out of his reverie and, from the other side of the room, whipped the straw from the juice carton and held it towards Matthias like an ancient challenge to a duel.

Matthias's face relaxed, the tension of a moment ago dissipating, his eyes crinkling at the corners as he returned, *'En garde!'*

Leo giggled and charged his father, but Matthias caught him mid-run, lifting him up easily and tickling him at the belly, so Leo's laughter pealed into the room and, before she knew it, Frankie was smiling. But it was a distracted smile, a smile that was only skin-deep.

'Excuse me, Your Majesty.' There was a knock at the door. 'It is time.'

'Of course.' Leo's smile muted itself when he addressed the servant, and Frankie saw in that moment the duality between private and public. The man and the King. The man who could smile and laugh and tease their son about long ago wars, and the King who presented a sombre and considered face to his servants at all times.

Had he been like that at fifteen? Or had he been allowed to mourn?

They were to be married in the Artheki Cathedrali, her secretary had informed her days earlier. It was five miles away, ancient, and all the Kings of Tolmirós had been married, christened and mourned within its walls for over a thousand years. That information had been inserted into the briefing and, though it was an unimportant detail, it had played on Frankie's mind.

She presumed then that Matthias's parents and brother had been buried there, that their funeral had taken place within the walls of the cathedral at which they were to marry. Had he spoken at the funeral? At fifteen years old, it wouldn't have been unusual, but her heart broke to imagine the young boy he'd been, and the pressure that must have been upon him.

She resisted the temptation to run an Internet search on the subject. Her curiosity was natural, but she would prefer her information to come from the source. Snooping around and reading articles online felt somehow wrong.

'Come, *deliciae.*' Was she imagining the way his voice caught as he addressed her? The way his eyes seemed to lock onto hers with emotion and an intent she couldn't comprehend? 'It is time for you to meet our people.'

CHAPTER NINE

'OH, MATTHIAS!' THEY were alone in a sleek dark limousine, with Liana and Leo following in the car behind. 'It's so beautiful.'

Beyond the black tinted windows of the car and the crowds that had lined the streets hoping for a real-life glimpse of the soon-to-be Queen, Frankie could see the streets of Tolmirós and they were setting her soul on fire.

'It's like something out of a beautiful story book. I had no idea!' Terracotta-roofed houses, built close together and higgledy-piggledy, one leaning this way and the next the other, were all washed in different colours of pastel paints. Little balconies had wrought-iron details and window boxes overflowing with bright purple and red plants. Many had refused to be contained to the small pots and were making joyous bids for sunshine and freedom, dancing their tendrils down the sides of the buildings, forming veins of green that shone in the late afternoon sun.

But the most remarkable thing to Frankie was the sense of history that was at every turn. These buildings were ancient. They whooshed past a church with a cupola and a bell tower, white with a shimmering blue face and enormous bronze hands. A statue of a naked man stood in front, and geraniums seemed to grow with complete abandon across a side wall. When she turned in her seat to get a better look, she saw a nun coming from the front gates, throwing something towards the ground. A moment later at least a hundred pigeons descended on the square. The nun threw her head back and laughed and then the limousine turned the corner.

Caught up in the wonderment of this picture-book streetscape, Frankie didn't realise that Matthias was watching her intently. She didn't see the way his eyes were scanning her face, reading every flicker of delight that crossed it.

'I had no idea it would be like this.'

His lips quirked. 'What did you expect?'

Frankie shrugged. 'I guess I didn't think about it. Until a week ago, Tolmirós was just some place on the edge of the Mediterranean. And since we arrived, we've been in the palace. I expected beautiful beaches and, I guess, a modern city, but this is…just…stunning.'

Pride flashed on his features and his nod was swift. 'The city of Novampoli was built in the nineteen-seventies. We needed a place that wasn't part of the port cities—much of our prosperity comes from being a safe harbour for shipping companies, but my father kick-started a technology revolution. Banking and finance are also primary industries for Tolmirós. We needed a city that would answer those requirements. The first few buildings were modest but within a decade or two high-rises began to shape the skyline. It is now a place of glass and steel, and the food there is second to none. I will take you there, when next I have occasion to go. You will like it.'

'Is it like Manhattan?' She settled back into her seat, smoothing the skirts of her dress simply for something to do with her hands.

'In some ways, but without the mix of old and new. It is more like Dubai, I think. A somewhat artificial-seeming city, in a place you wouldn't expect it. The whole island is a city, and an enormous bridge spans from the west shore to its neighbouring island, Emanakki.'

'I'd like to see it some day,' she said with a smile. 'I want to see everything.'

He laughed softly. 'And so you shall, Frankie. In fact, soon it will be your duty to see and know everything about our country.'

She angled him a look thoughtfully. 'Who were you going to marry?'

He arched a brow at her change in conversation. 'That seems irrelevant now.'

'I'm curious. Indulge me.'

'I think I told you that I hadn't yet decided…'

Feminine disapproval had her lips curling. 'Of course. You had a queen *smorgasbord* from which to select your bride. I'm just asking who it was likely to be.'

He smothered a smile at her comment and nodded. 'Lady Tianna Montavaigne was the front-runner.'

'Why?'

'She met the criteria.' He shrugged, as though it barely mattered.

But Frankie was persistent. 'In what ways?'

He compressed his lips and studied her for a long moment, his eyes tunnelling straight into her soul. 'She's royal, for one, though a distant cousin to the ruling monarch of Sweden. She's been raised to understand this lifestyle, the pressures of it, the need to be discreet, polite, dignified and private. She understands the realities of living life under a microscope.' He said the final sentence with a hint of disdain, but it was gone again almost as quickly. 'She is intelligent, beautiful, and we get on well.'

There was a pang of something in the region of Frankie's heart. 'Will she be disappointed not to marry you? Did she love you?'

He laughed and shook his head ruefully. 'It is always about love with you, no?'

Frankie's cheeks warmed as his eyes held hers thoughtfully. 'No, she doesn't *love* me.'

Frankie sighed softly. 'You act as though the very idea of marriage between two people who are in love is absurd.'

'Not absurd,' he contradicted. 'Just…romantic. Tianna knew what marriage to me would involve.'

'I just can't understand why anyone would agree to that,' she said with a shake of her head. 'A marriage without love seems so…cold. So…devastating.' She shivered.

'*You* have agreed to it,' he pointed out, watching her through half-shuttered eyes.

Her eyes flashed with pain and then she tilted her chin as though physically underscoring her determination. 'I… I know. But our circumstances are fairly unique. Were there no Leo, wild horses couldn't have dragged me into this.'

He nodded, as though her words were somehow reassuring. 'Tianna is in a relationship with her father's chauffeur. He's from Syria and came to the country as a refugee when he was a child. He's naturalised now, and she cares for him very deeply.'

Frankie blinked, her lack of comprehension apparent. 'So why in the world would she marry you?'

'Because he needs his job, because her parents would never condone the match, because she'd be disinherited and doesn't particularly fancy the idea of getting a job. There are any number of reasons to keep their relationship quiet. Marriage to me would have provided excellent cover for her to continue her relationship.'

'Oh, Matt, how can you speak so calmly about this?'

He sighed and squeezed her hand. 'I can't see there's anything wrong with making informed, intelligent choices when it comes to your future.'

The car began to slow, and the crowds outside their windows thickened. Frankie had been given a crash course in royal deportment. For hours each morning and again in the evening, she'd been drilled in the protocol that would be expected of her as the future Queen. It all jumbled in her brain now, but she tried to grab hold of it.

'Relax,' he murmured, leaning closer to look out at the view with her. 'The window will go down soon so you can wave to my people. They're excited to see you.'

Beyond the window, now that they were driving more slowly, Frankie could see signs with their official engagement portrait, taken on the balcony of the palace, her head pressed against Matthias's chest. There were handmade signs too, with her name all over them, and people wearing veils and throwing confetti.

Was Leo enjoying the spectacle? Or was he frightened by the noise? She angled herself in the seat in an attempt to look backwards but the limo was a little far away. 'Why aren't Leo and Liana in this car? There's plenty of room.'

He didn't look at her. 'In case something goes wrong.'

'Like what? He's never motion sick. He travels well...' Her voice tapered off as an alternative meaning unravelled in her brain. 'You mean in case our car crashes?'

He shrugged. 'Or theirs does. Or there's a terrorist attack.'

'So you won't ever travel with our son?'

He eyed her now, his expression implacable. 'No.'

'But you flew over here with him.'

He nodded. 'It was necessary on that one occasion. But I will not do so again. I have had this law written into our constitution.'

A shiver ran down her spine, and her chest heaved with emotion for the young man who'd felt it necessary to write in such a protection.

Surely this was a reaction to the loss of his parents and brother. She couldn't help it; she reached over and squeezed his hand, rubbing the pad of her thumb reassuringly over his skin. But he looked at her with a quizzical expression, and Frankie realised her eyes were moist. Emotions were running rampant within her.

'Surely that's a little extreme?'

His features were like ice. 'No.'

'But he's just a baby,' she murmured. 'He'd much rather travel with his mother or father.'

'He is my heir,' Matthias said through clenched teeth. 'Keeping him alive is my priority.'

She ignored the unpleasant suspicion he was speaking as a king who needed a living heir rather than a father who valued the survival of his child. Of course it was both. 'Then I'll travel with him in the future,' she said simply.

'Your place is with me,' he rebuffed gently, his eyes sweeping closed for a moment. 'And Liana is there for Leo.'

'You created this law,' she prompted softly, gently. 'So there wasn't one before this?'

His eyes fired. 'No. If there had been…' The words trailed off into nothing and now she was moving closer to him, needing him to hear her.

'If there had been,' she insisted, 'that boulder would have still been there. The car with your parents in would have crashed.'

'But Spiro would have lived.' His eyes glittered with hurt and pain and her heart twisted achingly.

'You don't know that,' she whispered softly. 'You don't know that your car wouldn't have crashed as well. You don't know that something else awful might not have happened later. There are no guarantees in life,' she said simply.

'You think I don't know that?' He turned to face her, his expression tortured, his features drawn. 'You think I don't understand how completely beholden we are to fate and sheer damned luck?'

His hurt was like a rock, pressing against her chest. 'So stop trying to control everything,' she murmured, lifting a hand to his cheek. 'I don't want our son growing up afraid of his own shadow. I don't want him being governed by protocols and edicts that overturn natural instinct. He's our son. He belongs with us.'

She pressed her head forward, so their foreheads connected, and she breathed in deeply, this connection somehow every bit as intimate as what they'd shared by the pool.

'It's my responsibility to protect you both, and I will do so with my dying breath.' The words shook with the force of his determination, and Frankie was momentarily speechless.

Then, with a surge of understanding, she cupped his cheek, holding him still. 'Is that what this is about? You think you couldn't save Spiro and now you're trying to guarantee that nothing bad will ever happen to us?' Her insight was blinding in its strength and accuracy. She knew she was right when he recoiled for a moment. But she moved with him, staying close, holding him to her. 'You were just a boy, Matthias. You couldn't do any more than you did.'

'How do you know?' he asked, uncharacteristically weary. 'You weren't there. You don't know anything about the accident…'

'I know that if you could have saved your brother or your parents, you would have. I know that if there's anyone on earth with the strength to almost make the impossible possible, it's you, Matt. You have to forgive yourself. Free yourself from this guilt.'

'Easier said than done.' He expelled a sigh and shook his head. 'I will not change my mind about Leo's safety. You'll have to respect that I know what I'm talking about.' He was himself again. Matthias Vassiliás—a king amongst men, intractable, unchangeable, determined. The emotionally charged air was gone and he sat back in his seat as if to say, *conversation closed.*

Frankie was about to argue with him, she wanted, desperately, to alleviate this guilt of his, but the windows began to move down slowly and she had only seconds to sit back in her seat and compose her features into an expression of assumed happiness, lift her hand and begin to wave slowly at the assembled crowds. The noise was deafening! People began to scream when the window went down, loud and shrill, but oh, so excited. The crowd applauded and children threw flowers at the car.

The conversation with Matthias pushed deeper into her mind, for later analysis, in the face of such a rapturous welcome. Matthias, beside her, seemed unaffected. He didn't smile nor wave, but simply watched Frankie and allowed her to have all the adoration of the people who'd come to see the woman who would be Queen.

She was so captivated by the crowds that she didn't notice the castle until they were almost on top of it but, as the car slowed to a stop, she glanced up and an involuntary rush of breath escaped her. 'Oh, Matt, look!'

His smile was just a flicker. 'I know.'

It was an ancient-looking castle, with enormous turrets that were topped with pointed roofs. As a child she'd read a book about Sir Gawain and she'd always imagined the castle to be something like this.

'It was the palace of a prominent family in the twelfth century. As civil wars gradually broke down the ranks of nobility, the palace reverted to the Crown. It serves as our parliament, and the west wing is used as a gallery for children to come and learn about the country's politics.

'I've never seen anything like it.' Windows had been

set in ancient brick, the glass rippled and uneven, showing its age.

'You should see it from the other side,' he teased but, before she could ask him what he meant, the doors were opened by a guard in a full liveried uniform and white gloves. The crowd reached a deafening pitch. Frankie moved towards the door but Matthias stilled her, holding her back in the limousine, safe from prying eyes for one more moment.

'Do you feel okay?'

She frowned. 'I feel…fine. Why?'

'This could be overwhelming. Do you need anything?'

His thoughtfulness, so unexpected, made her stomach swoop as though she'd fallen from an aeroplane. 'I'm honestly fine,' she promised. 'Really, I am.'

He nodded, a glint of admiration in his eyes as he released her hand. Remembering all that she'd been taught, she stepped from the car, concentrating on keeping her long skirt down for modesty, her head up, her eyes on the crowd, no dramatic facial movements that a camera would snap and a paper would publish for the fact it was unflattering. She also concentrated doubly hard on not falling flat on her face, which was harder than it sounded whilst wearing stiletto heels and what felt like miles of tulle and silk.

She'd been told they weren't to hold hands, nor to show any sign of affection. It was a protocol thing and, given their strange and somewhat dysfunctional relationship, she hadn't blinked at the instruction. So when he stepped from the car and put an arm around her waist, holding her to his side, she glanced up at him.

He smiled brightly, his even white teeth set in curving lips, a chiselled square jawline and every feature a standout, his dark eyes casting a spell over her, and she smiled back at him. Then he bent down and pressed a small kiss to the tip of her nose. The crowd went wild.

He lifted his head up but kept an arm wrapped around her waist in a way that she would have called protective, except the flames of desire that licked at her side were so much more dangerous than any other threat or fear she might feel.

He guided her to the crowds and she received gifts from the children who were lined up at the front. Dozens and dozens of cards, flowers, bears, and each one she admired and appreciated, before handing it to a protocol officer, hovering in the background. At the steps of the palace, Leo and Liana met them, having pulled up and made their way straight to the entrance.

Liana straightened Leo's shirt and then passed him to Matthias. With their son held in one handsome arm and the other around the waist of the woman he would marry, they stood there, smiling at the assembled crowd.

The smile on Frankie's face was dazzling, but it was a forgery.

Sadness for this man swarmed her chest, making her heart split and her mind heavy. She didn't want him to have suffered as he had. She saw now the depth of his grief—it was as much a part of him as his bones and blood. It had redefined his outlook on life. And love?

Matthias tilted his head towards her and it felt as though an elastic band was snapping inside her chest, her heart exploding out of its bracket.

He might not love her—he might not even be capable of love.

But if her sense of compassion for him taught Frankie anything it was that somewhere, somehow, without her permission, she'd done something really stupid.

She'd fallen in love with her future husband.

* * *

If the outside of the palace was mesmerising, then inside was just as much so. Enormous marble tiles lay in the entranceway, white and imposing, and a marble staircase rose from the centre. A harpist was playing as they strode inside, and more noise sounded, this time from within the palace. 'The party is on the rooftop terrace,' he said.

'Okay.' She nodded, but her mind was still exploding from the realisation she'd just had. She *couldn't* love him. No way. She was, surely, just getting lust and love mixed up, as she had back in New York. She barely knew him.

Yet somewhere along the way she'd fallen in love with a man who'd proudly proclaimed his disdain for the whole notion of love. He saw it as a useless impediment to life in general.

What a fool she was!

'You are okay?' he queried again, carrying Leo on his hip as though he'd been doing it all Leo's life.

'Uh huh.' She nodded unevenly, not daring to look at him again.

'Please, Frankie, do not be worried about Leo's safety. I will protect him, and you.'

She jolted her gaze to his, nodding. If only he knew what the real cause for her silence was!

They walked up the sweeping staircase in silence. She realised as they neared the top that Matthias had been right about something—she now barely noticed the servants that were standing on every second step, all dressed in formal military uniforms.

At the top landing, four guards stood, two on either side of enormous wide wooden doors, each carved with striking scenes that she'd have loved to have stood and studied. The doors themselves looked ancient.

As the family approached, the guards bowed low then saluted, all in perfect time with one another.

'Police!' Leo squealed, and one of the four guards lost control of his stern expression for the briefest of seconds, relaxing his lips into a spontaneous smile before focusing himself.

The tallest of the men took a large gold sceptre and banged it slowly three times against the wooden doors; they then swept inwards as if by magic.

The terrace, though filled with hundreds of people, was absolutely silent, and space had been left in the middle of the assembly—a corridor of sorts.

With his arm around her waist once more, Matthias guided Frankie forward. The group of people was silent. Frankie and Matthias were silent.

Leo was not.

'People!' he exclaimed gleefully, clapping his hand together. 'Lots and lots of people, Mama!' And everyone laughed, so Leo laughed, and then lifted his chubby little hands to cover his eyes for a moment before pulling them away and saying, 'Boo!'

More laughter, from Frankie too, who looked up helplessly at Matthias.

'And I worried he might feel nervous,' Matthias murmured from the side of his mouth.

'Apparently we have a showman on our hands,' she agreed, as Leo played peek-a-boo once more with the delighted crowd.

Conversation began to return to normal and, without the eyes of the world on them, Frankie looked around the terrace more thoroughly. It was then that she noticed something at first familiar and at second glance jarring.

'My paintings are here.' She was dumbfounded. For, hanging on the far wall of the palace, were some of her paintings. The sun was setting and it bathed them in the most beautiful natural light. She stared at the artworks with a growing sense of confusion. 'How in the world…?'

His look gave nothing away. 'You can no longer sell your paintings, Frankie. It wouldn't be appropriate. But that doesn't mean the world should be deprived of your talent.'

'I…but you…these were supposed to be showing in New York.'

He nodded. 'I bought the whole lot.'

'You bought…'

'It wouldn't have been appropriate for the show to go ahead, with news of our engagement.'

'But why buy them? If you'd said that, I would have called Charles and explained…'

'And deprived him of his commission?' He shook his head. 'He picked you to show your work; he is obviously very good at what he does. Why shouldn't he earn a reward for that?'

His perceptiveness and flattery pinballed inside her. 'I had no idea…'

'This was my intention.'

Hope flew in her chest, because the gesture was so sweet, so kind, so utterly out of left field. 'Thank you,' she said after several long seconds, as Liana approached. 'I'm truly touched.'

And, as if sensing that she might be at risk of reading too much into it, he straightened. 'It was simply the right thing to do, Frankie. Your art deserves to be seen, you cannot sell it any longer, or it would be seen that you are profiteering from your position as Queen. And this is now your country—of course the works should hang here, in Tolmirós.'

It was all so businesslike and sensible, but that didn't completely take the shine off the gesture. Because she found it almost impossible to believe that only pragmatism and common sense had motivated it. Surely, there was a thread of something else, something more?

He praised her artwork, but her artwork was *her*. Every painting was a construct of her soul, a creation of her being. To like it, to appreciate it, was to appreciate her.

'Come, *deliciae*, everybody here is eager to meet you. I hope you're not tired.'

He led her towards the Prime Minister first and for the next three hours Frankie met and spoke to more people than she could ever remember.

Matthias stayed by her side the whole time, intensely watchful, an arm around her waist at all times, shooting arrows of desire deep within her, his body warm, his eyes never leaving her.

When it came time for them to exit she was exhausted, but the fluttering of hope inside her heart refused to die down.

In a week she would marry the man she'd fallen in love with, and she refused to believe there was no hope that he would, one day, love her right back. He'd put his heart on ice, and who could blame him? He'd suffered an intense loss, a total tragedy, so he'd put his heart on ice…and Frankie was determined that she would thaw it.

CHAPTER TEN

'YOU DID WELL TONIGHT.' He watched as she strolled into their bedroom wearing a silk negligee that fell to the floor. All night he'd watched her, and he'd ignored every damned royal protocol, keeping an arm clamped vice-like around her waist because he couldn't *not* touch her. The urge had surprised the hell out of him.

At first, he'd wanted to reassure her, to protect her, just as he'd said in the car. Though she'd promised him she was fine with the event, the crowds and the attention, he'd felt she was nervous. He'd felt her energy and he'd wanted to soothe her worries. Then, when they'd stepped onto the terrace and she'd begun to charm her way around his parliament, speaking in halting Tolmirón that she'd been learning since arriving in the country, he'd felt something else. Something dark and sinister and distinctly unwelcome.

Jealousy.

He hadn't wished to share Frankie.

Every single person had wanted some of her time and attention and Frankie was so generous and giving that she would have obliged for another three hours, if he hadn't called an end to the evening with his speech. Even as he'd given the closing words he'd watched her—watched the way she stood, the way the evening wind rustled past her hair, catching it and pulling it out towards the sea, as though the wind and the ocean knew that she really did belong here in Tolmirós.

His eyes narrowed at the intensity of his thoughts, the depth of his feelings, and he suppressed them with determination.

'I had fun,' she said simply. 'It turns out I'm quite the attention-seeker.'

He lifted a brow but whatever response he'd been about to make fell out of his brain as she lifted her arms and began to style her hair. Long and waved, she lifted it onto her head into a messy bun, and the movement thrust her breasts forward, her nipples erect beneath the pale silk of the nightgown.

Oblivious to his heated inspection, she continued, 'You might have created a monster.'

He recognised that he had—but it was not the monster of which Frankie spoke. Matthias was in very real danger of becoming obsessed with Frankie.

Again.

But so much worse this time. He wanted her. All day and all night, his body craved her with a single-mindedness that he hadn't felt since he was a teenager and first learning the ways of his body's sensual needs. But tonight had shown him it was more than that. He didn't want anyone else to claim her attention. He didn't want her to talk and laugh and commiserate with *anyone*.

She'd spoken of her childhood and he'd listened, resenting the fact that she was sharing details he didn't know with a stranger.

There was danger in all those feelings and he rejected them, knowing they were not a part of his life, knowing he didn't welcome them.

'I'm kidding,' she said, and now she was looking at him, a quizzical expression on her brow. 'I just meant it wasn't as scary as I thought it would be.'

He nodded, eyes watchful. 'You're a natural.'

'Do you really think so?'

Her doubts opened vulnerability inside his chest like a chasm—a desire to shield her from ever feeling uncertain. He ignored the need to reassure her, to pepper her with praise and compliments and fill her with confidence in herself. For promises were inherent in that and he didn't want to make promises to Frankie when he had no idea of how to keep them.

'Yes.' He spoke the word like a whip cracking into the room. 'And you will have a busy week of such engagements.'

'Oh?'

'In the days before the wedding, diplomats and dignitaries will arrive to pay their respects to the woman who will be Queen. You will have many appointments.'

'I see.' She nodded thoughtfully. 'I remember.'

'You are not worried about it?'

'Well, I wish I had a better grasp on Tolmirón,' she said pragmatically, 'but, other than that, no. I'm not shy, Matthias. I have no issue talking to strangers.'

She dropped her hands to her sides and smiled brightly—Matthias's gut rolled. 'I saw that tonight.'

Her smile dropped. Damn it, the words had sounded critical, his jealousy not something he was able to disguise.

'But that's a good thing?'

His eyes narrowed. She poured herself a glass of water from the crystal decanter across the room and sipped it.

'Yes,' he said gruffly, finally, unable to take his eyes off her.

She padded across the room, so graceful and lithe. It was a warm night and the windows were open, so the hint of the ocean's fragrance was carried to them on the breeze. She climbed into bed, sitting up rather than lying down.

His fingers itched to reach out and touch her—the smooth, tanned skin of her arms drew his gaze.

'People are in awe of you,' she observed, tilting her head to look at him.

He shrugged lightly. 'I'm their King.'

'Yes, I know.' She seemed to be mulling that over. 'And tonight you seemed like it.'

'As opposed to?'

'Being King is so much a part of you. I guess I still find it hard to understand why you didn't tell me who you are. What you are. Three years ago. In New York,' she added, as if he didn't know exactly what she meant.

'It was a novelty to meet someone who didn't know,' he said truthfully. 'And I discovered I liked being treated like any other man.'

'Not like any other man,' she said, so softly the words were almost carried away towards the open window, then her ocean-green eyes latched onto his. Something pulled inside him. 'You weren't like any man I'd ever, ever met.'

He dismissed the words, refusing to let them matter to him.

'I mean it,' she said softly, her words reaching deep into his chest. 'You were so overwhelming.'

Her eyes held his, studying him in that way she had, as though she were pulling him apart piece by piece, and weighing every fragment of him in her hands. 'That's lust,' he dismissed. 'Desire.' And to prove his point he caught her hand and brought it to his lips, pressing a light kiss to her racing pulse point there. His eyes held hers as he moved his mouth to her palm and laid a kiss there, then to her thumb, which he nipped with his teeth. Her eyes fluttered shut and he felt her pulse kick up another notch beneath his fingertips.

'It was more than that,' she said throatily.

Frustration sliced through him. 'Desire is a powerful drug. Especially for someone who has no experience.'

'I'd met men I liked before,' she contradicted, dropping her gaze to the bed. He didn't want her to hide herself from him. It frustrated him. 'It wasn't like I hadn't ever been tempted by a guy. Or fantasised about what it might be like…'

Jealousy again. It was as unwelcome now as it had been earlier.

'But with you it was so different. It was as though everything I am was bound up in being with you. I felt like I needed you in the same way I need breath and water.'

'That is what it should be like,' he murmured, for it had been exactly like this for him, with Frankie.

'Like what should be like?'

'When you go to bed with someone, it should be because you want them with an intensity that almost fells you at the knees.' He regarded her with all the need he felt in that moment—and it was more than strong enough to cut his body in two.

Her cheeks flushed pink. 'So you…feel that…have felt that before? Before me?' She cleared her throat. 'With other women?'

So much was riding on that question—her hopes were so raw they hurt him. And so he lied, because it was the kindest thing for her. He lied because if he told her that he'd never felt desire like he'd known that night, like he'd known with Frankie, she would see something more in that—she would see a promise he would never give. 'Yes.' His eyes dropped to her lips and he thought about kissing her, he thought about showing her that nothing mattered more than their desire for one another. But she'd made her feelings clear and he had to respect them, even when it was practically killing him. 'That's what good sex is about.'

* * *

It was a dream he'd had hundreds of times. He was back in the car, the smell of burning hair and flesh, of smoke and smouldering metal all around him. Adrenalin raced through his veins as the limousine filled with flames. He was trapped. He knew this feeling well. He pushed at his belt; it didn't move.

His eyes were scratchy—the smoke, he knew now. His parents were dead, in the front of the car. His chest heaved as he looked towards them, saw his mother's beautiful face frozen still, horror on her features, almost as though she'd fallen asleep in the midst of a nightmare.

He turned to Spiro, bracing himself, wishing he could wake up, wishing he could reach back through time, into this dream, into the reality that had spawned it, and *do something.* But there was nothing—he was forced to relive this event again and again, the moment in which he had become truly alone.

Only Spiro wasn't there! Beside him, their faces bloodied, were Frankie and Leo.

He tasted vomit in his mouth and he stretched the belt, but it wouldn't move. His broken arm was an encumbrance he had no time for. With a curse, he called her name, but she didn't move. Leo was still, like a mannequin, so tiny, so frail.

He reached out and his fingertips curled around her fine blonde hair, clumped with blood, and blood filled his nostrils and eyes, vomit rushed through him. 'Frankie!' He called her name, urgently now, desperately, pushing at the seat belt again.

Nothing.

He was weak—powerless to help her.

Desperation tore him apart. 'Frankie!'

She lifted her head and looked at him, only her eyes

were not green now, they were dark like Spiro's had been, like Leo's were. 'You can't save us,' she murmured, rejection in her features. 'Just let us go. Let me go.'

He woke then, his forehead beaded in perspiration, his skin white. He turned towards Frankie on autopilot and almost cried out at the sight of her, fast asleep. But the dream was too real, the memory of it fractured and splintering into this time and life. 'Frankie.' He reached over and shook her arm.

She made a small noise then blinked her eyes open, looking at him.

'Matt?' In that tired, half-fogged state, she called him by the name he'd given her in New York. 'Is it Leo? What's wrong?'

Slowly, his breathing returned to normal. He looked at her for several seconds, reassuring himself that she was fine, and then he shook his head. 'Go back to sleep, Frankie. Everything's fine.'

Frankie stared at the little white bandage on her son's arm with a growing sense of rage and impotence. 'Liana—' she spoke slowly, in contrast to the way her temper was firing out of control '—what's this?'

Liana's eyes didn't quite meet Frankie's. 'From the doctor.'

'I see.' Frankie nodded, her chest heaving. She was getting married in the morning, and the last week had been both exhausting and distracting. She'd had less time for Leo than she would have liked, but she'd promised herself it would all go back to normal after the wedding. A new kind of normal, but normal nonetheless.

'Ouchie,' Leo said, looking up at his mother with big grey eyes and pointing to his arm. '*Big* ouchie.'

Frankie's heart cracked. 'Yes, I'll bet.' She bent down

and kissed her son on his cheek. He returned to his drawing. Frankie straightened and looked at Liana. 'Excuse me.'

She spun away from the older woman, striding out of the room and moving until she reached a guard. 'Where is Matthias? Where is the King?'

The guard looked somewhat surprised; she suspected her temper was showing.

'Ah, he is…occupied,' the guard apologised.

She pulled herself up to her full, not very imposing height and stared down her nose at him. 'Where. Is. My. Fiancé?'

The guard flinched and spoke into the little device at his wrist. Crackly words came back and then he nodded. 'He is in the west garden. I'll show you.'

Frankie didn't smile. She was seething. How dared Matthias take Leo's blood without so much as telling her? How dared he take her son's blood *at all*? Damn him and his DNA test!

Her anger seethed the entire way, through the palace and out of enormous glass doors, into a garden that was overgrown with oak trees and flowers. It was very beautiful. At the bottom there was a tennis court and Matthias stood down one end, hitting balls that were being served to him by a machine. As she approached, her eyes swept the surroundings—she had become adept at seeking out security guards now.

'Have us left in privacy,' she said curtly, not much caring who heard her dress down the King, but knowing on some level that the words she wanted to spit at him would be more satisfying if she could give full vent to her rage and that spectators would hold her back. Slightly.

'Ah, yes, madam.' The guard bowed and spoke into his wrist once more. Two guards stepped out of the periphery of the tennis court, moving towards their location.

Here, in the inner sanctum of the palace, security was lessened. No one could reach these parts without high-level clearance.

Frankie waited until the guards had moved back to the palace and then she closed her eyes and saw her son's little arm, imagined a needle going into his flesh, sucking blood into vials for the purpose of confirming something that any idiot with eyes in their head could easily see. And rage flooded her once more. She stormed across the lawn and slammed open the wire gate to the tennis court.

A tennis ball flew from the machine and Matthias whacked it hard, landing it with speed in the opposing side's corner.

'I need a word with you,' she snapped, crossing to the machine and staring at it. 'How do I turn this damned thing off?' She looked towards him expectantly. His eyes were watchful, his expression bland. He reached into his pocket, pulled out a small device and pressed a button. The machine went quiet.

'Yes?' he asked, still so damned calm; she wanted to shake that nonchalance from his shoulders.

'You had my son's blood taken without even telling me?'

He walked across the tennis court, his stride lithe, wearing only a pair of white shorts and a white shirt that clung to his broadly muscled chest. He was perspiring, the heat of the day intense, the tennis court in the full baking sun.

'I did tell you,' he said as he placed the racket down against the net and then came to stand in front of Frankie. His eyes skimmed her face, then dropped lower, before lifting to her eyes once more.

'When? When did you tell me you were going to get some doctor to do something so—so—invasive?'

His frown was infinitesimal. 'It is not invasive. Just a prick of a needle. The skin was numbed first and Liana was with him the whole time. She said he felt not a thing…'

'My God!' She stared at him as though he were some kind of alien. 'You didn't even go with him?'

His laugh was a short bark. 'My schedule is rather busy, *deliciae.*'

'That's your *son*!' she shouted, and rage pummelled her insides so she lifted her palms and pushed at his chest. His body was like steel, not moving, not so much as an inch. She made a guttural sound and pushed harder. Her rage grew.

'I am aware of that.' He spoke slowly. Calmly. 'I explained why the blood test was necessary.'

'But you didn't tell me *when* and I had no idea! I'm his mom! That boy has never had a single procedure in his life that I haven't been there for.' Hurt spun like a web in her chest. 'Every headache, every nose bleed, earache and injection, I have held his hand for. How dare you keep this from me?'

'Calm down, Frankie,' he said quietly. 'This is not a big deal.'

'Not a big deal?' She glared at him and hands that had been pushing him formed fists and she pummeled his chest. He watched her, his expression impossible to interpret, and then, he caught her wrists and held them still. But her anger couldn't be stemmed. She stomped her feet and her fingers formed claws and she tried to break out of his grip but he held her completely still. She charged her body at his and he caught her then, wrapping his arms around her, holding her body tight to his.

'Let me go!' she screamed. 'I can't believe you did this. I can't believe you took his blood! I can't believe you think you had any right…'

'He is my son,' he said into her ear. 'And you understood why the paternity test was necessary…'

'He's not your son!' The words had the effect of surprising Matthias sufficiently that he loosened his grip on her. She jerked out of his grip and pushed at his chest once more for good measure. Her breathing was rushed, coming in fits and spurts. 'How can he be, when you can speak of him with such callous disregard? You organised for a doctor to do something to a little boy that would have been terrifying and you didn't even go along yourself? Or tell his mother? What a heartless, unfeeling lump you are!'

A muscle jerked in his jaw. He stared at her without moving.

'You don't feel a damned thing, do you?' she demanded again, glaring at him, and emotions, feelings, needs pushed through her, surging inside her. Whatever sentimentality he lacked, she more than made up for. 'God, what an idiot I am to think you could ever change.' She stared at him with a falling heart.

He grunted something, words she didn't catch, and then he moved to her, pulling her around her waist towards his body and holding her there. He stared down at her and, before she could guess his intention, he'd dropped his mouth to hers, kissing her, punishing her, tasting her, tormenting her.

She groaned, but it was an angry groan, and then she was kissing him back, harder, punishing him right back, wanting to hurt him with the intensity of her kiss. Her hands ripped at his shirt, pushing at him impatiently. Anger seemed to have been the straw breaking the camel's back and all the feelings she had worked so hard to hold off flooded through her.

She was furious! She was so furious! But desire was

lurching inside her and she didn't want to ignore it. She wanted to use it to silence her rage!

'I hate you,' she said and in that moment she did. He stilled momentarily, then leaned down and lifted her, wrapping her legs around his waist. The power of his arousal did something to her body, weakening her, tempting her. 'I hate you,' she said again, but her mouth dropped to his shoulder, kissing his naked flesh even as her throat was raw with the ferocity of her anger.

'Good,' he said darkly, and she was so angry she didn't hear the resigned acceptance in his voice. 'So you should.'

She tasted his emotions; she felt them in every desperate lashing of his tongue, in the intensity of his grip around her waist, in the strength of his arousal. He felt—he just didn't know what to do with those feelings.

And she didn't care.

Thought had been put aside. Sense and reason were nowhere in evidence. All Frankie could do was feel and want.

She pushed at his chest and, with frustration, wriggled out of his arms; he guided her back to the ground, his eyes seeking hers for a moment. She ignored his look. She ignored everything. Her fingertips found his shorts and pushed at them; he stepped out of his shorts and shoes and then he pushed at her underpants, jerking them down her legs with impatience and desperation. She kicked them off but before her hands could find the zip of her skirt he'd lifted her once more, his eyes hunting hers with a question.

Her doubts had evaporated. She had only room for anger and need. She swore under her breath and nodded, biting down on her lower lip. 'Yes,' she groaned, as he moved her over his arousal and pushed inside her.

Her groan grew louder as pleasures so long denied moved through her body, and she remembered this. The intensity of his possession—the perfection of melding their two bodies into one.

He thrust into her, one hand on the back of her head, fingers pushing through her hair, dislodging it from the elegant style it had been put into that morning, the other hand clamped around her bottom, holding her where she was.

But it wasn't enough; she wanted so much more. With a grating cry she pushed at his chest and he stared at her for a moment, lost and confused. 'Lie down,' she commanded, and he did, pulling out of her for one devastating moment before they were one again, on the ground of the tennis court, the grass scratchy beneath her knees as she took him deep inside and rolled her hips, the power of this something she couldn't—wouldn't—ever forget. Beneath her, she saw his face grow pale and his breathing rushed, she saw desperate need fire in his veins and triumph was her companion.

Except there was no triumph in this—because she had lost. He had won. Sex was sex—there was no love in this.

She ignored the thought; the emotions it brought clawed at her throat and they were useless and unwelcome. She stared down at him, stilling slightly. 'Tell me this is meaningless,' she challenged, the gamble one she hadn't even known she was going to make. 'Tell me this means nothing.'

His eyes flared when they latched onto hers.

'Tell me while you're inside of me that this means nothing. That I mean nothing.' She felt tears slide down her cheeks, hot and fat. He caught her wrists and rolled her, flipping her onto her back and holding her still.

He moved inside her, gently at first, and then he kissed her slowly, trapping her beneath his body. Grief was equal to her desire. When would it not be?

He was skilled. Experienced. Despite the raging emotions in her chest, pleasure was inevitable. He rolled his hips and a wave began to build inside her, driving her to the edges of sanity, tipping her over it. She gripped his shoulders and he moved deeper. She cried his name out, over and over, as she fell apart.

But there was no recovery. No time to process what had happened. He kissed her lower, on her throat, and then his hands moved to the waistband of her shirt, pushing under it and finding the lace cups of her bra.

She was incandescent with pleasure. As he drove her to the edge, she kissed him harder and he kissed her right back. They tumbled off the edge of the world as they knew it, together. He exploded with the force of a thousand suns, their climax mutual and devastating.

And entirely inevitable, just as he'd always said.

CHAPTER ELEVEN

INSANITY HAD BROUGHT them together but it was dissipating quickly, leaving only confusion and regret in its wake. His body was heavy on hers and in another world, at another time, she would have lain beneath him all day, stroking his back, feeling him, wanting him anew.

But rage had been the catalyst for this and, with sensual heat evaporating, her rage surged afresh.

'I can't believe you did that.'

He pushed up on his elbows and looked at her with eyes that showed emotion—just not emotion she could make any sense of. 'You were…that was mutual.'

Her stomach plunged. 'I don't mean sex. I mean the blood test.'

Relief flashed on his features briefly and he lifted himself off her, extending a hand in an offer of assistance she ignored. She stood on her own and stared down at her outfit—it was in disarray. Shooting him a fulminating glare, she straightened her skirt and tucked her shirt back in place. Her underpants were across the tennis court; she wouldn't degrade herself by going in search of them.

He expelled a sigh. 'My parliament requires it. We've discussed that. It is done now, in any event. There is no sense arguing over an event neither of us can change.'

It was as simple as that to Matthias. Simple, pragmatic, black and white. Just like their marriage. Just like everything. 'You're unbelievable,' she muttered, looking towards the fairy tale palace with eyes that had started to see things as they really were. 'I thought this marriage made some kind of sense,' she whispered, letting her eyes close, and her heart close with them. 'I thought I could live with it. And maybe *I* can.' She could already see how addictive sleeping with Matthias would be. But it wasn't enough. Every time would destroy her a little more. 'But Leo shouldn't have to. Leo… Leo deserves so much better than this.'

There was silence. A heavy silence that throbbed with anger and disbelief. When she looked at him again he'd pulled his shorts on, but his chest was bare so she saw the way it heaved in an attempt to calm his breathing. Finally, he spoke. 'We are getting married *tomorrow*.'

'But we'll never be a family, will we?' The words were raw, thick with emotion.

The sun sliced across him, warm and bright. 'You will be my wife, and Leo is my son…'

'Sure he is,' she snapped. 'Once you have the DNA test results.'

Matthias's expression darkened. 'A DNA match will make him my legal heir; it will satisfy parliament. I do not need it to know who he is. Leo is my son. That fact has never been in dispute.' He spoke softly, perhaps attempting to soothe her, but it didn't work. She was beyond mollification.

'You'll never love me,' she said quietly. 'Will you?'

His expression flared with something like panic and her heart shattered. Yet she held her breath and she waited and she watched and, stupidly, she hoped. Finally, he shook his head. 'Love is not any part of this, as I have said all along.'

It hurt more than it should have. After what had just happened, she felt the rejection more keenly than anything else.

'And it never will be?' A glutton for punishment, apparently, she needed him to speak frankly. For him to be completely honest with her.

'No.'

So emphatic! So certain!

'So what just happened between us meant nothing to you?'

His square jaw tightened as he looked away from her. He was silent, and she took that silence as confirmation. It nearly tore her in half.

'And what about Leo?' she prompted, remembering his little bruised arm with fresh hurt. 'You do love him, don't you?'

The pause might as well have been an axe dropping. All her hopes crumbled in that moment. Reality was a pointed blade, one for which she had no shield.

'He's my son.' There was fear in Matthias's dark, swirling eyes. Fear and panic.

'For God's sake, he's not a damned possession!' she spat, forgetting her dislike for curse words and giving into the torrent of rage flowing through her like lava. 'He's not an accessory you can just put on a damned shelf! Leo is a living boy, a flesh and blood kid who doesn't give a care about your throne and your traditions and your damned cold heart! All he wants is to have a mum and a dad to play with—parents who adore him and are proud of him, who want to spend *time* with him, and delight in his achievements.'

A muscle jerked in his jaw and he spoke slowly, as though his own temper was pulling at him, begging to be indulged. 'That is not the way of royalty.'

'Says who?' she demanded. 'What was your own childhood like? I don't believe it was as cold as you are suggesting Leo's should be.'

'What do you know of my childhood?' he asked, deceptively calm.

She slammed her lips together and then her anger fired up anew. 'Nothing. But I know what mine was like. I know that my parents loved me even when they had no reason to.' Her eyes narrowed. 'I was given away, Matthias, by people who found it as easy to turn off their hearts as you apparently do, and I don't much like the idea of Leo *ever* knowing what that feels like.'

'Given away by whom?' he snapped, not understanding her implication.

'By my birth parents,' she returned, spinning away from him, her eyes caught by the hedge that grew around the tennis court.

'You're adopted?' he repeated, the words flattened of emotion.

'Yes.' There was defiance in her tone.

'Why have you never mentioned this before?'

'It didn't come up,' she said, and then bit down on her lower lip. 'And because I'm… I've lived with this shame, Matthias.' She whirled around to face him and pressed her fingertips between her breasts, as though she could score her way to her heart. 'I've lived with the knowledge that the people who should have loved me most in this world, and wanted me, didn't.'

A muscle jerked in his jaw and sympathy crossed his handsome face. 'I wish you'd told me this sooner.'

'Why?' she whispered. 'What difference does it make?'

They stared at each other in silence and then he moved closer, but she stiffened because her temper couldn't be restrained. Nor could her hurt.

'It is a part of you,' he said finally. 'A part of the woman you've become. It has been hurting you, and I would have liked… I would have liked to talk to you about it, to help you not suffer because of a decision two people made twenty-four years ago.'

'You make it sound like selling a house,' she muttered, shaking her head. 'My own parents didn't want me.' Her eyes were flinty when they lifted to his. 'Imagine what that feels like, then imagine how much I *don't* want Leo to ever know this pain.'

Her words lashed the air between them, and he stiffened visibly.

'People put their children up for adoption all the time,' he observed quietly. 'Oftentimes, because it is best for the child. Has it never occurred to you that your birth parents felt they were doing the right thing by you?'

'Of course it's occurred to me.' Her words were thick with emotion. 'I've spent my whole life trying to understand why my own mother didn't want me.' To her chagrin, the sentence burned in her throat, emotion making the words dense and acidic. 'I was determined I wouldn't repeat whatever mistake my biological parents made.' Her eyes assumed a faraway look. 'I always thought that when I had a family, it would be with a man I could spend the rest of my life with. A man I respected. A man who loved me too much to ever let me go. I thought that when I started a family, it would be with someone who would love my children like they were his purpose for living. Nothing less would be acceptable for me or whatever children I might have. I thought I'd fall in love and get married and I'd finally feel like… I'd finally feel like…' She had to suck in a deep breath to stave off a sob. 'I thought I'd feel wanted.'

The words stung the air around them, whipping through the atmosphere.

'Deliciae—' But what could he say? He wanted her for her son. He'd made that obvious from the moment he'd approached her.

Tears sparkled on her long lashes. 'And then I met you

and all my thoughts of saving myself for marriage went out the window. I discovered I was pregnant and had to face the reality of raising my child on my own.' She dashed at the tears that were threatening to run down her cheeks. 'It wasn't what I wanted, but I figured I could still give Leo the best of everything. And he had my parents, who loved me when they had no reason to.'

Matthias was as still as a statue, watching her with fierce concentration.

'Never would I have thought I'd be bringing my child up as a prince, the heir to a man who won't ever give him the love he deserves. A man who doesn't know how to love his own son.'

And now fresh tears ran down her cheeks, and Frankie didn't check them. She returned Matthias's gaze, her heart breaking, her soul splitting.

'I have never lied to you,' he said eventually, and she swept her eyes shut resignedly.

'I know that.' Her chest heaved. 'I knew it was unlikely you'd ever love me and, believe me, I have grappled with that fact. I have known that, in agreeing to this, I am consigning myself to the exact fate I've always sworn to avoid. You, and this marriage, are everything I didn't want for myself.' She straightened her spine, squaring her shoulders. 'But for Leo, to give him the father he deserves, I was prepared to put all that aside. What do my feelings matter when I can give him everything he should have?'

Matthias's eyes drew together, his expression not shifting. 'And what will he miss out on, living here with me? He is the Crown Prince of Tolmirós. He will want for nothing.'

'Come on, Matthias, don't be so obtuse. Children don't care about *things.* They don't care about *power.* He's just a sweet little kid, who wants to be loved. It's as easy as that.'

'I will do everything in my power to care for our son, you know that. I told you I will protect him with my dying breath…'

She shivered visibly. 'Do you think that's enough?'

His eyes glinted and slowly he nodded. 'It has to be. It is what I am offering.' He moved closer, so close they were almost touching and she could see the tiny flecks of silver in his dark eyes. 'I am what I am. I have never lied to you—I will never lie to you. I have been very careful never to make promises to you that I cannot keep.'

She bit down on her lower lip to stop it from trembling.

'I am telling you now that I will give our son a home, a future, and we will raise him as a family, just as I have always said.' His back was rigid, braced like steel. 'Our relationship is a separate concern to Leo's place here—as my son, and as my heir.'

'It's all the same thing,' she denied, shaking her head.

'No.' He lifted a hand, curling it around her cheek, stroking his thumb over her lips. 'You're offended I am not claiming to be in love with you,' he said quietly. 'And you're trying to hurt me by making that about Leo.'

'No!' she volleyed back urgently. 'I would never use our son in that way!'

He didn't relent. 'I have wondered why you are so hell-bent on idealism and commitment—why would a beautiful young woman deny herself the pleasure of sex in this day and age? And now I see. It is because you are always looking for a guarantee of security, for a promise you will not be abandoned again. You thought saving yourself for marriage would be an insurance policy of permanence.'

She drew in a harsh, raw breath at his accurate appraisal.

'You want to pick the safe option always, because you were put up for adoption and you want to make sure nothing like that will ever happen to you again.'

She opened her mouth to deny it, but the words were locked in her throat.

'How can you not see that marriage without love is a safer bet than one predicated on emotion? Emotions fade and change. How can you not see that what I am offering you is everything you want?'

Her eyes sparkled and her beautiful face fell. She shook her head slowly from side to side, but bravely held his gaze. 'If you think any of this is what I want, then you know nothing about me.'

CHAPTER TWELVE

'DO YOU THINK this marriage is what *I* wanted?'

'I know it's not,' she conceded, and the pain in her pinched expression practically tore him in two.

'I wish, more than anything, that you could have everything you've just described. I wish you could have met a man who deserves you.' He knew, as he spoke the sentence, that it was the truth. That he wasn't—and never had been—worthy of Frankie. 'I wish you hadn't met me. I wish I'd done what I knew I should have and left you alone three years ago.' He ground his teeth together. 'Hell, Frankie, do you think I haven't woken up every day regretting what I require of you? Regretting the fact that I am forced to marry you even when I know it's the last thing you want?'

'Then why are you?' she whispered.

'You know the answer to that.' His jaw was firm. 'I cannot let Leo go. He must be raised here, by you, and as my son and heir. Neither you nor I has any say in this.'

A small sound escaped her, and he thought it might have been a sob.

'I can't live here with you.' She pulled away from him, taking a step backwards.

'You must,' he said darkly, wondering at the way his stomach seemed to be swooping and tightening constantly. 'Marriage is the only option open to us.'

She nodded jerkily and she stared at him with an attempt at strength and defiance that made him feel even worse.

'I'm aware of that. I have no interest in depriving our son of a birthright he would more than likely choose for himself when he comes of age.'

Matthias tilted his head in concession, hiding the look of darkness that moved over his features.

'When you suggested this marriage, you told me I could live at another palace.'

'Mare Visum.' He remembered the conversation, and the fact he had made the promise in good faith. He hadn't cared where she might choose to live at that point. And now?

Matthias did care. He thought of her living on another island, separated from him by sea and miles, and he wanted to reject the suggestion outright.

'Leo and I will go there after the wedding,' she said, her voice almost completely steady, her eyes unflinching.

'Running away?'

She let out a small sigh and when she spoke it was with an impatience that made him feel about as big as an ant. 'I'm trying to find a way to make this work. If I was going to run away, I would have done it by now, believe me.'

Respect lifted within him, even as he warred with her words internally. To install Leo and Frankie in another palace did make perfect sense. They could spend their days happily, settling into a new lifestyle and culture, and he could continue as before. Nothing needed to change, except his country would rejoice in the knowledge of a blood heir to the throne.

It made sense. So why did he want to rail against the idea and refuse her suggestion? Why did he want to tell her he would never let his wife and child reside in a different palace to him?

The temptation to do just that terrified him, and so he nodded brusquely before he could give vent to the words that were racing through him. 'Fine.' He nodded. 'As you wish. After the wedding reception, you can be quietly moved to Mare Visum. Will this make you happy?'

For a moment her brave mask crumbled and she looked equal parts terrified and devastated. 'I'll make it work.' And then her expression hardened, like flint. 'You were right, Matthias. It turns out I'm capable of being a realist after all.' And she turned her back on him, walking slowly and calmly off the tennis court. He watched her go and told himself this would be for the best. He watched her go and told himself this odd feeling of uneasiness would disappear, just as every other feeling always had before.

Frankie was always beautiful, but dressed as a bride, her hair styled, a tiara on her head, surrounded by flowers and well-wishers, she was as stunning as he'd ever seen her.

No, that wasn't quite true. He closed his eyes for a moment and remembered the first moment he'd seen her, with no make-up, nothing special about her hair or clothes, but a smile that could power a space shuttle, and his gut pulled.

He remembered the way she'd looked when they'd made love that first time, when her face had glowed pink with rapture, her green eyes fevered with pleasure, and he had to bite back an audible groan.

He remembered the way she'd looked when he'd made love to her the day before, on the tennis court. So angry, so beautiful, so desperate with longing: the same longing that had carved him in two a long time ago.

But, while Frankie was beautiful now, there was a sadness in her features that cut through him.

He'd caused it. He'd caused it when he'd rejected her, just as she'd dreaded. He'd looked her in the eyes and told her he'd never really want *her*. He wanted their son, his heir, and she was a part of that deal.

All night it had swirled through his mind and he'd finally understood what had driven her outburst, what was at the root of all her reserve with him—she didn't want him to hurt her. She didn't want to care for him, to want him, to need him in any way, because she didn't trust him not to hurt her.

And because she wanted to be loved, and knew he'd never give her that.

Her green eyes were stormy, her lips tight, her skin pale. Standing as close as they were, at the front of the *cathedrali*, he could detect faint silver patches beneath her eyes, showing that she'd tossed and turned all night. Though she was smiling, it was unnatural and forced and there was a faint tremor in her hands as she held them clasped in front of her.

Perhaps he was the only one in the cathedral who would detect these insignificant changes but, knowing what was in her heart, hearing how she felt, knowing that this marriage was the diametric opposite of everything she'd ever wanted and that she was going through with it regardless, something pulled in the region of his heart.

He looked around the beautiful ancient building—the place he'd come to bury his parents and brother, when he'd stood in this exact spot and spoken to reassure a panicked nation, and he channelled that same ability to quell his feelings, to silence his personal needs.

Today, as on that day, he was guided by what his people needed of him, but he was also led by what Frankie deserved, by how he could go some part of the way towards fixing this for her.

Frankie would become his Queen, and then he would let her go, allow her to live as private a life as she wished. In that one small way, he could give her what she needed.

'I, Frances Preston…' she spoke loudly, as clear as a bell, just as she'd been taught '…take you, Matthias Albert Andreas Vasilliás, to be my husband.' She was glad to be saying her vows because they were generally seen to be emotional and the fact that tears danced on her eyelashes would be regarded as natural and normal. 'I promise to be true to you in good times and in bad, in sickness and in health. I promise to love you and honour you, for as long as we both shall live.'

Relieved to have said her piece, she met his eyes and flinched almost instantly. A noise sounded: Leo. She looked towards him unconsciously and her skin goosebumped at the sight of their son, the boy who would be King one day, watching on with such joy. *Please let this be okay*, she prayed, sweeping her eyes shut.

'I, Matthias Vasilliás, take you, Frances Preston, to be my wife and Queen. I promise to be true to you at all times, when you are well, and when you are not.' Frankie held her breath, knowing what was to follow, bracing herself for how it would feel to have him say the words she desperately wanted to hear and know them to be false. 'I promise to love you and cherish you, for all the days of my life.'

She couldn't help it.

She lifted her eyes to his face and saw there that he was simply performing a part, and that he was as loath to say those words as she was to hear them. Her heart didn't break. It had broken already—how could it break further?

But it disintegrated within her, being swallowed into her bloodstream, leaving only cold acceptance in its wake.

This marriage was a fraud in every way. The fact their chemistry was off the charts was just as Matthias had always said. Sex was just sex.

And finally the last vestiges of her childish hopes and naïve dreams burst about her.

Somehow, seeing the reality, made it easier for her to get through the rest of the ceremony. And, thankfully, the wedding reception was so full of dignitaries that there was always someone to talk to. Someone to dance with. Frankie took every opportunity she could to put some distance between herself and Matthias, doing whatever she could simply to pass the time, all the while knowing that she would soon be able to leave this damned palace, and her new husband, far behind.

She avoided him as best she could and she kept her heart closed off, but finally, at the end of the night, came the moment to dance with her husband. Every single guest and many of the palace servants stood at the edges of the enormous ballroom, and Frankie could fight it no longer.

For the next few minutes she had to pretend to be happy, and then they would leave and this would all be behind her.

Matthias walked to her with slow intent, his eyes holding hers in a way that made her blood gush and her chest hurt. He held a hand out and she placed hers in it, her stomach doing loops. She ignored those feelings and breathed out in an attempt to steady herself.

He led her to the middle of the dance floor and then the priest approached, a smile on his face showing they'd fooled him, at least. He held in his hands a small spool of silver thread. Once he was close enough he spoke soft words in Tolmirón, then began to loop the thread from her hand to Matthias's and back again. She remembered being told about this, but it had been so long ago she forgot the significance of it.

Some kind of tradition, though.

When their hands were bound tightly, the priest nodded and stepped away. Music began to play, soft and beautiful, and Matthias brought her closer to his chest, holding her there so she could hear the beating of his untouchable heart.

'This thread is from the Mediterranean silk crab,' he said. 'It is native to the caves of Tolmirós. Their silk grows deep beneath the ocean's surface. For as long as there are records, royal marriages have been blessed by this binding. It is said that dancing with the threads like this promises a long and happy marriage.'

Her fingers were aching beneath the beautiful silk. She inherently rejected everything he said.

'I see.'

She felt rather than heard his sigh. He didn't speak for the rest of the dance, but afterwards they stood with their hands bound, smiling at their guests.

'Is it over?' she asked quietly, her heart stammering inside her.

He tilted a glance at her, his face hiding whatever he was feeling, and then he nodded. 'We may leave.'

She kept her expression bland, her back straight, as they slipped out of the crowded ballroom to cheers and applause from all assembled. She walked beside him through the ancient corridors of the palace but as soon as they rounded the corner and were in the privacy of their residence at last, she pulled at her hand.

It wouldn't come loose. She pulled again, lifting her other hand to rip the threads free. Only they wouldn't disentangle, and it was suddenly almost impossible for Frankie to breathe.

'Please get this off,' she said, looking up at him with panic, pulling on it.

His alarm was obvious. 'Calm down, *deliciae*—'

'Don't call me that. Please. Get it off. I can't… I can't… I can't breathe.' She bit down on her lip, pulling on her hand until he held her still.

'You're only making it tighter. Just be still.'

But she couldn't. She kept pulling and he swore, reaching out and curling his fingers around her chin. 'You must be still.' He spoke loudly and firmly so that she stopped struggling and stood, her teeth chattering and her stomach in knots. Watching her the whole time, he eased a finger beneath the threads and found the loose end. He unthreaded them as quickly as he was able, but it still took longer than a minute and in that time Frankie's panic only rose, her huge eyes darkening, her face draining of colour. Finally, when he was almost done, she pulled at her hand and rubbed it in front of her.

'It's just threads,' he said in an apparent attempt to reassure her.

Only it wasn't just threads. They were married now, bound in all the ways a man and a woman could be united: tied together for life by law and by a child and, for Frankie, by love. But her love wasn't enough. It never had been—it never would be.

She needed to get away from him as soon as possible.

He glared at the painting and, for the hundredth time in the four weeks since Leo and Frankie had left the palace, contemplated moving it. He knew he should. He knew it had no place in his life, let alone here in the place he undertook important government work.

The painting had always been a distraction, from the day it had arrived, but at least before it had been a pleasant distraction. Now it served only to plunge him into a black hole of anger, a deep place of desolate realism.

She was gone.

It had been four weeks.

He turned his attention to the documents in front of him and read them again, then, with an impatient thrust of his hand, pushed them away. It was barely afternoon, but he stood and crossed to the bar on the other side of the room and poured himself a stiff measure of whisky. He inhaled it, then threw it back, his hand slightly unsteady when he refilled the glass.

What time had he gone to bed the night before? Three? Four?

He couldn't recall.

He glared at the painting from up close, seeing the brushstrokes and imagining the way her hand would have moved as she painted it. He hated the painting in that moment with a visceral rage because it embodied so much of who Frankie was, what she was, and he'd never felt more distant from her—nor that she was more out of his reach.

A knock sounded on his door. He ignored it; the knock came again.

'What?'

His valet Niko entered, holding a brown envelope. 'Today's security memo.' Niko placed the envelope on the desk and turned to leave.

Matthias grunted by way of acknowledgement, turning his gaze to the large envelope.

They'd been gone four weeks and in that time he hadn't called her once. He'd resisted every single urge to pick up the phone and speak to her. Any time he'd thought of so much as dialling Mare Visum palace to see how she was, to speak to Leo, he'd recalled the sight of Frankie trying to pull her hand free from their ceremonial wedding bind; he'd sensed her panic and despair and he'd known that to call her would be selfish. To speak to her might improve his spirits, might reassure him that she was making sense of their new lives, but it would hurt her, he was sure of that.

And so he'd ordered security packets. Daily. It was a way to stay informed of her movements. To see her life unfurl.

He crossed to the desk now, his stride long, his fingers moving deftly as they tore the top off the envelope.

Usually the envelope included a single A4 piece of paper

with a typewritten, lacklustre report of Frankie and Leo's movements. But when he reached into the envelope for the memo, he pulled out a newspaper article as well. With a frown, his eyes ran over the words, a sense of disbelief scrambling through him.

Eggs for the Prince! the headline screamed.

Matthias read the short article, describing the delight of a local café operator who'd discovered that the beautiful blonde woman and adorable dark-haired boy who'd wandered in for breakfast the day before were, in fact, Her Majesty the Queen and the young Crown Prince.

The photos, snapped on cell phones by nearby diners, obviously, showed Frankie and Leo doing nothing more exciting than eating breakfast. Nor did it show a single security guard anywhere nearby. She wore a baseball cap low on her brow, her ponytail pulled through the back, and Leo was wearing sunglasses.

So far as disguises went, it was pretty simple.

Matthias could tell it was his wife and son.

His *wife*.

He glared at the picture and his chest ached as though it were being scraped out and emptied completely of contents.

She'd wanted to be left alone, but he'd believed she would act in their child's best interests. To take him out without any protection detail… What the hell was she playing at?

Anything could have happened! Kidnap! Murder! An accident! And she'd accused him of not caring about Leo?

He ground his teeth together and, before he could realise what he was doing, he pulled Frankie's painting off the wall and hurled it across the room, satisfied when the frame cracked upon landing. He stared at it, broken and damaged, something that had once been so beautiful and pleasing, and tried not to draw a comparison to Frankie. He told himself he was glad. The painting was nothing but a damned distraction and he was done being distracted by this.

But the longer he stared at it, the more his gut twisted, until he felt only shame.

Shame, and a deep, profound sense of grief.

He swore in his native tongue and scooped down, picking the pieces up, trying to shape it back together, almost as though a madness of sorts had descended upon him. 'Damn it,' he cursed again, when it wouldn't comply. He'd broken something beautiful. He'd broken it beyond repair.

Carefully, slowly, he placed the painting down on the desk, his powerful hands reverent with the frame where only a minute ago he'd lashed out, acting in anger.

Without thought, purely on instinct, he reached out, pressing a button on his phone; Niko answered almost immediately.

'Have the helicopter readied.'

'Yes, sir. What is your destination?'

He pressed a finger to the painting, feeling the ridges made by the layers she'd added, each with care, each with love, and his eyes closed of their own accord. He tilted his dark head back, his expression held tight.

'Mare Visum.'

The colours weren't right. She ran her brush over the top of the canvas, streaking a fine line of grey over the black, so fine it was almost translucent, giving it a pearlescent sheen. Better. But still not quite right.

She took a step back to study the painting, her frown deepening. There was a kind of magic about the moonlit nights here, on the southern tip of Tolmirós. She'd watched the moon coming over the ocean each night since coming to live in Mare Visum, and she'd tried to capture the ethereal quality on her canvas but, again and again, she'd failed.

With a grunt, she grabbed her cloth and swiped it over the bottom of the canvas, smearing the ocean she'd painted only the day before so it looked like a murky swamp, then dropping her head into her hands.

She was tired, that was all. She wasn't sleeping well.

Her stomach rolled as her mind immediately supplied the answer as to why that was.

Matthias.

Her fingers dug into her hair, pulling it loose from the braid, and she made a guttural, groaning sound of impatience. For God's sake, as if it wasn't bad enough that her dreams were tormented by memories of her husband; now he was invading her waking world?

She'd tried so hard to banish him from her thoughts.

But every time she thought she'd done it—gone an hour or two without her mind wandering to damned Matthias—he was there, his handsome face in full Technicolor in her mind's eye.

With another sound of impatience, she pulled her hands away from her face and stared at the painting, then grabbed her paintbrush, dipped it in the red oil paint and lifted it, striking a single angry line through the painting's middle.

Maybe her gift was now destroying art, rather than creating it?

She lifted her hand to mark the canvas again.

'Stop.'

His voice held her still instantly and she spun around, her eyes finding his in the doorframe. He was watching her with a stillness that made her heart do the exact opposite—it was pounding hard and fast inside her, so fast it made her knees shake. She hadn't seen him since their wedding; she had no time to prepare for seeing him now.

'Stop,' he said again, and she realised she was still holding the paintbrush in her fingertips like a sword, with blood at its tip. She dropped her gaze to it, her heart pounding, her mind racing. She sucked in a breath and looked at him once more, her expression giving little away.

'I wasn't aware you were coming to the palace,' she said, the words slightly stilted. 'I presume you've come to see Leo. He's asleep. But he'll be...'

Matthias began to walk into the room and she held her breath then, watching him as he came right in front of her and slowly took the brush from her hand.

'Stop,' he said quietly, for the third time, his eyes roaming her face, his features symmetrical, both familiar and unfamiliar to her. He stood so close she could feel warmth emanating from his powerful, broad frame, so close she could lean forward and touch him, so close she could inhale his intoxicating scent.

So close.

She shook her head slightly, taking a step backwards, and his hand shot out, steadying her before she could connect with the still-wet canvas.

His touch on her skin was like a thousand volts of electricity; it ripped through her and she clamped her mouth together to stop from letting out a groan.

Because she'd dreamed of his touch; she'd craved it to the point of insanity and despair. 'Don't,' she whispered, pulling away from him, turning her back on him and staring at the wasteland of the painting.

He was no longer touching her, but her arm felt warm where his fingers had connected with her. She swallowed in an attempt to bring moisture back to her mouth.

'Leo will be awake soon, if you want to wait in the lounge.' The words were brittle, like a porous old seashell left out in the sun.

'I came to see you.'

Her eyes swept shut at the declaration and she braced

for whatever was going to come next. She had wondered how long she would be allowed to hide out like this, before being asked to return to some kind of normality, to the royal duties that accompanied her role. Only she'd expected it would be a lowly servant who would summon her back to the palace, back to her King's side.

She hadn't expected it to be Matthias.

She wasn't prepared for this.

'Why?' A hollow whisper.

He didn't speak. He said nothing and for so long that eventually she turned to face him, and now a spark of anger was igniting inside her. 'Why?' Louder. More demanding.

Because he'd invaded her sanctuary, and without any warning; he hadn't given her any chance to raise her defences and it wasn't fair.

She held onto that anger, using it, knowing how well it served her in that moment.

He opened his mouth to say something and then appeared to change his mind.

He moved closer, but not to her, towards the painting, and he frowned as he looked at it. Self-conscious—she never liked it when people looked upon her art as it was forming on the canvas—she felt almost as if she'd been walked in on while naked. A work in progress was raw, messy, chaotic.

She tried to see it through his eyes.

It was moody and atmospheric. The destruction she'd foisted on its lower half minutes earlier only added to its brooding intensity. The red line was striking.

'I bought it, you know,' he said, and she frowned because she had no idea what he was talking about. 'The painting you were working on when we met.'

'You... It sold to a private buyer.' She shook her head, lifting her eyes from the new painting to his taut profile.

'To me.' He looked towards her abruptly, so she had no chance to flick her gaze away. 'It sold to me.'

'Why? Why did you buy it?'

His smile was dark, self-deprecating, imbued with anger and scepticism. 'Because, Frankie, I found it very hard to put you out of my mind.' He spoke darkly. 'I bought it to challenge myself—you were always there with me, and yet I knew I could never contact you. I was testing my strength and resolve by keeping that beautiful piece you'd created close to me. Taunting myself with what I couldn't ever have again.'

It made absolutely no sense.

'You got into my bloodstream, like some kind of fever, and I refused to let you weaken me.'

She bit down on her lower lip, hurt shifting inside her. 'I didn't want to weaken you.'

'I know that.' He took in a deep breath, his chest moving with the action. 'I know that.' He lifted a hand then, as if to touch her cheek, but then took a step backwards, keeping his body stiff, his expression impossible to read. He was stern. Focused. She would have said *unemotional*, except she could feel waves of emotion emanating from him.

'You were at a café with Leo.'

There was a thick undercurrent to the words. They came to her from far away, making no sense. 'This morning?'

He gave nothing away. 'It was in the papers. A photograph of the two of you.'

'Yes.' She nodded, darting her tongue out and licking her lower lip. 'I was annoyed about that. I didn't notice a photographer.'

'Anyone with a cell phone is paparazzi these days.'

That was true. She nodded.

'Did you go out without security?'

The question caught her off-guard. 'I… It was… The island is tiny and the café an easy walk. Leo and I go to the beach often, without guards. I didn't think…'

And now, as though he couldn't help himself, he put his hands on her forearms and held her still. He stared down at her and she stared back, but her heart wouldn't stop racing; blood gushed through her so fast she could hear it roaring inside her ears like an angry ocean.

'You didn't think?' he asked, haunted, and he dragged her body to his, holding her against him, and she didn't fight him; she didn't even think about fighting him.

'What if someone wanted to hurt you? Or hurt him? What if someone kidnapped Leo?'

'I was with him the whole time,' she said shakily. 'Nothing was going to happen.'

'You don't know that,' he groaned, as though he could barely speak. 'You cannot take those kinds of risks, Frankie. You can't do it. Please. Please do not take these risks.'

'It's not a risk,' she promised softly, gently, her heart turning over for him.

'How do you know this?' His jaw tightened as though he were grinding his teeth. 'You can't. You're acting on blind faith and I am not prepared to. I won't live with this kind of worry. I can't.'

Sympathy curled inside Frankie. She reached up and ran her fingers over his cheek so his breath escaped him in a single hiss. 'I understand why you feel that way,' she said softly. 'You lost your family in terrible circumstances. You couldn't save them, and now you're worried something will happen to Leo and you won't be able to save him.' His eyes flared. 'But you can't keep him in some kind of gilded cage. Not here, not in your home. I want him to have as normal a life as is possible. You have to trust that I can keep him safe. You have to trust me.'

She could see as each word hit its mark, she could see

the way his face stretched with each statement. 'I have lost everyone I ever cared for,' he said finally, the words tight as though being dragged from him against his will. 'I have no intention of losing you or Leo.'

Stupid, blind hope beat inside her, but she refused to answer it.

'Tell me why,' she said, her whole body attuned to every movement of his.

'Tell you what?' He was guarded again, cautious. 'What do you want from me?'

She blinked thoughtfully. 'Tell me why you're so furious about this.'

'You are my wife—he is my son…'

She shook her head. It wasn't good enough. 'You were prepared to marry someone else two months ago,' she reminded him with steady determination. 'If something happened to us, you could simply remarry. Have another child.'

'Don't,' he ground out, and hope in her chest flared larger, brighter.

'What? You're a realist, remember? You can marry whomever you want and have as many children as you need. Why do you care about me and Leo?'

'He is my son!' The words were torn from him, and then he was dragging a hand through his hair, pulling at it, his eyes tortured, haunted, and she hated having to push him, but deep down she knew how essential it was.

'Yes, and you can't bear the thought of something happening to him, can you? It would kill you if he was hurt in any way?'

'Of course!' he roared. 'Damn it, Frankie, I'm done losing people I—'

'Say it,' she demanded, crossing her arms over her chest.

'I'm done losing people,' he finished, stepping back from

her, putting physical space between them as though that would defuse this.

Frankie wasn't going to back down though. 'I never expected you to take a coward's response, Matthias.'

'How dare you call me a coward?' He laughed, but it was a sound of desperation—a dying man trying to grab a life raft.

'I dare because I faced every single one of my fears when I married you. I married a man I love with all my heart, who claimed he'd never love me. I married you knowing I was relegating myself to a life of loneliness. I married you with only the smallest seed of hope that you might ever care for me how I needed you to. And now you won't even admit that you love our son? When it's the most natural thing in the world?'

He glared at her and her heart raced. 'I love him, okay? I love him so much I am terrified of how I'll live if anything ever happens to our child. I look at him and I see my brother—my brother as he was in the accident when I couldn't even reach him, I couldn't save him. I couldn't save them, Frankie. My whole family died and I couldn't do a damned thing. What if something happens to Leo?' He waved a hand over his eyes, then blinked at her with despair. 'What if something happens to you?'

She hated seeing him like this. She moved to him and put a hand on his shoulder but he stayed firm, unreceptive.

'Don't. I cannot ask you to reassure me, and I don't want to lie to you. I made a choice that first night I met you that I wouldn't love you, Frankie. I have made that choice all along, even when, yes—okay, fine—when every single cell in my body aches to say what you need to hear. Even when I know I probably fell in love with you the second we met.'

Frankie drew in a shaking breath.

'But I *chose* not to act on that. I chose not to let that control my actions.'

He stood before her, a king of men, and she saw only the fifteen-year-old he'd been.

She shook her head, lifting up on tiptoe and brushing her lips to his. He stood rock-still.

'I can't do this,' he said, but his hands lifted into her hair and held her where she was. He pressed his forehead to hers and she made a small sound, deep in her throat.

'You can't keep yourself shut off from life because of an accident,' she said simply when his pain was complex and ran so deep. 'Just like I can't live in fear of rejection all my life because my birth parents chose not to raise me. We neither of us need to be defined by our past, Matt.'

'When my family died—' he spoke quietly but their faces were so close she heard his words as though they were being breathed into her soul '—I wanted to turn my back on the kingdom. I wished I'd died too, Frankie. I wanted to die.'

'But you didn't. You became the leader they needed you to be…'

'Once. I did that once.' He pressed a kiss to her cheek and she turned her head, capturing his lips with hers. 'If anything ever happened to you and Leo, if I lost either of you, I don't think I could do this again.'

Her heart, so broken, so splintered, began to pull together and she knew then that she had to be strong—not just for herself, but for Leo and Matt as well. 'I can't promise nothing will ever happen to me. Or Leo. Life comes with so few guarantees. But Matt, you can't keep pushing us away. Not when we're right here, your wife and your son, so in love with you. You can't keep pushing us away just because something *might* happen, one day. You can't throw our family away because you're afraid. Not when, by being brave, there's a good chance we'll all get everything we ever wanted in life…'

He shook his head against hers, his hand moving to curl around her cheek, his other fastening around her back.

'I ruined it,' he said, the words husky.

She looked up at him, frowning.

'The painting. I was so… I do not know. Angry. Afraid. No, I was terrified. When I saw that newspaper article, I took the painting from the wall and threw it to the ground, and I stared at the broken frame, the once beautiful object I had destroyed because I was afraid, and I felt… I ruined the painting,' he said gruffly. 'And I cannot bear that I have ruined our marriage too. I cannot bear the idea that fear has made me hurt you and push you away, that I have put you through the kind of pain I have felt this last month…'

'You say fear, but I look at you and I see a man who is so brave. What you've been through and turned your life into? I don't know anyone else who could have done that.'

'Don't. Do not speak so highly of me when I have been a coward, pushing you away rather than admitting how I feel for you…'

'You came here today,' she said softly. 'You're here because you love me, aren't you?'

His eyes glistened black in his handsome face. 'Yes,' he said on a whoosh of relief, a smile crossing his face. 'I am.'

'Then you are brave,' she promised. 'And I love you.'

'How is it possible?' he asked, wonderment and weight in the question.

'Because you are good and kind and because I believe in fairy tales and for ever.' She pressed a kiss against his nose and his eyes fell closed. 'Because I'm an optimist, and because my heart is as much yours as it ever was.'

'Your heart is a fool,' he groaned huskily. 'To love a man so unworthy of you.'

'You are more worthy of me than you give yourself credit for.'

'I doubt that,' he said with a shake of his head. 'But I will spend the rest of my life trying to deserve you.'

He scooped down and lifted her up, cradling her against his chest, and she laughed at the sudden movement. 'What are you doing?'

'I have missed you, Frankie, in every single way. This last month has been an agony. I have longed to talk to you. To show you my kingdom—*our* kingdom. I have wanted to see your wonder as you discover what is so special about Tolmirós, and I have missed Leo with an intensity that is impossible to describe. I have missed you in every way, and right now I want to make love to you as I should have all along—hold you close and tell you that I love you, tell you that everything you have wanted all your life is right here. I want this day to be the first day of your fairy tale, Frankie.'

'I thought you didn't believe in fairy tales,' she couldn't help teasing.

'I didn't.' He was serious. 'Until I met you—and I found myself living in one regardless.'

He kissed her then, a kiss of longing and love, and it inflated her soul. 'You have given me everything I ever wanted—my wife, my son, a family, a future. And I almost lost you because I couldn't admit that. I've been such a *vlakás*.'

She had no idea what the word meant. 'Yes.' Her agreement was sanguine as she wrapped her arms around his neck. 'But I forgive you.'

'You were right about my upbringing,' he said throatily. 'I don't often think about my childhood. I try not to, anyway.' He furrowed his brow. 'But that day, when you were so angry with me, you said my childhood wasn't cold. That it was full of love. And you were right. My mother adored

Spiro and me. She would have fought like a wildcat, as you did, to protect her children.'

Frankie's stomach churned with sadness for this woman, this poor woman. 'I'd like to know more about her,' she said honestly, and lifted her hand to his chest. 'I'd like to hear about your family.'

She could feel his resistance; she could see that it was something he was fighting, but then he nodded tightly. 'I think I'd like to talk to you about them. In time.'

It was enough. She lifted up and pressed a kiss to his cheek. 'We have all the time in the world, Matthias. I'm not going anywhere.'

EPILOGUE

NINE MONTHS LATER to the day, baby Emilia Vasilliás was born—a beautiful little sister for Tolmirós's thriving Crown Prince Leo.

Matthias had been by his wife's side the entire time—from the moment they'd discovered she was pregnant, only a week after her return to the palace, all the way to the delivery.

As he'd promised, in his office he was King, but he was also a man. A husband and a father, and as he watched her deliver him of another beautiful child he was mainly a bundle of nerves.

He hated seeing her in pain; he longed to be able to carry that pain, to experience it for her, so that she didn't need to feel the agony she was enduring. But she was so strong, so brave, and after hours of labour a baby's cry broke through the hospital and they looked upon their princess for the first time.

'She is beautiful, like you,' he said, the words thick as he placed the bundled-up child on his wife's chest.

Exhausted but delirious, Frankie stared at her daughter, emotions welling inside her. 'She's so like Leo was,' Frankie murmured, a smile on her lips, tears on her lashes. 'The same little nose and look, your dimple,' she said, looking up at Matthias. Her heart exploded at the sight of the big, strong King with suspiciously moist eyes of his own.

'She is divine,' he agreed, the words thick with feeling. 'A princess for our people.'

'A sister for Leo.' Frankie grinned, stroking their baby's dark pelt of hair. She pressed a kiss to Emilia's forehead and then relaxed back against the bed. 'How perfect she is.'

'How perfect you are,' Matthias corrected, kissing Frankie's cheek. 'A true warrior queen.'

Their marriage was blessed with three more children—a family of seven—and each birth was rejoiced at and celebrated by the people of Tolmirós, just as the country cheered when Leo, a young man of twenty-eight, announced his engagement to an Australian doctor. His parents were beside him when he married, and by the time Leo welcomed his first child onto this earth, Matthias's life was so rich and full, his family so extensive, that he loathed to think of a time when he had almost turned his back on what could have been. He remembered, of course, the instinct to push Frankie away, to close himself off to love because he had lost so much once before.

But brave warrior Queen Frankie had seen through that and she'd fought for what they were, regardless of her own fears and insecurities. And for that he loved her almost more than anything.

Fairy tales generally ended with the idea of people living happily ever after, but Matthias no longer thought about endings—he thought about each day as it came, and he lived with gratitude and peace. Come what may, he had been blessed, and blessed again—more than all the fairy tales in all the land.

* * * * *